CASTLE GILLIAN

By MAURICE WALSH

CASTLE GILLIAN

BY

MAURICE WALSH

W. & R. CHAMBERS, LTD.
LONDON AND EDINBURGH

First Published . . *1948*
Latest Reprint . . *1950*

All the characters and events in this book are fictitious,
and no reference is made advertently to any living
person, by name, implication, or description

Printed in Great Britain
by T. and A. CONSTABLE LTD., Hopetoun Street,
Printers to the University of Edinburgh

CONTENTS

CONTENTS

Chapter I

CASTLE GILLIAN NO MORE

Sylvia Gayne, my cousin thrice-removed, and myself had been quarrelling once again. Usually we had a pleasant little war on our hands, but Sylvia was deadly serious this time.

Now she walked sullenly at my side, and the path amongst the trees was so narrow that, sometimes, she touched shoulder with mine, and jerked away again. So we came down the gentle slope of the wood and on to the railed foot-bridge across our little Gullane River. As usual I paused to lean on the wooden rail and look down-stream. The water ran clear and smooth between undercut banks of wild garlic for a furlong or so, and then hastened down a long slide, over and around quartz slabs, to shoulder under the high-cocked stone arch that carried the main highway half a mile below.

A balmy, still evening, just before bird-song time, early in May, and in the stillness I could hear the remote sough of the waters from the throat of the slide. Then the mirror of the pool below me shivered and broke where a trout leaped, and circles of ripples widened to murmur "lap-lap" tonelessly on the undercut of the bank.

"Beglory!" said I, "that was a two-pounder—ten ounces anyway—and I'll feed him a cockybondhu come gloamin'."

"Oh hell!" said my thrice-removed cousin Sylvia in her deepest contralto.

I felt a hard grip on my shoulder, and came round on my heels willy-nilly. I am on the shortish side for a man, and Sylvia is a tall slip of a girl for a girl, taller than I am by half an inch. But that mere half-inch had now lifted to half a mile so far she looked down on me along her nose. She had her knuckles on her hips, and her young buds of breast stretched the silk she was wearing. And she was blazing. When Sylvia blazes it is her grey eyes that blaze, not her face. Her face retains its delicate old ivory, except around the mouth that goes dead white. Even her lips show loss of colour unless she has her war-paint on. She hadn't this evening, or, rather, she had licked most of it off biting the tip of her tongue. She tossed the spray of her fine flaxen hair down at me.

"Keep to the business in hand, Gill Morris, you hound!" she said deeply. Ordinarily, Sylvia has a light and pleasant voice, but in anger or emotion it goes deep, and is twice as pleasant, so that you want her to keep on being angry and vociferous. She put a finger under my nose, and said:

"Look you, Gillian! I wouldn't marry you, as you are, if you were the last man top o' earth. I won't marry you no matter what my father says, and that's flat."

"Your father will say plenty," I said, slapping her finger aside, "and he'll be looking for reasons, moreover. You don't love me I know——"

"Sometimes I don't even like you," she stopped me. "And you don't love me either—or anyone but your silly drifting self?"

"Silly Gilly! Silly Sylly!" I mocked her. "This is a family business, and love don't matter. You'll have to think up some better reason than lack o' love, my lass."

"I don't need to think." She hesitated, and the first breath of evening air stirred her fine hair over one ear. A thrush piped a tentative note, and the big trout splashed again in the pool below. I kept rubbing her on the raw. I said:

8

"Before we leave love, what about Garret Ward?"

"Damn Garret Ward!" she snapped, and let herself go. "I am talking about you, and you are no good any more. The war ruined you. You're a drifter and refuse to take hold in a breaking world. You let your sister, Mary, break her heart in that blasted stables, and you are not any good even as her stable-boy. You are the son of your father talking about his Kismet; and you'll take to drink like him one of these days, and be touching me for booze money. You have bad blood in you, Gillian Morris."

"Same like you, cousin," I said. "But you've known all that for some time."

"The effect is cumulative." She used an intelligent word when she liked. She had the bit in her teeth now. "You are a fleering, sneering, sardonic pint-pot of a black devil, with no interest in life except dull land and slow fishing—and you don't care for fishing really, if a gaff is handy. Gillian of Castle Gillian of the blood horses, my eye! You wouldn't know the difference between a blood horse and a spavined mule."

"I would so," I protested. "I'd know by their ears, and I'd prefer the mule, spavins and all. Look here! Are you sure, once and for all, that you are not marrying me?"

"I must be sure," she said more quietly, and came down to my own stature. "You are an ambitionless clodhopper, and you call me a hedonist. You want to marry me for dad's money and the life it will bring you. I'd rather our dying families to die out—or find new blood."

I wondered if I was beginning to know anger in myself. If I was it did not show in my voice.

"New blood! Garret Ward's blood? No! he has some of our blood too, but steal you the hound from my sister, and welcome! You are better looking than she is, and you have all the money the devil ever spit on."

9

But I could not anger cousin Sylvia beyond a certain point. She came back at me, calmly now.

"I'm hurting you, Gill, and I mean to. Leave Garret Ward out of it, but I could do worse."

"You couldn't—not ever!" I told her firmly. "Adding Ward's badness to the Gaynes' would be plain hell."

"That's where you can go this blasted minute!" she cried. "I'm off to tell my father."

She swung a swift left hand at me, but I dodged it of long practice. She turned with the swing of her arm, and stamped off the bridge and up the path towards her father's house of Castle Evan; and I was left tapping the floor-boards with an iron-tipped heel. The sound they made was hollow, and I was feeling pretty hollow too.

She strode like a country girl, long and smooth and lissomely, a tall slip of a girl, and shapely; and the light blue dress she was wearing was like a veil on her shapeliness. I kept on watching her, and her pace up the slope never slackened.

Gillian, my son! I thought, *that young rip don't care a cuss for you. By the powders o' war! if her temper lasts she'll tell Uncle Tom, and he'll flay her.*

Tom Gayne, her father, was not my uncle, but he was avuncular. His dead wife had been our cousin. Indeed, the two families had been blood-related for three centuries, and it might be that inbreeding that had left us where we were: with only one son in the two families. And not so long ago that same son had been told that he was no good. He wasn't either, I suspected.

I looked over Sylvia's head shining in the sun, and away up there between the wide-spaced holm-oaks I caught glimpses of the white top-storey and the copper-green dormer roof of Tom Gayne's house of Castle Evan. Sylvia was approaching it at the rate of knots. I turned my back on Sylvia.

It was as if the whole landscape had swung round with me. For I was looking up a straight path between wide-spaced holm-oaks, and I caught the white and copper-green gleam of a house at the head of the slope. But the gleam was not as bright as the gleam of Castle Evan. That was my father's house of Castle Gillian.

Away back in the seventeenth century, the brothers Morris—Gillian and Evan of the Celtic fringe—had settled in Ireland, and, by the favour of a certain king, possessed themselves of the whole valley of the Gullane, divided it equitably between them, north and south of the river, and built two houses from the same plan. These houses were rebuilt in Georgian days, and now stood facing each other across the valley to display the unimaginative solidity of Georgian builders. Uncle Tom Gayne, thanks to his Big Business, still possessed most of the original acres, but they were only his playground; my father, Gillian Morris, had lost half of his, and was doing badly by the other half. Half, indeed, was an ample domain for any continent man, but not enough at all for a man with a drouth. Thirst is not a bad thing in itself if a discriminate palate goes with it; it is what usually goes with it that plays havoc. We knew all about that havoc, my sister Mary and I.

The trout were on the rise; I did not look to see their back fins cut the water. The soft, may-blossomed air moved in my shock of black hair; I did not scent its fragrance. The thrushes were singing and a blackbird piping his four notes, but I did not listen. I just plodded up the slope towards my father's house. I did not go with the verve or grace of cousin Sylvia, for, hurry or no hurry, my slightly-bowed legs were not made for graceful movement. I just plodded on evenly against the brae, and I was not hurrying to tell anyone anything.

The shelf whereon stood Castle Gillian was separated from the slope by that type of sunken fence that is called a haw-haw. It was half-full of last year's leaves, and I crossed it by a stone bridge that had plain stone gateposts but no gate. The lawn, without shrubs or flower-beds, had not been cut since the previous autumn, and carried a thick sole of emerald grass that was now being cropped by a neat, black Kerry cow. Hens and chickens ran everywhere, and sultan cocks strutted, and, sometimes, made clarion challenge.

I walked across the grass to the Kerry cow, and she flicked a tail and tossed an upstanding horn as I ran a hand along her barrel; and as I walked away she followed me like a dog as far as the packed-gravel spread fronting the house. I had no interest in blood horses, but I liked cows, and I knew that a middling good dairyman-farmer was spoiled in me. Sylvia had been unfair. I could be a farmer if I had a chance, but I had no chance any more—or enough will either.

There was nothing castellated about Castle Gillian. It was a tall, three-storeyed, white-fronted Georgian house, with a copper-green dormer roof and many, many-paned windows—and many panes broken. The astragals of the windows looked inadequately fragile, but they were of solid bronze that, to save burnishing, had been white-leaded before my time and not touched since. Tacked on to the front of the house, in what looked like an afterthought but was not, was a big pillared and pilastered portico at the head of three broad steps of stone. At the left of the house was a long wing of wall pierced by an arch leading through to the stables; and behind the house the slope went on upwards and curved over in a larch grove tender in young green.

There was a peaceful sleepiness about it all. I could hear the soft sigh of the evening air adrift in the fronds of the larches; a couple of nesting wood-quests were crooning a love song in the branches of a cypress at the gable-end; and from the stable at the back came the muted clink of a head-chain running in its staple.

The house faced south by west, and the evening sun, shining aslant, cast on the Caithness flags the long shadows of the pillars and of three people in the porch about a rustic table. They were my father Gillian, my sister Mary, and the black devil who would be courting Mary if she let him, Garret Ward—or courting any woman out of sheer devilment, and most women would let him. Whether he was trying to court Mary for devilment I was not yet sure. He was distantly related to us by blood, and I disliked and feared him—physically.

My father was leaning back in a wicker chair drinking Irish whiskey in his tea. He would drink whiskey in anything. The blue-tinted waterford decanter, without a stopper, was half-full of a liquor that had a suspicious colour. Strong drink had spoiled my father's palate, and he could no longer tell strong whiskey from weak; so, at every chance, Mary used to baptise the decanter, and doctor the paleness of the mixture with black tea. I often told her she was wrong, for a man should be allowed to shorten the road by his own short-cuts. He had always been a drinker, but not a besotted one till tragedy came his way. Since that terrible spring morning, coming home from a Hunt Ball, when he had killed his wife out of a high-wheeled gig over the Gullane Bridge, he had never seen a sober day—and never would.

Even relaxed in his chair he was still a fine gallant figure of a man in his old brown homespuns; and his face, lean and high-nosed, showed no trace of the inner ravages of hard liquor. He had a fine bush of white hair just touched with cream, for he had been auburn in his youth. He was what I would call a cold drinker; when fully-loaded we knew it only by the absolute pallor of his face. At this hour of the evening he was no more than half-loaded.

In his youth and manhood, by all accounts, he had been the gallant master of wine, women and horses. But, having lost his one woman, other women no longer interested him; he had brought one of the most famous racing stables in the country to the brink of ruin; and Irish whiskey was his lord. He knew it and accepted it. He was not one of those topers who pledge themselves to give up drink to-morrow, or next month, or during Lent, or when the weather grows warm. He just drank much the same as he drew breath, and we made no protests any longer. Everyone liked him, and we, his children, whom he had ruined, loved him.

I went up the three worn stone steps and across the flags to Mary's side. She wrinkled her nose at me pleasantly, and said:

"Where's your Syl?" She was not my Syl. I said:

"Off to complain to Uncle Tom, after throwing a left in my face."

"Tried to kiss her, he did?" suggested Garret Ward.

"You go to hell, Sultan!" I told him, and he only laughed at me. I had once seen him kiss her, and she did not seem to mind.

I sat on the arm of Mary's chair, and the cane of it sagged, so that Mary sat up expecting both of us to go over, but I propped her and ran a hand through her soft, free black hair, and she nudged me with her head. Mary and I were of the dark breed, like our mother who was with God.

I looked across and grinned at Garret Ward leaning

14

against a pilaster, cup in hand and black eyes watching
Mary. He grinned back at me, and we understood each
other. He would love to sit as I sat, a hand in Mary's
hair, and her head nudging him in the diaphragm. He
daren't try—bold as he was—not yet at any rate.

I wondered what he saw in Mary to make his eyes
greedy. I was her brother, and I suppose brothers
seldom see beauty or appeal in their sisters; but I had
heard good judges say that blonde Sylvia Gayne could
not stand by Mary Morris's dark vividness. I thought
that was nonsense. I knew she had nice soft black hair,
and a soft, delicately flushed duskiness of hide, and eyes
that were violet in lamplight; and I knew that she had
a tough, supple, long-legged body, and that she could
throw me if I gave her first grip. But that was all. She
was wearing a faded red silk blouse stuffed into grey
slacks, and her scuffled brown brogues showed traces of
the stables.

But, apart from her looks, I also knew that Mary
Morris was the finest girl God ever made, and I wasn't
forgetting Sylvia Gayne either. She was invincibly game,
and despair could never touch her. She was the leader
of a forlorn hope to save the house and lands of Castle
Gillian, and I, her older brother, who should have been
leader, tagged along in the rear, loyal to her in my own
cussed way, doing as she bade me without any illusions,
and knowing how hopeless was her task.

Garret Ward straightened up from the pilaster, and
the sunlight flowed along the strong line of his jaw. He
came across to the table, put his cup down, spread his
riding-breeched legs, and looked down at Mary and me.
He had thick, awkward-looking legs, even in riding-
breeches, and his feet splayed.

"Mary and myself—and Uncle Gillian—were talking
business, Gilly," he said. My father was not his uncle

by a long shot, but he called him that, same as I called Tom Gayne, Uncle Tom.

"I'm not going," I said. "Is there a drop o' tea in that pot, Mary Jane?"

She leant forward and felt with a firm brown hand. "Cold as a stone! Timmy will bring some more. Did you pull Sylvia's hair?"

My father leant aside in his chair, so that his head was beyond the jamb of the open door, and his rich husky voice echoed down the cavern of the hall.

"Timmy! Timmy Tadg Shawn! to the fore!"

It was as if the shout had exploded old Timmy out-of-doors. He came scuffling. He called himself a butler, no one else did. He surely was a caricature of one, the last relic of old decency. He wore grey flannel pants that had been made for me and did not reach his ankles, red carpet slippers, a morning-coat green with age, a near-white dickey and collar, but no tie. He flaunted a fringe of white beard from ear to ear below a shaven chin, and his domed skull was as naked as a billiard ball. He was grumbling steadily to himself without any respect for persons.

"Holy God! there was no call to go burstin' me eardrum with all that hullabulloo. Hadn't I my eye out for Gill, an' only waitin' for the kettle to bile." He laid down a common earthen teapot, moved a shoulder to cover my father's line of sight, picked up the decanter, and shuffled for the door.

"Put it back, you old villain!" said my father calmly.

"Aisy—aisy!" protested Timmy. "Sure I was only going to add a taste of whiskey to it for ye." I saw him hood his near eye at Mary.

"Put it down!" ordered my father shortly, and Timmy did so, and shambled off grumblingly into the wilderness of the house. The bang of the door at the back of the hall echoed emptily in a house half-empty.

Mary poured tea for Garret Ward and me, and looked at my father. He shook his head, his hand on the neck of the decanter. His cup was half-empty, and as he refilled it with dilute whiskey, the neck of the decanter clinked against the rim of the cup. He took a deep gulp of what must have been a nauseous lukewarmness.

"Try a taste, Garret?" he invited. "It improves cheap tea."

"Not on your life, sir!" said Ward. "Whiskey is no vice of mine."

"The world knows that," said my father, "and could name one or two more to your choice."

"And yourself not a bad judge of the same, Uncle Gillian?" said Garret Ward pleasantly.

"Surely!" agreed my father, "but a man can afford only one."

I did not like to sit looking up at Garret Ward. It gave him a dominance over me that I could not stomach. And, certainly, Garret Ward was dominant. He was not a big man—not much taller than I was—but he was heavily built, with thick shoulders, and thick waist too. His round firm neck supported a peculiarly solid head, and his crisp, short hair fitted close to his skull like a black lacquer. A black devil looked out of his black eyes under close-growing black brows, and his nose was flattened and turned slightly askew. A tinker gave him that nose at Caerline Show, but he had about killed the tinker. He was not handsome in any way, and what women saw in him I could only guess at. He certainly had some power over women, and did not hesitate to use it.

I got to my feet, picked up my cup, and moved across the porch to lean a shoulder against a pillar. I sipped hot tea, and looked across the green lawn and over the tops of the holm-oaks. The oaks did not come quite up to the rim of the shelf, and over them I could see the windows and copper roof of Castle Evan, less than a mile away. The long shadow of it would be cast out on its clipped lawn, for it was turned away from the evening sun; and if Sylvia was looking across at Castle Gillian she would see our windows shining bravely in the evening glow. She would probably be now doing her bit of business with her father, and getting herself laughed at. Over here Mary and Garret Ward—and old Gillian Morris—had been talking business too, but no one was inclined to laugh. What business had Garret Ward with Castle Gillian?

III

They were silent about the table behind me. My father's wicker chair creaked; probably he was reaching for the decanter. From the stable-yard came a faint and doleful whistling. That would be Sandy Ythan, our head-groom, doing his evening stables. He was whistling the "Flowers of the Forest," which is the Scots lament for Flodden Field, and might now be his lament for Castle Gillian. The Kerry cow was at the edge of the gravel mooing softly at me. Her big dug was full, and she was asking for relief. Any minute now Timmy would be out to the milking. I spoke over my shoulder.

"Don't mind me! Ye were talking business?"

"It might concern you too, Gilly my lad," said Garret Ward.

I turned round then. He was half-sitting on the edge of the table, hands in breeches' pockets, and a cigarette on his lower lip. Mary was smoking too, and her eyes were considering me. My father was slowly, but with steady hands, filling a clay pipe—he used one per day—and he was looking at me too. They were all looking at me. I said:

"But how does our business concern Garret Ward?"

"More than it concerns you," he said bluntly.

"Welcome to the fold!" I said. "Are you wolf or shepherd dog?"

"Some fine day I'll teach you manners, you young pup," he said, but without heat. I was only a year or two younger than he was, but I did feel a bit of a pup.

Mary reached an arm behind him, lifted the decanter off a long, legal-looking envelope, and held the envelope up for me to see. I had noticed that envelope already, but I had seen others like it, and was not interested particularly.

"Attorney's letter, Gill!" she said without emphasis.

I nodded. "Not a final notice?" I said.

"Final as ever was," Mary told me. That was not so good.

"Does Garret Ward know how final it is?" I enquired.

"Why not?" said Garret Ward. "I know that Padderson must have his three thousand come term day in September or he'll foreclose. If he does——" His flung arm embraced all our side of Gullane Glen— "this, all of it, goes under the hammer, and the Morrises are out of Castle Gillian forever and a day."

"And you in it? What do you use for money?" I said.

I couldn't nettle him that way. "And I in it," he said equably, "and I can find the money. But if I am in it——" He stopped and threw his cigarette over my head. "That is the business I am talking about, and if Gilly don't keep a quiet tongue in his head I'll shut his mouth for him."

I had nothing to say to that. I put my cup down at the foot of the pillar, sat on the top step, and turned side-face to them. I leisurely filled a pipe and listened to Garret Ward. He had a deep, taurine voice, and when he paused I could hear a thrush singing across the lawn, and the chirp of sparrows from the stable eaves.

"The facts are simple," said Garret Ward, "but you

are so near 'em or so used to them, that you don't altogether grasp how cut-throat they are." He turned to Mary. "Castle Gillian is in the marrow of your bones, Mary, and you can't see yourself losing it——"

"I don't intend to lose it," said Mary calmly.

"Fine! and I'm showing you how to hold on. You have plenty of land left, bottom meadows and limestone pastures, to make this what it once was, the best training stables in the South. You have at least three dozen loose-boxes, and once on a time you could have used more. How many are occupied now, Mary?"

"Ten," said Mary without hesitation.

"And ten half-trained horses using 'em! I'll be a bit of a brute, Mary, and tell you that you are not able to put the final polish on a horse—flat or 'chase."

"Bit of a brute goes—and dam' liar as well!" I said. I wouldn't have him belittling my sister—and let him try and shut my mouth if he wanted to. Instead he gave a growl of laughter.

"Have a care, pint-pot!" he warned, "but I stand corrected. I know, Mary old girl, that you can train a horse to the last hair in its tail. What I meant was that you haven't the facilities to finish off a horse; and, more than that, a woman-trainer cuts no ice with owners. You have one good man in the stables—the Jock—and two louts—and Gilly is not interested."

The devil knew I was not interested, never would be interested in horses as racers. But did he know that I was taking no stock in forlorn hopes, that I, actually, was beginning to look forward to the evil day because it was so inevitable? Then Mary would be a free woman in spite of herself, and the two of us—— Well! we had the world before us. . . . And our father would have enough in the remnant of assets to drink himself comfortably under the ground. And there was Sylvia Gayne.

She wouldn't marry me if I was the last man top o' earth? All right! That left me free too. . . .

Garret Ward was talking glibly and convincingly. The hound must have conned over his words before mouthing them.

". . . You don't cut enough first-crop hay to rough-feed ten horses; your oats in stook got caught in the rain last September, and went malty; and you can't afford the little luxuries to put on the final polish for a race. You have ten horses to train, because a few old owners are loyal to you—or to your father; but you can't expect any owner to keep on being loyal if you don't win a race occasionally. Have you won any?"

"A point-to-point at Templeside last March," said Mary tonelessly.

"Yourself up on a hunter in poor company. Last season you had one second over the sticks, and a third in a flat mile—and that was all. And, what is more significant, you haven't a two-year-old in the stables! That means that the source of supply has dried up. You are at the end of your tether my dear, and, if nothing happens, you'll be sold up before winter. That's plain speaking—too plain maybe—but it is time you realised where you stand. That's all I need say, isn't it?"

He had said plenty, indeed, but most of it should be no news to Mary. She had heard much the same out of my mouth, but I don't suppose it ever registered with her, she was so possessed by the notion of restoring the glories of the once famous establishment. Well, something might register now out of the mouth of Garret Ward.

I looked sideways at her. The girl was as calm as a post, relaxed in her old chair, her long legs out, and ankles crossed. She put two fingers in a breast pocket where she carried loose cigarettes, took out a crumpled one and put it between her lips. Garret Ward leant over and lit it from the tip of a fresh one, and, as he looked down at her, emotion moved in his face. She looked up at him out of her rather deep-set dark eyes under their straight brows, and her face gave no sign at all. She spoke quietly in her clear modulated voice that had a firm note in it that was close to harshness.

"You have a good deal more than that to say, have you not, Garret?"

He moved his head slowly in considering assent. "I have told you frank and free where I know you stand. Now I am going to tell you where I stand—and where I hope to stand."

He straightened up from the table and walked across to the side-rail of the porch. His shadow flowed up a pillar, and the evening sun, turning orange, glinted on his polished riding-boots. He did not lean on the rail, but stood with his back to it, legs wide, hands deep in the cross-pockets of his tan breeches, and solid head and shoulders hunched forward. He said, his voice rumbling:

"I am talking to you now, Gillian Morris! You'll listen?"

That was to my father. He never called me Gillian. I was Gilly, and it had a contemptuous implication.

And there it struck me that, though Ward had been addressing Mary, it was my father he had been talking at most of the time, implying all the things he, and he alone, had done to Castle Gillian. I looked at my father. The indictment had not stirred a hair in him. He no longer cared. He sat aside at the table, his chin in his pale cupped hand. The evening glow in his creamy bush of hair made it almost translucent as he moved his head in a dignified assent to listen to Garret Ward. I felt something close to awe. He was like some fallen god assenting to hear the plea of some lesser Lucifer in the abyss which was his dominion.

But Garret Ward was not awed. His deep voice was easy and conversational.

"This place is in the marrow of your bones too, Uncle, and I'll make a proposal that might appeal to you. You know my place over at Monaglass? It is big enough and good enough, but not quite good enough for blooded stock—too much peat and not enough limestone. The Ministry for Lands wants it for division amongst some dam' crofters, and they can have it at a price—and the price is about fixed. I have three brood mares with three foals at side, and you know who they are by and out of. I have a yearling and a two-year-old, and four horses in training—all useful or promising. That is twelve in all, young and old, and a stable jockey thrown in. Uncle Gillian, when I get rid of Monaglass I want to breed and rear and train my horses here at Castle Gillian—where my people belong."

Mary stirred in her chair, and put him a quick question :

"Buying us out?"

Garret Ward paused for a long time before he replied. I heard old Timmy shuffle across from the arch in the wall, and his shadow lengthened prodigiously on the gravel. He gave the little Kerry cow an impatient shove and, before Garret Ward answered Mary, I heard his grumble, "Shove over, you consaited divil! thinkin' I have nothing else to do but attind to your bellowin' an' the fit on you."

"No-o!" said Garret Ward at last and slowly. "No! not buying you out! Not lock, stock and barrel! even if you are agreeable—and you're not. Listen, Uncle Gillian! I'll settle with Padderson for his three thousand, and I'll put another two thousand into the stables; and in return you'll assign me a controlling interest in Castle Gillian, house, stable and lands."

So that was the business. Garret Ward leant back on

23

the railing, and put his hands on it, so that his barrel of chest strained against his vest. The evening sun was shining red through the shell of his ears, and I noticed that one of them was bigger than the other, and stood out from his head. I looked at my father. His propping hand did not leave his chin, but his lips moved, and his voice was casual through the huskiness of alcohol.

"A controlling interest! fifty-one per cent.—or more?"

"More—much more," said Ward promptly. "A two-thirds controlling interest signed and sealed——"

"For five thousand pounds? Dirt cheap at the price, Garret!" There was not even the bargainer's surprise in my father's voice.

"Three thousand to Padderson," corrected Ward, "and two thousand in the business! Get more in the open market if you can—you have five months to try." A quirk came into his voice. "Can you think up another partner, Uncle?"

No! my drunken father would never find a partner, and Garret Ward knew that. If the place went on the open market Gillian Morris would have to sell outright. But Garret Ward also knew that any bargain that left part of the place to the Morrises would appeal to my father and Mary, for, indeed, Castle Gillian was as the marrow of their bones. Garret Ward went on talking.

"I'll put all my cards on the table, so that there can be no mistake as to what I want. If I come to own two-thirds of Castle Gillian I shall of course retain that name——"

"Wait!" I stopped him. "Retain the name if you like, but as majority owner you can enter all horses as trained or trained-and-owned by Garret Ward. And that's the end of Morris of Castle Gillian, thou brazen son of Shylock!" It struck me then that he had a Jewish cast of countenance, but, to be fair to a much-maligned race, there was not a trace of Jewish blood in him—as far as I knew.

"That's for future arrangement," he said equably, and went on. "Now I come to the important point and I want you to note it, Uncle. I know Mary's value as a trainer, and I want her to train with and for me. You will contract her to train for me for one year as from the first of October next. At the end of that year, if Mary is then my wife, you will give us an option to buy your third share. That is all! Excuse plain speaking, and thank you for listening so patiently." He lit another cigarette and blew smoke through his flattened nose.

My father and Mary had, indeed, listened patiently. Why not? If Garret Ward had been anyone else I would consider his offer reasonable—more than reasonable—for a place we could not maintain, and might have to sell for a song.

I pivoted round on the sun-warmed flags, my back against a pillar, and my hands about my pulled-up knees. My father was lying back in his chair now, his slightly unfocussed eyes on Garret Ward. The decanter was three parts empty. Ward's proposals had not moved him in any way. Nor had they moved Mary. Reclining in her old chair, ankles crossed and hands behind her head, her long supple figure took the eye. Her dark eyes were brooding on Garret Ward.

Jerusalem! Is she falling for him? I thought with dismay. "Thanks, Garret!" she said almost mildly. "Have you no proposal about brother Gillian?"

I sensed some irony in that, but he didn't. His laugh showed how confident he was that he had the game in hand.

"Oh, Gilly? We'll marry him off on Silly Gayne. Isn't that the arrangement with Uncle Tom?"

It was, but not any longer, I said to myself.

"The editorial *we* already," I said aloud, and thrust a chin at Mary. "Mary, have any implications penetrated that obstinate black head of yours?"

"I have listened to some plain speaking," she said, not getting me.

"Do you know what it means?"

"Of course——"

"You don't. It means that in less than a year and a half cousin Garret Ward will own all Castle Gillian, including yourself—if he wants you."

"Including myself?" Her dark brows half-hooded her eyes.

"And that has two implications," I hinted. "Go and consider them, you dumb cluck!"

"Don't mind the viper, Mary!" Ward was not taking umbrage. "I'm not rushing you—that's all."

"But he has a curb chain on you all the same," I said.

My father sat up and held up the stem of his clay to Ward.

"You do not want an immediate answer I presume?" he enquired calmly.

"Certainly not, sir! Take all the time——"

"Five months at most," my father interrupted him. "Very good! As the Scots say, we'll take the matter to *avizandum*, and the discussion is now closed."

My certes! as the Scots say, to hear that rich, deliberate husky voice, one would think that it was he, and not Garret Ward, who had the situation snugly under his thumb.

I think Mary was glad that the discussion had ended that way—for the time. With the whip of a slip of whalebone she was out of her chair.

"Sandy Ythan has been whistling for me this quarter-hour," she said, "and Caerline Show day after tomorrow!"

She gave my tousle of hair a soft tug, took the three steps in a fly, and made loose-footed for the arch in the wing-wall. Crisis or none, the routine of the stables must go on.

"I'll spell you, my dear!" That was Garret Ward, and as he brushed by, he gave me a playful but solid clunk on the crown—not the first by a long count.

IV

I re-lit my pipe and sat on. Let Garret Ward do my share of the work at Mary's side, and his own work on Mary too! I puffed slowly and fixed my eyes on the angle of my father's lean jaw. He was gazing up into the grimy, groined ceiling of the portico where dusty old cobwebs hung in what are known as Irish curtains. We seldom talked to each other any more. The thrushes were singing still, as they would go on singing till the summer heat stilled them, unconcerned with the fate or fall of Castle Gillian. . . . The old round of nature would go on, no matter what happened to the dynasty of Morris. Well! a man could drift round with it. . . .

In the quietness of the evening I could hear the lances of milk striking frothily into Timmy's milking pail, and Timmy was rhythmically crooning an old lullaby to help the cow yield the last of her strippings. That croon I had heard Timmy sing to Mary as a baby.

> "O-o-h! there's two and two more,
> And two in the cradle,
> And two in me lap,
> And two and two more.
> O-o-h! I'm weepin' an' wailin'
> And rockin' the cradle,
> And nursin' a baby
> That's none of me own."

"True for you, Timmy Tadg Shawn!" said my father, softly husky, his voice slurring a little. "Gill and Mary

27

were the only babies you ever had." And he went on musing remotely, though now his remarks were in my direction: "I wonder, Gillian, was it a good thing for you to go out to war?"

"'Tisn't good for any man to go to war," I said; "but I know what you mean, sir, and you are wrong. I was never the one to save Castle Gillian. I'm not the true horseman stock, and maybe I should thank God for that."

"Yes!" he said, ignoring the bite. "To train horses a man must have training in the blood and bones of him. If he hasn't, the horses find out and fail him."

"And you found me out too, sir, and that—well! it did not help."

"No blame to you, boy! But there was your sister——"

"Pity she wasn't a boy and born when I was, you mean?"

"She might have saved the place from slipping."

I came to my feet without using a hand. I would not let him go, this once tin-god with feet of clay. I spoke as quietly as I could. "Mary could not save the place. The place is all right. There's no finer place, anywhere, and it is still here and waiting."

"It was I that lost grip and went slipping, you imply?" He just murmured the words, and I was sorry then.

"Your son failed you," I said, "and you were left with a young daughter——"

He brought his eyes down from the ceiling and smiled at me. "Don't start making excuses for me. I sunk Castle Gillian, and when I found that Mary knew about horses I tried to take money from the books with half-trained racers. Slipping judgment, Gillian lad! and here we are—on the rocks."

"But not yet broken-backed," I said. "Find Mary five thousand pounds clean cash and she'll float the old ship." But I knew that I was lying. Mary might carry on in a limping way with five thousand; but Garret Ward was right: a woman-trainer cuts no ice, and the place would never really revive until a dominant man was in control. I did not want that man to be Garret Ward—and there was no other man.

The stem of his clay pipe broke in his fingers. He rubbed the bowl at the side of his nose, and his eyes focussed me.

"You heard the five thousand offered——"

I took a step nearer him. "What do you think of that offer yourself, sir?"

He shook his head at me, and his voice shook a little too. "I was boasting, boy. I take nothing to *avizandum*, for I no longer think. When, at last, I found that I had nothing in me to draw on, I sat back and let Kismet do its damnedest. That is what I am doing now." He threw the bowl of the pipe over my head to crumble on the pillar behind me, and a fragment rapped me on the poll. I took another step nearer.

"Then Garret Ward will get his own way?" I said.

My father had come out of his tower this evening, and stayed out a bit longer. "Listen, my son!" he said, his voice again slurring. "If there is no other way out, and your sister—not you, but Mary—if she is agreeable I'll do exactly what Garret Ward wants."

"Then she'll be Garret Ward's wife—or she'll be worse," I said harshly.

"If that is her way, and it is so writ for her."

I lost control for a moment. "Damn your Kismet!" I said. "Does it see your son taking an eight-o'clock-in-the-morning walk?"

He moved his head. "No, Gillian! If the time came, one might save a son from that."

I considered his words, and was not sure that I got their meaning. Behind me across the gravel I heard the

29

slap of Timmy's palm on the cow's rump. "Kick me would ye? Go and chew the cud, you ungrateful baste." And then there was the shuffle of his slippers towards the arch in the wall.

"Leave it, son!" said my father. "I have been looking on at you choosing your own road in a dying world. Don't think you can make a fresh choice in the next five months, and lead Mary thereon. Her problem is her own, and it is bigger than yours."

"And too big for Mary," I said.

My father sat forward. He was looking behind my shoulder. "Hello! Here's Tom Gayne and Sylvia— your own problem."

V

I turned on my heel. Yes! Tom Gayne and his Sylvia—not my Sylvia—were coming across the lawn, Sylvia a little behind, and giving the impression that she was being dragged along. As was her habit, as well as mine, she slanted towards the Kerry cow that flicked a tail for her and waited to have an ear pulled. Her father came straight across the gravel and up the steps into the porch. I found the table behind me, put my hands back on it, and looked down at my toes. I wondered what was in Uncle Tom's mind, but I might not find out. He looked and spoke like a forthright man, but was not.

"'Morrow, Gillian!" he greeted my father in his genial bluff way. "Them two brats of ours have been fighting again, and I won't have it, bydam!"

"Bydam you will, Thomas!" said my father lazily. "They'll fight till the day they die—and be unhappy in Paradise if one of 'em is in Hades. Have a drink?"

"Not yet. Och! I don't mean the usual sparrin'. This is more serious." The orange glow of the sun was cut off from me, and I knew he was standing over me. "'Morrow, young Gillian!" he said.

"Good morrow, sir!" I gave back, and lifted eyes to him.

He was as tall as my father, but not lean like him: a big bulky figure of a man in a white woollen homespun; double-jowled, ruddy-cheeked, with light eyes, and not a trace of white in his light scanty hair. To look at Tom Gayne and Gillian Morris together one would pick Tom as the drinking man; and, indeed, he took his share, but with continence. He shook his head down at me, and grumbled:

"Boy! have you no sense at all?"

"Not a scrap, Uncle Tom," I humoured him.

"I'm thinkin' that same! Don't you know the rule: a bottle by the neck, a woman by the waist? Hit 'em and hold 'em, and kiss 'em hard and often."

"If you're talking of Sylvia," I said, "she'd knock my block off."

"I am, and she mightn't. Bydam! Ye two youngsters puzzle me. Tell me, did you ever kiss her at all?"

"I forget," I said.

"Just as well, if that's the sort of kiss it was. Never mind! Here she is now to speak her piece, and I'll leave ye to it." He stepped back and aside, and put his hands behind his back, as an interested spectator would.

Sylvia was coming up the steps, slowly and casually; but I knew, by the pallor round her mouth, that she was still agitated. Her lips were now an orange splash, and she had used her powder-puff, and her eyes were lustrous; but yet I knew that she had been "letting the tear down fa'." I leant propped back on my hands, and she came close up to me. The dying sun made a halo of her hair, and the orange glow behind her outlined the long lines of her through her blue dress.

31

"You are a good-looking hoyden, anyway!" I said.

"Go to the devil!" she said, her eyes lighting, "and if he is good-looking so are you. Oh!" She put her hand up to her mouth. "No! I'd better begin over again."

I shook my head at her. "Girl, dear! you didn't learn your piece well. Didn't your da's slipper hurt enough? Hey! Keep that left paw to yourself."

"Oh dear! oh dear!" She gripped her indignation back. "I will not fight with you, Gill Morris."

"You won't? What are you here for? Don't say it! I never knew you were a coward."

She pulled herself up. "*You* call me a coward, that I have seen cowarded every day of your life."

We had ignored the two old men, and they left us to it.

"Will you let me speak, Gillian?" she said in her deep voice.

"I like you better than that," I said. And it was then, in a sudden flash, that I made up my mind. I surprised her. I was on my feet and so close that she started back; but my hands came down on her shoulders and held. She trembled under my hands, as if she disliked me touching her, and that hurt me, and made me want to hurt her too.

"Look you, Sylvia!" I said, tight silk in my voice. "I like you fine, and sometimes you don't like me. Good enough in its way, but not good enough for a fire-corner! We are sick of being thrown at each other's heads, and I am not playing any longer. You are not in my market for I have nothing to buy you with—nothing in me any more to offer to Castle Evan or to you, and you said it to-day. Wait! I don't want your father's money to play with, or get drunk on, or to prop up Castle Gillian. To hell with your father's money! I think too well of you to marry you for it, cold blood to cold blood. And that being the way, I am not marrying you, Syl. Are you listening? I wouldn't marry you if you were the last woman top of earth."

That was a long speech for me, and a brutal one too. Sylvia, eyes wide and lips parted, was shaking under my hands, but all she said was:

"Oh, Gillian!"

"Oh, Gillian! and ho, Gillian! You're a free woman now. Go home and make your own bed for yourself."

I swung her around quickly, and gave her a firm shove; and she went, slowly, almost heavily, down the steps and across the gravel; but, when on the grass, she suddenly came alive, and took to her heels, lifting her long legs neatly and economically as a girl does. Was she cursing or weeping? No, not weeping! When Sylvia wept she could be heard across the glen.

I turned then to face her father, and I was ready to outface him too. He was not looking at me, but at his flying daughter; and there was something like hurt in his face.

"She can run like Deirdre in Glen Etive, that lass," my father said composedly. "Where do you go from there, Tom Gayne?"

Tom Gayne did not answer. He came over to me to be faced and outfaced. He was inches taller, and he bent down and forward to look close into my eyes. His face was stern and his eyes hard, and I tried to outgaze him. I found that I could not. My eyes flickered and sank, and when I lifted them again he was standing straight, and his mood had changed. He was smiling.

"Very well so!" he said placatingly. "If that's the way ye carry on—two young fools hurting each other! Why were you hurting her, Gillian?"

"I wasn't hurting her," I said hotly, and a spurt of anger helped me. "I'll not have her thrown at my head. By God! I'll not have her browbeaten by you or anyone else."

"Browbeaten! Thunder an' turf! You young bully——!" His mood again changed. "All right! All right! Sure all I want is for the two of ye to be friendly."

I looked at him suspiciously. Was the wily old devil getting at me in another way? He sensed what was in my mind, and spoke hastily. "No—no! Damn the game I'm playin'! Why should I, after I know the way the land lies?"

But did he know? I said: "You won't rush Sylvia, Tom Gayne?"

"Divil the rush! Look, young fellow! don't you browbeat me. By this and by that! If I live to be a hundred—and I will—I'll never again open my mouth in anything that concerns ye two fly-off-the-handles. But, all the same, ye are cousins, and I don't want any bad blood between the families." His mood changed again, and he took me into his confidence. "She is the only one I have, Gill—she and you brought up together —and I'd like you to be friendly with her, and keep an eye on her for me. That's all. And, sure, you could be taking an odd wallop at each other, and no harm done!"

There was something in his gruff voice that moved me. I answered to it impulsively: "Uncle Tom, I'll be friendly with her in spite o' hell—I'll be friendly with her in spite of herself."

"I wouldn't doubt you, Gillian! You are your mother's son—God rest her!" he said warmly, and slapped me on the shoulder.

"Amen!" said my father. "A nice bit of work, Tom!"

Tom Gayne swung to my father, threw back his big head, and laughed hugely. "Begobs, Gillian Morris! after me throwin' the daughter at your son's head, an' havin' her pitched back at me, I'll take a drink from you—and I need it. This'll do—I like my whiskey neat." He picked up Mary's cup, emptied the dregs into the saucer, and poured whiskey generously. There wasn't a half-inch left in the decanter. I watched him with interest, and there was a snigger at the back of my throat.

"Here's to us all, on us!" he toasted, and took a deep gulp. Then he pulled up his shoulders, and shivered all through him, his eyes batting and his throat gagging. "Holy Saint Christopher! I'm p'isoned," he managed to say. To a drinker of neat spirits diluted whiskey is most nauseating.

"That's powerful strong whiskey, Uncle Tom," I said hurriedly.

He looked at me fiercely, ready to explode. His big body hid my father, and I shook my head and formed the word "Mary" with my lips. He was an old sportsman. He grinned understandingly, and turned to my father.

"Be the powers, Gillian!" he said, "that whiskey of yours has the divil's own kick."

My father nodded as he emptied the decanter into his cup. "I noticed that, Tom. That scoundrel, Maney, at the Cross, must be palming off immature spirits on me. I'll talk to him."

"Begobs do!" advised Uncle Tom. "But sure whiskey is nane the waur for an extra kick, and I would never turn my back on it. Here's to us once again, an' God ha' mercy on me!"

He tossed it off like a man, shivered again, drew a long breath, and put the cup fumblingly on the table. "This is not my lucky day," he said. "Ah well! I'll have to be leavin' ye now to be sayin' a word to that girl o' mine before she burns the house down—only a friendly word or two, Gillian lad. Faith! the two of ye frighten me."

35

He leant to my ear. "If I get rid of me eternal soul into the Gullane River, I'll come back and haunt Mary—God bless her!"

He departed hurriedly, and I watched him go, his shoulders hunched, and a hand over his paunch. He probably would be sick too, but that would be beneficial to a man of his full habit.

VI

I heard a rustle and a creak behind me. My father was on his feet, his hand on the neck of the decanter to hold him steady. He focussed his eyes on me over his high-set nose, and I wondered what he would say to the son who had thrown a bonny lass and her tocher into the discard. But, true to his code, he said just nothing at all on that subject.

"May evenings carry their chill for thin blood," he said. "I'm going in."

There was no chill that mild May evening, and his thin blood might register on a spirits hydrometer. But the decanter was empty, and he would need to refill it; and he would empty it again before he slept.

He lifted the decanter, pivoted cautiously, steadied himself, and walked line-straight for the hall door, as if he was walking on a plank just wide enough. His footsteps echoed emptily from the old black-and-white tiles of the hall. Then I heard other steps shuffle, and old Timmy came out, holding a big tin tray like a breastplate. The earthenware rattled crackedly as he piled it on, and his cracked old voice grumbled away to itself.

"Some people work, and some people don't, but all of 'em talk all the time. I heard some of it."

"I knew you were behind the door," I said, "but aren't you deaf in one lug?"

36

"But don't I know the lug, and haven't I sense enough to turn th' other wan?"

"Listeners hear no good of themselves!"

"True for you! I heard enough to know that Timmy Tadg Shawn might be out of here come harvest time."

"What's wrong with Garret Ward?" I asked him, taking a short-cut.

"Nothin' that might not be wrong with many a dacent man. But there's the power o' the dog as well! An', moreover, some of his blood don't match with our blood." Timmy was not kin to us, but our blood was his blood all the same.

"You're a perverted old snob," I told him.

"Small right for you to be calling me names I can't retort to be dint o' education," he complained. "But, high or low, I knew Nedeen Ward, an' he makin' his money sellin' delf ware, afore he married into your cousins the Terrys of Monaglass—much as his grandson would be insertin' himself in Castle Gillian."

"And you wouldn't stay? Where would you go?"

"Wherever you go—and where else?"

"A far road, Timmy!" I said gently.

"It mightn't then," said Timmy as if to himself, "unless he went for it the long way round, an' I'd be waitin' for him near the end o' the road."

I knew what he meant. "Go park yourself in hell, you old devil, and wait there!" I cursed him, vaulted the side-rail of the porch and moved towards the arch in the wall.

He called after me. "Divil yourself! I'll have the supper ready if you're still atin'—that bit salmon you and Miss Syl gaffed nefar'ous the mornin'."

The sun was behind the shoulder of far-away Shirlan Ben, and the toneless, lonesome light of the gloaming was drifting down on all the valley of the Gullane. The

37

heavy masses of the holm-oaks seemed to close over something ominous and withdrawn, and all the near-by birds had stopped singing; but away up the slope among the larches, where the rim of the sun might still be in view, one brave thrush was throating a final vesper.

I went through the arch into a cobbled yard, with the kitchen door to the right. At the corner of a tumbledown peat shed a fine cupressi grew out of what looked like solid rock, and beyond it was another arch leading directly to the stables. And under the up-curving branches of the tree my sister and Garret Ward were facing each other and talking. His broad back was half-turned to me, and neither of them saw me or heard me coming. Sylvia used to tell me that I had a treacherous walk, because I moved cat-footed and in-toed; though the natural man in his bare feet is silent-footed as any cat, and in-toed too.

I saw and heard them all right. I did not hear much, for the talk was near its climax. Ward was speaking, and his heavy voice was confident and almost playful.

"No use kicking against the pricks, my dear Mary. My offer is on the board, and it is above the board also."

I saw Mary's fine hair shake, and knew that her steadfast eyes were on him. "No, Garret! I will not tie myself while there is still space to turn in."

"Yes—yes! Turn as much as you like, and I'll be there." He extended a broad hand. "Look, Mary! I'll take a chance with you. Say the word and I'll pay Padderson his three thousand to-morrow."

Mary shook her head again, and more definitely. "No! I could take your money on one condition only—and I am not ready."

"You will be ready?" Confidently persuasive, he put a hand on her shoulder with a small pat. She tried to draw away, but her heel caught on a root, and, to prevent her falling, his hand went round her shoulder. Before she knew, she was inside his arms. But he hadn't her yet; she brought her hands up quickly and propped her wrists under his chin. He tried to draw her close, face and breast, and I saw her arms slacken and go rigid again. Her head was back, and her voice was as cool as water.

"You can't storm me that way, Garret. Please let me go!"

I drew in a long breath, and took two paces forward. *This is the show-down at last!* I said to myself, and there was an ugly empty feeling at the pit of my stomach. It was fear, but I would try and take Garret Ward nevertheless.

It was not the show-down, for he at once let her go, and stepped back himself. He laughed.

"I will not storm you," he said. "You'll come of your own free will—when I am ready." His voice went throaty. "Gosh, girl! I want to kiss you warm—I'm off!" He clapped his big palms, turned on his heel and went off through the arch to the stable-yard where his saddle-horse was.

I walked straight up to her. She was not embarrassed. She grimaced at me, and ran her hands through her hair.

"Blast him!" she said exasperatedly. "He has the pull of Lucifer, star of the morning."

"The power of the dog only," I said. "Do you want him?"

She met my eyes fairly, and did not hesitate. "I don't. I don't want anyone, or anything but Castle Gillian—and it flourishing like a green bay tree."

"Between now and October?"

"As long as God lets me!" Her voice was harsh, and her brows down. "A month, five months, fifty years, and I going out feet first! I'll play the game out."

"Come off it!" I said. "You're only a pawn in the game."

39

"Neither pawn nor queen, I make my own moves."
She did not often show emotion, but she showed it now.
"To keep hold of Castle Gillian I might cold-bloodedly
marry Garret Ward, mover-of-women. I might even
come to do worse—for now I know what you meant by
your two implications. I'll hang on here as long as I
can—all my days if God lets me—all my days if God
rejects me—with you near me across the glen at Castle
Evan. You have it now, Gill!"

I had the talk where I wanted it, and lifted a hand as
she moved to leave me.

"Wait! Suppose I am not at Castle Evan?"

She gave a little snort. "Where else would you be?
you and your Sylvia—and, maybe, a new small clann
of Morrises!"

"I will not be at Castle Evan," I told her then. "I
am not marrying Sylvia."

She laughed at me, her eyes crinkling, and when she
laughed she was a new and lovely girl, because of the
contrast with her usual seriousness. She simply would
not believe me, and I had to make her.

"Another small war?" she enquired carelessly, taking
a step away.

"I am not marrying Sylvia Gayne, I tell you," I said
steadily.

That held her. She looked closely at me, all serious
now. She was even inclined to be angry.

"You stubborn young fool!" she called me. She was
five years my junior, and I was twenty-nine. "I have a
good mind to shake some sense into you." Her firm hands
came down on my shoulders, but my shoulders were stiff
under them. That vexed her, for she was some conceited
about her active young vigour and her strong horsewoman's hands. "Stubborn is right!" she said. "By glory!
I'll stand you on your head and let the spleen run out."

She slipped one hand under my arm, and tried to pull me close. But I was in no mood for horseplay, and remained as stubborn as a post in concrete. I made no move to grapple her, and she could not move me an inch. That sobered her. Her hands slackened and tightened again affectionately, and she looked close into my eyes. Her voice coaxed me:

"Why, Gillian lad, who hurt you? Sylvia, the little rip?"

"She didn't"—that was a lie—"but I am not marrying her."

"But poor old Sylvia! Syl is a darling——"

"I'm not marrying her, I tell you, and I wish you'd listen to me for one minute."

"All right, Gill! I'm listening," she said soothingly. "Tell me what has gone so terribly wrong."

"Nothing at all has gone wrong," I said, and put my hands over her shoulders. We stood there holding each other, and I tried my best to force my will through my hands. The gloaming had closed round us, and Mary's eyes were black in a white face. I gathered my thoughts, and spoke carefully and slowly:

"Whatever Castle Gillian had once, it has no soul of its own any more. It is only a vampire of a place sucking the life blood out of you, holding you, body and soul, until you lose them both in an evil bargain. I can't stand that for you, Maureen Oge. Are you listening to me?"

"I am listening, Gillian."

"But not heeding! Look! This is only a place, not an entity; and we are only sojourners, not possessed nor possessors. As a mere place, why not sell it in the open market and clear our feet——"

"And our father?" she put quickly.

"An empty husk, he can't and he won't bind us. Let

him go and live with Uncle Tom, if he can't leave Gullane Glen."

"And Sylvia?"

"Let Sylvia go her own road, and find a man for herself."

"I thought she had one?" she suggested softly, not to vex me.

"She hasn't—she never had, and now she knows it."

"You told her?"

"I told her." But I didn't say that Sylvia had told me first.

"Poor Syl!" said Mary.

"Oh damn!——"

"Wait! What about us—you and me?"

"We would make the long trek out of dying land. Australia or New Zealand is the place for us. With your knowledge and tricks-of-the-trade you'd go places in Australia, where, I am told, the people have sold themselves to horse-flesh. And can't I farm? Dammit! don't I love a sheep, don't I love a cow, don't I love a pig even—anything but a useless blood horse?" I had about run myself dry.

Bending to me in the twilight, she looked close into my eyes, and I could see a quiver about her mouth before she spoke. "Is that all?"

"It is, and it went in one ear and out the other."

"It did not, brother." A note that sounded like exultation was in her voice. "I am glad to make your acquaintance, for the first time, young Mr Morris. Would you sacrifice so much and so much for your pig-headed sister?"

"No bloody sacrifice about it!" I said brutally. "Can't you be serious?"

"I am, and so are you. But if a sacrifice is called for I don't want you to collar the job."

"What the devil are you talking about?" I said, and gave her a good shake.

"Maybe you don't know," she said with a touch of sarcasm, and gave me back the shake. "I'll not be rushed, even by you, Gillian. One has to take thought and time to choose the holocaust, and, as our father said, I'll take this to *avizandum*."

"You're only hedging!" I protested.

"I am not," she said, almost fiercely. "I understand, as never before, all that is implied. It is I, the woman, that has to decide—as usual. I will give you your answer when I give Garret Ward his. That is all." Her voice again changed, and went low and husky. "My poor old Gillian! and my poor old Mary as well!"

I fear we went sentimental then. Her cold little nose was in my neck, and her breath quivering in my ear. She was crying in her own quiet way, and I was tugging softly at her hair, that was tickling me, and I was swallowing small hard potatoes.

And I did not go fishing for that two pound—ten ounce—quarter-pound trout.

Chapter II

THIS IS ROBIN MORRISON

I

I DID not see Sylvia Gayne for two days. The down-and-up path across the Gullane was deeply worn, and usually we were back and fore two or three times a day. But the girl was holding aloof now, and I was not yet in the mood to start redeeming my promise to her father.

I saw Sylvia again on the first day of the big Spring Show at Caerline. I went there, ten miles on my old cycle, supposedly to see Mary compete for the Goodsel Cup, the premier prize in the fifteen-hand jumping class; but, actually, I went to see the cattle, the agricultural implements and the gadgets.

I had a good morning amongst the beasts: the massive soft-eyed, sound-fleshed beasts lumbering placidly into and around the show rings: and the lively little classes like the Kerry and the Ayrshire, always on the edge of prancing and tossing a horn. After that I went for the Machinery Hall, and had another good time. The sun, pouring diffusedly through the glass of the high-domed roof, gleamed on polished steel, nickel and chromium, and enriched all the colours of the rainbow garishly mixed together—like a splendid, barbaric, impressionist picture in the modern French style. Here was what I liked in a show, not trick jumpers.

There were some new machines and refinements that appealed to me. After a world-disastrous war, farm implements and machinery were again the interest of engineers who for six years had been inventing gadgets

44

to kill their fellow-men at the behest of the War Lords for the love o' Liberty. There was a one-man motor-plough on the motor-cycle principle that I coveted, that I would buy if I had the money, that I would dicker for if I had even a first instalment. I could use that machine at Castle Gillian.

The plain, honest, food-production side was mine, and this was my slack season. Our drills of potatoes were already peeping, the white turnip showing a pale green, the oats breered in bluish emerald; and when I had the swedes down and the spuds earthed I would have an easy time till hay-saving started in late June. After that, to October, there would not be an hour I could call my own. And after October? In my vain moments I used tell myself that I toiled to help Mary play out her losing game, but, back of all, I knew I liked farming for itself; and, sometimes, I told myself that marriage with Sylvia had its attractions, because at Castle Evan I could let myself go and farm high, wide and handsome. That was all finished now.

I talked with an exhibitor here and there, and had what he called a *sederunt* with an intelligent Scot showing and selling ochre-and-red threshing-machines.

"Is it true, sir," I asked him, "that since the first threshing-machine was turned out—by a Scot probably—no material improvement has been made—that it was about perfect from the start?"

"I wouldna go as far as that, young man," he said cautiously. "There have been bits o' refinements in oiling and electric fittings. But I will say this: the first machine designed in the toon o' Aberdeen by my great-great-grandfather did its work as efficiently as this will do it, and with identical similar guts in the belly o't."

"Manalive!" I said, "your twice-great-grandfather was no' a business man."

He chuckled. "I canna see the point in that crack, sin' he made sure none o' his kin would see what you'd call a poor day."

I pointed to the machine. "How long should that do good work?"

"Give it fair play, as long as the parson's one-hoss shay."

I joined him in his chuckle. "That's where your forefather made a mistake," I said. "He should have kept a few refinements up his sleeve, and brought out a new design every three or four years, same as the motor companies. Where would you be now?"

"In hell with the auld-kirkers! Man, you're by way of an unbeliever! If you must have private enterprise, and you canna do wantin' it, you must trail a bait to draw your customers."

"And there's the ritual without an ethic in the code of the great god Mammon."

"Dinna blame Mammon ower muckle! Us Christians know a groat from a bawbee. Hey, Aelec!" he hailed an assistant. "I'll no' be long. I'm for convertin' a heretic, or vice versa."

We went into one of the refreshment bars and talked, and did not convert each other. Moderately, he drank Irish whiskey, which he had got to like better than his native Scotch on his many visits to our Irish showgrounds —and a good judge too. I drank some thin porter, and did not like it. And we talked so much that I was nearly late for Mary's jumping.

By the time I got round to the white railing in front of the grand-stand she had got through the first round, successfully, and was already in the enclosure for the second. She looked well on horseback. She was long-legged and long-stirruped; her hands were good, and her arms not flapping wings; her backbone was a limber slip of whalebone, and she did not jounce wide-buttocked in the saddle. She was riding her piebald almost-pony Crabpie, a fifteen-year-old trick jumper that had been consistently winning showground events for seven seasons. It won this event too. It could have gone over the course bareback. Mary had only to keep her balance while the piebald steadied itself, and jumped, and rocketted, and changed feet, and tucked its hind legs in. In addition to the cup, to be held for a year, was a prize of twenty sovs—not real sovereigns any more, but treasury notes of an almost debased currency. Twenty pounds would come in handy, but it was a long way short of the thousands Mary needed.

Showground jumping was not Mary's line of country, but it helped to keep her in the public eye, and brought an occasional new client to a stable that not so long ago could and did choose its clientele arbitrarily. Mary, first and foremost, was a trainer of racehorses, flat and 'chase, and showground jumping is tricky and leisurely compared with the dash and fire of steeplechasing, where a horse has to take the fence in its stride, and devil take the hindmost.

After Mary's success I lost any interest I had, and moved out into the wide parade below the stands, wondering whether I'd start for home or take another turn among the Aberdeen pollies. It was there I spied Sylvia.

The jumping was on for the rest of the afternoon, and the folk were drifting across the parade towards the stands. It was a bright spring day, with a bright spring sky where little white clouds sailed; and far away over the roof of the stand I saw the long ridge of Shirlan Ben, green and brown and limestone grey, with the sun shining on it, and the cloud shadows racing. The sun shone down on the parade too, and made a galaxy of colour, for it was ladies' day, and the ladies were as gorgeous as a pride of peacocks. How is it that man is one of the few species, including the falcon and the spider, where the male leaves the bedizenment to the female? It was not so in virile Elizabethan days, when a man was a man-and-a-half, and a woman knew her place.

Sylvia, when I saw her, was as taking to the eye as any female there. She was wearing a flowered dress of many colours, a rather wide hat with a small helmet crown, and carried a bright parasol over one shoulder. Her face against that background was lovely and alive and fully war-painted. There was, as always, some soft allure about her, and the tender curves of cheek and chin belied a tough and persistent core. She was the Lady Debonair.

I could not understand how such an eye-easy young shaft of girlhood was alone in that multitude of young males. Usually she was not. Also, I saw, by the turn of her head this way and that, that she was on the look-out for someone. That someone could be no longer I, but there I was, and she was walking straight down at me. I didn't catch her eye once, but I knew she had seen me by the way she pulled herself up and set her eyes on some horizon far over my head. I stopped in front of her, and when she tried to brush by I was still in front of her, so that she had to step back to avoid a collision.

"Get out of my road, Gill Morris!" she said, and I knew by the deep timbre of her voice and the fading of colour round her brilliant mouth that she was still hurt.

"I won't get out of your road," I said, "and you can't make me." That did not look a good way of offering the olive branch, but I knew Sylvia's reactions by this time.

"Can't I?" said Sylvia, accepting the challenge promptly.

"You can't," I said, "and if you try I'll wrestle you right here amongst the populace—and some of them are looking and listening already."

48

She drew in a long breath. "What do you want?" she asked, as if she had all the patience in the world.

"I want to be friends—for the day."

"Friends! Friends, indeed!" She was finely indignant. "After all you said to me?"

"Cast your mind—if you have such a thing—a little further back——"

"So you were only paying me back?" she put quickly.

"No, I wasn't!" I said just as quickly. "Look! now that we've kicked the cart to smithereens couldn't we run free and friendly for a couple of hours?"

"No! you shamed me at your own door, and I'll never forgive you."

"Never is a long time. Ah well! if that is your way!" I stepped aside. "I've done my part, and you can go on looking for whoever you were looking for, and be damned to him!"

"Amen to that!" she agreed warmly, took a step, hesitated, and came round again. "All right! I'll make a truce — for to-day. What'll we do?" She grinned at me cheerfully.

The change was so abrupt that I at once grew suspicious. *By heck! she was looking for me*, I thought. I wouldn't put it past her old fox of a father to have worked on her as he had worked on me. *Poor old Gilly! like a lost soul across the water—don't be hard on the lad if he makes up to you! Sure maybe he didn't mean it,* and so on. Something like that. And here she was in her womanly way putting the onus on me condescendingly. However, I had given my promise, and I would keep it—for the day. I said:

"I'll tell you what we'll do for a beginning. You'll stand me a shilling ice, and I'll stand you two goes in the roundabouts."

"A tanner's worth! No, siree!"

"But I've only five bob between me and destitation—as Timmy calls it."

"I've a ten-bob note somewhere. All right! I could do with an ice. Say, Gill! Was Tyzack Lane in camp at the Bridge this morning?" she asked eagerly.

"No! If he's at the Show, he'll be there this evening."

This is the first time that the name of Tyzack Lane has been mentioned in this chronicle. It will be mentioned again, and often.

The pecuniary transactions between Sylvia and me were as peculiar as our other relations. I will say this for her: money, ordinarily, meant nothing to her; if she had it it went, and if she hadn't she simply didn't need it. Of course she could have all she wanted, but, often as not, she forgot to take any along. But we had a code of our own. Years ago, for some obscure reason connected with the poverty of Castle Gillian, I ruled that any borrowings between us must be on strictly business principles, and I drew up a scale of charges that were plain usurious. Sylvia still stuck to that code—for the good of my soul, she said. Usually I had no money, or, if I had, Mary took it from me, as soon as she found out, and used it on her beloved stables.

After our fashion, when Sylvia and I tangled, we ignored our surroundings, and talked as if we were in the middle of a ten-acre field. People passing by were smiling at us, and giving us pleasant glances. Now I swung to her side, and we went off shoulder to shoulder towards the Amusement Park. I thought the sun was shining a bit brighter.

II

The Amusement Park was a hard-packed paddock back of the showground, and was the usual thing seen at our country fairs: swings and roundabouts of varying ingenuity, shooting galleries, soft-drink stands, mystery tents, innumerable gambles, Tyzack Lane's circus, and Jacus McGrath's boxing-booth.

We were going in at the gate of the park when a bass shout came from behind, and a strong hand thrust me aside.

"Got you! Been hiding out on me, Silly Gayne?" That was Garret Ward, elegant in riding kit, supremely confident, his flat-nosed face massive and arrogant. He had Sylvia by the arm, and was looking down at her round the rim of her parasol; and she was laughing up at him rather mockingly, perhaps challengingly: laughter light and eyes asparkle. I wondered if she had been on the look-out for him, back in the showground. Well! it was no business of mine any more.

"We'll shed Gilly?" he half-queried playfully.

"No! I owe him a shilling ice." Sylvia's voice was light and pleasant now.

"Give him the bob?" he suggested.

I put a challenge up to Sylvia. I thrust a palm under her nose.

"The bob! I'll have it."

Promptly she flashed her hand at mine. "Not on your life! I want an ice too."

"Good enough!" said Ward. "I'll run to three ices. Come on!"

And he took her off with a swing. She looked over her shoulder, some anxiety in her eyes, and gave me a quick beckon of the head. For one whole second I was minded to turn on my heel and go marching, but that would show Garret Ward that he could touch me on the raw. I didn't mind what Sylvia thought. So, hands in pockets, I slouched along behind them.

They went arm in arm, and they looked all right. He was taller than she was, but not by much, and his firm

51

bulk and her lissomeness were like an oak tree and an ash sapling. He was a fine figure of a man from the knees up, but he walked splay-footed and that is not so good in a man. *He would be slow on his feet against a fast boxer,* I thought. In fact, he had a passion for boxing, or rather bruising, for his method was to get inside and stay inside, and break the good boxer in two with short-arm jolts. He was a terror to the proprietors of boxing booths.

I withdrew myself into myself, as was a protective habit of mine. Sun and shadow flowed over me as from a remoteness, and sound came faintly as from a great distance. The mechanical blare of machine-made music, the raucous voices of showmen, the staccato rattle of wheels-of-fortune, the sharp crack of small rifles, the pleasant shouting of children on the roundabouts, the high, rather cruel, gull-like skirling of girls on the swings: all made a susurrus of sound; and the folk that occasionally jostled me were in another dimension.

And then Garret Ward and Sylvia slowed in front of me, and I came up to their side. Sylvia was speaking over her shoulder.

"The Lanes are in. See their canvas!"

I came alive then. Over the cone of a roundabout I could see the canvas of a two-pole circus-tent in alternate strips of green and white.

The Lanes were our friends of long standing: Tyzack Lane, Oonagh Blake his wife, and Jacus McGrath his half-brother. Once a year, for as long as I could remember, they had established temporary headquarters at our Gullane Bridge, and, to us children, the luxury of Castle Evan and the careless living at Castle Gillian were as nothing compared to the fascination of the showman's camp. Mary, Sylvia and I made it our very own, and were accepted without question; and our people knew that we children would come to no harm where Oonagh Blake was queen.

"Let's pass the time of day," Sylvia said. She released her arm from Garret Ward's, came to my side, and took my arm firmly. I knew why she did that, and it was quite thoughtful of her. She and I were friendly with the Lanes, and Garret Ward definitely was not. He had some sort of feud with Jacus McGrath. Tyzack Lane took no part in that feud. If he ever did——! Garret Ward had better look out, even though Garret Ward feared no man.

We moved round the circling ponies and across the open to the brightly-painted, intricately-ornamented ticket-booth at the side of the canvas entrance passage to the tent. The afternoon show would soon be on, and the white, shapely, plump hands of the woman in the booth were deftly taking in money and serving out tickets and change to a moving line of customers.

She was a generous, nobly-built woman in her late middle years, Oonagh Blake, wife of Tyzack Lane. She was wearing a tailor-made costume of dark green, out of which rose a neck round and smooth as a column to support a finely-proportioned head, with the sensitive mouth, the broad cheekbones, and blue eyes of Galway. Even that fine neck seemed barely sufficient to support the great waves of red hair that would be completely unruly but for a green ribbon holding it inadequately in check. She was like a gorgeous red and white flower, fully grown but not yet blown.

An electric organ was blaring behind us, the roundabout was noisy, and it was not easy to make ourselves heard; but Sylvia lifted up her gay treble, and her parasol whirled aloft.

"Hullo, Oonagh darling! You're welcome back."

Oonagh lifted head, laughed richly, and waved a

welcoming hand. Her voice was as clear as a bell, and her arm gave us possession of the whole circus.

"Are you going in, my children?" Garret Ward was a pace behind us, and her words and gesture did not include him. If he had been standing at our side, they would not have included him either.

Oonagh Blake spoke like a lady, she looked like a lady, she was a lady. She had been a secondary school teacher with a degree when she met Tyzack Lane, the coming young pugilist, and married him, not impulsively, but with clear understanding that he was the man for her. And she had never looked back. She was the wife of a showman, lived in a caravan, and was proud of her husband. She had every reason to be. Tyzack Lane could, indeed, leave the road any time, and settle in any place he wanted to. He didn't want to. The show business was his business, and he would touch nothing else. That was his absolute code. And it was his wife's code as well.

Tyzack Lane was there too. A man of middle height, he was leaning a massive shoulder on a corner of the booth. He lifted a quiet hand and gave us a grave smile. Tyzack was economic of speech. He had a grave—almost saturnine—blue-shaven face, coal-black eyes, and his short-cropped, plentiful black hair had no trace of grey in it. He wore a semi-morning-coat of the finest, dark-grey broadcloth, and carried a wide-leafed grey hat in one hand. Presently he would go into the circus and act ring-master for a while.

Tyzack Lane was the son of a showman of gipsy blood, and his mother was Irish, and that's one "quare" mixture. In his young manhood, about the time he met Oonagh Blake, he was in the world-class as a middleweight. It was said that, at his best, the only man who could give him a fight was his younger half-brother Jacus McGrath. They had never met in the ring. As Jacus

54

himself put it: "Holy Saint Jacus! me hit Ty Lane in public! I'd rather hit me mother."

Tyzack Lane had had one son and several daughters. His sons-in-law probably controlled most of the road-shows in the South, and Tyzack had a controlling interest in every one of them. He had grandchildren galore, male and female, but only one grandson who was the apple of his eye. That was Dionysius—Dinny for short—the son of his son, who was dead. I had seen him die. We shall meet Dinny later on.

Sylvia gave my arm an interrogative tug. "Going in?"

"No!" I said. "It will be hot as hell under the canvas, and I want that ice."

Sylvia again lifted up her voice, and her arm was flung in the direction of Glen Gullane.

"You're in camp, Oonagh?"

"To-night," Oonagh called back.

"Be seeing ye, then. Where's Jacus?"

"Down the line." Oonagh laughed. "You'll hear him in a minute."

Sylvia tugged my arm. "Let's look him up." That is what she said, that is all she said, but if she hadn't said it I would have no story to tell. Yes, Sylvia was the directing genius from the very beginning.

Garret Ward came up to our side, and we walked on down the line of shows. Ward had held himself aloof while Sylvia had exchanged greetings with Oonagh Blake. But he would not hold himself aloof with Jacus McGrath.

We hadn't gone a hundred yards when Garret Ward threw back his head, and paused to laugh.

"Listen to old Jacus letting off steam!"

We heard him. A short distance ahead a high, strong, tenor voice lifted above the susurrus of sound. Every word was distinct.

"Step inside, my hearty men! and take a look and a peg at Robber Morrison, the middle-weight champeen o' all Scotland south o' Tweed. No weights barred under one-hundred-and-sixty pounds! Light or welter, stand up to him for three rounds and take me hard-earned fiver. A five-pun' note for only three rounds of two minutes. Who's for it? In ye go, and have your bob ready at the door. Ho-ho! Any middle-weight that puts the Robber away in three rounds takes a tenner. No one barred. Who's for the tenner? . . ."

Garret Ward flexed his shoulders, and laughed again. "Fine! He's got another punching-bag for me. I took that tenner off Jacus last year. Do you mind the lacing I gave that tinker light-heavy?"

"You'll see the nose he gave you any week you shave," I said.

Sylvia laughed lightly. "Your nose is fine, Garret! It makes you unique. Before you acquired it, you were just a plain brute, now you are an intriguing one."

That might contain enough tribute to his masculinity to please him, but it was the word "intriguing" that would please him most. Garret Ward, except in boxing, never wanted to have his way by brute force. And he had his way all the time.

"If you don't know," I told him, "that tinker died four months ago spitting arterial blood."

"His own fault!" he said, indifferently enough. "A man with a weak middle should 'ware boxing."

"Boxing? You don't box, Garret," I said.

"I get results." He gestured towards the booth. "You used to box—care to try me a few rounds?"

Sylvia spoke hastily while I hesitated. "Have you never met your match—among men, Garret?"

"Not yet, my dear—and you can leave out the addendum."

56

"It stays for a future occasion," Sylvia said. "You'll meet your match some day, Garret—everyone does."

"Why not? A match to a matcher! that's the game. If you're there you'll root for me, old girl?"

"I'll be there, and I'll root too," said Sylvia. "Hoy, Jacus! Stop your bellowin'!"

We had stopped before a square, patched-canvas booth. On a soap-box left of the looped-up door-flap was perched a squat old man with a blue jowl. He had Tyzack Lane's cast of countenance, but the gravity was inclined towards truculence, and his eyes, instead of being coal-black and expressionless, were of Irish blue and irascible. He wore an eye-searing suit of black-and-white checks in a mesh of red squares, and a brown bowler hat was pressed hard down over his thickened ears. I should not have called him old; years or age would never weigh that man down.

A few customers were still going in, and an old fellow with a battered face was taking shillings at the triangular opening. The booth must be about filled, for I saw trouser-legs just inside; and a gale of laughter, with a jeering note in it, came through.

The man on the box was Jacobus McGrath, but he was not called Jacus because of that, but because of the expletive he so frequently used. He had the devil's own tongue, was no respecter of caste or class, and, as they say, had a heart o' corn. There was no need for him to run a boxing-booth. It was his plaything, the same as the circus was Tyzack's. He had a notion that our boxers were losing their old toughness, and that the only way to restore it was through the rough-and-tumble of a boxing-booth.

He looked down and across at us, and his blue eyes lit up on Sylvia. Sylvia, from her earliest years, could do what she liked with Jacus, though he protested hell-

57

deep while it was being done to him. My sister Mary was Tyzack's favourite.

"Who's bellowin'?" he demanded hotly. "Jacus, Miss Syl! You're in bad company, and I dunno which of 'em's the worst."

Garret Ward's bass sounded rough after that clear tenor.

"Found another bruiser for me, Jacus?"

"Found him long ago, Garret Ward, only he's bidin' his own time," said Jacus, a cold note in his voice. I did not get his meaning.

"What about your Jock middle-weight-champeen?" Garret Ward asked tauntingly.

Jacus hesitated. "He's nearer Gill Morris's weight," he said then. He nodded to me. "You wouldn't be for tryin' a coupla rounds, you divil?" he half-invited me.

When younger I had often boxed in Jacus's booth, but I was no longer disposed to risk having my block knocked off by old or young professionals. I shook my head at Jacus. I knew that he knew that his Scot was not a match for Garret Ward, and that he was only trying to save him from demolition. Garret Ward sensed that too.

"Have it your own way, Jacus—you're only an old boast!" he said jeeringly. "I'll put a tenner against yours, and take the hide off your Jock?"

That challenge was too much for Jacus. He gestured a thumb, and his tenor was savage. "Go on in, an' be Jacus! you might smell brimstone before your time." He leant to his doorman. "Pass 'em through, Billy! but take a bob off them if they'll give it. They won't." We didn't.

"Come along and see, Syl?" invited Garret Ward. "I need some exercise."

Sylvia looked back at me.

"Don't!" I said. "His match is not in there, and Jacus knows it. It won't be nice."

Destiny was still pointing a finger. "You'd never know," Sylvia said, flapped her parasol shut, and followed Garret Ward. I followed Sylvia, and Jacus stepped down off his box and followed me.

III

There was a golden glow inside the booth: that subdued, diffused light coming through canvas that gives a queer sense of hush. There was no hush inside that tent. Men were laughing—and they were all men. Sylvia was the only female present, but Sylvia was a law unto herself and went anywhere.

The arrangements were economically simple. There was no elevated ring with posts and ropes. Four of Jacus's team held a rope flank high to make a rough square, and another acted as a timekeeper without a watch, and as a referee if things got rough. Once only had I seen that restraining rope tangled up in a free-for-all.

Inside that twelve-foot square of packed clay two men were boxing, one of them furiously. The laughing men round the ring ran more danger from the furious one than did the man slipping round him. One of Jacus's team was playing with a big country lad, but not brutally: just slipping, ducking, feinting, popping a big glove here and there to head or body, while the big lad plunged and reeled, and swung furious haymakers into empty air.

The lad at last grew tired of useless and ridiculous effort. "To hell with it, Sloper!" he panted. "Wouldn't you stand and be hit?" Forthwith he peeled the gloves off, bashed them on the ground, plunged head first under the rope, and cut a swathe for the entrance, leaving his jacket draped on a cornerman's shoulders. Before the lane filled in Garret Ward slipped through and under the rope. Sylvia followed but stayed outside, close to a cornerman. I slipped round the edge of the crowd after Jacus.

The boxer who had played with the country lad was not Robber Morrison, the Scot. He was a veteran lightweight, good old Sloper Jones, and I knew him as well as I knew myself. I had often boxed with him in and out of this booth. He saw me now between shoulders, and lifted a glove in greeting.

"Hey, Gill! Come and try one?"

"Go to glory, Sloper!" I said.

A man who knew me called, "Go on, Gill! You used to paste the Sloper."

But I slipped through a loose flap in the back wall of the booth, after Jacus, into a small dressing or rest place. Behind me a silence came over that tentful of people. Garret Ward was in the ring, and they all knew Garret Ward. They would see some real action now, not an amiable old veteran refusing to hurt a boy.

There was a battered enamel basin, a ewer of water with a not-so-clean towel across the top, a basket of old and soiled gloves, a crooked wicker chair, and nothing else. Yes, there was! There was a man of about my own age reclining in the wicker chair, reading a green-backed "Penguin." The chair creaked as he sat up, and I caught the gleam of a deep-set grey eye.

There came a strange expectant hush into that little patch under the yellow-lit canvas. Destiny was pointing a finger at me too. That man and I had been fated to meet at this hour in this place, and our meeting was to change many a life. He spoke lazily, with a laziness that I recognised, the laziness of the post-war man of thought suffering from the post-war disease of the thinking man:

Indifference. Man, the mammal, was failing, as the Reptile had failed, and this man was sitting back and watching the passing of the breed. A second-rate glove-slinger in a boxing-booth! That did not make sense.

"The Lord forgive you, you old gipsy man calling time!" he said to Jacus in a soft cultivated drawl. He chucked the green-back amongst the boxing-gloves. "Another chapter and I had the murderer pegged down. Nevah mind!" He yawned and pulled himself to his feet, the old chair creaking protestingly. "Have I to absquatulate another aborigine? Is this he?" His deep-set grey eyes went over me. "Useful looking customer! About my weight, thanks be, but a bit of a gorilla, ain't he? Buttons his leggin's standin' up."

That was no showman speech, and yet the speaker looked a veritable roadman. He was of good height, well but slenderly built, with a tousle of brown hair, and a face that was already tanned to almost the same colour. His cheeks were hollowed out below strong cheek-bones, and his chin was flat and wide. He hadn't shaved for, maybe, two days, but the film of blonde stubble scarcely showed against his brown hide. He was wearing leather-strapped, whipcord riding-breeches, and an old Harris-tweed jacket over a low-cut cotton singlet. Below the tough brown of his face the whiteness of throat and chest looked extraordinary delicate. And those cool grey eyes were as cool as cool water.

"Hardly more than a welter!" I said. "Is he any good, Jacus?"

In perplexity Jacus had a habit of lifting his brown bowler an inch off his head and ramming it back again. He did that now.

"Good enough," he said, "but not as good as he thinks he is—no man is."

"Good enough is not half good enough," I said. "He

hasn't a middle worth a cuss, and he'll get himself broken in two."

The brown man laughed. "By you, Mr Man? You're welcome for to try."

"Gill is not your man, Robber," Jacus said, "but I wish to the blue Jacus he was! A purty three rounds, and no harm done—barrin' me losin' a fiver! This is Gill—young Gillian Morris of Castle Gillian."

"Of the stables?" There was some interest in his voice now. "I have heard of young Mr Gillian Morris, and a team-mate of his: a young Amazon woman." His voice mimicked Jacus's tenor in every cadence. "Holy Jacus! them two! an' nawthin' too hot or heavy for 'em!"

"The mildest thing I could say!" said Jacus. "Gill, this robber is Robin Morrison out o' the Highlands. He lives with us in Ty's camp."

"And inevitably 'Robber' in the company he keeps," added Robin Morrison.

That was a deft introduction by old Jacus. Anyone taken in to live in Tyzack Lane's own camp must be of our crowd beyond all doubt. Of all the showmen and relations in Tyzack's tail only two lived with Tyzack and Oonagh: Jacus McGrath and Sloper Jones, and Sloper was needed to drive one of the tractors. There was also, of course, grandson Dinny.

I gripped Morrison's hand firmly. "Don't take on a man twenty pounds heavier—and a killer besides," I said. "Don't let him, Jacus?"

Robin Morrison cocked an eye at me. "A killer! How do you know? Tried him yourself?"

"No, I'm afraid of him," I told him honestly enough.

His eyes centred on me. "That's not as bad as it sounds. Who is this holy terror anyway?"

"Garret Ward of Monaglass if you want to know,"

said Jacus a trifle shamefacedly, "and I'm not askin'
you to fight the scut."

"Garret Ward!" The Scot was interested now.
"Sloper told me about him. Didn't he help to kill
Tinker Billy Brien?"

"And the tinker scaled one-hundred-and-seventy," I
said.

"Damn that tenner!" exploded Jacus. "I'll forfeit
it. I don't want you to take him on."

For answer Robin Morrison twisted lithely out of his
Harris jacket. He had good long brown arms that did
not bunch into hard-bound knots, and the build of a
cagey hit-and-get-away fighter, but what use would he
be against a pile-driver like Garret Ward?

Robin Morrison picked up a brace of gloves, slapped
them together, and flicked Jacus softly on the chin with
one of them.

"We don't back down from catawampuses, Mr
McGrath, not within shoutin' distance of Ty Lane. I
heard you shooting your mouth out there a mile off.
Nothing barred—put him away in three rounds for a
tenner! You ole fox! were you anglin' for Mr Ward,
and guile your middle name?"

"Were you, you vengeful old scoundrel?" I flung at
him.

"Jacus lord! listen to them!" His tenor went high,
and he pranced. "I been on the look-out for a light-
heavy all the year, an' what good is a welter to me in a
county that breeds big basters? Drop them bloody
gloves, Robber Morrison!"

Sloper Jones put a cropped, scarred head through the
flap. "Is the fight on?" he enquired mildly. "They're
gettin' noisy." We could hear them.

"Go to blue blazes!" cursed Jacus, and Sloper went.

"I'll ha'e a look at the victim over the guard," said

63

Morrison, and, forthwith, turned and ducked out under the flap. Jacus and I looked at each other.

"I didn't think you'd do a trick like that, Jacus!" I said.

"I didn't, either." His blue eyes glared at me, and words were scorching him, but he swallowed most of them back. "'Tis that limb of a High-lander that's a pig for obstinacy! and as for you, Gill Morris, I'll complain of you to Oonagh Blake this holy and blasted night!" He suddenly picked up a pair of heavy gloves, and bustled under the flap. I followed him.

Robin Morrison was already in the ring facing Garret Ward, and he was tapping his gloves softly together as if in contemplation. Ward's hooked nose, twisted withershins, made his mouth seem more contemptuous. His jacket and vest were off, and his shirt-sleeves folded to show his thick forearms sheathed in fine black hair. Across the ring I saw Sylvia. Her mouth was open, and her eyes were shocked. Not heeding the sudden silence she called out:

"Don't let them, Gill! It is not a match."

But there was nothing I could do then. These two men had met for the first time, and this fight was ordained. Garret Ward laughed.

"Got yourself another tinker, Jacus?" he boomed. "Is this the best you can do?"

Jacus, at the ringside, rammed home his bowler. He was troubled, and his voice went high.

"If you don't think him good enough, don't fight him."

"I don't force anyone," said Ward. "Care to go three rounds with me, tinker?"

"All in the day's work," said Morrison indifferently.

"Sir to you!" Ward ordered.

"Sirrah is the word I might use," Morrison gave back coolly.

That touched Garret Ward, but he did not wince.

"A gentleman tinker, by Jove!" he said. "Let me have those gloves, McGrath, and I'll take some of the polish off. And have that tenner handy."

"Go to the divil!" said Jacus, and his voice echoed under the canvas. "Value for your bobs, lady and gents! Three two-minute rounds between one Garret Ward, God help him, and Robber Morrison, who'll help himself. I'll be judge and time-keeper, an' if anyone hits below the belt I'll know it—and he'll know it. Now then! a little more room? These are big lads, and need it. Heave ho! boys."

The four cornermen strained back on the rope, and Jacus and I, shoulder to shoulder, strained with them. That was a good move, for in a small ring the lighter man has no chance. I calculated that nothing less than half an acre would help Robin Morrison.

It was warm in there under the canvas. I felt my brow damp, but that might not be due to the heat. I had met the Scot for the first time, and I did not know who he was—but he was never a tinker; he might have fallen far, and deserved the fall, but I did not want him beaten up. And, deep down, I did not want Garret Ward beaten up either. I wondered why that was.

IV

The fight was on, and it was a fight, not a boxing match—on one side at any rate. It went the three rounds, and Jacus won his tenner, but his man was only just on his feet at the end of it. At the very beginning, as the better boxer, he nailed Ward good and hard, and got away untouched. But Ward, in fight, was a berserk and indestructible. He kept boring in on his flat feet, and tried to overwhelm the lighter man with savage short-arm punches to the body; but the lighter man danced away, and side-stepped, and back-pedalled, and made full use of the ring. And he boxed all the time, hitting quickly, mostly with a left jab, and never unbalancing himself by a full blow. He looked cool, almost indifferent, barely interested. His job of work was to stay three rounds, and he stayed them—just about.

That lightly-built man could surely box, and I wondered how an expert like Jacus could say that he and I would make a match. He'd have jabbed my head off in three rounds.

But boxer though he was, and smart on his feet, he could not stay away from Ward all the time; and at the end of the first round I saw that he was wilting under those short-arm smashes, even though he took most of them going away. When Jacus called time, and he might have scamped a few seconds, Morrison came across to us, smiling confidently, but he was not too steady on his feet. I ducked under the rope, went on one knee, and pulled him down on the other, as in the old days of bare-knuckle pugilism. He drew in his breath shortly as if his ribs hurt.

"Thanks, son!" he said pantingly. "That lad likes a fight, but I'll stay with him."

"Circle a bit more to your left," I said, and looked round his shoulder at Garret Ward. He stood wide-legged at the other side of the ring, his black-filmed arms massive across his stomach, and his barrel of a chest heaving. He was not in training. He grinned bare-toothed across at Jacus, and there was a trickle of blood at a mouth corner.

"Give him all the time you like, you old ruffian! I'll get him," he called, and one or two men laughed.

And he very nearly got him too. Morrison was down three times, but two of the blows that sent him to the

66

floor he had been going away from, and it was the shove
of the big glove that toppled him over. Garret Ward's
nose was bleeding now. He was tiring, and his blows
began to lose pith. But near the end of the round he
got in his first solid jolt to the short ribs, and Morrison
went down solidly. It was almost a foul blow. For a
moment I thought he was down for good, but then I
saw that he was watching Jacus's count. He could have
got up at nine, but at the end of a slow eight Jacus
called the end of the round.

The tent was noisy now, and men were shouting.
That holy terror, Garret Ward, had done his savagest,
but the Scot was still there, and had given the big fellow
a lacing. Sylvia was still there too, a hand up to her
mouth, and a hand holding the elbow of a corner-man.
She did not like it. She had dropped her parasol.

Morrison was glad of my knee. I rubbed his flat
stomach and he breathed through his open mouth.
Jacus leant to him.

"Don't come up to time, you divil!" he whispered.
"He'll put a rib in your lungs—same as Tinker Billy."

"Look at him! He can't hurt me now," Morrison
panted.

That might be so. Garret Ward had about spent
himself. He was not holding on to anything, and his
splay feet were solidly planted, but his heavy arms hung
heavily, and he had difficulty in getting enough hot air
to fill his lungs. Two fast and furious rounds take it out
of an untrained man as much as climbing in high
altitudes.

"Had enough, Ward?" Jacus called cheerfully.

Ward did not reply, but made an imperious, inviting
gesture with a glove.

"Time!" shouted Jacus. He was risking his man, but
he was not giving the other time to get his wind back.

That final round was the best, and the evenest too. How Morrison survived the first minute of it I do not know. He surely was tough, and had grand control. Ward tried to overwhelm him by sheer force, but his punches were no longer lethal, and after a minute there was nothing more in him. If the Scot had a kick in his right he might have put the big fellow away. He hadn't, or he didn't try, though a man with a blood lust invited him to. Out on his feet, he boxed as he had boxed all the time, moving round to the left, avoiding clinches, propping a long left, holding his right down to guard his ribs. There wasn't a mark visible on him, but I knew there would be ugly red blotches under his cotton singlet. Garret Ward was showing blood enough for both.

And then Jacus called the end of the round, and I drew a long breath. I didn't applaud with the applauding crowd; I was too intent on Robin Morrison. He came steadily enough towards us, his face smiling aloofly, but I saw that his eyes were not focussing, same as if he was blind drunk. He held on his feet, but a touch would have knocked him over. Jacus and I moved quickly, and got a shoulder each side, but not obtrusively. The rope was lifted high, and men made room for us. One man tried to thump Robin on the back, but Jacus brushed him flat on his face.

We got him into the dressing-tent, and there he let all holds go. Lying out in the wicker chair, he closed his eyes, opened them again, and grinned feebly at us.

"All for a tenner! And I don't even get it," he murmured.

"You got the full value of it, be Jacus!" said that man.

"And gave some change," said Robin Morrison, and passed completely out.

Jacus rammed his hat down, and started cursing

himself softly. Veteran Sloper Jones, with the cauliflower ears, was on his knees by the chair. He pulled up the cotton singlet, and with knowing spatulate fingers was feeling over the bruised ribs. I was unlacing the blooded gloves, and saw the red blotches wide as a plate.

"Hoops of iron! not a crack anywhere, Gill," Sloper said with husky satisfaction, and began massaging the flat stomach muscles.

"Bleedin' inside he'll be, livers and lights," said Jacus pessimistically. "That's two men killed on me be the one man! What'll Ty say to me, an' what the hell are you going to do about it, Gill Morris?"

Before I could think up an answer to that asinine question, a voice spoke above my head:

"The poor lad is going to be sick—his mouth is sweating."

"Go wipe Garret Ward's nose!" I said.

"Lying on his back, a key down his neck in a pie-tent," Sylvia Gayne said.

Robin Morrison opened one grey eye. "I heard you out there first time, young Amazon, and you were dead right," he said, and then his voice became the voice of Jacus. "That one! Nawthin's too hot or heavy for her."

Sylvia opened her own grey eyes. That man with the two voices—one of them cultured—surprised her into silence.

I heard the squeak of a cork out of a bottle. Jacus had a flat half-pint bottle in his hand, and the cork was in his teeth. He put a hand under Morrison's poll.

"Laive a mouthful for meself, and God love you," he said out of the side of his mouth.

That gulp of brandy had a completely eruptive effect. Robin Morrison sat up like a Jack-in-the-box, crowed like a cock in the intake of his breath, said faintly, "Excuse me!" and put a hand over his mouth.

"I told you," cried Sylvia, and acted like one o'clock. She leaped for the basin, thrust me flat with a knee, got the sick man's head down, and propped it with a hand on the brow. She had her parts, Sylvia Gayne. Let a veil be drawn.

But Jacus enquired anxiously: "Is he puttin' up blood with his gizzard?"

He was not. He was toughly put together that man who looked like a tinker and spoke with a nice Highland draw. After a while I said to Sylvia from the ground:

"He is Robin Morrison. He lives with Tyzack and Oonagh in the Bridge camp."

"Then he belongs to me," said Sylvia promptly.

"No, he don't! I saw him first."

"All right! I'll share him with you," said Sylvia.

"God ha' mercy on me," murmured Robin Morrison.

Yes, he would need all the mercy and help there was, but none of us knew it at that time.

Chapter III

THE CAMP AT GULLANE BRIDGE

I

ROBIN MORRISON and I were sitting on tall stools outside the counter in the soft-drink bar off the Agricultural Hall; and on another stool, between us, sat Sylvia Gayne, imbibing some pink concoction through a straw. She looked ever so gentle, and had a soft allure about her that might deceive any man. It did not deceive me. The sun shone yellowly down through the wide skylights in the roof, and made a glory of her hair. Her elegant hat was lying carelessly under a chair; she had lost her parasol, but probably Sloper Jones had it safe for her; and she would have lost her tartan bag too had it not been slung over her shoulder. She was aye dropping things, and forgetting all about them.

Robin Morrison and I were nibbling our second ice-creams in brown wafers. He sat very straight, one hand propped on the bar, and he drew his breath carefully into the tops of his lungs. And he looked more the road-man than ever. He had on a faded blue shirt now, but no collar, and a blue bird's-eye kerchief was in a tight knot about his throat. His fine brown bush of hair had needed cutting three weeks ago. But, still, he was one of ours unquestionably. As a member of Tyzack Lane's own camp we accepted him as a matter of course.

Sylvia lifted her straw, blew softly through it, and one pink drop fell into her empty glass. "I won't have another —I think," she said consideringly. "No! but don't let anybody ask me." Her pleasant voice did not change. "Why the disguise, Mr Morrison?"

"Mind your own business, you impudent rip!" I protested.

"But she is." Robin Morrison chuckled, stopped abruptly, winced, and turned cautiously to Sylvia. "Hair and hide all my own, Miss Gayne."

"Sylvia to you, Mr Morrison—not Silly all the time!"

"Not once," said Mr Morrison. "You can call me Robber if you like, but Robin will do as well."

"I mean, you are not a professional boxer, like Slope Jones, are you?" went on Sylvia on her own road.

"Not yet at any rate. But I'm pretty good, ain't I?"

"You needed to be," I said. "What is your fighting weight?"

"Not sure, but at a pinch I can ride at one-hundred-and-forty."

"Ride! Ride a horse?" Sylvia was interested.

"I'm no' bad—and that's Scotch for the best ever—gi'e us a guid conceit of oorselves!" He smiled at her, and she clapped her hands.

"I know," she cried. "Your father had a g-r-e-a-t big racing establishment, and you, Master Fauntleroy Morrison, riding your Shetland pony, and heir to it all. This is going to be good——"

"Oh hell!" I said. I knew she had Castle Gillian in mind.

"Next instalment, please?" said Robin.

"Evil days! Oh, such evil days!" went on Sylvia sombrely. "But, indomitable, you rose to the occasion. Fauntleroy became Robber, and you are out to make a million, being world champion, in disguise, not to soil your noble name. Right? What book was that, Gill?"

"Take your pick of a thousand."

"That's a good story," proclaimed the Scot. "Pity there ain't no racing establishments north o' Forth!"

"Middle-weight champeen o' Scotia south o' Tweed,

be Jacus!" I said. "Where did you learn to box?" I was some curious myself.

"There is quite a bit o' Scotia south o' Tweed, you know!" he said. "Simon Burns would have been heavyweight champion if Deaf Burke hadn't killed him. I could always use my mawleys, and I was in the army, same as yourself—I saw it in your eyes."

I nodded. "Yes! I saw it in your eyes too. One of the bunch who are no longer interested."

"Except in a vine and fig tree somewhere. They'll still grow in spite of split atoms—or will they? I'm lookin' for to see."

"Wait!" cried Sylvia, who was on her own tack. "The other alternative is *the* one!" She tapped the cold shining counter. "A mile high on the ladder, and your lady-love married a rake, so you fell down, after blooding his nose—same as you bled Garret Ward's. Holy Jacus! I promised to meet him half an hour ago. Never mind! Now you are climbing up again, and your widowed-lady waiting for you—or is she? You can call me Sylvia." The imp was jumping about in her addle-pate.

Robin shook his head. "Sorry to let you down—Sylvia! Romance is out! I didn't climb or fall. I'm just writing a book, plain Jane and no nonsense." He was quite serious now.

"Staying with Tyzack for local colour?" I suggested.

"Not exactly that!" For such a cool customer he was unusually shy at this moment. "You two are nice people——"

"I never called you no names," I protested.

"You see, I had a sort of a vision," he said still shyly, "and I live among primitive people—for perspective—for focus——"

I stopped him. I wasn't going to probe this shy man. I said:

73

"You lived with a primitive for three rounds a while ago—and lost your focus, dam' near!"

"Sure as a gun! That sort won't die out." He pointed to Sylvia's empty glass. "Try another pink assassin on your case-hardened duodenum, Sylvia?"

"No, please!" Sylvia was suddenly considerate, and went off on another tack. "Do you like roundabouts, Robin?"

"Who told you?" He sat up and winced.

She shook her fine hair. "No! not a roundabout with stove-in ribs. How much cold coin have you left, Gill? It's your turn?"

"As far as it will take us," I agreed, and put my small fistful on the counter. It was largely copper, and I fingered it and felt hurriedly in my pockets. "Thunder! I'm out a shilling. Only three-and-eleven."

"No use!" That hair of hers scintillated as it swung. "Robin is our guest, and I want to take him to see *Odd Man Out*. He won't have to laugh his sides sore. I have five bob left. Lend it to you for a week?"

"No interest?" I stipulated. She had soaked me more than once according to our code.

"For the first week only."

This was business, and we were quite serious. Robin Morrison looked puzzledly from one to the other of us.

"Look here!" he said. "I've heard about you two. Aren't you—closely related——?"

"My third cousin, and that's the hell of it!" I told him.

"I don't mean——"

"Oh, yes!" said Sylvia. "Until day-before-yesterday we were engaged to be married, but we had a heck of a row——"

"For the good of my soul," I added.

"And we parted brass rings—the hound!" said Sylvia deeply.

74

"You are not engaged any more, you mean?"

"That's right," I said. "It was only a family job."

"We are not even friends," said Sylvia. "This is only a truce for to-day."

Another thought struck Morrison. "This—Garret Ward—he wasn't in it?"

"Could be," I said.

"Not particularly," said Sylvia. "I got Garret taped."

"Watch out, or she'll tape you too, Mister!" I warned him. "Whatever you do, mind her left. Good as you are she'll bust another rib. She has a sand-bag—I saw it—in her room—or she'd be plain fat."

He leant forward carefully and looked at me closely; and then he looked at Sylvia closely. We were not meeting his eye very well, either of us, but Sylvia was the better of the two. Then he lifted his chin and started to laugh, tried to stop himself and couldn't. His face was twisted with anguish, but, still, he laughed. We found ourselves laughing with him.

"He's a Scot, sure enough," said Sylvia. "That's at a crack I made an hour ago."

"Not so long ago," said the Scot, holding his sides. "I was prepared, but you two are a new species to me. Sure, I'll stay with you as long as I can, but take me aisy for a start." He bowed carefully to Sylvia. "Permit me the privilege? I want to see *Odd Man Out*, and I'll stand the seats."

"No! you're our guest, and it is Gill's turn," said Sylvia firmly. "But next week you'd better have buttons to your pockets. Let's be going."

II

So we went to the pictures, the three of us, and had our withers wrung by the slow and tragic death of a party gunman. And after the pictures, the sun was well in

75

the west, and we were as hungry as hawks. We pooled our resources, and Sylvia shook her gleaming hair about her eyes.

"Damn all food racketeers!" she said. "Sausages and mash—one helping each—that's all that runs to, and you know what the sausages are *not* made of. I can do better than that, and Gill is tired of salmon mayonnaise for supper—without the mayonnaise."

"You get used to it," I said, "but I am only hoping to."

Sylvia interrogated Robin. "Your team—Tyzack—they'll be back in camp by now?"

"Should be."

"Fine! We'll give you a lift."

"There's a bus, I think."

"Come on! My bus is outside the showyard."

I knew what was in her mind, and it had my approval. I said:

"You have the devil's own neck, Syl."

"While you lick your chops," she gave me back.

So we went off in Sylvia's useful, touring two-seater, propping Robin Morrison between us. My old cycle was slung on behind in its not unusual place; we even kept a length of cord in a side-pocket for tying it on.

The road to Gullane Glen runs and twists ten miles on the flanks of the hills, and we tooled along at an easy pace. Surprisingly enough, Sylvia, unless a hurry was on her, was a careful driver, and favoured a sedate thirty, the air in her soft hair, and a song in her mouth. A hurry on her, I wouldn't be found in the car with her, if I could avoid it, for I am a timid man by nature. We were in no great hurry this evening, though we were hungry.

On our right and below us was the wide, farm-dotted, verdant plain of Moymore, softly-hazed and long-shadowed in the evening sun, and swooping across three counties to the big, humped, purple-and-blue Midland Mountains. And close on our left lifted our own little round-topped hills, clothed from roadside to summit in a gorgeous mantle of furze in full bloom. That mile-wide, miles-long, folding mantle of gold, swallowing the orange of the sun, took one's breath away; and all about us was the faint, dry, almost-acrid perfume that was the veritable odour of ancient earth under the sun. I heard Robin Morrison draw in his breath, and his voice was in my ear:

"One might choose this as an abiding place, and find a simulacrum of peace."

"And be a slave to it all your days, same as my sister Mary," I said roughly, angry against the pull the place had on me too.

"Sister Mary! I've heard of her. Martha ain't she?"

"I dunno—the one that works. A long-legged dam' fool, besides being the finest girl God ever made."

"A contradiction in terms, wouldn't you say?"

"It states but the case," Sylvia put in, and, throwing back her head, intoned a verse of a song made by an Irishwoman:

> "For joy of mine she gave grief of hers,
> And girded my brow with a crown of furze."

Sylvia's singing voice was about the deepest contralto I had ever heard. It did things to me. Her bright hair was blowing about her face, and she put her hand up to clear her eyes. Suddenly she exclaimed, and the car leaped and slowed again.

"Gill, you hound! Where's my ten-guinea hat?"

"Under a chair," I said.

"Oh, that's all right! Tom-the-Bar will retrieve it for me. I never lose a thing, really."

"Your parasol, you liar?" I reminded her.

"A casualty. Someone stood on it—twice."

In nine miles or so, where the hills folded deeper, we topped a rise, and passed on our left massive wrought-iron gates, inhospitably closed, and guarded by a gate lodge. A smooth drive disappeared between holm-oaks. Sylvia tossed a spray of hair.

"Tom Gayne's place, Castle Evan! I live there—he's my father."

Robin Morrison slanted an eye back and up at a granite gatepost supporting a wild boar tusking a shield.

"Now I know," he said. "You did sound some like an effete aristocrat who had got beyond codes."

"You got her, but she don't get you," I said.

"I do so, and you're both wrong," said Sylvia. "I've a code of my own, and I'm working it overtime just now."

"Gullane Bridge I'm looking for—you could drop me here?" suggested Robin.

"I'm still using you," said Sylvia, and took the down grade easily.

At the bottom of the slope the fold opened into the valley of the Gullane, and there was the high-cocked bridge across our little river. We humped and dipped over it and drew up close to the wing-parapet on the left. Sylvia got out with a swing of her long silken legs.

"Here we are, my poor fella!" she said commiseratingly to Robin, "and sorry we are that you are nearly dead in our hands. Leave it to us!"

Robin looked at her suspiciously.

I got out too, and stood by the parapet, looking up the river as was my habit. There was the long slide of water coming down between the holms over the milky quartz slabs, glistening in the evening light and soughing remotely to itself; and there above it was the hand-railed foot-bridge where Sylvia had told me I was no good, and that she would not marry me if I was the last man top of earth. That was two days ago, and now it was evening

78

again, and again it was bird-song time. Above the sough of the waters I heard a thrush singing. The old round was going on.

Sylvia was leaning over the parapet at my side, and her voice was clear as a gull's, but not soulless like a gull's.

"Hullo the camp! Is this Robber Morrison's wake?" A dog barked friendlily.

I leant over the parapet too. And there, twenty feet below, was the camp of Tyzack Lane on our lands of Castle Gillian.

III

In the angle made by the road and the river, on the near side of the holm-oaks, was a small grassy field clumped thinly with furze bushes, and margined along the bank by sage-green sallows. It was in that patch of ground that Tyzack Lane had camped each year for all the years that I could remember. Sometimes he camped only for three weeks while his shows covered the three C's— Caerline, Cantrip and Casleinch; frequently he camped for several weeks; and one great season he had made it his winter quarters.

With that small clan we had allied and feuded in the days of our youth and adolescence, so that now we knew each other for friends, and went armed front and rear against each other's pranks. Sylvia was for playing one now.

There was Tyzack's resplendent caravan in gold and cream, with all its modern gadgets and contraptions; an old-fashioned van painted bright-red; and two tractors. I looked again.

"By gum! Tyzack has got him a horse," I said. A motor horse-box, dusty brown, was set away among the whins, and, close at hand, a tall dark-hided horse was busily cropping our grass. As I looked it took two slow paces to fresh herbage, and I noticed that it was yielding

79

to the off foreleg. It was a blood horse of the light hunter or 'chase type, and I was not interested—not yet.

I had not looked down on that camp for three years. That last time I was on furlough in the middle of the war; but it might have been only yesterday that I had stood here and watched the camp at its routine, before dropping a *divot* close to Jacus over his cooking pots; and I wondered how a wise one, here and there, had managed to go on living sanely in a chosen way. I, no longer, had a chosen way.

Jacus, his shirt-sleeves folded to show his powerful old fore-arms, was again at his cooking pots. Strangely enough Jacus loved to cook, and craved for the praise he never asked for and never got. His portable calor-gas oven and hot plate were set up in a buttress-angle, and Jacus was stirring a pot with an iron ladle. I sniffed. *Bacon-and-chicken*, I said to myself. *I wonder are they Mary's.*

Tyzack Lane was sitting in the doorway of the caravan, reading a green-and-white paper-back. He read any-thing and everything, and had a habit of reading aloud to his wife while she knitted. His wisdom, however, did not come out of books.

Oonagh Blake sat below him in a canvas chair, a cigarette on her lower lip and wisps of smoke drifting in the glow of her red hair. Oonagh was aye knitting, and she was knitting now: a pull-over of an intricate thunder-and-turf, Celtic-scroll pattern. She probably knitted a score in a year, and never sold one; but in every show-ground in the South one might see a showman's child wearing an "Oonagh-gansey." I had had one or two resplendent ones myself, but Mary and Sylvia took them off me as more fit for female adornment, and I was just as well pleased, for I hadn't the nerve to wear them in the public eye.

Another canvas chair was set up at Oonagh's left hand. At the tail of the caravan, in the shade that the May-flies avoided, Sloper Jones, in a green-and-gold "Oonagh-gansey," moved about a big camp-table on trestles, and I caught the gleam of silver and steel on a red-and-white checked cloth. I smiled then. There were six perma-nents in camp, but that table was set for at least two more. As Sloper shifted about flat-footed and effortlessly one could see why he was called Sloper. His real name was Lloyd—Lloyd Jones—and he was ashamed of it.

And finally there was Dinny, christened Dionysius. In him the dark gipsy dominant had come to the surface. He was fifteen and small for his age: a wiry, brown-skinned lad with the crisp black hair and black eyes of the breed. He had no job at the moment, and was circling round the dark-hided colt; and a black half-retriever-half-spaniel was circling with him. Sometimes he gave a tug at the horse's tail, and the horse took no notice. If I did that to a horse at graze I'd get myself kicked into the middle of next week.

Dinny was the son of Ethan, the son of Tyzack. Mary, Sylvia and myself used to worship Ethan, who was some years my senior. He, taught by Jacus, taught us all the nature lore we know—most of it nefarious. He married early, like most showmen, and had one son when his wife died. Ethan went wild after that. Then came the war, and he and I joined up. I saw him killed on Salerno beach.

The orange sun poured its glow over that pleasant scene. It was only a temporary camp, yet there was something homelike and staid about it, and the very thrushes seemed to be singing for it as of old custom. I wanted to be staid too, and in this very valley.

At Sylvia's clear halloo everyone looked up, and the camp stilled to attention. Then Tyzack and Jacus looked at each other, and I saw Tyzack rasp a palm across his blue chin, the only sign he ever gave of any emotion. There was a queer psychic tie between the two half-brothers. Tyzack was a silent man, and he used Jacus as his thought-transmitter—not his mouthpiece, for the words Jacus used were all his own and flagrantly over-coloured.

Jacus straightened a stiff back, and pointed the iron ladle at us. In the hush I heard a drop of grease sizzle on the hot-plate. His tenor pealed:

"The Robber—is he killed dead?" He drew the last word out.

"The stem o' life is still in him," cried Sylvia cheerfully. "We are bringing him down to you."

Robin Morrison was out of the car now and close behind us. Sylvia hooked his arm solicitously, and her voice was a croon.

"Easy, darlin'—easy! We'll see you safe home. Gill, you hound! Give him a hand."

I did as I was bid, for that was our rule when a play was on. Indeed, we had many queer rules in our code. For instance we would not go anywhere together without first fabricating an excuse. Any excuse, on the spur of the moment, would do. Now Sylvia wanted one of Jacus's hot suppers, and was using Robin Morrison as an excuse to get us into camp. Probably Robin guessed that.

"You are still using me?" he said agreeably. He let us prop him between us round the end of the stone wing and down a slippery slope of grass to the camp. All eyes were on us, but I don't suppose we deceived anyone but Dinny. Dinny was the only one to move and he came at full pelt, the dog barking about his feet and escaping a flying kick. Dinny was frightened, I saw by his eyes.

"Oh, Robber! you're not killed dead on us?" he appealed.

"Oh lord!" said Robber in his throat. "This will not do."

I flared round at my hare-brained cousin, but she was bending down to Dinny. She said nothing, but something passed between them, for the lad put up a hand to cover a sudden grin.

"Japus, Miss Syl! You gave me a fright." He spoke nicely as his grandmother had taught him, but in excitement a savour of his uncle's speech crept in. He sniggered softly, dodged round behind us, and butted a head lightly between his Robber's shoulder-blades.

Sylvia's play was finished. Tyzack went back to his reading; Oonagh smiled at Sylvia and resumed her knitting; Sloper swung a chair from the table; and Jacus hopped a foot and poised.

"The stem of life is in him, the poor fella! Very well so! Chicken broth for his supper, the dyin' man, an' dam' the thing else!" He scuttered round to his stove, and turned again abruptly. "Now that he is here to die, let us not be detainin' you, me lady—an' take Gill Morris with you!"

We deposited Robin in the canvas chair by the doorway; Sylvia found the edge of a chair at the back of her knees and sat down; and I sat on the grass, my shoulder against Oonagh's knee. I had sat that way as a boy, and, now, I felt sorry that I had grown up.

"Did Jacus complain about me, Oonagh?" I asked her over my shoulder.

"Well! yes—a little."

"But why?"

"My dear brother-in-law is sometimes in a hurry," she said in her soft Galway voice. "You were too long away, and must get time to adjust yourself. Leave it, boy!" I felt a soft finger run up into my tousle of black hair. I hadn't an inkling of her meaning.

Robin Morrison turned cautiously in his chair and pointed.

"My detective yarn, Mr Lane?"

Tyzack reached him the green-back without a word, and Robin pushed it back.

"Page sixty, are you? Another ten and you have the nigger."

"Page four," said Tyzack briefly.

"Never!"

"You should have noted a certain tone in one voice." Tyzack's voice was as deep as Garret Ward's, but more resonant. He went on reading placidly.

Sylvia sat up and sniffled, and her voice lifted:

"Chicken-stew! I smell it. Who raided Mary Morris's hen-roost?"

"I didn't, anyway," piped Dinny virtuously from the back of Robin's chair.

Jacus stalked at me on tip-toe, the ladle at charge. "Gill Morris, has the bloody British army taken the dacency out of you—but, sure you never had it? You wouldn't stand up for me in a court o' law?"

"I would," I said, "but fair is fair. That was a fair question, Tyzack, wasn't it?"

Tyzack nodded solemnly. "No one is called on to fit the cap."

"Thunderin' Jacus!" yelped Jacus. "Sure, Mary Morris, the dacent girl, hasn't a chicken worth pluckin' in the month o' May."

Sylvia hooted. "Guilty! How did you know? And, another fair question, who knew she has year-old pullets just as tender?"

"I plucked 'em," said Dinny.

"And I claim a cousin's share," demanded Sylvia. "I appeal to Oonagh Blake."

"If I have to share with you, linten-locks," said Oonagh.

"I don't deserve that in this camp," said Jacus in his most offended voice. "I never sent no one out hungry, and I won't now; but if there's a tough drumstick in the skillet I know who's for it. Jacus! do I smell burnin'?" He scuttered back to his stove.

We all knew that Oonagh had an arrangement with Mary about a supply of chickens, but Jacus always fell for the accusation of chicken-stealing. He lifted up his voice again.

"Sloper Jones, you lazy flat-foot! Hand me them plates, and will ye all sit in and choke yerselves while it's hot."

IV

Had time stood still? Was it now or three years ago that I was eating on this white-and-red cloth? The same evening seemed to have come again in its circle; the same air drifted softly round the tail of the caravan; the birds were at the same song; and the river, as of old, was remotely communing with itself in its own dimension. But I knew myself as older, and life was beginning to weigh me down, and I knew—the coward in me knew—that a test was waiting for me round a near corner.

But I was as hungry as ever, and the ritual of eating was not changed. Jacus served each of us with a deep plate of thick chicken broth, and if we wanted a second helping—and most of us did—we each helped ourselves. Then into the same plates, cleaned up with a manchet of bread, Jacus ladled hugely chicken-bacon-potato stew, and again we rehelped ourselves, if we wanted to, and none of us wanted to, except Sylvia and Robin. Sylvia, for all her lissomeness, could eat my head off.

There was one exception, I should have said. Oonagh Blake was not allowed to help herself. Jacus saw to that.

He looked upon Oonagh as something superior in flesh, blood and texture. She was the lady, the queen of the road, and she must not be allowed to soil her hands with menial tasks.

There was little small-talk at that fine meal, but over a cup of strong Indian tea we lay back replete and talked lazily, all except Dinny and Sloper whose chore it was to wash up at the riverside. The rattle of dishes came faintly to us round the side of a sallow clump.

"That was a booful meal," said Sylvia, checked herself, and added carelessly, "but, of course, chicken-stew cooks itself."

I pushed my empty cup away. "Pity the tea was biled!" I said.

"Yourself should know," rasped Jacus, "for divil the thing else you get from ould Timmy Tadg Shawn."

That was true enough, but, then, I liked boiled tea.

Sylvia pointed a languid arm. "Where did Jacus steal you the nice colt, Tyzack? and who hurt him?"

"The owner hurt him—and who else?" said Jacus, and Tyzack pointed the stem of his pipe at Robin Morrison.

"Yes, Benbecula is my horse—and my all in the meantime," said Robin Morrison.

"Yes! you said you were a horseman," Sylvia said. "That's a strange new name, Ben—Ben——"

"Old as the hills! Benbecula, an island not far from my clan country!"

I looked at Morrison consideringly and he met my eye.

"That's right!" He nodded. "A man has to eat—meantime."

That was fair enough. I knew two other men who took their summer holidays—three months of them—and paid all expenses, going round to the various shows with a good trick jumper. But this Benbecula did not look like a trick jumper; he was too tall and rangy and young. And so thought Jacus McGrath.

"Ate, be Jacus!" he exploded. "Not on the winnings of a five-year-old, and him not accustomated to stone-wall jumps. And look at him now—and look at you! atin' be the dint of the beltin' you get four times a day from country buckeroos."

Robin felt his ribs gingerly. "You surely sicked a country buckeroo on me to-day, my dear old friend."

Jacus yelped. "That's a flamin' lie! I never saw Garret Ward comin'. An' why wouldn't Gill Morris keep him off—and he by way of a friend?"

"Not with our-dear-old-friend bellowing challenges a mile off," I said.

"Stop there!" cried Jacus. "I'm not your friend—nor old neither—an' as for the Robber——"

"Never mind!" Robin interrupted. "Benbecula will be sound in another week—I hope—and I'll take no more beltin's from you."

"In a week—in ten weeks—never!" Jacus scoffed. "A lame shoulder tied up in a horse-box over the rough mountainy roads! Give him three months in a soft paddock, and see if that shoulder is chronic. Ask Ty Lane, if you don't believe me?"

Tyzack moved his head in agreement with his half-brother, and Morrison ran a hand through his own tousled hair.

"Steps will have to be taken, then," he said quietly.

"Never mind, *agrah!*" Oonagh said understandingly, using the soft Galway brogue. "Sure what is a bite and a sup amongst friends going the friendly road; and aren't you the world-and-all to Dinny, and good for him?"

"Makin' a consaited little jock out of him!" said Jacus.

"A born horseman, Dinny!" said Robin, and rose to

his feet. There he lifted up a voice of astonishing volume. "Dinny—Dinny Lane! evening stables!"

Dinny and his dog exploded out of the sallows, and the three went off towards Benbecula, and Benbecula sidled away playfully amongst the whins.

Tyzack knocked his pipe out, got up from the table, eased himself into a canvas chair, and shut his eyes placidly; a man of his years would take a snooze after a full meal. Oonagh resumed her knitting in her own chair; I lit a cigarette for her, and sat at her knee filling a pipe. Sylvia pulled her chair round, and lay back somnolently, her hands clasped over her flat stomach. And Jacus, after fussing about his stove, ambled across and sat in the doorway of the van; his pipe was in his hand, and he looked hard at me.

"Only grass-cut Virginia!" I said, and threw my pouch to him.

"It'll burn the tongue in me head, but I'll try it this wance," he said. He had said the same thing time out of mind.

We were all comfortably silent. There was now no jingle of ware from the riverside where Sloper would have finished washing-up. Swallows—no! they were black-fronted swifts—were shuttling high-up in the evening sky; and the sun, glowing red, was coming down into the notch of Gullane Glen. *This thing, this life is all right now*, I thought. *Now—now—now! if we did not look before or after—and fear the after*. That after would have to be faced, and I must share my fear now. I nudged Oonagh Blake's knee with a shoulder.

"What is it this time, Gillian?" I had always nudged her that way before telling her things, and I had always told her things. I looked down at my brown hands, and said:

"We are near the end of the road at Castle Gillian, Oonagh. Maybe you heard?"

"There was some talk that I did not heed," she said quietly. "The end of the road?"

"Or the start of one I don't like. We must find three thousand pounds before the end of September."

"Padderson the horse dealer? Mary told me about him."

"And hell his eyetarnal bed!" cursed Jacus warmly, and added confidently, "Mary Morris will find that money, if 'tis under a stone even, and make Castle Gillian go one, two, three—if only she had a man about the place!"

"The man and the money are on offer, Mr McGrath," I said with some sarcasm.

Sylvia sat up, no longer somnolent, and there was hurt in her voice.

"You never told me about this, Gill?"

"Hadn't a chance—only two days old! I'm telling you all now. The man offers five thousand pounds for a controlling interest, with Mary as his trainer—and his wife, or so he says."

I was watching Sylvia. Her eyes were wide on me, and she was paling about the mouth.

"I don't want to know the child-robber's name," shouted Jacus.

"You do," I said. "His name is Garret Ward."

"Glory be to hell! we bled his nose good for him to-day."

I felt as if someone was watching me intently and turned my head sharply. Tyzack Lane's eyes were shut and his breathing easy, but his eyelids twitched once. He was listening too.

Sylvia reclaimed my attention with a jump. She was on her feet, her eyes blazing.

"No—no—no!" she cried, her voice deep and poignant. "Not Garret Ward?"

"Garret Ward it is," I said evenly.

"Not with Mary—our Mary! Not Castle Gillian!" She stamped. "I will not have it."

"The choice is with Mary, isn't it?" I kept my voice cold.

"No, Gill! You must not let her choose." She leant to me and went on with a rush. "She does not know Garret Ward. Neither do you. I know him. I found out for myself. At worst you think him a big forthright brute. He's worse. That's only his shell. Underneath he's a sadist—a pervert—and sly. He likes a sly cruelty—like a cat and a mouse, before the cat kills. He's evil I tell you."

"And you found out?"

"I found out. You were away. He practised on me." She pulled herself up proudly. "But I had a sure shield." Then her shoulders sagged, and her voice went low. "I am no longer sure of that shield. Oh God! if it breaks!"

She turned away and her shoulders shook. I never saw her so moved. I thought she was going to weep, and I could never stand the way she wept.

"Stop that dam' nonsense, Sylvia Gayne!" I almost shouted at her.

She turned on me at once, and her mood completely changed. She laughed at me. "Nonsense? Very good! But I'm still in the game, and I have been playing Garret Ward at his. If you'll do nothing, Gill Morris, watch me!"

I watched her now, and she watched me. I could hear the quiet breathing of Tyzack Lane. Across in the whins Robin Morrison and Dinny were talking and laughing, and a whiff of embrocation was wafted on the air. And again Sylvia changed her mood, and I knew that change of old. I had seen it so often. She used to pout out her lower lip, and shut her grey eyes to slits, and, then, suddenly burst out into a new inspiration of mischief or adventure. I waited for that burst now with some trepidation. It did not come. She waved a hand carelessly.

"You go on talking, Gill!" she said indifferently. "I'll go and have a look at this Benbecula colt."

She turned and strolled off amongst the whins, and the low sun outlined her lissomeness through her flowered dress. *Are you looking for another victim for your bow and spear?* was my thought.

V

Jacus McGrath scratched under his hat. He knew Sylvia too. "Be Jacus to glory!" he said. "I'll have to watch me P's and Q's with that one, or find meself in jail for murdher—they wouldn't hang me."

Oonagh Blake, above me, came out of her own thoughts and twitched a knee. "Let us be sensible," she said calmly. "You say the choice is with Mary. She hasn't chosen yet?"

"Not for five months, she says."

"Very good!" I felt a knitting-needle pushing through my hair. "You are rising thirty, little Gill, and it is time you had grown up."

I knew so well what she meant. I was twenty-nine and Sylvia twenty-five; it was time we were married; and then I would have the right to help Mary. That was what everyone thought, except Sylvia and myself.

"I'm grown up," I said, "and I am not marrying Sylvia Gayne."

"Since the last falling-out?" said Oonagh indifferently. No one would take us seriously.

I jerked from her knee and to my feet. "Sylvia Gayne and I are not marrying—ask her!" I said slowly, holding in irritation.

Oonagh Blake's voice had a stern note in its smoothness. "Be careful, grown man! or you'll force your sister into an evil man's arms."

"Lordalmighty!" I stopped myself, and strutted off bow-legged towards the river. I have good hearing. Behind me I heard Tyzack say deeply:

"Give the boy time, woman! Only the first round, and he's a slow starter!"

Round the belly of a sallow bush I found Sloper Jones lying on his back on the green slope of the bank, his broken hands under his head, and his deep-socketted eyes slitted on the high pale sky. He would lie like this until it was dark, as he had often lain, and he might sleep here too, as he had often slept. Old Sloper Jones, still good enough for a few rounds with amateurs, was a quiet and retiring man, that had once been a terrible man in the ring. He, at any rate, would not hint at my duty.

My eyes followed the run of the water that flowed fast and free till, checked and worried by the buttresses of the bridge, it heaped and gurgled sullenly in the throat of an eddy that was always changing and always the same.

"A penny for your thoughts, Sloper!" I said.

He moved his head in his palms. "Old they were," he said in his husky voice.

"About the time you were within a bout of a title?"

"No' then! nor the time Ty Lane picked me out of the sweepings of the road, and made half a man of me. What I was thinkin' was that this was an old, old place."

"And people growing old with it?"

"And well they might! but you know"—he paused—"there in camp a while ago I knew that this place don't care a dam' for the old—for the done old ones that try to strangle it. It's all for ye young chisellers."

This was no ordinary thought for an old fighter, and it was a true thought too. All places that are old and loved and have evolved an entity are for the young only. Once age possesses and youth rejects the old places, they are no longer old, they are only desolate; as some parts of this island already were—as Gullane Glen might be. Sloper Jones went on musing huskily:

"'Twas when ye three young ones came hippling into camp play-actin', and Dinny made for ye, that I knew myself for an old man before my time. And I been lyin' here thinkin' to myself that 'tis time for a new generation in this old place, and that 'tis up to Gill Morris, home from the wars."

There it was again! I wasn't safe even from Sloper Jones. Up to Gill Morris, home from the wars! I swallowed anger. I repressed an urge to kick the piled plates into the river. Instead I touched Sloper with a toe and spoke softly at first:

"Too late already, old-man-before-your-time! You like this place—all Welshmen love the hills—but the tide of desolation is already flowing into Gullane Glen, and you cannot stop any tide from flowing. I'm not trying. I'm not playing. Damn you! I'm not playing. I'll be out of here by October—and this camp will never be back."

"Very well so!" said Sloper, gloomily calm. "Tell that to young Sylvia Gayne. She's the one. Eh, man! Listen to her voice like a clairinet!"

Yes, in her laughter out there, there was a fine, clear, clarion note. Suddenly added to it was a high yip-yip from Dinny, and that was immediately followed by a pained bellow from Robin Morrison.

"Almighty! someone is kicked," I cried and leaped.

"Only one of Dinny's close finishes," called Sloper, and laughed.

I was already round the curve of the sallow. And, then, I was laughing too. They were bringing the colt in, but

93

not soberly. Robin Morrison was hanging on to the head-halter with one hand, and holding his bruised belly muscles with the other; Dinny, perched jockey-fashion on the colt's withers, was riding his mount right out with his hands, and the colt, forgetting his lameness, was cavorting along between the whins; and Sylvia, pealing laughter, was busy getting out from under.

Dinny sat up, and the horse quieted.

"A good finish that time!" he piped pridefully. "Two lengths clear—and going away."

"No, you whelp!" denied Robin, still rubbing his stomach. "The last of the pack and tailing off."

"Holy Joe! What did I do wrong?"

"Your hands were fair, but you swayed all over the place and unbalanced your mount."

"All right so, Robber! We'll try it over again."

"No, you don't!" shouted Robber promptly.

Jacus walloped the side of the van to thunder. "Come down off that dot-and-carry-one, you limb of sin!" he yelped. Then his voice wheedled. "Come on down and gather in the dishes like a good boy. I have a bit of candy somewhere."

Dinny was down and in amongst the sallows. Sylvia turned and saw me. She looked as nearly embarrassed as any time I could remember, and the diffident way she looked at me told that she was hiding something that could not be hidden long. Her eyes strayed to Robin Morrison, and a finger moved towards her lips.

"I'm for home, my dears!" she decided suddenly. "Thanks a lot—I'll be seeing ye. Gill, strip your bone-shaker of my Rolls."

Half-way up the bank she turned and looked down over my head, and her light poise took the eye.

"Nine o'clock in the morning, Robin," she called. "I'll be there."

"Nine o'clock it is, chieftainness," he called cheerfully.

So our Sylvia was playing a game of her own. But it was not my game. Was it Robin Morrison's game? He was a cool, ironic, likeable man, but so had been one or two devils I had known. Come to that, Lucifer himself must be a whale of a friendly devil to be any good at his job.

I felt a bit lonesome, as if shut out of something.

CHAPTER IV

THE STABLE-YARD AT CASTLE GILLIAN

I

THE Castle Gillian stables were not the modern ones of brick, chromium and asphalt. They were thoroughly utilitarian, spacious without being draughty, and as solid as the hills behind them. There was the big square yard of packed gravel, firm of grip, and perfect for showing off a horse's action; three sides of this square were closed in by loose-boxes: roomy, two-storeyed, stone-built, slate-roofed, with half-doors and loft-doors painted a deep red; the fourth, or west side, was the wall of the peat shed pierced by a single narrow arch leading through to the kitchen premises and the front of the house. North and south were wider arches, wide enough for a cart, tall enough for a mounted man, leading to the training grounds and paddocks. That was about all. Every wall was lime-washed, and every wall needed a fresh coat. That was one of my jobs this morning.

We were short-handed, and some of us, but not Mary, were getting used to slipshod methods. Faithful Sandy Ythan and his "two louts," as Garret Ward had called them, had brought in six horses from exercise and taken out the remaining four. Mary, with my help, did the grooming. Usually she went out to exercise, but, sometimes, to give the boys a chance, she did a week of stable chores. I did the mucking out of the loose-boxes.

This morning, in my slipshod fashion, I had finished before Mary, and had taken to whitewashing, a job I did not like particularly. I could hear Mary hissing away groom-fashion to the steady sweep of her dandy-brush. A head-chain click-clicked through its lead; a bay head, white-starred, extended over a half-door, and rubbed a jawbone lazily on the smoothed wood; a wood-quest crooned away-up amongst the larches. A quiet, sunny morning, and slumbrous for such an early hour. It would be another warm day, and it was warm enough already to silence the birds, except one cocksparrow, in the eaves, chattering in surprise at the five nestlings that his mate had hatched out that morning.

A magpie, sleek in black-and-white, jerked over a roof, cursed me harshly twice, and looked about for loose corn. *One for sorrow!* I said. Another flicked over, cursed me some more and joined its mate. *Two for joy!* I said. *Not hatching yet, or you would not be together!* A yellow cat slunk away round a corner. The teasing magpies had broken its courage long ago. Those two, or two like them, had owned Castle Gillian time out of mind, had their home in the top of a spruce back of the stables, brought out a clutch of four in June, cherished them till October, and then chased them ruthlessly off their domain. *By gum!* I thought, *there's a pair of old ones that don't give way to the young.*

I had started whitewashing close to the southern arch. Half the yard was still in shadow, and I looked over my shoulder to where the edge of the shadow cut aslant across a doorway. That line gave me the time more surely than watch or formal sun-dial. *Past nine o'clock in the morning, and where are Sylvia Gayne and Robin Morrison?*

A horse's shoe clack-clacked on some close-set small cobbles under the arch, and Sylvia and Robin were right there. And between them they were leading Morrison's tall horse, Benbecula.

Thunder an' turf! is this their game? I knew the game already; and had an odd sense of relief. I half-turned from them, and, whistling tunelessly through my teeth, became engrossed in my whitewashing; and I remembered the beginning of a great yarn. So did Robin Morrison.

"'Mornin', Tom Sawyer!" he greeted me.

"Hush!" Sylvia sounded conspiratorial, and I straightened up and looked at her. Our truce was ended, but she had no need to say: "You're a bloody disgrace to the eye, Gill Morris!"

Maybe I was at that. I was wearing the trousers' part of a battle-dress that had been from Sicily to the Adige, unlaced brogues on bare feet, and a shirt loose at wrists and neck because there were no buttons. But I had shaved, and Robin Morrison had not, and he still wore his blue bird's-eye in a tinker's knot. Sylvia herself was resplendent in yellow slacks; and my gorgeous "Oonaghgansey" outlining her young breasts.

"Go to blazes!" I said.

"Hush!" she whispered. "Where is Mary?"

"In there—there she is, and God be good to ye!"

Mary's head had appeared round the jamb of the loose-box door, and her intent, rather stern, violet eyes were not on Sylvia or on Robin, but on the tall horse. She came all the way out now, and pointed her dandy-brush.

"That's a good-looking brown gelding," she said. "Who sent him?" She assumed that she was getting a new customer; and from the glance she gave Robin Morrison she would not take him for other than a carelessly dressed groom. A brown gelding, she had said! The horse looked black to me, except that his cheeks toned into a deep-brown muzzle. It is that muzzle tone, I believe, that decides the colour of a horse. Sylvia said coaxingly:

"Isn't she a serious, lovely old darling?"

She was all right, Mary, standing slim and tall in her slacks and red blouse. The blouse was open at the neck to show the clean white round of her young neck; and her soft hair had one shade of copper in the black of it, and was tied loosely behind her ears with a red ribbon; and her work had brought colour to her softly dusky cheeks. And she was as serious as Rhadamanthus.

Robin Morrison shut his mouth, and turned to me, his eyes batting rapidly. "Is that your sister?" he asked, awe in his voice.

I nodded, and he said: "But why wasn't I warned?"

"Look out!" I said. "She is as hard as nails. I'd ha' warned you if I knew."

"I don't mean that," he said, and turned back to Mary.

Mary was not interested in him. She gestured with the brush, and Robin said "Yes, ma'am" mildly, and led the horse six slow paces across her front. The yield in the off-fore was scarcely noticeable, but it was plain as a broken leg to her expert eye. Sylvia was at my side, and grasped my arm so quickly with both her hands that the whitewash brush fell and splashed her brown shoes. She was excited, and her hands were twitching.

"Ah-h-h!" said Mary. "Who has been misusing this nice brown horse?"

"Me, ma'am," said Robin humbly, and Mary frowned. A wastrel groom could have no excuse for laming a good horse.

"And the owner took your hide off, I hope?" said Mary tartly. "Who is the owner?"

Sylvia, holding on to me, broke in. "Look, Mary! This is Robin Morrison. Wasn't Gill telling you?"

"No, Syl! Gill never tells on you——"

"Gill, darlin'! give us a hand?" Sylvia squeezed my arm. "She's in her cold business mood."

Mary glanced coldly at Robin Morrison. "What am

99

I supposed to do with this lame horse—Robin Morrison?"

"Wait a moment, stupid!" I broke in quickly. "This *is* Robin Morrison. He looks like the wrath o' God I know—but he is *Mister* Robin Morrison out of Scotland. We were with him all day yesterday, at the show, Syl and I——"

Sylvia came in with a rush: "And he is camping with Ty Lane at the Bridge—and he is writing a book—and he owns that colt—and he bled Garret Ward's nose glorious to behold in Jacus's booth. *Mister* Robin Morrison, meet Miss Mary Morrison! Oh hell! I mean Miss Morris."

That was quite a smart speech for Sylvia. Any man who had come out of Tyzack's camp, and was writing a book, and owned a nice horse, and had bled Garret Ward's nose, would interest Mary as no ordinary groom. She looked at him, really for the first time, where he stood facing her at his horse's head, his grey, deep-set eyes steadily on hers. And he was as serious as she was. I never saw two more serious young people. And that aloof indifference of his was scarcely noticeable though it was still there. He spoke in his low pleasant drawl.

"I was told, but what is telling? The family improves as we go along." He bowed and gestured a hand towards himself. "I should be gnashing my teeth in the outer darkness, Miss Morris."

By gum! I thought, *he is excusing his personal appearance. He made no excuses yesterday.*

Mary did not fail to notice that cool, pleasant, cultured Highland voice. She hesitated before she spoke.

"Horses are my business—Mr Morrison. What do you propose——?"

Sylvia burst in impatiently. "That is what I am trying to tell you, if you'd listen to me." She dropped my arm, kicked the brush at her feet and strode at Mary. Face to face they were of a height, and I did notice that the dark one was the more vivid of the two. "Listen, Mary! 'twas I persuaded Robin to bring you his horse, and I didn't tell Gill. Gill is a dumb cluck——"

Mary would not have that. "That's what he calls you, darling—and he doesn't mean tongue-tied either."

"The slug! Shut up! I'm talking about Robin. That's his horse, Benbecula. He hurt its shoulder jumping a stone wall at Tarmon Show——"

"Oh! a showground lepper!" The horse dropped two points.

"And going round in a horse-box over bumpy roads——" Sylvia went on.

"I see! A pot-hunter?" Robin Morrison dropped a couple this time.

"Blast it! I told him that you had a nice soft, river paddock for sore shins and sprains, and that you had oceans of room, and a heart o' corn, and you'd cure his horse in a month. So I persuaded him to come along and talk to you."

"He hasn't got a word in edgewise," I said, "but you are doing fine for a dumb cluck."

"I am not speaking to you, you slug!" said my nice cousin.

"Thank you, Syl!" said Mary quite warmly. "It was right good of you to canvas business for me."

Sylvia put her hand to her mouth in that way she had, turned round, and came at me, her eyes dismayed. "Snakes, Gill! we're sunk," she whispered. "Business! Does the girl think of nothing but filthy lucre? Robin Morrison hasn't a bean."

"I could have told you all that yesterday," I told her.

"Don't make me mad. Whisper, Gill darling! Stick in a word and I'll pray for you."

I did not call her any name. What was the use. I said:
"Let's see how the game goes, first."

Mary was now robed in her business buckram. She
moved slowly round to the horse's shoulder, said a
soothing word, and smoothed a brown hand from withers
to elbow. I could see the hide twitch and still under her
hand. Her fingers prodded softly here and there; she
gestured her head, and Robin walked the horse slowly for
her; she walked with it, her hand moving knowingly
over the weak places. Then she nodded and stepped
back.

"Yes-s! there's nothing much wrong—I think—but
you'll never cure that shoulder in a horse-box." She was
the brisk business woman again. "Right you are, Mr
Morrison! You have come to the right place. I have a
suitable paddock, and, if that shoulder is not chronic,
I'll make it sound as a bell for you in three months—
not a day less. I'll have your horse in half-training by
that time, and you should be able to jump him in four
months. It will cost you only four guineas a week."

"Mother o' Mercy! Listen to Shylock," whispered
Sylvia desperately. "Damn you, Gill! have you lost
your tongue?"

"She has to try, hasn't she?" I said. I was watching
the Highlandman. He was taking it well, and kept his
eyes away from his deflated temptress. He shook his
head consideringly, and his voice was weighty.

"No, Miss Morris! I couldn't pay four guineas a
week—at the moment."

"How much can you pay?" she asked smartly.

She had him in a corner. He couldn't pay a Scotch
bawbee—at the moment. He rubbed the back of his
head perplexedly, but he was game.

"In time I might rise to your four guineas, Miss
Morris," he said, "but at the moment I'm—ah—yes—

financially embarrassed, and couldn't pay anything." The antic careless spirit lifted ahead, and he grinned. "Yes! I could. What about a prayer or two, and a bit of respectful worship from a distance?"

Mary looked at him coldly. She had Robin and Sylvia taped. I think she had them taped from the beginning. She nodded.

"I see—I see! So Sylvia persuaded you? She would. And she was afraid to tell Gillian." She swung round, and gazed sternly at Sylvia, who backed into me, and fluttered her hands helplessly before her face. Mary's voice was fierce. "What do you take me for, soft-heart, mutton-head?"

"Oh, Mary, Mary! my heart is broke," wailed Sylvia, "and I told him you were the best in the world."

"Did you now? I'm not. Business before pleasure is my motto." And there she threw back her head to show her lovely long throat, and started to laugh. It was not scathing laughter. She was no longer the business shark, but a pleasant young woman laughing amongst her friends. I found myself chuckling. Sylvia's shoulders were twitching, and she was beginning to snigger. But Robin Morrison was perplexedly contemplating this new and pleasant girl. Her sudden change of ground had surprised him, and he was no longer easily surprised. Mary stopped laughing and lifted her hands nicely.

"Business session over!" she proclaimed, "and no dividend declared! All right, Syl! I'll back your play. Your Mister Morrison can run his horse in our bottom paddock for as long as he likes—until October, say." She had just remembered what might happen in October.

Sylvia clapped her hands. "What did I tell you, Robin Morrison?" she exulted. She looked over her shoulder at me. "And I don't thank you for anything, you dumbbell!" I was not minding her. I was still watching Morrison.

He was a Scot, and not yet lord of indifference; and as a Scot he was none too sure about accepting what looked like charity from a young woman who, a minute ago, had been trying to screw four guineas a week out of him. And at the same time he could not well spurn Sylvia. Mary saw his hesitation, and became impersonally casual.

"I like horses, that's all," she said. "Your horse appeals to me, and I wouldn't like to have his ruination on my conscience for tuppence worth o' grass. The paddock is empty, and you are welcome to use it, as my cousin told you."

"I—I don't know how to thank you, Miss Morris," he said diffidently.

Sylvia whispered, "Gosh! she's knocked him all of a heap."

Mary's interest returned to the horse. She had seen and trained many better horses, but this particular one seemed to get her in some way. Knowing her so well, I could see the germ of an idea already budding in her mind. This was a poor man's horse, and she was a poor woman! That put them in the same boat. She had given him the run of a paddock, and that was all she could do—or was it? *By glory!* I thought, *she is wondering if she can do anything with that horse. Anything to help the owner? No! Anything to help Castle Gillian? Of course!* My sister Mary was beginning to grasp at straws.

Sylvia was inclined to be restive, and I said:

"Put the lid on it, pot-aboil!" and poked her in the middle of the back.

She leaped a foot, and came round on the pivot with that long left aswing, but I was well out of distance as it went by, and then got close in to imprison her arms.

"Pax! I said it first."

She relaxed strangely under my hands, and then jerked her arms free, and turned her back on me. The other two took no notice of us.

Mary was walking round Benbecula, getting a good squint at it from all angles.

"A good thrust," she murmured, "and lepping shoulders! Shouldn't go on its nose readily—even pecking over stones in amateur hands. About five, isn't it?"

"Just about, and it did peck over a stone wall in my hands," Robin told her. He was livening up again.

"So I gathered," said Mary carelessly. "You have him registered?"

"Yes—br.g. by Becfola out of Benmee."

Mary opened her eyes. "Why that's the true Blackthorn blood! That's not for showground jumping! Ever try him over bush fences in his stride?"

"No, but at four he could take hurdles full pelt."

"And you took a year to spoil him! That blood is wasted pot-hunting." She faced Robin and put him a slow question. "If it is no harm to ask, what do you intend to do with your Benbecula horse, Mr Morrison?"

There was a pause then; a pause that had some significance. The idea that was in Mary's mind was flickering in my own. *Damn that magpie!* A sorrowful one had flicked over a roof and cursed me. Benbecula cocked an ear knowingly and nudged a brown muzzle into his owner's chest, as much as to say: *Answer the lady, dumb one!* And he answered very deliberately, but I knew, by the quick motion of his head, that until this minute he had not thought much about the future of his horse. He was writing a book, he had said, and was living on his horse and Tyzack Lane, and was no longer looking forward in a crumbling world. But now, as it were, he was getting another glint of daylight through a milestone. He could play Mary at her own game.

"This horse is all mine, Miss Morris. If I have to, I'll sell him once he's properly schooled. And still! I'd like to keep a lien on him. You know? Lease him, after trial, on the usual terms."

Mary, legs wide and thumbs in the belt of her slacks, said smoothly in true horse-dealing fashion, "If that horse has to learn to race, the sooner you lease him the better."

"I was thinking much the same thing myself," said Morrison just as smoothly.

Sylvia turned her head. "Don't open your mouth, you pup!" she warned me.

There was no need. Mary made up her mind, there and then, that she had gone far enough on this occasion.

"Time enough to think of leasing when you have a horse with a sound shoulder," she said, and became the brisk young woman with jobs to do. "We'll give your Benbecula a look at that bottom paddock later on. Meantime we'll try him in a loose-box. Is number five bedded, Gillian?"

It was. That bedding was one of my chores. So Mary and Robin boxed Benbecula. I heard her say conversationally from inside the box, "You stay with the Lanes, Mr Morrison?" She was going to do some probing in her woman's way.

I resumed my whitewashing.

II

Sylvia was at my side watching me.

"Like a turn?" I invited her. "I want to fill a pipe. It will cost you only a shilling for five minutes."

"No, you——! Yes, I will." She was looking down at her splashed shoes, and I knew she was blaming me; and I knew what she'd do with the brush.

"No, you won't! Keep back, or I'll make a whited sepulchre of you!"

"Oh, please yourself! Say, Gill! What is going to happen next?"

"The thing that happens next will follow as the night the day," I said, keeping the satire out of my voice. "You have it in the bag, my darling, just as you planned."

"What do you know about my plans?" she asked suspiciously.

"You can't fool me, cousin. I'm consumed with envy watching you nobly saving the ancestral home of Castle Gillian. Look! I see it all just as you dreamt it. Mary will train Benbecula into the horse of the century, enter it for the five hundred pounds 'chase at Lislawn in September, and every last one of us will have our shirts on it as an outsider at twenties. It can't lose, and we'll pull down five thousand—nay! seven thousand, and the villain is foiled. Foiled, by heavings! For Mary, flowing with love and gratitude, falls into Robin Morrison's arms and all goes merry as a marriage bell. Keep back, I warn you!"

"Make fun of it if you like," she said smugly, "but I did do some planning all by myself——"

"Like hell you did!" I hit her. "You only thought you'd play some more with the nice Highlandman. Very good! Possibly he'll leave his horse here, but himself will be off with Tyzack Lane. And Mary might mend that horse too, but how good is it? A five-year-old light hurdler! The country is full of 'em, better bred, better schooled, sounder in limb, and better cared for. It might win a bumper race, and Garret Ward might buy it come October. That's all! and don't you put foolish notions into Mary's head."

"Stop it, Gill!" she said seriously. "We must do something about October?"

"Must we?" I was bitter again. "Find three thousand for Padderson on a furze bush? Not likely! Garret Ward has offered five thousand as soon as he sells Monaglass, and you know Mary? The bit in her teeth, she might take it."

"For you——" began Sylvia, who did know Mary.

"I'll not be within five thousand miles," I said with a growl.

"You are going away?" Her voice went low.

"I am going away, Syl," I said steadily, "and I might be in a hurry too."

Whether she understood that, I do not know, but her eyes blazed at me, and she went pale about the mouth. She came close in at me, pulled the brush out of my hands, and threw it against the wall. Then she caught me two-handed by the neck-band of my old shirt and I heard it rip. Her voice came from away down.

"You talk to me about cheap melodrama, Gill Morris! I'll choke it out of you."

When she was in that mood I never exerted my greater weight against her. I let her force me back, and she went within an ace of putting me under the hooves of Sandy Ythan's horse coming in under the arch from exercise. She whirled me round just in time and let me go. And Sandy, reining aside, said in his own Aberdeen Doric:

"'Gree, bairnies! 'gree! Ye'll soon be sundered."
It was an old Scots admonition to children.

"And you're another false prophet, Ythan, curse you!" she railed at him.

But I had a queer feeling at the base of my neck, and it was Sandy's admonition to children that put it there. Agree, children, agree! You'll soon be sundered. Sylvia and I never agreed, and yet, come to think of it—— Ah, well!

Four sets of hooves clattered echoingly under the arch,

and dulled on the packed gravel. The Benbecula colt, head over half-door, nickered anxiously to the new arrivals, and Sandy said:

"Guid be here! What have we now?"

I did not go back to whitewashing. I wanted to see how our Lowland groom reacted to his Highland brother off the road.

Sandy's surname was not Ythan. His full name was Alexander Bethune. Ythan was the name of his beloved home-river, somewhere in Buchan. Unlike the run of Buchan men, he was short, small-set in the bone, tough as heather, and irascible as a terrier. His riding breeches were of Glenfeshie tartan tweed, and so were his jacket and the long-peaked cap over hot blue eyes. He was so good at his job that many stables had tried to lure him away, but not even his stern Calvinist Deity could wean him from drunken old Gillian Morris, with whom he had seen great days and evil days.

He was riding one horse and leading another. His two stablemen were each leading a horse behind him. The older, Dan Shea, was a bully lad of twenty-odd, riding eleven stone; and his brother Lant, who had once promised to be a useful lightweight, was growing up so quickly that he could never hope to be anything but a stable hand, a fact that, as Lant put it, broke the melt in him.

Sandy Ythan saw the brown-muzzled, long Irish head extended over the half-door, sat straight-up in the saddle, and looked at his mistress. In the tail of his eye was Robin Morrison, who, if he had a horse, must have stolen it. His voice was irritable.

"What have ye been about, Miss Mary?"

Mary's gesture took in the horse and Robin. "Got me another horse, Sanny. This is the owner." Mary was pulling a quick one on Sanny.

Sandy took one quick look at Robin Morrison by the loose-box door, rolled off his horse, and nearly tripped himself with the leading rein.

"Waters o' Dee! who wished a tinkler's horse on us? Wait'll I vet him afore waur happens!"

Sandy hurriedly boxed his horses and came out banging doors. His lads did likewise, for they did not want to miss anything. Sandy made forthright for Benbecula's door, and found himself face to face with Robin Morrison.

"Out o' my road, tinkler!" Sandy barked.

Morrison lifted a calming hand, and his Highland draw was more pronounced than usual. "Bide a wee, my cantyman! For your ain sake you'll be moving softly with a horse first time in a strange loose-box."

Sandy actually reared back and appealed to high heaven. "Goad be here! Is it a Hielan' tinkler that's cursed on us? Are you a Williamson or a MacFee?"

"No' me! Are you frae Aiberdeen toon, twelve mile roond it, and whaur so rather?" This was Sandy's veritable speech and habitat.

"Ye impudent loon!" he yelped. "What was I no' doin' with horses afore ye were foaled under a whin? Oot o' my way! or ye'll be with a dingin' lug!" He ducked under Robin's arm, and shouldered him away from the door.

"His fate be on his own head!" said Robin agreeably.

As the brown head disappeared into the box it had its ears back, and a white gleam in its eyes.

"A vice! and what other would you expect?" proclaimed Sandy.

"He don't care for the dour Lowland taint of you," said the Highlandman.

"Wait ye!" threatened Sandy, as he snicked back the bolt and dodged inside.

It was as if he had touched off a six-inch shell. There was a clatter and a rattle and a thunder, and a smack of iron on wood; and Sandy Ythan came through the doorway like the devil through Athlone—in standing lepps—his cap in his fist, a triangular rent in a tartan shoulder, and the sun glinting on his bald dome. Someone laughed.

"Sakes be!" he cursed inadequately. "A maneater that's in it!"

The brown head was in the doorway, but before the horse could break out, its owner had it by cavesson ring and top-knot. He brought it out prancing some, soothing it with hand and voice, and led it across the yard and back again. The limp was noticeable now, and Sandy's voice was shrill.

"A killer, a crowbait—stable-shy—and a'e showder gone as well! Wae's me, Miss Mary! Ye didna dicker for a cast-off wi' a tinkler loon?"

Mary surprised him. She was there facing him, taller than he was, and bent like a taut bow. Her firm brown fist was under his nose and moving for action. Sylvia caught my arm, and her voice pealed urgently:

"No—no, Mary! Sanny didn't mean to."

"But the horse did," I said.

Mary did not thump him, of course. Her voice was low, but it had a grate in it. "What do you think you are doing, you sawed-off, bellowing, little polled bull of Buchan?" She got off that without a splutter. "If you make a rogue of my horse, I'll tear your blisterin' Ythan tongue out by the roots and feed it to you with red pepper."

"Who has the blisterin' tongue, I'd like to know?" I asked softly, and Sylvia chortled.

Sandy stepped back hastily, and his gnarled old hands fluttered up protestingly. "All reet, Miss Mary! All reet! *Your* horse, did you say? All reet—all reet! Never mind me! But what will auld Gillian Morris say?"

"Ask him! Here he is," I called, and added to myself, *and his new boss with him.*

III

My father and Garret Ward had just come through the narrow arch from the house. Ward was in riding kit, his shoulders wide and smooth, and his feet slightly asplay. My father was in his easy-fitting old homespuns that never wore out. He was taller than the younger man, his bush of ivory hair away up in the air, and his lean aquiline face hiding the inner, broken-down defences. He was sober at this hour, but he would have had at least three morning drams.

The two stable boys disappeared into loose-boxes; Ythan waited on to see what auld Gillian Morris would say; I turned to retrieve my whitewash brush, and found Sylvia lavishly at work with it.

"Spread it!" I said. "We haven't all the lime there is. And that's a bob off."

"Listen, Gill! Will they tangle again, them two?" She was a bit excited.

"Hoots, girl!" I said. "Yon was only a glove bout in a boxing-booth."

Robin Morrison was easing Benbecula in a circle. Garret Ward cut across it, and the horse stopped. The two men faced each other, and I could see Ward's quite amiable grin. He might go berserk in a fight, for that was his method, but after the fight he became his cool, collected self. It was that cool, collected poise of his that got under my skin. It was more than cocksureness, for it went deeper. He was sure of himself, and he knowingly made sure of others—men and women. Mary was the one woman he was not yet sure of, and her appeal lay in that uncertainty. I noticed that his flat nose was a shade swollen, and a shade under one eye.

"Hullo, fighting tinker!" he greeted cheerfully. "I nearly took you that third round, didn't I?" He knew Morrison was no tinker, whatever else he was; he was just hoping to touch the Scot where he lived. Sylvia was right: there was a sly cruelty deep down in Garret Ward.

Robin Morrison said equably: "Just about, Mr Ward."

"Try you again some time, and take a tenner off old Jacus!" Ward said.

"Not if I see you first," said Morrison firmly.

Ward laughed, and turned his attention to the horse. He knew horse. "Nice horse! Nice lame shoulder! Chronic, no doubt?" he said. "Yours or Ty Lane's?"

Robin Morrison might be probed by Mary, but not by Garret Ward. He did not answer directly, but gestured a hand towards Mary.

Mary was observing the two through crinkled eyes, comparing them, and she was beginning to wonder about Robin Morrison. Now she went as near telling a lie as makes no matter.

"That horse is in stable from now on, Garret."

"For mending?"

"I'll mend him all right," said Mary confidently, "and I hope to race him too."

You're a cute dodger, Maureen Dhuv, I thought. *Giving the false impression to Garret Ward, and selling a pup to Robin Morrison. Women are all the same!*

Ward did jump to his conclusion. "Good lord! You haven't bought the poor brute?" he cried.

"Why not?" gave back Mary casually.

Garret Ward controlled himself firmly. "You're the boss, of course, my dear! But I wouldn't have the beast in my stable, eating his head off, without first making sure of that shoulder. What do you think, Uncle Gillian?"

My father had strolled across, his trainer's eye on Benbecula.

"A nice animal, fore-and-aft!" he said in his husky, gentlemanly way. "Wo, boy! Wo—o!" He moved softly forward, patted a twitching neck, and ran a slow feeling hand from shoulder right down to fetlock. He spoke musingly. "No! one would not find a bone and hoof like that below a chronic shoulder." He glanced at Robin the groom. "How did it happen, young man?"

"Over loose stones in a jump, sir—" Robin answered.

"But how long ago?" Ward rapped in.

"The hound!" said Sylvia in my ear.

Morrison answered promptly, "A month ago at Tarmon Show."

"Could be!" said Ward laconically.

"Hardly mature enough for stone jumps," said my father, and turned to Mary. "You have taken him in, girl?"

"Yes, Dad! I'll tell you later." She would tell Father, of course, but she would tell Garret Ward nothing, not after he had questioned her horse-sense.

"Put him in the river paddock," advised my father, "and after a month give him a gentle course, and you'll know."

"Just so!" agreed Garret Ward, but he added, "At the worst we can pack him off to the zoo in October. Hope you got him cheap, old girl?"

Mary did not answer that. She could not get a horse any other way, and Ward implied that. He resented Mary acquiring another horse without consulting him, and he implied what he might do on his Ides of March.

Keep on, brother, and you'll cook your own goose, I thought.

However, Garret Ward was not particularly interested in horse or owner at that time. He was here to see Mary, and now he said:

"I'm at a loose end this morning, Mary. I came over to take out a horse for you." That would not be a bad way of breaking himself in at the stables.

Mary hesitated, and made up her mind.

"Thanks, Garret! I want to see if *Rowan Red* can give your extra poundage to *Steeplecrown-Hat* over a mile. Wait till I get a jodhpurs on! Sandy, send Dan round with the horses." Now she looked at Robin Morrison. "You and I will talk later on, Mr Morrison," she said meaningly.

"I'll need to learn a few new words, ma'am," said Robin Morrison.

Mary smiled and went off towards the house-arch in that brisk, snappy stride that girls show when they wear slacks. No girl at all can walk as gracefully as a man. My father mooned round the square, looked into a loose-box here and there, and drifted back to the house. That is all he did any morning.

Garret Ward strolled across towards Sylvia and me.

"Hello! Siamese-twins!" he greeted us.

There was some reason in the name too. Sylvia and I had been brought up together. Since she had learned to walk she had followed me round, whether I liked it or not, and had taken her share of the beltings like a brick. So now, when we were in the same company we, of old instinct, gravitated together. But man and wife? That was another kettle of fish, and we were not touching that old man's dish.

"You're the Queen o' Sheba in all her colours, my darlint," he said to Sylvia, admiring her Oonagh-gansey.

"I got a job this morning, Mister—you keep going!" Sylvia said.

"So I see." He came between us. "I'll hire you come Michaelmas." That date was a fixation with all of us. Michaelmas is at the end of September.

Sylvia poised the brush. "Want me to make a whited sepulchre of you, Garret?"

Smartly he caught the handle below the brush, pulled her forward, chucked her under the chin, and swung her round and away. He gave me a solid thrust of shoulder, and strode off towards the house-arch. Before I could do anything, Sylvia came swooping round with the brush, and I had just time to duck under it. My head was in a convenient place, so I gave her a soft butt in the diaphragm. After that the limewash bucket went over.

IV

Robin Morrison reboxed his Benbecula, pushed at the brown head over the half-door, and moved across towards us. Sandy Ythan disappeared into a loose-box. I could hear the sibilance of soothing voices keeping time to brush strokes, the clap of a hand on a polished hide, an admonitory "shove over," and the thin whistle of the Ythan man at one of his two tunes:

> "Once mair to hear the wild birds' sang,
> To wander birks and braes amang,
> 'Midst friends and fav'rites left sae lang
> At the back o' Benachie."

He hadn't been back for forty years, but the song was as nostalgic as the *Cruachan Beann* of the Campbells.

Robin Morrison looked from one to the other of us. There was a speculative look in his deep-set eyes, as if he had been set a problem that had got behind his indifference.

My unlaced shoes were full of limewash, and I was engaged in emptying them out. I'd probably have blisters. If Sylvia was wearing nylons under her slacks she would need a new pair. Her last lot had been smuggled from New York via Shannon.

"He gave me no help, this hunk!" complained Sylvia, rubbing one ankle against the other. "Gosh! it tickles. And you were a bit tongue-tied yourself, Mr Robin."

"But I wasn't warned. I got right out of my depth with that dark beauty."

"You got your horse settled in, didn't you, thanks to me," Sylvia boasted.

"Till October," I reminded her.

Morrison wrinkled his rather heavy brows. "I don't want to butt in," he said, "but this October, now? Your sister mentioned it, and Ward, and now you—as if it were the crack o' doom."

"It is, for Castle Gillian," I said.

"Didn't Oonagh Blake tell you?" Sylvia put in.

"Oonagh told me plenty, but she don't gossip about your private affairs, young lady. Forget it; it is no business of mine!"

I made up my mind to keep my mouth shut, but I reckoned without Sylvia.

"It is this way, Robin," she said impulsively. "Garret Ward wants to marry Mary and Castle Gillian in October." That was not correct, but near enough.

"But she don't need to marry him if she don't want to?" said the Scot, mildly interrogative. The Scots are noted for minding their own business, but their business covers some territory. Sylvia further explained.

"Mary—or Uncle Gillian" (that was an afterthought) —"must find five thousand pounds before October— mortgages or something—and Garret Ward offers it— and himself."

"For a controlling interest," I amplified.

"My father would give the five thousand like one

o'clock," said Sylvia aggrievedly, "only that is not in the dam' code of the Morrises. Some scoundrel Morris about ruined Castle Evan four generations ago, and cold cash is taboo. Such nonsense!"

"Miss Mary Morris is a business woman; I noticed that in passing," said Robin whimsically. "Am I to assume that she would chance this Garret Ward for the sake of his five thousand pounds?"

"But you don't know all that Castle Gillian means to Mary Morris!" Sylvia tried to explain.

"Don't I?" He lifted his head and pivoted slowly round on his heel.

There, over a stable ridge, was the tall old house, with its copper-green roof swallowing the sun; there was the living green of the larches climbing the hillside; over there was the curve of Castle Evan hill clothed in the gold of the furze; and far away was the ridge of Shirlan Ben taking the sun on its ribbed limestone. The birds were not twittering, nor the wood-quests crooning, nor the magpies cursing; there was, though it was morning still, a slumbrous quiet over the place, and that quiet would last and thicken all the long afternoon. Sandy Ythan was whistling his other tune, the lament for Flodden and the lonesomeness of it was in tune with the place, but it was a soothing lonesomeness that had a deep content under it.

"Maybe I do," said the Highland Gael ruminatively. "This is the hole that a girl has chosen, and she would stay in it, even if she has to share it in cold blood. Don't I know it, looking for a hole of my own?" A new note of gloom had come into his voice.

He turned on his heel and walked slowly away. Sylvia called after him. "Anyway, your Benbecula is getting a chance till October."

"Behind me, temptress! This place is dangerous and

doomed, and I'll ride from it fast and free till Benbecula falls under me on three legs." He lifted a slow hand, and went on in his straight-footed way towards the brown head of his horse over the half-door.

Sylvia said in a mild, tired little voice, "I think I'll go home."

"Do," I said, mildly too. "You did a good job o' work, even if you failed."

"I don't know. I'll not be seeing you again, will I?"

"Hair or hide of me you won't be seeing again this day," I told her.

"You could be polite about it, couldn't you?"

Her voice was low, and her tell-tale mouth gave her away. I didn't want her to go like that. I put my finger under her nose.

"Listen, you! The day will be hot, and the trout won't rise, but, come gloaming, I know a good fish that might take a fly I tied for him. Look! if you come flauntin' that gansey about the Luidin Pool I'll drownd you——"

I was too slow that time. I took her left in the short ribs, and was late with my counter. She turned from the arch, and her voice was high.

"I'll be there, but you won't see me. When you come up for air I'll be gone."

V

I would have to mix a fresh bucket of whitewash now, and I must clean up the mess on the packed gravel. Let them wait! I moved across to where Morrison was pulling his horse's top-knot. Sandy Ythan came to a loose-box door, and shook his head at the splash of white on the gravel.

"Your lass and yourself are no' safe the one company," he said.

119

He looked at the Highlandman consideringly. Dambut! he looked the fair wastrel, but was he? Sandy had kept his ears open, and was beginning to wonder, about this Hielan' tinkler loon. The Highlandman spoke quietly:

"Come and get acquainted with a horse, Mr—Ythan, isn't it? Once I was through a bonnie bit place called Ythan Wells——"

"He has talked of no place other for forty years," I said.

"Bethune is my name, but I dinna get it," Sandy said. "Were you trampin' the road yon time?"

"Ay, was I! With a company of West Coast kilties training for war. Bethune is of the Highlands too— McBeth, Beaton, Bethune surgeons to the clans."

"Ay so! I've a brother a doctor, but I wouldna risk a dose o' physic from him an' I dyin'." Sandy gave him a choleric blue eye. "A West-coaster, wi' ponies twelve hands high, makin' me acquaint of a horse! Tak' a runnin' kick at yersel', laddie!"

Morrison snicked back the bolt, took hold of the cavesson ring, and led his horse round to the manger-end of the box.

"Come into my parlour!" he invited.

Sandy was in the doorway looking cautiously in. An inexperienced man might make a quick dart to the horse's head, and cause another rumpus, but Sandy sidled along by the partition, keeping an eye on the horse's ears that twitched only once. I leant a shoulder on the jamb, and filled a pipe, but I was ready to jump.

"There noo, my laddie! Take it easy! easy, boy!" The dark hide twitched under Sandy's palm, and the head would have jerked up but for the firm hold on the cavesson.

"Try a wisp o' straw on him," murmured Robin. "Wait! Let's try it my way?" He took a length of string from a pocket, and I knew he was used to horses. Trainers, grooms, even Mary, carry odd lengths of string in every pocket. He tied one end of the string to the cavesson ring, and the other to the ring-bolt of the feed-box.

"That's a horseman's trick, anyway," commended another horseman, teasing a wisp of straw between his hands.

"My father taught me that—and he owned a horse or two," Robin said.

At the first touch of the wisp the horse jerked away, and the string broke. Many a young horse has panicked at the relentless tug of a head-chain. Robin soothed the horse and tied the string again, and again the string snapped, and again. After that the wise beast understood that nothing dreadful was going to happen, and stood up to Sandy's wisp. Soon the two men were quietly grooming, and quietly talking under the belly and over the barrel; and the horse, hearing those quiet voices, and feeling the pleasant tickle, relaxed and drooped a head.

"The hurt showder your side—chronic is it?" Sandy remarked.

"Mr Morris said a month would tell," Robin hedged.

"Maybe so!" Sandy tried again. "Was I hearin' that this beastie belongs to Ty Lane?"

"I ken what you heard," said Robin. "No doubt Miss Morris will give you the facts."

"Fair enough!" Sandy said, not taking umbrage. "It is her business to tell or tie," and went on minding his own business. "Would it be fair to speir if you are in Ty Lane's camp your ainself?"

"Certainly! I am in Ty Lane's camp."

"In his ain camp at the Bridge."

"Just right there."

"Ayman! Tyzack is aye pickin' down-and-out chiels off the road." But Sandy was well aware that none of Tyzack's many waifs would be cherished in the home camp—none but old Sloper Jones. He went on probing. "You'll be a showman too, I jalouse—a boxer maybe?"

"Off and on," agreed Morrison.

"And was I hearin' right that you had a bit of a tulzie wi' Garret Ward?"

"Your hearin' is slightly affected, Mr Bethune-Ythan— nice double-barrel name that. Three rounds in a boxing-booth don't make a tulzie."

"You gie'd him that blue e'en?"

"And a bluidy nose, forbye! Like to see my belly— ouch? Say, Gill Morris, would you give me the verdict over yon three rounds?"

I scraped a match and let it light up. "Just about! Yes, I would. But don't you take him on barefisted, brother!" I warned.

"That *would* be a tulzie, and I'll be dam' careful."

"Man-o'-man!" said Sandy. "All tinkler loons are handy wi' their neaves."

"Have to be," said Robin agreeably.

"Tinkler or no'," said Sandy, "when I'm no' lookin' at you, you sound like a gent."

"Dogs abuse, my freen'!"

"And your father kept horses?"

"He did, and I know what you're driving at, you old devil?"

"Devil yourself! You don't?"

"You think—like others—that I have fallen from a high estate and enjoy grovelling in the mud?"

"By goshikins! Barrin' the gentry words sic' was my very thought. Ay! I met your likes in my time, but nane wi' your guts or gumption."

"And you'd rather I was a straight tinkler, eh?"

"You're nimble-witted, my man," said Sandy. "Over a wee, horsie!"

Robin Morrison straightened up, and kept meditatively rubbing a hand down Benbecula's crest. Sandy, grooming done, leant against the feed-box and let the horse sniff his horseman's smell. I relit my pipe, and wondered if Morrison was going to let the old groom retain his false impression? And then the Scot made up his mind about something. I knew that by the way he lifted his head with a small jerk. He lifted his voice too, and I knew that, though addressing Sandy, it was to me he was telling things.

"Who made you my confessor, dear old Father Alexander?" he enquired quirkily.

"I'd have you know I'm a staunch Auld Kirker," said Sandy huffily.

"And far frae heaven! You got me wrong, I think. I'm no' your tinkler loon, and I'm no' a wastrel loon either. I stand on the ground I always stood on. I come of Arisaig in Moidart—mostly MacDonald country."

"A bonny place, I hear tell—but papish as the plains o' hell."

"Same as your Gordon country. My father kept a riding-horse or two, and so does my brother, for the place is still there. There were six sons of us, and two are dead in a desert with the dead of the Fifty-First; and most of us had to wander for bread. I got some schooling at Fort Augustus——"

"Ah! the Benedictine Mass place, head of Loch Ness?"

"But I never saw the monster, being truthful more or less—even though I took to Journalism after that."

"Writing pieces for the papers?" There was a new note in Sandy's voice. He had the national respect for letters—any sort of letters—even Journalism.

"Pieces for the papers is right! Free-lance for a while, and I was sporting correspondent to the *North Riding Times*. Wait! I have a good memory for horses. I saw a horse named Larch Pole win at Thirsk, trainer and owner, Mr Gillian Morris. How long ago was that?"

"That was 1936," said Sandy promptly. "The good old days, and God be wi' them!"

But we were slipping long before then, I thought.

"The good old evil days, for evil was even then seeping," said Morrison. "But I was young and thought I could run my own furrow in the world of letters, having no ancestral wealth to fall back on; and three years later I went to war, and that was the beginning of the end of things."

"Man—man!" protested Sandy. "Aren't we beginning over again? I would I was young like you, and my time before me."

"You are lucky, my father! Time is standing still—didn't you know it? Standing still and waiting for another war to make a finish—and I 'm no' playing——"

"Then you are a wastrel!" said Sandy firmly. "That's no talk!"

"But I'm no' playin', I tell you!" His voice hardened. "You cannot divide the world between what is called Communism, but ain't, and Private Enterprise yclept Democracy, and call it universal peace. Peace that is a desolation! No, sir! I'm no' playin'. I'm only looking for a hole to watch the farce from till the curtain falls. That's me, Mr Ythan-Wells: a lad without a bawbee, and one horse to call his own!"

"Lookin' for a bit burrow over here?" queried Sandy crisply.

"I'm looking for to see—in this land that cannily wouldna fight, and sent so many thousands out to die."

"Is that why you bide with Ty Lane?"

"Could be! but Tyzack and Oonagh and Jacus are too far ahead for me."

"There's young Dinny Lane?" I put in.

"Ay! there's Dinny," he said sombrely. "Dinny is a problem for a man. I like Dinny—a lad of parts, and a born horseman! I am troubled about Dinny. We know what too often happens the third generation of roadmen—with too much money to squander."

He straightened up, gave his horse a clap over the croup, and came out into the yard. Sandy followed him, and the horse snapped his head-string and turned round.

Robin Morrison looked from Sandy to me and might be addressing either of us. He was noticeably diffident, almost shamefaced.

"Tyzack will be in camp at the Bridge for some days," he said. "I know that Benbecula horse, and he knows me. I wonder could I ask Miss Morris if I might come round for a day or two until the horse gets used to the place?"

"You could ask Gill Morris, couldn't you?" said Sandy, who was a man's man.

"No!" I spoke quickly. "Ask Alexander Bethune, who is head-groom, and lord of the Man's Room."

Sandy was a prudent, slow-thoughted man, but his countryman had got him. He grinned. "We can be doin' fine with a helpin' hand. You'll be welcome to come and go—and bide if you like."

"Thank you, sirs! I'll be seeing ye." He lifted a hand in salute, and walked off at his even pace towards the south arch. His horse made to walk out after him, but Sandy slapped the door to just in time, and the horse whinnied anxiously. Morrison did not look back.

I tap-tapped my pipe against a shoe heel, and wondered. Robin Morrison, who was to ride away fast and free, had changed his mind. He was leaving his horse at Castle Gillian, and had been giving us some credentials so that himself would not be unwelcome. No Highland-man would so talk about himself for any other reason.

"Might be I was mistaken about yon chiel," mused Sandy at my shoulder. "He's Hielan' o' course," said the Lowlander, "and you couldna' be tellin' the quirks in a Hielan' head. Still, man, still! any lad that tangled wi' Garret Ward is no enemy o' mine. That's his own horse then?"

"Mary will tell you."

"You're as good as tellin' me. Ah, well! We'll gie the beast a fair show."

"Till October?" I said.

"Ay! I ken what might happen then. Miss Mary told me." His voice had venom in it. "Garret Ward meddlin' in oor affairs—an' cock o' the walk! Goad! If I didna love auld Gillian Morris, I'd curse him on my bended knees—same as a bluidy papist."

"You don't like cousin Garret I would say?"

"Hair nor hide—but I'm no' the one to hinner him." He looked at me, and looked away again.

"Another way of saying I'm that one?"

"There's no one other—but I'm not sayin' you're the one."

"Blast you! You two-voiced old horse-coper," I cursed him, and walked out of the yard.

Chapter V

SYLVIA SETS AN EGG TO HATCH

I

I HAD not seen cousin Sylvia for three whole days. She hadn't come fishing the Luidin Pool, nor come down to thank me for the ten-pound salmon I had sent up. Her thanks, indeed, would go something like this: *Three weeks in stale water, ne'er a hook mark in its mouth, and a cut in its tail where the loop nicked it—but thank you all the same!* I was somewhat disturbed about her, but not ready to admit it. Instead I said to myself:

I promised Uncle Tom to be friendly. And anyway, she has been down once, so it would be no harm to return the visit to show there's no ill-feeling. After that she can go to blazes!

So I padded across in the evening on the path that many Morris feet had worn: down through the holm-oaks to pause on the foot-bridge across the Gullane, and up through the holm-oaks where the sun spread orange splashes on the polished green leaves. The ditches of the haw-haw fence were not choked with dead leaves, as ours were; the stone pillars of the foot-bridge were fitted with a wrought-iron gate; the green-green lawn beyond was velvet-smooth and resplendent with formal flower-beds, mostly of wallflower and tulips, edged with primula-wanda; and clumps of red rhododendron cast long shadows.

I told myself that I preferred our thick-soled lawn, where our Kerry cow was as familiar as a dog, and chicks raced wing-wide after clucking mothers, and a bold Leghorn cock crowed at a bold Rhode Island cock morning, noon and eve. There was a perfume of cut grass mixed with the cloying scent of wallflower; and I knew Uncle Tom would have hay-fever.

The tall house of Castle Evan was a replica of our own, but the white of it was so white that it had a hint of blue, and the fine bronze astragals of the windows were shining. The house faced north, and got one slanting glimpse of late sun in late spring. It was getting that glimpse now, and the pillars of the portico cast long shadows by the side of the wall.

As I came to the foot of the scrubbed steps, Uncle Tom came out of the open door, and his shadow raced hugely up the wall. He was wearing his whites, and he was blowing his nose in a red handkerchief. He leant against a pillar, and his face was not quite as red as the handkerchief.

"'Morrow, Gillian!" he gave his usual salute. "Damn country life and hay-fever!" He preferred to live in his house in town.

"'Morrow, Uncle Tom!" I said. "Where's Syl?"

"She saw you coming," said Uncle Tom. "She is gone up to her room."

"Is that the way with her?" I said. "Do you think I should go up and give her a beltin'?"

"You could try." He sneezed. "They are never too old for it."

"Did Dad's whiskey make you sick, Uncle Tom?" I asked then.

"Sick? I thought my last hour was come. I should ha' been warned."

"I knew a bit of convulsion wouldn't hurt you," I said.

"You impudent pup! And so old Gillian can no longer savour his liquor? Man, that's a pity! The best judge o' good whiskey in four counties, I only knew one better—a writer chap he was, but otherwise fair enough. How are things across at Gillian?" His shrewd eyes were holding me, and I think he was making talk to give Sylvia time for a second thought.

"Things are looking up, Uncle Tom," I said. "Mary got another horse."

"And the loan of a man with it? Sylvia told me, and she taking credit for it." Sylvia did not hide things from her father. None of us did.

"Did she tell you about Garret Ward, Uncle Tom?" I asked.

"She did. Is he after the lass or the land, eh?" He hid behind his red silk.

"The land first, I would say. Do you think Mary good-looking, Uncle? I don't. But she's no worse than your long-legged Sylvia with her graceless old tow-top! Would you like Garret Ward in Castle Gillian, Uncle Tom?"

"To go out of it feet first, I would." Then he chuckled. "Mary is only your sister in the house, Gill, and my Sylvia a tomboy to play with. 'Tis the faraway cows have the long horns." He sneezed again, waited, and as I was silent, went on. "'Tis Mary he wants—any man would— I would myself—but the land and stables are no drawback either. You don't like the scheme, do you? No! Does Mary? Yes, I know Mary! And what can you— or I—do about it?"

"You are answering your own questions, Uncle. Answer that one too?" I said.

Hands in pockets, and feet solidly planted, I looked up at him; and he looked down at me over his red silk handkerchief.

"All right! I'll answer it," he said firmly. "Castle Gillian wants five thousand pounds, and Castle Evan has it to give. Well?"

"We all know that, Uncle Tom," I said. "But listen!

Did you ever hear of my great-great grandfather, Evan Morris?"

"Let that flee stick to the wall, boy!"

"For everyone to see. Old Evan of Castle Gillian took ten thousand off Castle Evan by plain fraud, and never even tried to pay it back—and it is still due—and this house was left on the rocks, until you married my cousin, and floated it off on your money. Do you think my father or Mary would take a penny from you, Uncle Tom?"

He thrust his head down at me. "You are the son of the house, Gillian! What about yourself?"

I knew what was in his mind. I moved my head slowly. "No, Uncle! Nothing doing! I'm not in the money market, and I'll accept no sacrifice. I have nothing to give and there is nothing I will take. And another thing: your five thousand would be only a stop-gap, for Castle Gillian will never come alive until there is a dominant man in control—and I am not that one."

"By God, boy!" rapped Tom Gayne, "you'll find Garret Ward dominant enough."

"That's to be seen," I said, and turned on my heel.

I had given Sylvia time enough for her second thought.

"I'll be toddling along, Uncle Tom," I said. "Tell Syl that the next time I make an appointment with her at the Luidin it will be for the sole purpose of drownding her."

"I wouldn't blame you, boy," said my uncle heartily. "But wasn't she for drownding three nights ago?"

"Manalive! did I put the fear o' God in her at last? That's good news. So long, sir!"

I turned on my heel and took a couple of steps. A high, clear, chill voice came from behind, and made me turn again.

"What are you doing here, Gill Morris?"

That was Sylvia. I had assumed that she was listening in the hall for some time, and so I had said a couple of things for her ear. In her pale-blue dress she was full in the slanting evening glow, and the sunlight was caressing her, and I didn't blame it. She was surely long-legged, but she was not graceless, and her tow-top was gilt with transparent gold. I said:

"I was only going down to the camp."

She was not in her low-voiced mood this evening. "You are taking the long way round, aren't you?"

"I thought you might give me your hand through the tulgy wood."

"Good man yourself!" commended Uncle Tom.

"Supper will be over," Sylvia said, "and I've had mine—that salmon was spent."

"Mine wasn't," I said, and half-turned from her. "Well! I'll not be inconveniencing you. See you some time—Tibb's eve, maybe!"

I walked away, but not fast, and Uncle Tom was laughing and sneezing behind me.

She was at my side before I got to the haw-haw gate.

"I was going down to the camp myself," she explained. "I want to say a few words to Robin Morrison."

"You will not," I said firmly.

She flared. "Who is to stop me?"

"Not a few—a spate," I said. "Look! don't start another devil's agency. Robin Morrison is nearly a gone coon already."

"Lord, Gill!" She was interested at once. "Has he fallen for Mary?"

"Not him! She is working him to death, that's all."

"Huh to you! I'll come over and see for myself."

"I've no dog to set at you," I said.

We went down to the river by the path. Last time

131

she had been scarifying me, and jerking her shoulder away; now she took my arm in her impersonal, friendly way, and we talked as we always had talked. We crossed the foot-bridge to our side, and went down through the wood, well away from the pungency of the wild garlic after a day of sun. There was no undergrowth beneath the holms; it was cool and pleasant in there, and there was a diffused yellow glow like the light on a chancel floor; and once a shaft of low sunlight struck Sylvia's hair and splashed it to spun gold. And the sough of the water down the slide was near, yet remote.

"Robin is leaving his horse, then?" she queried. She wanted to be sure of that.

"For the time—I think so——"

"Weren't you listening? What did he say?"

I told her. All our days, Sylvia and I had been telling things to each other. It was so natural that we did not stop to think. I told her of that talk Morrison had with Ythan, and how I was meant to hear it. She put me no questions but at the end she dropped my arm, and paused to rest her hand against the bole of a tree. She was not looking at me, but down at her shoes. They were magpie colour, and had that ridiculous pouting aperture at the toes. I could see a toe twitch as she mused.

"Dinny is fond of him," she said as if to herself, "and he is fond of Dinny. Just so!"

"Aren't we all fond of Dinny?"

"But he is troubled about Dinny. He would like to do something for Dinny—the born horseman—of the third dangerous generation."

"Stop it!" I said. "You'll get us into trouble with the Lanes, and I'll not stand for that."

"Gosh!" she exclaimed indignantly. "What did I say to get anyone into trouble?"

"You're hatching something under your rye thatch."

"I am not," she lied. "And if I am, who set the egg to hatch? And if it's a bad 'un who'll get the blame?"

"I will," I said.

"Garn!" said Sylvia, started from the tree, and marched off down the slope. I followed after, thinking hard, but failing to see where or how I had set an egg to hatch.

II

The camp was as it had always been, in its evening, staid, calm. We stirred it for a moment. The black mongrel came barking, and Dinny came skipping, his black curls bobbing, and his black eyes brilliant in the low sun. Sylvia bent to him, and the first thing she said was:

"Say, Dinny! Are you missing Robber and Benbecula all the livelong day?"

Sylvia is not thoughtless with children, but that was not a good thing to say to a lad who loved a man and his horse. Dinny's face grew serious at once.

"Dinny knows the horse has to be mended," I said.

"I do so," agreed Dinny, "and the Robber comes home for the night—bate to the world." He jerked a thumb. "There he is! and he'll be asleep in a minute."

Robin Morrison rolled to his feet out of a canvas chair, and yawned unashamed.

"The post is again beleaguered," he said.

Sylvia gave the formal salute: *God save all here!* and sat down in the canvas chair, but she did not relax. Robin leant over the back of the chair, and almost unthinkingly lifted a tress of her spun hair with a forefinger, and blew a soft breath; and the spray of hair floated lightly in the air. Oonagh was at her knitting; I sat against her knee, and felt the cool tip of a needle run up my scalp. Tyzack woke up, gave us a glance, picked a book off the ground, and opened it at a dog-eared page. It was a small volume of The Thinkers' Library, and, from where I sat, I thought it was Winwood Reade's *Martyrdom of Man*. That martyrdom was well on its way this year of our Lord. Sloper Jones would be in his usual place on the river-bank. Jacus McGrath was polishing the top of his gas-cooker; he didn't deign us a word or a glance, but his polishing took on a sudden briskness. We were close enough to these people to be accepted silently and remain silent.

I filled a pipe and listened to the old sounds of the river: the steady sough of the slide, and the hollow gurgle under the sounding-board of the arch. The tobacco-pouch was taken out of my fingers, and Jacus was sniffing it.

"Jacus! only two fills in it, and it smells better than most times." He spread his legs, looked down at me fiercely, and jerked his head towards Sylvia.

"Whin that wan keeps her tongue behind her teeth she has roguery in her mind. Which of ye stole the Robber's crowbait?"

"Look out!" I said. "She has stealing still in her mind."

"Don't I know it?—and she well on the road, God ha' mercy on him!"

He meant Robin Morrison, but I did not. I think Sylvia was only waiting for her clue, and there she had it. She sat up a little straighter, and her head flicked Robin's fingers.

"That is one bright idea, Mr McGrath," she said, and turned to Tyzack. "When do you break camp, Tyzack?"

A quiet smile lit the gravity of Tyzack's face, and, without looking up, he lifted four fingers.

"Four days! earlier than usual; and you'll work round to the big show in Dublin, and, your season over, you go into winter quarters. Why not here? You did once, and I remember it because of all the beltings I took."

Once one time Tyzack had made this Bridge field his winter quarters; and it was then young Ethan Lane had shown me the many honest ways of catching a fish or snaring a bird; and I had to run Sylvia twice a week to try stop her following us and getting herself drowned. But follow us she did, despite all coercion.

She changed course again for no reason that I could see. She leant to Tyzack. "You were never the man to desert a sinking ship, Tyzack Lane."

Tyzack slowly lowered his book, and gave her one of his steady, black-eyed looks. Sylvia went on her own road.

"And look at all Mary's chickens going wild on her for want of lifting by an old two-legged fox! And man, Dinny! You should see our orchard of Irish peaches and Comice pears!"

"Gosh alive!" said Dinny, curled in the doorway.

Jacus shoved my nearly-empty pouch forcibly into my breast-pocket, and pointed his over-full pipe at Sylvia.

"If a direck attack was made on meself—just wance— I could take steps, judeecial or otherwise, but 'tis no nice thing for a elegant young lady to be incitin' a young chiseler to rob her da's orchard. Not a nice thing at all, and I put it to anyone here?"

Sylvia ignored Jacus, as we frequently did. "Tell me, Oonagh!" she said on another side-track, "how often was Jacus married?"

"Twice—wasn't it twice, Jacus boy?"

"Three times," put in Tyzack briefly.

"Wan was a mistake and soon rectified," amended Jacus complacently.

"I can remember four of his sons myself," said Sylvia.

"Six—all sons he had," said Oonagh.

"Eight," said Tyzack.

"Eight as I know of," said Jacus off-handedly.

"And where are they now?" questioned Sylvia. "Two I know are running a show for Tyzack."

"An' two dead fightin' for the bloody British Empire," said Jacus. "An' two more—Jacus! I don't know where them two are this minute—jail maybe!"

"And a dozen grandchildren running wild——"

"They got the bad drop from the mother's side," explained Jacus.

"Ay! they often grow wild—the grandchildren, don't they?" mused Sylvia sadly. "Wild—wild, in the third generation! Isn't it a grand thing for Dinny that he has a fine, dumb, solid old bear of a grandad to plan his future?" Her voice was as smooth as milk, and she turned head towards Dinny. "Don't you grow up wild like your Uncle Jacus, my born young horseman!"

"Sure there's no harm in my Uncle Jacus," said Dinny, "barrin' his tongue. I wonder now, when I grow up, would my grandad buy a horse for me—same as Benbecula?"

"As I said," said Jacus under pressure, "I don't care nothin' for the indireck attack on me, seed, breed and gineration; but putting consaite in a young lad's mind is contrary to human nature, and I'll not listen to it." He scuttered round to his stove and manhandled it furiously, smoke from his pipe pouring about his ears.

Tyzack laid his open book on his stomach, and looked solemnly and unwinkingly at my temerarious cousin. I felt a small pressure of Oonagh's cool hand on my neck. Robin Morrison straightened up from the back of the chair, took a wide, wary curve on careful feet, and brought up facing Sylvia. He looked at me, and pointed at her.

"Marry her, please?" he besought urgently. "Marry

her, and keep a tight rein—she's dynamite, she's a breaker up of homes."

"Go to glory, you men!" said Sylvia. "I was only having a quiet chat with Oonagh Blake."

"That was all, my dear," agreed Oonagh.

I was just going to ask Robin if he would like some fishing, when Sylvia forestalled me. She said suddenly: "Would you like to have a look at a nice fish, Mr Highlandman?"

"In your company I would," said the Highlandman agreeably.

She was on her feet in one lithe twist.

"Come up to the Luidin Pool above the foot-bridge and I'll show him to you?"

Jacus shouted encouragingly. "Take her out o' here, Robber, before I lose me temper. Me rod—and doings—are in the roof of the van—and I'll be up after ye."

She hadn't yet said her few words to Robin Morrison, and apparently they were for his ear only. But first she had dropped a stone into a pool—into a couple of pools.

I got to my feet too, circled the van, and turned the clump of sallows to the river-side. It was a custom of mine to pass a word or two with Sloper Jones. As usual, he was lying on his back on the slope, and, again, his slitted eyes, under craggy brows, were looking into the deeps of the sky, that was still full of light but turning bluer. Up there, scattered rooks were winging weightily towards Uncle Tom's rookery. Any day now, Sylvia would offer me the breasts of young rooks under a crust of pastry, and call it pigeon pie. She had tricked me that way only once, and I was sick for a week. Our old Timmy could cook bacon and cabbage, and boil potatoes in their jacket, and brew fowl into soup; any other dishes were trash to Timmy, and he was about right. Bacon and cabbage with clothed spuds is a dish to stand by. I used to dream about it in Italy of the spaghetti and olive oil.

"You like this camp, Slope?" I said.

"As good a camp as the next," said Sloper indifferently, "only you'd need eyes in your poll to save your skin—and I'm mentioning no names."

"No need! As good a camp as the next? What you mean is that you don't like camps at all?"

"I like any place where Ty Lane is," he said loyally.

"Camping here, camping there! you don't love it, Taffy?" His father was Welsh.

"I'm young no longer, Gill," he half-explained.

"How much older are Ty and Jacus? You Welshmen are aye the same: you like an anchor. You go to London to run a drapery or a milk-cart, or box bantam to make your little pile——"

"I made mine and you know where it went?"

"That was your drop of thirsty Irish blood. Most of you go back to a small house in a Llan with a capel Zion up the hill where you sing in lovely unison to a god so harsh that he has no ear. A house near the hills for you, Sloper Jones!"

He lifted his head better to look at me. "Is it a job you're offering me?"

"Once I might, but not any more. You ask Syl; she's the job-getter!"

"She's the one!" He showed his gapped teeth in a grin. "Didn't she get a job for Robber Morrison, and he's not easy to suit. A cool man and a friendly, and gay when he likes; but there's a lonesomeness in him somewhere—like as if he had lost confidence in himself. But so have you, Gill Morris!"

I did not deny that, and Sloper lay flat again.

"The times are bad," he said, "when women play the game alone."

138

"Till the crack o' doom," I said, "as they always played it, and always lost. I think Syl is playing a game with Robin Morrison."

"Why not? You're not jealous, are you? No. You lost interest in things. So did Morrison. So did I. No, be the powers! I have an interest in young Dinny Lane."

"So has Sylvia," I told him.

"Do you tell me that?" He lifted head again and considered me for some time. "I dunno what's in her mind, but I'm guessing. She loves a gamble. See she don't lose it, Gill Morris?"

"Go get yourself a job!" I said, touched him with a toe, and walked away. I went home without looking for the fishers. If Sylvia was setting an egg to hatch, that was no concern of mine. My mind was made up, and I was only waiting for October.

Chapter VI

ROBIN MORRISON BREAKS BREAD

I

If Sylvia was playing a game I saw nothing of it for a further three days. She had dropped a few preparatory and intriguing words to the Lanes, and left them to fructify, but there was no sign of fruit yet. She certainly had introduced Robin Morrison and his horse to the stables, but she had had nothing to do with Morrison staying on and on. It was Morrison's Scots conscience that had worked there. Mary had tried to jump four guineas a week out of him, and, if that was her usual charge, justice demanded that he work some of it off while he had a chance. I do not think that sentiment had anything to do with his decision.

Tyzack Lane was breaking camp to-morrow, and there was a choice of three things that Morrison might do: take himself and his horse off: go himself, and leave his horse: or stay on and work off some more of his obligation. Sylvia would be aware of these three choices too.

These three were in my mind that Sunday evening as I strolled with Robin down to our river paddock; and I knew that the decision was near. Also I knew the other decision Sylvia would want, but I did not see how she could bring it about. All I knew, from Robin, was that she was playing about with Dinny Lane: fishing, guddling brown trout, birdnesting, eating early strawberries with him in her father's hothouse, racing ponies with him in the rocky pastures behind Castle Evan. Uncle Tom bred Connemara ponies for fun, and was a member of several pony associations.

Well! the camp was breaking up to-morrow, and Dinny would be away; and probably Sylvia would stroll down in her inconsequent way, and our old life would go on. No! Not the old life. Probably she was weaning herself and me of old habits, now that we were free of the family arrangement. A gradual estrangement was bound to come; different interests would widen the gap, and after October—there was nothing after October. I was inclined to be a bit gloomy—but I always was.

It was a fine, fresh Sunday evening after a rainy morning, and the grass was again dry. The thrushes were singing everywhere, and a blackbird, usually silent in May, was trying three mellow notes. A wisp of mist faded and died above the ridge of Shirlan Ben, and the furze on all the hills stole the glory of the sun. Up the slope behind us the dormer roof of Castle Gillian was golden-green above the dark green of the holms.

Our river paddock was fringed on one side by copses of hazel, and on the other by a line of black alders along the river-bank. There were some good cannibal trout below the alders, but casting a line was almost impossible. Sylvia and I had probably left a hook in every tree. Any high spring freshet overflowed the banks, and sent tongues of water into the paddock to make it a nice texture for sore shins and swollen pasterns. There was only one sick horse in it now, and that was Benbecula.

The paddock was not a large one—five or six acres—and was surrounded by a rail-fence, painted white to prevent a skittish horse injuring itself in a bad light. I leant on the top-rail and smoked; Robin vaulted over, and walked slowly out over the coarseish grass. Benbecula lifted head and whinnied; and then, head and tail erect, cantered a circle about its beloved biped, and came soberly to hand. The lameness was barely noticeable, and in cantering it was not noticeable at all. Robin's hand came out of a pocket and the horse lipped it daintily. That was a fist of sugar from Robin's own ration, and sugar ration was none too plentiful.

Robin petted his horse for some time, slapped it, shoved it playfully away, and walked across to me. He was no longer Sandy Ythan's tinkler loon. He was clean-shaven, and Dan Shea had clipped his hair about neck and ears to leave a fine bronze bush of it above his broad brow. He was wearing his Sunday garb of grey flannels, with a blue shirt and a red tie, and there was peace in his deep-set grey eyes. I was used to him now, and no longer noticed the aloofness—if it was there at all.

He perched himself on the top-rail, set his feet pigeon-toed on the lower rail, lit a cigarette, and put his elbows on his knees. That was a horseman's attitude. Wherever horses are and men who follow horses, you will find men sitting on rails on Sunday afternoons, smoking and watching horses at graze. After a while I spoke out of my thoughts:

"That horse will miss you?"

He gave me a quick side-glance, as if I had touched something in his own mind. "What do you think, yourself?" he asked.

"He will miss you all right," I said.

"That is not what you were thinking," he said. "You were wondering whether I would go off with Ty Lane to-morrow, and leave Benbecula here. What do you think yourself?"

"I think that your fine indifference is only veneer, and that your Scots conscience is nagging you underneath."

"That is no answer."

"Yes it is. Take yourself off and Dinny Lane will no longer be on your conscience——"

"What the hell can I do for Dinny Lane?"

"Devil the thing, but there it is! Give your horse a

chance to mend, and you are troubled that you are taking
four-guineas-worth a week from Mary for nothing. You
aren't, really. Tuppence-worth o' grass, as Mary said,
but you are pig-headed!"

"That from you? But if I leave the horse, what
happens—after September?"

"What's that to you?" I said bluntly. "Your horse
will be mended, or he is not mendable. If you want to
know, I think Garret Ward will own a controlling share
of Castle Gillian: and, what is not quite so inevitable,
he will marry Mary. Isn't he over every second day to
break himself in?"

He considered that for a long time. His face was very
still, but little flickers of light and shade ran across his
eyes. At last he threw up his head in that way he had
when he reached a decision.

"That's settled, then!" he said firmly. "I will give
that horse a chance, and take myself off—and I will pay
that dam' four guineas some day."

"And that will be one more episode behind you!" I
said tartly.

He nodded in gloomy agreement. "Yes! Just an
episode. There are no turning-points any more—no
tides—no crises—just small episodes."

"And you 'll go on looking for that hole?"

"Passes the time, doesn't it?"

"You might not know it when you come to it?"

"Or find a 'No Trespass' sign," said Robin Morrison.

II

There was a rustle of leaves behind us, and my sister
Mary brushed round a clump of hazel. She had been to
church in the forenoon, and, as usual, had gone to her
own room after lunch, to read—or sleep—after a hard
week. Frequently we saw no more of her till next morn-

ing. Here she was now, wearing one of her few good dresses, and she was all woman. Robin Morrison, twisting round to see her, nearly fell off the rail.

"Body and soul of the glen!" he cried unashamedly. "Is this what the thrushes are singing for?"

She smiled, a little more colour was in the damask of her long cheeks, and her violet eyes were brilliant. She looked taller than when in slacks, and more fragile, though I knew she was as tough as whalebone. Her dress was some sort of pink, darker and dustier than salmon, a definite sort of shade without the insipidity of real pink; and it emphasised her vividness and vitality. And she had a band of the same colour in her hair, that in its soft richness had again that hint of red under the kiss of the sun.

"I knew I'd find you looking at a horse somewhere," she said pleasantly, and put her hands on the rail between Robin and me. He kept looking at her, his mouth a little open.

"Don't dislocate your jaw, Robin," she told him, "and give me a cigarette!" She called him Robin now, like we all did.

"You shouldn't ought to be allowed to surprise a fellow like that on a quiet Sunday," he said. With a neat overhand action he put a cigarette between her lips, scraped a match forcefully, and held a light for her. There was a soft air moving in her hair, and the match-flame wavered, so that, to shelter it, she put her cool brown hands over his. She looked up at him under her dark brows, and smiled; and his teeth were clenched, and his jaw muscles ridging. He looked away, and looked back again; and shook his head solemnly.

"I took you for a boy, Mary Morris, and I knew you were a bit of a rogue at a bargain," he said frankly, "but did anyone tell you that you are beautiful?"

144

"Not one! Do you think so, Robin?" she asked simply. They were as natural as daylight, and completely ignored me.

He nodded gravely. "You are so beautiful that for a beginning I wouldn't want to touch you—except that way." He put his middle finger softly on the back of her hand, and drew it away again; and Mary looked down at the fading white spot his finger had made. She shook her head slowly.

"Ay! for a beginning," she said. "But if one has beauty one can't own it for one's self. Beauty is always in the mart and always sold at a price. And then! often spoiled, often hoarded, often wasted in a closet long to quiet vowed. That was a bit of 'Paracelsus'—ain't I smart?"

"You've brought your Sunday tongue along too," he said. "If I were you I'd be careful in choosing a market."

"The choice is not mine," she said, "but why should I be careful?"

"So that you be not mouldering your books and lutes among as when a queen long dead was young. We were not allowed to read Browning in the school I went to—so we read him."

That song from "Paracelsus" was Mary's favourite. She was always trying her voice in the strange cadences of it. But Robin gave it a wistful forlornness that was new. She looked up at him, and some current passed between them. Damn! I could almost see it. *I dunno! I thought, but this was never the way Sylvia and I carried on. Still, I suppose two young people like them would be philanderin' words to pass the time. Two young people! poor as church mice, and if they fall in love there'll be the devil to pay—and Garret Ward holding the scales! But no! Mary is too level-headed, too pig-headed, too obsessed by this blasted incubus of Castle Gillian.*

Benbecula lifted a head, and Mary reached a long hand out to it. Muzzle forward it came straight to her, and she scratched its broad forehead between the eyes. It sawed its head up and down, set back a few paces, turned side, sunk head and one hip, and went into some deep thought of its own—or, probably, it was only going into a snooze within the murmur of its people's voices.

"That shoulder is much better already," Mary said, and, her voice never changing from its easy tone, she went on. "In about a fortnight, Robin, I might be giving your horse a gentle schooling if I only had a light lad to mount him. Lant Shea is getting fair mountaineeous, as Ythan says."

I do not think there was anything behind her words, but Robin and I knew where there was a lad to mount Benbecula.

"Has Sylvia Gayne been talking to you?" Robin asked curiously.

"No!" She opened her eyes at this sudden switch. "Why? I haven't seen Syl for days." She poked my elbow. "Had another tiff, Gill?"

"Syl and I don't need to fight any more, you numb-skull!" I said exasperatedly. "I told you that."

"Oh! so you did," she said calmly, and turned to Robin. "Talking of beauty, young fellow, how does our lovely Syl strike you?"

"Strike is the word," said Robin feelingly. "Every time I see her on the skyline, I look to see if my lines are open behind. They aren't—Gill Morris is threatening my rear."

Mary chuckled. "She did take possession of you, didn't she?—for your good, of course! She loves to arrange things, our Sylvia. She even arranges old blustery Uncle Tom, though he don't think so. But she can't arrange our Gillian. Can she, Gill? A dumb cluck, ain't she?"

That was irony or satire, or someting, and it did not appeal to me. I said warmly:

"She ain't as dumb a cluck as Mary Morris, and time will show it."

Those two looked at each other, and started to laugh. Blast! they were already seeing things together that had no laugh in them for me. I started up from the rail and turned to leave them . . .

III

That clump of hazel was again rustling. But nothing or no one came into the open. My heart stirred. Would it be Sylvia, the vixen? I was about to call out vituperatively when a dog whimpered. It was the whimper of a dog that was being held, and wanted to get away.

Robin turned his head and gave a sharp whistle; the rustle became violent, and then the copse exploded and erupted Dinny Lane's black, mongrel, springer-retriever. It came like a streak, cleared the rail, barked shrilly, whirled, and took Robin Morrison on the hop; and he went over backwards in a complicated, active somersault that landed him sitting. The dog was all over him, licking hands and face. The horse pranced, and went off at a gallop, tail up and neck curving aside, came round in a curve, and halted snortingly, to face us, twenty lengths out.

Robin struggled to his feet, holding the dog by the scruff, but the excited little fellow twisted free, and went barking joyfully round the clump of hazel. Mary stopped laughing.

"A horse and a dog, Robin! Who else?"

Robin lifted up his voice. "I wonder, now, could that

be someone poaching rabbits on a Sunday? No! 'Tis a friend coming to see a friend. Show a leg, young fellow?"

Young Dinny Lane, thrusting a foot at his dog, came round the clump shamefacedly. But he wanted a clean bill, and blurted out:

"I wasn't poaching at all, Miss Mary—only myself and Sut taking a walk for ourselves."

"Surely, Dinny!" said Mary brightly, and went forward, her hand out. "Sunday or not I want to see Sut chase a rabbit—we're eaten alive by them. How are you, boy? and what kept you away from us so long?"

Dinny looked up at her, and held on to her hand; and his face twisted, and the twist was all grief. He was the lonesomest lad in all the world, and the sorriest for himself. He looked at Mary, and he looked at me, and out into the field where Benbecula was nickering to him, but he did not look at Robin Morrison at all. He tried to hold himself, but failed; no one could against all that forlornness. He dropped Mary's hand, turned blindly, butted his head into Robin's side, and grappled him with his hands. Sobs he tried desperately to smother, and his voice was broken lamentably.

"I couldn't stand it no longer! Not another minute could I stand it! I tell you I couldn't! Be the lonesome river mindin' the camp all day with Sut, and my little Benbecula gone on me. An' they saying you wouldn't be coming back any more. . . ."

"Hush, boy, hush! Who would say a foolish thing like that?" Robin's voice was husky.

"I dunno," Dinny hesitated. "My Uncle Jacus was saying it for one." So was someone else, but Dinny was loyal. He looked up now at his idol, his eyes brimming, but his voice held to steadiness. "Don't send me away, Robber? I'd rather be dead."

Robin rubbed a hand through Dinny's black curls.

His face had lost colour under the brown tan, and there was a hurt grimace about his crinkled eyes; but his tone was easily confident.

"Right you are, my lad! We'll make a bargain, the two of us: where you go, I go; where I stay, you stay. And no more nonsense about it!" That was a variation of Ruth.

Dinny blinked his eyes, and rubbed his nose on his sleeve. Mary took my handkerchief and wiped his face briskly. "Blow your nose now! That's fine!" She slapped him on the shoulder. "Your little Benbecula horse wants to talk to you. Off you go—and shake a hoof!" Benbecula was sixteen hands one, and Dinny four feet ten; but that tall horse would be always Dinny's little horse.

Robin slipped hands under Dinny's oxters, and swung him deftly over the railing; and Dinny, glad to get away after his exhibition of feeling, lifted heels and ran, his Sut dog whirling and barking before him. Benbecula galloped a half-circle prankishly, and the three came together in the middle of the paddock. No doubt they collogued.

Mary, quite nicely, tried to make light of the incident. She took another cigarette from Robin, and blew smoke at him.

"A horse, a dog, and a boy! Your tail is growing, Highland chief?"

Robin leant over the rail at her side, and pointed his chin towards Dinny. "That lad is my trouble," he said gravely.

"And don't you go on deceiving yourself, Morrison my son!" I half-derided him. "You were no' playin'; you would sit in your hole and let the legions thunder past. Would you hell? Tangling your life with the life of a son and grandson of showmen! afraid of what so

149

often happens to sons of the road! And what can you do about it? What can you——?" I stopped, and cursed myself silently; for I was using Sylvia's very technique. "Don't mind me!" I said and knocked my pipe out so hard on the rail that the stem broke. It was only a home-made cherry-wood stem, and I could whittle me another.

But my final question had interested Mary. She put Robin the same question quietly. "Yes, Robin, what can you do about it?"

Robin Morrison had scarcely heeded me. He was looking at Mary contemplatively, and a small strangely shy smile came and went at one side of his mouth.

"What can I do about it! What, indeed?" He gestured a hand at me. "Gill Morris has a hard-edged tongue, but who let a certain young lady hog-tie me in a boxing-booth and drag me along this far? Well, here we are, and what are we going to do about it?"

"Leave me out of it," I said.

"At your word, sir!" He saluted me with lifted hand. "You are out of it, and Sylvia Gayne is out of it, and I am out of it too. The only one who can do anything is Mary Morris."

"Good gracious!" exclaimed the surprised Mary Morris.

Robin turned from her and pointed towards where Dinny Lane was chasing Sut around Benbecula. His voice was convincingly firm.

"There's the lad to mount that horse for you, Miss Morris."

"Young Dinny Lane?" cried Mary.

"Not so young—though he's little," Robin said, and went on persuasively. "He hasn't grown an inch in a year, and his small bones are already set. All whipcord and whalebone, he'll never need to waste to ride one hundred and ten pounds. A born horseman, with perfect balance and velvet hands, he used to jump Benbecula over whin bushes, bareback. Bareback, mind you!" He turned head to Mary, but his finger still pointed towards Dinny. "Speaking to a horsewoman, as a business man to a business woman, I say that young Dinny Lane would be an asset in your stables."

I do not think that was the first time she had thought of Dinny at Castle Gillian. She was not surprised now, and she took her time to answer, while she put a frond of dark hair that the air was teasing back under her head-band.

"Dinny Lane an asset in *my* stables!" she said slowly. "Have you not heard what might happen to my stables in October, Mr Morrison?"

"I have heard that, and I've heard that you'll play the game as it lies—day after day—five months or fifty years," he said just as slowly.

That stirred Mary, but she insisted on being reasonable. She shook her head.

"Apart from all that, there's Tyzack—and Oonagh, to say nothing of Jacus. They would never part with Dinny?"

Robin waved his hand lightly. "That's another card in the same game, and Sylvia Gayne is playing it for you."

The time had come for me to play a small card in the same game too. I said: "The Lanes are going to-morrow, and, if you go with them, not even Benbecula will hold Dinny here?"

A few minutes ago he had said that he was leaving; now he looked at me unashamedly, and changed his mind unashamedly, too.

"I like this place," he said, "and I'd love to stay on for a while longer—if Miss Morris wouldn't mind?"

Mary moved her head sadly, and that frond of hair again got free and tossed across her forehead.

"But I can't keep you," she said.

"Enough said, my dear lady!" said Robin Morrison evenly.

"No—no! I didn't mean that. I mean I can't pay you—I have nothing to pay you with——"

"I owe you four guineas a week?"

"I was cheating—I'd have taken two."

"And you don't get two—and also you'd have to feed me some victuals once the camp is away."

"There's plenty good plain food, thanks to Gill and Timmy," said Mary.

"Yes, ma'am! I tried one of your pullets before I knew you. There was nothing wrong with it." He laughed, and held up his hand, and his voice had a dominant quality in it that I had not heard before. "Wait! Let me get my own bit of cheating in first? I know what is in your mind about that horse of mine, Mary Morris, and I'll tell you what's in my mind. If we can abduct Dinny I'll stay on a month to see if that shoulder mends. If it does, you—and this is strictly business—you'll engage to school and train Benbecula, and, if you think him good enough, race him under the stable's name and colours. All expenses paid by the stables, and the stables taking half the winnings—if any, and not a penny more. A bit of a Shylock, ain't I?"

This was Mary's line of country sure enough. She was getting a horse to train, and a man to help, and a chance at some money. But it would not do to be too eager. She said consideringly:

"Well no! Not a Shylock. But——"

"Let it lay, business woman!" he stopped her, and put a firm finger on her forearm. "Take it easy. We are in no hurry. Take your jumps when you come to them. Wait till all the strings are in your hands. Let us plan—not too far ahead—but, still, with no thought for disaster—next October, or next year, or in fifty years' time. Bless me! these are your own maxims, and to-morrow is another day."

He took Mary right along with him, and she was glad to go. She livened up and smiled at him.

"Fair enough, Mister! I'll plan, but not too far ahead—just one hour. I'm going up to the house to make a nice salad for our supper. In an hour—and bring Dinny!"

She lifted a graceful hand, and went off gallantly and briskly between the hazel clumps. Brisk she always was, but often enough there had been a sort of doggedness in that briskness that told of the *cui bono* in her mind. Not now. All her sails were set, and the breeze was in herself. And to hell with the rocks in the channel! and the Barbary pirate round the point. Why not? Foresight is good enough, and honesty not so bad, but *mañana* gives more solace than either. *Behold the lilies of the field! Eat, drink and be merry!* these were not said foolishly. It was no business of mine, anyway. But Mary believed in miracles. Mary was already building a castle in Spain. Castle Gillian had to be saved. Why not by a broken-down 'chaser—and the 'chaser's Highland owner?

IV

It was a little later that Robin called to Dinny poking about in a bush after Sut after a rabbit; and Dinny came running, his eyes all question.

"Yes, Robber?"

"We are going up to the Big House—for our supper," Robin told him, and Dinny, not sure where he stood, did not question further. He stuck close to us for a while, but, presently, Sut jumped a rabbit out of a tuft, and dog and lad streaked off in pursuit. Sut made most of the noise there was, and Dinny made the rest of it, but the rabbit sailed away unconcernedly. Robin's head was down as if weighted with thought. He was no longer the onlooker.

"Bitten off more than you can chew, fella?" I said.

"Chewing an edge of it," he said, and jerked up his head. "Say, Gill! have you a hole-and-corner where Dinny and I could hide out to-night?"

"Not a hole-and-corner," I said.

"Oh! You don't approve," he said blankly. "Sorry about that!"

He misunderstood me, but I took him along. "Listen!" I said. "Did you ever know a turncoat to make anything of himself?"

"I don't want to make anything of myself," he said without a trace of resentment, "and can't I go back to my original colours if I want to?"

"God save us from the contorted Scots mind! As I said, I have no hole-and-corner for you, but you'll have heard of our Rookery."

"The single men's quarters? Dinny told me. Yes, the Rookery?"

"I'll show it to you, and you can have your choice of twenty nests."

"Sorry, I took you up wrong," said Robin. "Most people do, even Sylvia sometimes."

We slanted up through the holms, took a path round the back of the house, and entered the stable-yard by the southern arch. Even the horses knew it was Sunday. After early morning they had nothing to do all day. Lazy heads were here and there over half-doors, and one or two of them snorted at black Sut. Dinny was close to heel now, and his black eyes were avid.

"What a darlin' of a place," he said reverently. "And

gosh! can't you smell horse?" It was not his first time in this yard, but he was seeing it from a new and possessive angle.

"You'll be stable-rat after supper," Robin promised him. After supper on Sundays we replenished feed-boxes and mangers, for horses sleep very little at night, and do most of their eating then.

/ I led across through the narrow arch to the yard where was the peat-shed and the big cupressi. In the end wall of the house was the open door leading to Timmy's cavernous kitchen premises. But there was a closed door too, and it was set so close to the back corner that one might wonder at the thinness of the near wall of that big house.

To that door I went, and put my hand round the corner-stone, where a deep chink held the massive, century-old key. The bolt went back slowly with a final thick click, and the door opened silently right to the foot of a stone stairway.

"Body o' me!" exclaimed Robin. "What a stairs. And what a climb after a hard day!"

"Or a harder night," I said.

"Many necks to its credit?"

"None on record. A few collar-bones, mine included. You can fall only fifteen steps at a time."

That long, long stone stairs, and it was not a narrow one, slanted away up and up through three floors, and it was built right in the solidity of the wall. It actually made a diagonal to the rear rectangle of the house, for, beginning just inside the door, it finished at the dormer corner where there was a tall window, with the top branches of another cupressi showing through it. The whole length of it was well lighted, for at the head of each fifteen steps was a small square platform with a window in the outer wall. There was no opening in the inner wall below the top

155

floor, and that meant that the top floor was cut off completely from the rest of the house. A cool draught of air was flowing down, for many panes were broken all the way up.

"Let us climb!" I said, slowly mounted fifteen steps, and stopped on the first platform. The dog, not used to stairs, barked in the open doorway, and then came in an anxious scramble.

"That door below," I said, "used to be locked at sunset in semi-feudal days—till a lad in love broke his neck out a window. See how feet have worn these stones!"

I mounted another fifteen steps and halted. "No shemales allowed inside this stairway," I said, "except the chatelaine of the castle. That's Mary now. She comes up regularly with a leather to see how Lant tidies up. He gets the leather every time. Listenin', Dinny? It's the latest lad's job."

"I'm good with a sweepin'-brush, my gran'ma says," said eager Dinny, close at my heels to the next platform.

"There have been some quare doin's up above," I said. "Master and man on their own feet, and the man often enough master! The smallest democracy in the world, and better than most. The head-groom was floor-master. Sandy Ythan is now, and he is a tough yin. I saw as many as twenty young devils up there when I was a whipper-snapper. Now there are only four of us —five with old Timmy."

"Seven, I'd say," whispered sanguine young Dinny.

I went on up to the top landing. The tall end-window was facing me. Through the cobwebs I could see the branches of the cupressi near enough to tap the panes in a breeze. One pane was completely gone, and the soft evening air came through. At my right was a closed door. By the side of the door on the not-very-white wall was a long list of names one below the other, with dates and times. The top ones had been pencilled over more than once to preserve them. I pointed it out.

"That represents twelve-fifteen generations. This stairway was and is used for taking fat off apprentices—twelve times up-and-down, a groom with a leather each end, and sometimes a broken bone on transit. It didn't take an ounce o' fat off Lant Shea—and you won't need it, Dinny."

"I'll have a go at it, whatever," said Dinny.

"Surely! you might make a record. See! here are some of the good times on the up course. The down course was not considered, or a lad in a hurry might jump fifteen steps and rupture himself. There's the record: *Evan Morris, 6th June* 1842—*Nine seconds, flat.* He was my great-grandfather—maybe two greats—and a rogue to boot!"

"Where do you come in, Master Gill?" enquired Dinny.

"Nothing over eleven seconds recorded. I could only take three steps at a time."

Robin Morrison pointed over my shoulder and chuckled.

"Whose name is that?"

"You would see it. Yes, that's Sylvia. She did it when sixteen—ten seconds plus from a flying start. It will stand this generation."

"You said no shemales were allowed?"

"That's right too, but Sylvia got the decision in the third round. We tried to keep her out! I'll say we tried!" I pointed to where the pane was missing. "The third time she climbed the tree and broke through. There's a weal down the middle of her back—ask her to let you see it some time!"

"No, suh! I saw her get that long left in on you."

I opened the door to a big room full of evening light.

At the other end the westering sun was shining aslant through three big dormer windows.

"Single men's domain!" I said.

It was a huge room, sixty by thirty or so, and the shouldered ceiling looked low though fourteen feet above the floor. That rugless floor of yellow pine gave a dip and a heave here and there, and was patched in places. As a man's room, it was untidy and some dusty, but there was a sort of comfortable aura in the great space of it, and a homely odour of oil and leather, harness soap and inevitable horse.

The furnishings were remarkable, and some of them might be museum pieces. Probably an expert could arrange a comprehensive, if ramshackle display, going back a couple of centuries. Any piece that had gone out of use in the main house had been brought up here to be patched up or burned. A chair, a couch, a sofa, a chaise, a chiffonier, a sideboard, a table caught the eye at once as distinctive; odd lots were stacked in a corner or propped against a wall to give room for boxing or even football; a grandfather clock and two wag-at-the-wa's ticked out times that never agreed; polished silver trophies and cups covered the tops of two sideboards.

The walls, wherever there was space, were covered with prints and reproductions, and hung with old racing saddles and bridles, some with a history. There was the four-pound saddle that had backed a famous winner out of the stable seven consecutive times in one season. That was before my time. There were photographs and paintings of famous horses in and out of the stable, photos of close finishes, sporting and hunting prints, quite a number of sentimental reproductions that had nothing to do with races, photographs of boxers in all poses from the time of Paddy Ryan to Joe Louis, and one modern corner devoted to film stars, mostly female. Dan Shea had

158

fallen for Ann Harding, and her picture was repeated half a dozen times. But we all knew that it was Mary that Dan worshipped from afar, for, apart from colouring, Mary was not unlike Ann Harding in a serious mood. There was not one even near-risqué picture. There used to be, but Sandy Ythan had a conscience nearly as susceptible as an Irish censor's.

Two big brass lamps hung on pulleyed chains from the ceiling, and there were two cavernous, open-hearth fireplaces in the inner wall. The gable-end wall was windowless, had many cupboards and presses, and one wide door in the middle. That door was bolted and padlocked, for it opened to emptiness where a pulley-chain ran down to the ground, for the purpose of bringing up peats and heavy articles. Once it had brought up a horse on a drunken bet. Before my time the door used to be left on the bolt, and apprentices and lovers found it could be used for getting down in a hurry; and it was so exploited till a daring one broke both legs and one arm. It is noteworthy that Authority always holds that Liberty invariably degenerates into Licence, and forthwith starts framing restrictive acts and religions, and after two thousand years calls the result Christian Democracy.

Between the fireplaces was another door, wide-open to show a long passage running the length of the house to a window in the gable-end. Right of this passage there was only one door; on the left there were several. That was the Rookery.

Neither Ythan nor his two lads were in residence this Sunday evening. Sandy had cycled ten miles to a Presbyterian Service in Caerline; the Sheas had cycled the same distance to see a film. The Scot had passed a restrictive act against Sunday films, but, lacking a penal clause, it had fallen into abeyance through long disregard.

We walked down the room, the boards echoing under

159

our feet, and Dinny had hold of Robin's sleeve. It was not the first time he had been up here, but the vastness of the room cowed him, used as he was to open air and the narrow cosiness of a van.

"Gosh!" he whispered. "You could play football!"

"It has been played," I told him, "and I can still feel the strap that Ythan used on me." I pointed through the passage door. "That's the Rookery in there. Right, is the apprentices' dormitory, left, the rooms for their bosses, damn 'em! Three are occupied, and you can take your choice of eight or ten."

"Right! Dinny takes junior side, and I'll be a boss," said Robin.

"We'll get you some blankets and linen from Mary," I said.

Mary's sheets were surely linen, her grandmother's linen from flax grown and steeped and cloved and spun and weaved and bleached on our own lands of Gullane: white as a hound's tooth, thick as tweed, cool as water, and fresh with ozone.

Robin moved round a big chair into the alcove of a dormer window; I followed him; and Dinny, like a Bilbao greatly daring, sidled off to explore the Rookery.

We were high up in the tall house, sixty feet above the lawn, three hundred above the valley; and the view was splendidly wide. Across the glen, on its shelf above the holms, stood the white house of Castle Evan, with its copper dormer golden-green below the golden-orange of the furze on the slope above it. There was no one on the lawn or porch; and Sylvia's flag was not in her window. Sylvia and I had a system of signals, highly developed, to tell each other what was on, where to go, and what to do. It often saved us the fag of a down-and-up mile.

My scrap of red flag was tied to the butt of an old fishing rod in the window corner, and as it caught my eye a thought struck me. I lifted the lower half of the middle sash, thrust the flag out and brought the sash down to hold it in place. Right enough Sylvia was in residence, and she must have been on the look-out too, for in ten seconds her more ornate red-and-white flag was out. That made me wonder. She might very well have known of Dinny's bolt, and was now waiting for results. Her flag went up and down twice staccatowise.

"See that impudence!" I said.

"An obvious arrangement," Robin remarked. "You didn't invent it?"

"No, it is old. That's Sylvia!"

"Of course. If it's no harm to ask, what did she say that time?"

"Go to hell!" I told him.

"A polite sort o' cuss, ain't you?"

"Sorry! I told you to go nowhere; that was Sylvia telling me where to go." I thrust shoulders out the window and wagged my flag. "The same to you," and I went on signalling. I signalled for quite a time, emphasising one point of the compass, and Sylvia sometimes pulled me up for a repeat. Then I pulled in my flag and shut down the window. The flag across the glen said "damn" three times, and disappeared. I looked at Robin, and hesitated.

"No need to tell me," he said, "but at a venture I would say you were yelling for co-operation."

"You might find out to-morrow," I said, "and I was not yelling either." But he was pretty near the mark all the same.

Robin swung a hand. "You've all the view there is up here," he said. We had. South and east, beyond the valley mouth, the great, verdant, sun-hazed plain of Moymore spread to the blue humps of the Midland Mountains; westward curved our own valley, with the river winking silver and gold amongst the alders, and the slopes clothed in the profligate gold of the furze; and over the shoulder of our small hills stood up for Shirlan Ben, its quartz streaks glistening in the gravity of grey limestone.

"History would be made in a house and glen like these," said Robin Morrison, "as it was once made by seven men in my Moidart."

"It was," I agreed. "An early Morris, like your Simon Fraser, backed a horse to win and lose: William of Orange to win, but he sent a son to Aughrim field and the Wild Geese; and he kept his head." I pointed across to Castle Evan. "Gayne, by the way, is the first outland name over there—and it was Gayne money that saved the place."

"It could be changed back easy as winking," said Robin easily, and his gesture took in the whole valley. "And this is the place you would be leaving?"

"It is, and I am not again turning my coat for anyone."

"No! For the first time I am really understanding the hold this place has on your sister. She would sacrifice much to hold Castle Gillian—or even part of it."

"No dumb vampire of a place is worth that sacrifice," I said.

"You don't want her to marry Garret Ward?"

"I do not."

"Does she want? Sorry, I should not have asked that."

"Why not? She doesn't want to marry anyone now." I looked at him slyly. "But she might, later on, and feel like a snared bird."

He looked at me through slitted eyes, turned and tapped the glass of a pane, and spoke thoughtfully.

"I think it might be a case of pull-baker-haul-devil between you. The place has as much a hold on you as on her. She wants you near her, and that's as plain as daylight. And you think that if you go away she might hesitate about sacrificing herself; so you frequently insist that you are going——"

"I am going, blast you!"

"So you say. There's only one way out that I can see."

"What way is that?" I asked curiously.

"We are in the process of finding out," he said, and laughed. "I can see as far as the first corner and we are not round that corner yet—except in a certain one's imagination."

It was there that Mary's clear, high halloo came up the stairs, gathering resonance as it mounted.

"You are invited to break bread with us," I said.

"I invited myself," said Robin, and walked away towards the door.

And that was how Robin Morrison was induced under the roof of Castle Gillian.

Chapter VII

SHOWMEN IN THE STABLES

I

The morning's work was over; the horses were half-dozing in their boxes after exercising and grooming; and there came that halt in activity that always comes about noon; and I knew it was noon by the line of shadow across the gravel. The sunlight seemed to doze over two-thirds of the yard, there was a feeling of somnolence in the air, and now and then a wood-quest crooned sleepily amongst the larches. The dog Sut was asleep in the sun.

Sandy Ythan and the Shea boys had gone to the harness-room round the corner. Mary, Robin Morrison, and myself were lazying and smoking about the door of an empty loose-box—most of our loose-boxes were empty —but Dinny Lane was not lazying. He had taken over my postponed job of whitewashing, and had worked round near us. He looked and felt important. That morning, with Robin, he had been allowed to exercise a quiet four-year-old, and had his first lesson at lungeing. He would be feeling completely at home in our friendly atmosphere, only for a small apprehension at the back of his mind. Any sound from outside startled him, and he kept a weather-eye lifting towards the northern arch. Personally, I was beginning to wonder if Tyzack Lane had broken camp, and was leaving Dinny with us without protest.

Jacus McGrath apprised me otherwise. His high, tenor bellow came pealing under the arch while he was still out of sight.

"Oh, ho-o-o! are you there, me fine Mister Maw-rison?"

"'It is, it is the cannon's opening roar,'" Morrison quoted Byron.

And there was Jacus's squat, shepherd-plaided figure, leg-spraddled in the mouth of the arch, one hand clenched at shoulder-level, the other thrust forward, fingers spread —like Jonah cursing Nineveh. His tenor pealed:

"There they are! Who's the chicken-stealer now? Who's the robber be name and nature? Who is the horse-coper—and the kidnapper at the end o' the day? Here I am, be Jacus! and answer me that."

Tyzack Lane, in his quiet grey, appeared quietly behind him. He was smiling gravely, and he said nothing; but we knew that Jacus would express his views in his own outrageous way. I looked for a third behind Tyzack, but no third appeared. *Blast!* I said under my breath.

Jacus held his poise of high drama for seconds, and then came straight at us, his arms held away from his sides ready for all emergencies. Tyzack came sedately behind. Jacus's voice lifted in a fierce wheedle:

"Dinny! Dinny Lane, *agrah*! Watherboy, where are you hidin'? Come away out till I have the hide stripped off of you! Where are you at all, at all? Come on out to your ould uncle, and the melt broke in him!"

There was no response from Dinny. I had not seen him disappear, but he was gone, and so was his dog. I side-stepped Jacus's lunging shoulder; Robin backed away, his open hands on extravagant guard; Mary stood in the middle of the doorway, legs wide, hands on hips, head truculently forward. Jacus reared back, and brought up facing her, and he was equally truculent. But he would never manhandle the Mary that he had often carried pick-a-back. Mary addressed us remotely:

"Was that my red cockerel that I heard crow? I had two, and I haven't heard them for a week!"

But Jacus would not be turned aside by personalities just yet.

"Is it me darlin' Miss Mary Morris that's in it?" he said warmly. "Be Jacus! but it is! in a shameless pair of Gill's pants—and she too proud to come and see us. How are you, ma'am?"

He thrust his hand impulsively out, and Mary took it—and was undone. She came out of that doorway in a swoop, found herself spinning, skirled, and brought up in Robin Morrison's arms. And Robin lifted her and set her neatly on her feet. And I think his arms were reluctant to be free of her.

"Well held!" said Mary, shoving her hair out of her eyes.

"Do that again, Jacus?" invited Robin.

But Jacus was craning in at the door, and I was looking over his shoulder. There was no sign of Dinny, but there was a big wisp of bedding under the feed box, and that was no place for it; and the mongrel Sut was standing over it poking it playfully with its nose.

"Sh-h!" sibilated Jacus. "That's our Sut after a rat. Sick him, Sut!"

He tip-toed across, moved the litter carefully with his foot, and pounced. And Dinny, as a first precautionary measure, started to bawl, but there were no tears.

"Shut-up, you schamer!" shouted Jacus. "Have I hit you yet?"

He hauled Dinny to the door, and I backed away. We knew enough of Jacus's technique not to interfere until we saw his hand. He played another card. Tyzack had come slowly across the yard, his hand to his chin in that way he had when his mind was not made up. Jacus ran Dinny a few steps, and slung him straight into his grandfather's arms.

"There he is for you, Ty Lane!" he shouted, "and there is no need for us to be wasting our breath on dummies."

Dinny clutched his grandad with both hands, and buried his head in him. Tyzack's mouth twitched.

"It's all right, boy!" he said quietly, and smoothed the boy's hair; and we knew by Dinny's shoulders that tears were being smothered.

"Very well so, if 'tis all right!" cried Jacus. "Don't let us be wastin' another minute. We've got what belongs to us, an' let us be goin' while the knot is still in their tongues."

He strode away six furious paces, looked over his shoulder, and stopped. Tyzack had not moved. He stood, his hand on the boy's shoulder, and looked gravely at Mary, and Mary looked gravely at him. They were two very grave people, and understood each other. And this was an important moment—for one young life. Jacus came softly back on the balls of his feet.

"Is it how you want me to give them a piece o' my mind?" he enquired mildly. "'Tis a thing I seldom do, but I'll oblige you this once." His voice blustered. "Look here to me, Mary Morris! You might be able to coax a bird off a bush—and I wouldn't blame the bird—or the High-lander either—but you can't coax me."

"No, Jacus dear!" said Mary amicably. "But all my life you coaxed me."

"Stop that now!" he cried, dismay in his bluster. "Only a minute ago you threw a red cock in my face. Wouldn't you be blamin' a red fox, and the place ate alive by them?"

"Or a fox with a plaid pelt, Jacus!"

"I'm a patient man, as is well known," said Jacus

under pressure. "But supposin' I did lift an eye towards a tough rooster, what is it to the stealin' you have in mind? Answer me that? Coaxin' away an innocent bit of a lad, mad about a crowbait of a horse and the owner o' the same——"

Mary addressed Tyzack, her hands appealing. "But look, Tyzack! what harm was it for Dinny to stay the night with a friend? And didn't I send word to Oonagh?"

Tyzack moved his head. "Last night was all right, my dear, but to-day——!"

II

It was there that I got a solid clunk between the shoulder-blades, that made me gaggle and nip my tongue. I thought it was Garret Ward giving me one of his irritating wallops, and swung round angrily, fists clenched. I was just in time to take a left in the ribs, and Sylvia Gayne danced away from me.

"You lazy slug-a-bed!" I shouted, and rushed her so quickly across the yard that she hadn't time to dodge. I got two fistfuls of her hair, but before I could tug she had an ear of mine in each fist. We looked into each other's eyes, and daren't begin. Then her hands gentled, and her mouth too.

"Pax! I said it first," she said in her low tones, and her cool hands smoothed down along the angle of my jaw. I let her soft hair run through my fingers.

"Your flag-wagging last night kept me busy all morning, you lazy hound!" she said.

"In your dreams?" I said.

"Of course. How are things?"

"Robin stays if Dinny stays——"

"I got that, silly! I mean how is Mary making out?" she enquired.

168

"Trying to coax Jacus, but I think Tyzack is doubtful."

"Yes, he's troubled about two things. I was at the camp all morning, and Oonagh is on my side. Mary can pull Tyzack, or no one can. Let's see?"

We walked over to the others. They had been watching our byplay with condescending amusement, all except Robin Morrison; he was scratching his poll, and there was a light of understanding in his eyes. Sylvia walked directly to Mary, and shook an admonitory fist.

"Shame on you, you hussy! twisting my Jacus round your finger. He's my meat, and I'll not have it!"

"Holy Jacus! where am I now?" cried that man.

"Leave it to me, partner!" said Sylvia confidently. "What is all the trouble anyway?"

"None that you don't know, my dear," said Mary wisely. "I was about to ask Tyzack to leave Dinny here for a while with Robin Morrison."

"Would it be good for him?" Sylvia wondered.

"My father would be pleased about it—I told him," Mary answered indirectly. That was right smart of Mary. Tyzack Lane had an aloof respect for Gillian Morris, in spite of my father's one vice.

Jacus put his finger on one of the two things that troubled Tyzack. He said quieter than usual: "We are in no need o' charity, young woman."

"Charity your granny! Jacus McGrath," said Mary hotly. "This is a business talk."

"Laive me poor granny in her own hot corner," implored Jacus.

"Make it business, Miss Mary?" said Tyzack.

"Business and friendship too, Tyzack. Indenture Dinny as an apprentice to the stables, and I'll give him a profession that he loves——"

"Wait ma'am—wait there!" exploded Jacus, a finger under her nose. "How long will you be teaching professions in Castle Gillian? Professions be Jacus! And tell me, will there be a man coming in here in the fall of the year that a Lane wouldn't stomach in the pits o' hell—or the plains o' heaven, itself? Answer me that?"

Jacus had put up the second thing that troubled Tyzack. Mary would have none of it. There was an impelling, harsh note in her voice.

"I am talking of now—now—now! What happens in five months or five years is in God's keeping. Look, Tyzack! I am not speaking for myself—but how do I know? Give me Dinny, and, at least, Robin Morrison and I will give him a start in a profession that he'll be proud of. That's plain business, and take it so. That's all."

Jacus was finished, but he would create a diversion. His voice was sorrowful. "And is no one at all thinking of poor Oonagh Blake, and the heart broke in her?"

Sylvia promptly hooked a finger in the top button of Jacus's plaid waistcoat. "Will you leave it to Oonagh, then?" she shot at him.

"I will and I won't," said Jacus.

"You two-tongued old devil! Very well! Take Dinny!" She pushed Jacus scornfully away. "Take Dinny! and someone besides your granny might be waiting to welcome you in a warm corner."

"Thanks be to me guardian angel that saved me from a pair of women the likes of ye in the days o' me misspent youth!" cried Jacus, piteously fervent. "All right! not another word will I say—not one dam' single word!"

Yes, he had extravagantly said what was in his half-brother's mind, and it was now up to Tyzack. And Tyzack showed the decision he had come to in his own quiet way. He held his grandson at arms' length and looked down at him, gravely smiling.

"Well, boy! You'd like to stay on with Miss Mary

and Robin?" I thought there was a sad note in that deep voice. Youth is aye selfish.

"If you let me, Granda," said Dinny nicely, and then he did please his granda. "But sure, ye'd be back campin' at the bridge—as Miss Sylvia said—and what a grand time we'd have?"

"Winter quarters, Tyzack! That's a right good idea," cried Mary, forgetting the sore month of October.

Tyzack nodded to Dinny. "Got a job to do, lad?"

"Whitewashing I was——"

"Go to it!" Tyzack chucked him under the chin, and Dinny scuttled. The day had been won, and Dinny knew it.

Robin Morrison and I had prudently kept our mouths shut and let the girls have free play. Now Robin lifted up his voice and his hands, and his face was gloomily serious.

"No—no—no! I don't like it."

That surprised us all. Tyzack's hand went to his chin; Dinny's brush clattered in the pail; Jacus drew in his breath and let it out again without exploding; Mary frowned perplexedly; I thought the Scot was turning his coat again; and Sylvia leaped in, her hair flying like an oriflamme.

"Don't you spoil the good work, Robin Morrison!" she flared at him.

He ignored her and concentrated on Mary. "That camp at the bridge, fall and winter, I don't like it, Miss Morris!"

"You mean it would distract Dinny from his work?" Mary asked, still perplexed.

"I don't mean that at all." He spread his hands. "It is so obvious. Add a two-legged fox to a four-legged and you'll not be left with an egg, or a chicken to lay one."

"Sold once more for a wooden-head!" cried Sylvia, and her laughter pealed. So did Mary's. Even Tyzack was chuckling, and Dinny was hick-hicking into his limewash pail.

"This is the last indireck assult to break me camel's back!" cried Jacus, "an' I'll take the law into me own hands for good and all. Watch me!"

He swept off his hat as if about to throw it in the ring or pitch it over the roof, changed his mind, and rammed it back again. The first and only time he had pitched his hat belligerently Sylvia and I had made a football of it. Then he made the motion of spitting in his fists, and sparred up crouchingly at Robin. Even now, his every movement showed what a formidable man he had been in his prime. Robin declined the issue. He side-stepped promptly behind Mary, and pushed her into Jacus's arms. Immediately the three were in a tangle.

I saw at once that this was some byplay on Jacus's part. I had never known him to use physical force, and I knew him well enough to know that there was something he wanted done. I thought I was the only one who saw it done. He bristled the two back against Tyzack's broad chest.

"Easy all!" said Tyzack, and it was then I saw him slip a hand into Robin's outside jacket-pocket. Jacus drew back at once.

"Very well so!" he said magnanimously. "Never let it be said that I hit a man hidin' behind a girl's petticoat."

Mary was laughing, but she was blushing too, as she slipped out of Robin's hands.

It was then that old Timmy Tadg Shawn gave the dinner call. It was the mid-day meal, and it was the principal meal of the day after the tradition of the house. Timmy stood in the mouth of the small arch walloping a tin pan with an iron ladle. There was a huge old gong

172

in the front hall, and a bronze bell above the kitchen door, but Timmy liked a nearer approach.

Mary had hold of Tyzack's arm and drew him along. "This is like old times, Uncle Ty," she said. "We'll all dine together, and you must see Father."

"That will be nice, Miss Mary," said Tyzack, who knew his manners.

"As much as a bite 'ud choke me," protested Jacus, "but sure I'd better be dead than driven into a loon-atic asylum!"

"Bacon and white cabbage for me!" cried Sylvia, and put a tentacle on Jacus.

III

We clung to a few traditions at Castle Gillian, and one of them went right back to feudal times: the main meal was eaten at noon by the sun, and the whole household sat down together, with the owner at the head of the table and his head-groom facing him at the foot. That made for good, democratic teamwork, and clean hands, and good manners, and live talk; and it is a pity that the custom has died out amongst our few Big Houses aping metropolitan fashions. It is still common amongst the farmers of the south where, as with us, only one set meal was taken; the others were hit or miss, and might be taken as hunger moved one, or not at all—and strong tea was part of all. Probably we had tea four or five times a day at Castle Gillian.

We no longer used the vast old dining-room with its depressing dark-red walls and black-oak furnishings. Instead we ate our mid-day meal in the gun-room inside the back-door, and conveniently near the kitchen. There was a scuffled mahogany table and sideboard shifted in from another room, and a nondescript collection of chairs.

In glass-fronted presses were several guns: a Queen-Anne muzzle-loader, a flint-lock, a pin-fire, a converted chasse-pot, some modern twelve-bores and point twenty-twos; and a clutter of fishing-rods and tackle. There was cork matting on the floor, and sporting prints on the walls, and the windows had no curtains.

I forget what we had for dinner that day. Probably the usual, plain and plentiful: a big ashet of home-cured bacon, honey-coloured in the fat and nutty-salt in flavour; a fowl or two for any that wanted some; a mound of white cabbage that had been boiled with the bacon; and a boat-shaped, wicker basket of potatoes bursting from brown jackets. We never had any fish, except for the movable feast of supper and on Fridays; and no soup until Michaelmas and after, when on Sundays we had goose-soup, boiled goose, and the inevitable bacon and cabbage. I suppose one does grow tired of a same diet of meat, but I never knew anyone to grow tired of bacon and cabbage, with boiled potatoes. There was seldom a sweet; sometimes Mary made a rhubarb or apple cake for Sunday, or Sylvia brought down a peck of strawberries or rasps. Sylvia's dish was bacon and cabbage, and she seldom got it at Castle Evan. It was strange how metabolism worked to metamorphose pig-and-greens-and-starch into a lissome shaft of young womanhood.

Old Timmy Tadg Shawn did not serve at board, nor did he sit down with us. He clumped the dishes down, and the head-groom carved for our bottom-end of the table. My place, as son of the house, was at the right hand of the head-groom, and I could recall the days when, as a lesson to apprentices, Sandy Ythan had regularly sent me off to re-wash my hands. My father carved for Mary, Sylvia, and his guests. Timmy, crooning and grumbling, ate standing up at the sideboard. Every two or three bites he came fussing about his god-with-feet-of-clay. "You're not atin' a bite, Gillian Morris!" He probed a fowl with a fork. "Look now! there's the oyster piece, and it delicate enough for a mother-on-milk. Ate that now, like a good boy!" And my father would say, "Yes, Tim! I'll come round to it—fill that glass for me." And the moment the old fellow's back was turned the tit-bit was transferred to a neighbour's plate.

My father, indeed, ate very little. Yet he was not emaciated or wasted in any way. I have read somewhere that whiskey has a food value, but is slow of absorption, and that a practised hand can usefully digest some two glasses in ten hours. My father was so long-practised that, probably, most of his nourishment came from alcohol. That must be why he never got hoggishly drunk, but always retained a fuddled dignity.

Alcohol gets its victims quickly or not at all. Drinkers die early, or go on imbibing gaily for longer than the normal span. What usually kills an old toper is a too-sudden attack of virtue and the taking out of a fire insurance. And, come to that! give me a drinker for thought. But, of course, only a select few can treat whiskey as a servant in full employment. My father certainly could not, but he would probably live to be eighty. In no circumstances like the present would Castle Gillian last him out, and therefore it was essential that the old place be taken out of his hands. He knew that, and since I had failed him, he wanted Mary married to a man who knew horses. Garret Ward did, and he would accept Garret Ward, but only as a doubtful bargain. There was our problem.

Tyzack Lane and my father respected each other, but they were not intimate friends, simply because their orbits never touched. Besides being a breeder and trainer of horses, my father was an old-time aristocrat, and had an innate sense of caste; but he would not recognise snobbery if he saw it, because snobbery had no meaning for him. Tyzack Lane, on the other hand, was the real showman, who despised ordinary business as mere huckstering, and he was also a natural gentleman; caste, outside his own world, meant nothing to him, but in his own world he was as real an aristocrat as my father.

My father greeted Tyzack and Jacus with affable dignity, and sat between them at the head of the table. I gauged his drink by his moods. Affability stood for four glasses. Mary sat next to Tyzack, and Sylvia to Jacus; and Robin Morrison sat below Mary. That was his chosen seat, and he retained it all the time he was with us; and he used talk across her to my father. He surely knew about horses, and racing history, and strains of blood, and crossings for speed and stamina, and things I was only guessing at. And he knew about books in a modern way.

The modern readers no longer read Lamb or Hazlitt or Dick Steele, or Richardson, or even Swift, Defoe or Fielding—or Smollett. Thackeray tires them, they merely pretend about Dickens. Scott is as dead as a door nail, and they never even heard of Hawthorne. Galsworthy is about their farthest off starting-point, and he is already slipping into the wilderness with Meredith, Hardy, Bennett and Chesterton—and Belloc, poor fellow. There are some books that stand up like rocks in that wilderness: *Robinson Crusoe* perhaps, *Gulliver* doubtfully, *Les Misérables*, a Tolstoy. *Lorna Doone* certainly, and the *Master of Ballantrae*; *The Lost Pibroch*, *Huck. Finn* and a few more. And most of them, strangely enough, are on the romantic side. A man here and there might read up dialectics, or jump back six centuries to study a scholastic and his immortal soul, and wonder, if a nebulous first cause does exist, why any god ever bothered to evolve a soul in the most brutal of all animals.

My father's reading came as far as the hither side of Charles Reade, and washed Mark Twain's shore. So that Robin and he made contact only on the edges. With Tyzack Lane it was different. That strange showman had read widely, if without method, and, while ordinarily sparing of words, he would freely enough talk books with anyone. He and my father were talking books now, and I heard them quoting strange old ballads like: "The lift grew dark, the wind blew loud, and gurly grew the sea"; and:

> " A noble so brave and a maiden so fair conversed as they sat on the green.
> The name of the knight was Alonzo the Brave, and the maiden's the fair Imogene. "

And it struck me that, had they moved in the same orbit, friendship between them would be as natural as breathing.

My father occasionally replenished his glass and urged his two guests to help themselves, which they did not after one trial. Robin was talking to Mary—he usually was. Sylvia was hoping that Jacus was enjoying the creations of Timotheus the Chef, that is, if his usual indigestion was not troubling him.

"I'll know to-morrow," he retorted. "Jacus! you could sole a shoe with the lean o' this piece o' fat bacon."

Sylvia turned her attention to our end of the table. Someone had lost an admirer! Were Dan and Lant at the pictures on Sunday? They were. Who was seen coming out of the Red Branch with a strange girl in tow, a girl in a white print dress? Evidently Dan, by his colour. The girl in the white print dress, I knew, was Sylvia's maid, and Dan might flirt with her, but it was Mary that he really worshipped from afar. Sylvia held Lant in thrall, but he was loyal to me too. Only yesterday he had said: "Blazes, Master Gill! why don't ye make it up? Sure we'll have no fun at all if Miss Syl keeps her own side o' the water!"

If I haven't shown the sort of place Castle Gillian was I should stop writing now. An old house in its decline, but still with its code, its traditions, its atmosphere that made it an entity—no matter what I said: a comfortable, easy-going place made for work and play: a democratic place ruling itself on almost anarchistic lines: a house for young people, and a numerous clann of them: a house for old men to sit back and tell of doughty deeds (with a stretcher) and watch youth blossom from the true stock: a house to cling to: a house Mary might sell her soul for, and hope for a miracle. But I was the sceptic, and I did not believe in miracles.

IV

After that sound meal we drank hot strong tea, and the boys munched butter-scones with it. Then Lant and Dinny gathered dishes and went kitchenwards to help Timmy. Dan used to do that too, but now he was in the man's place; he lit a cigarette, bobbed a head towards my father—or Mary—and went stablewards with Ythan. Mary and Robin went out together. Already they were doing things together as the most natural thing in the world. My father said to the two elder men:

"I want a word with you men. Come out on the porch, and bring your glasses."

That left Sylvia and me, and that was usual too. I did no stable-work in the afternoons. Presently I would go into our kitchen-garden and plant out two hundred cabbage seedlings. Next week I'd be sowing swedes.

Sylvia was leaning forward on the table, her forearms

under her young breasts, and she looked to be in a day-dream, her grey eyes far away, and her lips softly apart. Probably, she was only replete.

"Come out of it!" I said. "Are you aware of the peck of trouble you have wished on this house?"

"With you and Mary to help," she said lazily. "A peck of yeast only, and you wait till the mash settles!"

"That's how vinegar is made," I told her.

Old Timmy ambled in on his carpet slippers, and looked round, humming behind his teeth.

"Is it there the two of ye are?" he mumbled. "Do you know, young Dinny Lane is a handy willin' lad with the delf. Me heart was broke with Dan Shea makin' smithereens o' cup handles, an' him too big for me to wallop. But faith! I took it out o' Lant's hide. Do you know what I'm thinkin' this minute?"

"Hold it!" I said, "though there's no lady present."

"Sittin' there at yer aise after a prime meal, ye're like the man and woman o' the house—and the baby havin' a sleep in his cradle under a tree on the lawn, as I have seen it in my time."

"You've got a nice imagination, Timmy boy!" said Sylvia, chuckling softly.

"'Tis a good thing to see the table filling up agin," went on Timmy. "It reminds me of old times, God be with them. Do you know, if it keeps on I'll have to get a woman in to help me?"

"You might have to marry her, Timmy?" Sylvia hinted.

"If I had to—but sure the opposite arrangement would suit me just as well!"

"You dangerous old Sultan!" I called him.

"Why not? That sort was not unknown in Castle Gillian, or Castle Evan aither. Do you know this now: there's a new feel in the place: there's a weight lifted off it—an' all since that nice Highlandman set his foot in it. I can hear heart-free laughin' in the yard any hour of the day. God be with the good old days! an' they might come again—an' meself here to share 'em for a short while, God rest my soul in glory."

"Amen to that, Timmy!" responded Sylvia.

"Will the good days come with Garret Ward, you old dreamer?" I put.

He pointed a finger at Sylvia and crossed it with another. "Cross him like that for me, Miss Syl! Cross Garret Ward that way—till Gill Morris is ready."

"I'll do my damnedest, old hero!" said Sylvia deeply.

"Go back to your bed!" I rasped at him, and he ambled off humming between his teeth.

Sylvia got to her feet and yawned deeply. "Gosh! I could sleep for a week. I have to lie awake thinking for both of us."

"Don't!" I urged. "You did that once, and I was on my back for three months with a broken leg."

"Listen!" she said. "Uncle Gillian is talking to the old boys and I want to hear——"

"You can't do that——"

"Come along and stop me," she challenged, and swung for the door. I followed her.

She went out on to a flagged passage, and up three steps, and through a green-baized door to the cavernous front hall, with its black-and-white tiles, groined roof of pine, and double stairway. There were many immense unpolished brass jars holding sprays of young bracken, a big open fireplace with a bronze hood, and above the hood were the shields and badges of all the Morrises. A queer thought struck me: *What was the Morrison badge?* It was *Sgod cladaich*: driftwood. Fair enough! Robin Morrison was a drifter, and he had drifted in here. To drift out again?

Sylvia sat down on the doorstep, and curled her legs. My father in his chair by the rustic table could not see her, but Jacus, leaning back on the side-rail, filling a pipe, gave her the lift of an eyebrow. Tyzack was seated opposite my father. The sun was high in the south, but half the porch was in cool shadow. I walked across into the sunlight, and faced my father. He was leisurely filling one of his clay pipes, and his eagle face was serene. There was a decanter on the table, a glass half full of pale amber, and two empty glasses.

"Am I in the way?" I asked. "If I am I'll go and haul——"

"No, boy," said my father. "You—and Sylvia—are welcome." He hadn't seen or heard Sylvia, but he had noted Jacus's lifted eyebrow.

I sat down on the sun-warm top step, shoulder against a pillar, and looked at a hen scratching amongst her chicks in the grass-grown gravel. Our Kerry cow, that had been lying down, got to her feet, tossed a horn impatiently, flicked tail at a horse-fly, and made for the shade of a bush growing out of the haw-haw. There wasn't even a rook in the sky at this dead hour of the day. My father was speaking in his rich husky voice, and he was not yet slurring his words.

"Yes, we three are of one generation," he said, "and I know how you helped educate some youngsters." He chuckled.

"And look at us now!" murmured Sylvia.

"Ye were good at yere a-b-c's, the pair o' ye, but not out o' the first book," said Jacus.

"Just so!" said my father chuckling. "I'm told Mary was your lass, Tyzack? You taught her some useful things, and now she is keen to impart some useful things to grandson Dinny. I shall be happy to have him in my stables, if you are agreeable?"

"I am agreeable, and thank you, Gillian Morris," said Tyzack quietly.

"Splendid! And if you are agreeable I shall indenture him formally, and, what is more, be happy to give him the benefit of any little knowledge I possess——"

There was my courteous father talking hot air. He might have more knowledge of blood horses than any man in Ireland, but he could or would no longer impart it.

——"And I think," he went on, "that it will be good for the lad to be here with Mary and Gillian—and Sylvia too——"

"Not forgetting Robin Morrison?" said Sylvia firmly.

"Thank you, my dear!" He waved a hand. "That is the young man I want to talk about. He interests me, and my daughter has taken rather a fancy to him——"

"So have we all," said loyal Sylvia.

My father emptied and refilled his glass, and addressed himself to Tyzack. "Mary is only a young girl after all, Mr Lane, and there is no older woman to order her life— (Sylvia was swallowing a chuckle; she was thinking of any woman ordering Mary Morris's life)—and, if you don't mind me saying so, it is my duty to consider any strange man coming in off the road?"

Tyzack moved his head in slow affirmation.

"That he has come out of your camp speaks highly of him, I know," went on my father. "Ythan took him for what he calls a tinkler, but he was never that, of course. He is a man of education—a gentleman fallen from his estate, perhaps? or a gentleman of fortune—eh?"

"Divil the fortune!" said Jacus.

"He is writing a book, Uncle," put in Sylvia. "He's fine, Robin is."

"Well, Tyzack! what do you know of him?" queried my father.

"That's his own business, my friend," said Tyzack.

"It is not in your code to decry a man?"

"If you want a reference I'll give it," said Tyzack almost voluble. "Robin Morrison is the second son I always wanted and never had."

"Let that go," said Jacus, "and I've said me last word."

My father looked at me. "Any remarks from you, Gillian?"

"Not one," I said, and changed my mind. "Morrison is all right, but if I were you I'd boot him out right now."

"Gill Morris, you hound!" cried Sylvia aghast.

"Yes, Gillian?" my father queried.

"If you don't," I said, "Mary and he will fall in love with each other, and you know what that means?"

"I see—I see!" said my father imperturbably. "He certainly knows horse, and is wasting his time even with you, Lane. And writing a book is surely wasting his time. All the books have been written long ago." He hesitated a moment. "He is not a man of means, then?"

"Not that I know of," said Tyzack.

"A lame horse, and divil the thing else!" amplified Jacus

Old Gillian Morris is a romantic dreamer too, I thought. *He sees Morrison in love with Mary, and five thousand pounds coming out of his hat.*

"He hasn't got a bean," Sylvia said.

"If he has a tenner to his name 'tis as much as he has," said Jacus.

"Not him," I said. "Last night he and I were considering ways and means of touching a notorious female Shylock."

"Whoever she is she'll want to see your collateral," Sylvia said cagily. "No dozed fishing-rods any more, but a point twenty-two considered."

My father chuckled and reached for his glass; and Sylvia twisted lithely to her feet, and came round to face him.

"Uncle Gillian," she said impulsively, "Tyzack knows about Garret Ward. Let the hound stick to his Monaglass; we don't want him in our glen."

"But he is selling Monaglass, my dear, and must find another place——" (Here I noted that Tyzack Lane sat up and smoothed his chin)—"but you can speak to Mary."

"And whistle a jig through a milestone!" Sylvia said bitterly. She bent to him and her voice went deep. "But look! if we found the five thousand——?"

"Tut-tut! We don't pass and take gifts across the Gullane any more, young woman." He tugged her blown hair softly. "Money for value received, my dear! You find a man with five thousand pounds, who wants a part in a training stable, give him your *imprimatur*, and bring him along."

Sylvia straightened up. "Gosh! Money and pride are twin devils," she said warmly.

V

Out on the lawn, a red cock straightened up, clapped its wings and crowed. It was a lonesome, eerie, clarion call in the dead middle of the day. Across the grass a black cock answered the challenge. These two would have a sparring match, but that would be later in the day; the sun was too drowsy to do anything about it now.

As is well known the crowing of a cock in daytime portends a visitor, mostly unwelcome. Here came the visitor, and he was not welcome. Footsteps sounded on the gravel, and Garret Ward came up into the porch, giving me a touch with the side of his foot as he passed.

He was controlling a temper which had been ruffled somewhere. He took no least notice of Tyzack or Jacus, but spread his legs out-toed before my father, who looked up at him unconcernedly.

"This place is becoming a regular showman's paradise, Uncle," he said, a sneer behind his careless tone.

Tyzack Lane eased back in his chair again, gave one under-brow glance up at Ward's profile, looked across at Jacus, and gave a certain down-twist with his left thumb. I knew some of their showman's sign language, and that sign meant: "pipe down."

My father gestured with his pipe-stem. "Two friends of our young people, Garret—you know them?"

"Not your friends, sir?" said Ward. He meant that a man would lose caste in claiming showmen as friends. He gave a bark of laughter. "One of them has been trying for three years to find a bruiser to take the hide off me."

"I am workin' round to him," said Jacus.

"I don't think I'll give you another chance, old Jacus," said Ward.

"I'll make it," said Jacus.

Again Tyzack gave him that "pipe down" sign, and Jacus clamped his lips together. I knew that there was a three-year-old feud between Jacus and Garret Ward. I was away fighting for Democracy (God help us) when it started, and never got to the bottom of the story, for both sides were reticent. There was a woman in it, a young, flighty red-head out of one of Tyzack's shows, and a granddaughter of Jacus's to boot. She disappeared for two days at Caerline Fair. On the second day Tyzack and Jacus paid a visit to Monaglass, Garret Ward's bachelor house. They could have taken fifty men in their tail if they wanted to. No outsider knew what took place inside the house, but the flighty one was back in her camp the following day. After that Ward gave Tyzack Lane a wide berth, but he revenged himself on Jacus by trouncing his second-raters.

He now turned his attention to my father, and I think that his idea was to show him up before our low friends.

"Some time ago I made you a certain offer, Uncle Gillian, contingent on my selling Monaglass," he said.

"I took it to *avizandum*, I believe," my father gave back equably.

"But that offer did not contemplate this place being infested at the time of its acceptance."

"If and when is the usual term, Garret," said my father easily, and refilled his glass steady-handed.

"Go on cooking your own goose, cousin," I said.

He whirled on me and loosed some of his temper. "I'll cook yours in another minute," he rasped.

I turned in, and drew my feet up. My heart was hollow, but I could get a shoulder under his breast-bone and crack his head on a pilaster. I hadn't to try that time. Sylvia laughed clear and high.

"Mich'elmas is the time for goose, Garret! Wait till then."

Ward turned and steadied himself. "Anything to please you, Silly, but you'll not care for cooked goose when I have basted it."

"Depends on which goose," said Sylvia.

"Easy, children!" said my father. "Are you thinking of withdrawing your offer, Garret?"

"Certainly not," said Ward promptly. "That offer holds through thick and thin, and Monaglass is about sold; but you are welcome to look for a better offer right up to settling day. Can *you* get another partner in Castle Gillian, Uncle?" He accented the "*you*."

"If I do you'll know it when the pact is signed and sealed, my friend." My father took a sip of his whiskey instead of the usual gulp, and that was the only sign he gave that he was touched.

"Fair enough!" said Ward, "but I think you'll have to consider my offer at the end." He moved his hands in reasonable persuasiveness. "That being so, I think that I should at least be informed of any new commitments in the stable."

My father tapped out his clay pipe meditatively. No emotion moved in him that I could see, and his voice did not change from its husky equability.

"You have no say in running the stables, Garret—not yet—but things are going on as usual, are they not?"

"If you call deterioration the usual thing," Ward gave back, "Mary got herself saddled with a lame horse, but we'll let that ride. That horse can be dealt with if it's no good. Then she took a showman into the stable off the roads. I don't like him hanging round Mary; for he's worse than a showman, worse than a tinker; he's a man who has fallen out of his place, and I found him grovelling in the mud in Jacus McGrath's boxing-booth."

Jacus covered his mouth with his hand, but Sylvia spoke for him.

"And he bled your nose, nice and handy, Garret."

Garret Ward waved a careless hand. "All in the day's work, my darling! And he can be dealt with too. And finally, Uncle, I understand you are thinking of indenturing young Lane as an apprentice."

"Surely you have nothing against that lad?" my father said.

"Not a thing. I have nothing against anyone—no resentment whatever. I merely want to pull this place together, and I frankly think that showmen or showmen's sons do not make for the prestige of a racing establishment. That is all." He stepped back and looked down at Tyzack Lane, who looked up at him out of steady black eyes that told nothing. "Yes, Mr Lane! if this place is to revive, it calls for a new dispensation, and it is going to get it."

He turned on his heel and came towards me. I turned out on the step, kept my head down, and a hand ready; and my mind was made up that, if he moved a foot towards me, I would hand-trip him, and pile on him out in the gravel. But instead he tapped me smartly on the crown of the head, and strutted off quickly for the stables. Strut is the right word there, for he walked from the thighs, bent his knees very little, and turned his toes out —a good style for fast walking, but not for activity.

VI

"Jacus alive, Ty Lane! why did you muzzle me?" Jacus had a grievance.

"Because that man wanted you as a sounding board," Tyzack told him.

Tyzack got to his feet, and lifted a valedictory hand to my father. "So long, Mr Morris. This makes no difference to our arrangements."

"I never thought it would, my friend," said my father.

Tyzack flicked my ear as he went down the steps. "On the road by nightfall, son—come down!" he said.

Jacus put his hand on my shoulder and his smoky breath tickled my ear. "Take it aisy, boy!" he whispered consolingly, and jerked a thumb towards Tyzack's broad back. "Garret Ward is past praying for this bloody minute, and Ty Lane bides his own time."

Sylvia said: "Wait for me, Jacus! 'Bye, Uncle!" She gave my hair a soft tug. "Be seeing you some time, Gill?"

I was sorry to see her go. Yes, I was always sorry to see Sylvia go. She was a tall sylph of a girl in her blue dress, walking between two squat formidable men; she had an arm of each, and was busy talking back and fore, and she was the dominant figure of the three.

From the stable-yard came the distant clatter of hooves going out under one of the arches. *That's Garret Ward taking himself off*, I thought, *but there is a second horse.*

My father's chair creaked. He was on his feet, holding on to the empty decanter, and he sadly moved his head from side to side. "I thought I had gone beyond shame, Gillian. Not yet! I am going in."

I sat on and filled a pipe, and I refused to think. Drowsiness was wrapping round me in the warm sunlight, but I shook it off, got to my feet, and pigeon-toed for the stable-yard on my way to our garden patch.

Robin and Dinny were the only ones about, and they were playfully sparring. I noticed Dinny's neat footwork, and the smart way he hopped in and away. He would need speed at his poundage. If an apprentice is not good with his hands he is in for a bad time until he reaches his accepted level. Lant Shea was about Dinny's age, but pounds heavier, and some evening soon he would give Dinny his first blooding. Dinny wouldn't have a chance with Lant.

"Jacus to glory!" I yelped. "Is this the way the work goes, an' Mary Morris's back turned."

Dinny leaped a foot, for he thought it was his uncle speaking. Then he laughed. Robin came across towards me, one hand in a jacket-pocket, and his mouth open.

"Whisper, Gill! Do you keep a tame *leprechaun* in residence?"

"There used to be fairies in Glen Gullane, but not any longer, and Walt Disney borrowed our last *leprechaun*——"

"But look!" He took his hand out of his pocket.

"Two noble five-pound notes—and last night we couldn't raise the required half-dollar!"

"Even fairyland has given up the gold standard," I said. "He was one fine, big, buck *leprechaun* too."

"Tyzack—eh?"

"Yes. I saw him slip it across."

Dinny lifted his voice in protest. "You shouldn't tell, Master Gill. I saw it too."

Robin was looking down at the crumpled five-pound notes, and there was a softening about his austere mouth. "Well! Well! Well!" he mused aloud. "Maybe one shouldn't ever hole-up after all."

"You are a renegade," I said, "but I'm still a partner of yours—financially?"

"Sure! Say, Dionysius, what are we supposed to do with all this wealth?"

"I dunno," said Dinny, "but my grandma was sayin' you might be needing something extra for Benbecula, and it wouldn't do to be too hard on Miss Mary."

"Oh my! and not a word about a couple of thirsty souls?"

"No, but Uncle Jacus said he knew two buckeroos would be beatin' a path regular to the pub at Gullane Cross; and granda said something about a muzzle on an ox, whatever he meant."

"Sound man!"

"Two buckeroos, Uncle Jacus said!" Dinny kept a straight face, "and not a word about an ice-cream."

"You're in on the ground floor, my son. Say, Gill! How much do we give Mary Morris?"

"A fiver, and not a penny more," I said promptly. "And look here! not a word about the other or—whoosh! the tenner is gone, and we die of thirst."

"Teach your grandmother to suck eggs," he said scathingly. "I got sisters too." He gave Dinny a lift.

"Go raise your own thirst, shaver!" And Dinny trotted off to finish his whitewashing.

"Where's Mary?" I asked though I knew.

"Gone ariding with Alonzo the Brave. Say, that lad has been swallowing down bile all day—why, I wonder?"

I told him, though I was playing Sylvia's game. I said:

"He thinks that showmen are not good for the prestige of *his* training stable, and shall be dispensed with when the occasion arises. Thinks a certain down-and-outer should not be allowed to grovel in the mud within arm-grab of his Mary Morris, and steps shall be taken at an early date."

"He said all that?"

"At greater length."

"Did Tyzack Lane hear him?"

"He did, and never opened his mouth, and wouldn't let Jacus open his either."

"Then God ha' mercy on Garret Ward the other side o' hell! Do you know this, Gill Morris? It was easy enough to shove me out of here any day at all. Now I don't go until I'm thrown out neck-and-crop."

"That's the way you'll go in October," I said.

"Very good! Meantime I have a job to do."

"You have," I said, and collared him. "Come and raise your own thirst in my garden patch?"

He did too, for he was an amenable man.

But that evening, when he was quenching his thirst with Ythan and me at Gullane Cross, he produced one solitary one-pound note, and met my eye brazenly.

"I got that fiver changed," he remarked carelessly.

"You did?" I said suspiciously. "All right! Let's see the other four singles?"

"Ah well! She—I mean, they are being held for us."

"And there's an end of 'em," I said resignedly.

"Ay so!" Ythan chuckled. "The last hoor, Miss Mary

and myself was makin' out a list of gear we can be doin' with."

"Look here, Mr Morrison!" I told him. "You Norse-Irish-Highlandmen have a soft streak in you, and Mary knew it."

"I am inclined to agree with you, Mr Morris," he said amiably. "A good thing we have a second string in your Sylvia."

"Blast it! that's not fair to Sylvia," I said, "and she's not my Sylvia either."

Chapter VIII

MARY FINDS A MAN IN THE STABLE

I

I was in an old armchair in the alcove of a dormer window in the Man's Room at the top of the house, and I was reading one of Robin Morrison's books—not a book he had written, but a copy of a book he had reviewed. His few things had been sent up from the van before it took the road, and amongst them were some review copies of modern books. The one I was reading was called *The Drinking Well*, by a well-known Scots writer, and I was interested in it. This was the sort of thing I wanted, the work I would like to try if I had a chance: make two blades of grass grow where one grew before: get rid of some of the furze and most of the bracken, and go in for drainage, and mixed farming with sheep, cattle, and corn. And I would be no dilettante, gentleman farmer either, even if I had all of the Castle Evan acres to play with. I wouldn't have, of course; and I would not stay in Glen Gullane at all if Garret Ward was in control at Castle Gillian.

In another chair near mine Sylvia rested on her shoulder-blades, her crossed ankles on the window-sill to show the taper of her nylon legs. There was a pile of old *Posts* on the floor at her side, and she was reading a serial, cursing some as she had to turn a score or so of pages. Now that there was no outside compulsion we had more or less resumed our old cat-and-dog existence, though cat-and-dog does not nearly explain our relationship.

As I have said Mary and Sylvia had rights on the man's floor: Mary as chatelaine, and Sylvia by right of conquest. But having wrested that right from us, Sylvia did not abuse it. She was not always raising Cain. Here she was, now, sitting amicably beside me, and not interrupting. This sitting together and ignoring each other on fine evenings was becoming another of our customs. After an hour or so we might go fishing, or Mary would stroll in with Robin Morrison, and start an argument.

The day had been dull and clouded, but, now, the sun broke through in orange bars that slanted in through the window and dazzled in Sylvia's eyes, until she moved her head and set her hair on fire. She looked sideways at me and smiled.

"Well, guidman?" she said.

"No, I won't," I said. "I want to finish this book."

"I never said a thing."

"And anyway the water won't be right till to-morrow night."

"Hush!" she said. "Listen!"

I was already listening, and now turned head round the wing of my chair. With us in the big room were the two Sheas and Dinny Lane. The day's work was over in the stables, but an apprentice's work is never definitely over short of bedtime. We had discontinued fires this mild weather, and Lant and Dinny sat on blocks inside the cavern of the near fireplace polishing the metal of some training harness. Dan Shea sat astride a chair, his arms over the back, and directed operations, but his directions were mostly adverse criticism. He had taken his promotion seriously, and was inclined to be bossy. He had just called his brother "a left-thumbed son—of a female dog," and told Dinny to use less polish and more spit, consarn him. Suddenly and without context he put Dinny a casual question:

"Can you fight, young Lane?"

"If I have to—what for?" Dinny answered unsuspectingly.

"For fun, what else?" Dan said. "Will you box me brother Lant?"

"Why so? Look at the size of him!" Dinny wanted nothing but friendliness.

"Och! Lant's only a tub of guts, and you'd easy manage him. Supposin', now, he gev you cause?"

"I'd—I'd crucify him," Dinny said warmly.

"Give him cause, Lant?" ordered Dan.

"Why not I?" said Lant cheerfully, and, without rancour, belted Dinny across the shins with the leathers of a saddle. In return Dinny swung a whole head-halter just out of range, and then, the two warriors were on their feet, circling out into the room, and swinging indiscriminately at each other, but not yet angrily.

Dan's mouth was open wide in laughter. Dinny shut it for him. A swoop of the halter, going over Lant's ducked head, took Dan on the side of his, and Dan and his chair went over in a crashing, vociferous heap. It was by no means the first chair broken in that room. After that poor Dinny, shuttled back and forth between the brothers, looked to be in for a manhandling. Sylvia was on her feet in a complicated, leggy twist over the side of her chair.

"Blast! I'll have to bleed Dan's nose for him again." She used to induce Dan into a bout with her, and invariably ended it by one slight tap on a nose that bled at a touch. Finally, Mary forbade him to put on the gloves with her.

I caught her hand and held her back. "Wait!" I said. "Watch this!"

II

Mary, Robin and Sandy Ythan had just come in at the far door from the stairs. Robin had one look, saw his cub being mauled, and came swooping, his feet echoing on the bare boards. He swept the two lads apart, and took Dan by the neck: vest, shirt, collar, and tie, and probably some hide, in one comprehensive clutch.

Dan was a strong lout, tall as Robin, and heavier, and he was no coward. His right hand came up clenched, but the Scot slapped it down smartly. His voice was nicely controlled.

"Take it easy, Dan Shea! I'll show you how things should be done. Sit down there!"

Dan found himself slumped on an old chaise, and he looked up open-mouthed at Robin's back. He shook himself just as if he had touched a live wire, and grinned sheepishly. Robin swept the broken chair aside with his foot, and beckoned Dinny.

"You'll try Lant out, young fellow!" That was an order.

Dinny was on the edge of tears—tears of rage. "Give me fair play, and let me at him!" he shrilled.

"You'll have some gloves, Ythan?" Robin called.

"Ay have we." Ythan hesitated. He was head-man in this room, and his control was being usurped. And then he spoke with a quirk in his voice. "All reet, big boss! 'tis time the laddie was blooded!"

He went to one of the many presses in the gable-end wall. It contained shelves of old gloves, most of them black and battered, some split open, but a few sets still serviceable. Sandy felt them over and picked out a set.

"They'll no' do muckle hurt wi' these," he said, and slung them across to Robin, one by one.

Robin matched them and thrust the smaller pair at Dinny. "Go on over to Dan! He'll lace them on. Come you here, Lant!" He patted Lant's shoulder. "Take him if you can, my lad!"

There was a pause then. I found I was still holding Sylvia's hand, and dropped it. She sat aside on the arm of my chair and looked over the back of it. Mary had not come far forward. She was chatelaine, but, after all, this was the Man's Room, with its own code. She was over near the wall, her elbow on a sideboard, and her attitude was aloofly observant.

The set-to that followed was no desperate one, but it was warm enough while it lasted. Dinny surprised me, and he surprised Lant too. Lant started it all-agrin, he was so certain of lambasting little Dinny, but in half-a-minute Dinny wiped the grin off his face. Dinny was a Lane and a boxer by seed, breed and generation, as Jacus would say. His bones were set, and his muscles wiry, and he surely could use his hands and his feet. He danced about on his toes, and that was the Morrison technique; sliding in and out, and he was Sloper Jones. He took a round-arm wallop or two going away, but he surely gave Lant his bellyful.

I didn't care to see boys leathering each other to exhaustion with heavy gloves. Neither did Robin Morrison. He was watching carefully, gave them three minutes or so, until they were forced to ease up, called "Time!" and held them apart. He had to restrain Dinny.

"Give me one other peg at him!" That was what Dinny wanted.

"Well, Lant?"

"Whatever you say, sir!" panted Lant. "Me nose is bleedin'." He had the family weakness.

"So it is! That will be enough this time." He swung Dinny round. "Off with the gloves, cockerel! Dan will attend to you." He stripped Lant's gloves, talking to him quietly. "You'd have taken him in time, Lant—you've a useful right swing—some day I'll show you some straight hitting, and Dinny'll know about—no, your nose is not bad at all." He lifted his voice. "Here, whipper-snapper!" Dinny came over, and Robin put a hand on his shoulder and another on Lant's. "You two will shake hands like fighting men. Go on! No grudges in Castle Gillian."

The lads grinned at each other, and shook hands, and Robin gave them a swing and a shove. "Off you go and wipe each other's noses!" Obediently the boys trotted off through the open door leading to the Rookery. In there at the back was the bath and shower and reducing-rooms. Robin walked across to Dan on the couch, and laughed pleasantly.

"That's how to do it, Dan, and no ill-feelings! This is one fine friendly house, and you and I will shake hands too."

Dan was on his feet, his hand out impulsively. "Sure I wouldn't hurt Dinny for the world," he said. "While I have 'em stripped I'll give them a good scrub." Robin Morrison had another lad in his tail—two lads.

Sandy Ythan was chuckling derisively, and Robin looked his way. Sandy saluted him in mock deference.

"A bonny bit o' work, my fine Hielan' gent!" he scoffed. "Were ye thinkin' yerself back in Moidart, laird o' a' the rocks and heather?"

Robin's hand went to his toss of hair. "Sorry, Ythan! You are the boss, and I did forget myself for a minute——"

"Four by the clock, but dinna mind me. There's yon lassie, and she's boss of us both! Were you thinking o' her at all?"

"The lord be here!" said Robin in a startled voice, and walked directly across to Mary. The flat sun was shining orange all about her, and I never saw her look so lovely—or so solemn. Robin bowed to her with old-world dignity.

"Sorry, my dear chatelaine——!"

She straightened up, and her shadow flowed as she moved towards the door. She spoke gravely over her shoulder. "A natural usurper, Robin! I am beginning to be afraid of you."

He stood looking after her until she turned down the stairs. I do not think he understood, then, what she meant, but I, her brother, did. She had realised for the first time that she had a man in the house who could be dominant, and ignore her in being so, and that it was the most natural thing in the world.

Robin turned to us, and his voice was doleful. "Put my foot in it, didn't I?"

"Both of them," I said.

"Eh, man, man!" mocked Ythan. "Think o' our Miss Mary afraid of a Hielan'man!"

Robin took that seriously. "No—no! She is not afraid of me." He punched his chest. "She isn't—she couldn't—she mustn't be! She has enough to fear already. Oh, blast!"

He made for the door in long strides, and Sandy called after him, "That's the way! Eat humble pie, and like it!"

I sat back and looked up at Sylvia. She was smiling down at me, and she would start crowing if I let her. I kept my voice low.

"A nice mess you've made of things," I said. "You know what's going to happen now, don't you?"

"Of course," she said smugly. "Them there two will fall in love as sure as shootin'."

"And then?"

"And then what?"

"They are poor as church mice—did you think of that?"

"Why should I?" But she was beginning to be disturbed.

"Because, when Mary thinks it over," I said, "she'll decide that she can't, she daren't, she mustn't. You know Mary?"

"Lord, Gill!" She was seeing.

"And to cut the painter, as it were, she'll up and marry Garret Ward out-of-hand—just like that."

"She couldn't, Gill?" she whispered.

"She could—and I've a darn good mind to put the gloves on with you for three minutes."

Ordinarily she'd jump at that, and take her lacing. Now she shook her head. "No! I don't want you to hurt me any more."

"Then you'd better give up being a hay-headed mutt of a tin god."

She was on her feet flaring down at me, her eyes brilliant and her mouth pale. "I will not," she said deeply. "I will keep on trying—and trying—and trying—and never get what I want—never—never—never! you dam' pint-pot of vinegar and gall and wormwood—and—and—pusillanimity!"

"Six to four on that one!" I said.

I rolled over the arm of the chair, so that her long left barely flicked me. By the time I got to my feet she was half-way down the room. Sandy was again at his chuckling.

"Women bodies are kittle cattle," he said. "I found that out early on, and look at me now!"

"Ay, look at you now! Head-groom in a busted stable!"

"Ay so! but, man, man! the guid days might be here again."

"Anither bluidy optimist!" I mimicked him. "The place is fair steerin' wi' them."

I stalked off after Sylvia. But Sylvia had gone home; and Gullane Glen, glowing weirdly in the red light of the gloaming, was sad and lonesome. Maybe it wasn't the glen was lonesome.

Chapter IX

INTERLUDE OF HALCYON DAYS

I

If I keep on like this I'll never finish. I have scribbled thousands of words to cover a couple or so weeks, and I have four months and more still to cover. Still, a big book has been written to cover twenty-four hours, and, anyway, the next three months are only an interlude.

I have got Robin Morrison and Dinny Lane into Castle Gillian; Sylvia Gayne putting thoughts into people's heads; Tyzack Lane circling on the road; Mary playing the game out with Garret Ward; my father watching his Kismet at work; and myself—Dammit! I was no better than my drunken father: I was only looking on too.

The stage is set for the second quiet act, an act as dull as ditch-water. No, not ditch-water! as quiet as a deep-flowing stream whose current surely reaches its own sea. Nothing much happened; we just drifted; but the inevitable happened just the same: Mary Morris and Robin Morrison drifted into love.

It was the most natural thing I ever saw; so natural, so instinctive, that they themselves did not know for a time whereto they were drifting. We all knew it before they did, but we said nothing. There was nothing we could say—or do. That was the devil of it! We could not help them in any way.

"Nought would she aye love but a horse and a house," said Sandy Ythan, "but this was bound to happen frae time immemorial." There was the Calvinist believer in predestination. "The puir wee things!" said Sandy Ythan. The Scots often speak commiseratingly of young people in love.

I should not have said that we all knew. Garret Ward did not, or did not seem to notice. They did not carry their hearts on their sleeves; the Gael in love is the least effusive of all breeds; and Garret Ward, sure that he had all the strings in his hands, could not contemplate a rival, or, at any rate, a successful rival. A man of many affairs, he had ousted many a rival, and the Scot, at most, was only another.

Sylvia and I were not far away the evening that Robin and Mary really discovered what was wrong with them. It was a Sunday evening in the dusk. There had been heavy warm showers and some thunder most of the day, but the evening had cleared up, and the woods and hills shone in a washed splendour of sunlight. Mary and Robin had, as usual, gone down to have a collogue with Benbecula; they had taken Benbecula into partnership, as it were. Dinny and I had stolen off to the river when Sandy's back was turned; the Presbyterian would not countenance fishing on the Sawbath, and we thought it best to humour him as a rule. I was sure that the higher water in the Gullane would induce the first run of sea trout to come upstream. And so it did. I sent Dinny up with word to Sylvia, and when she got down I had already landed three nice ones on a pennel tackle.

Sylvia, I remember, was in slacks and thigh waders, which were not necessary, and a mistake besides, for in a short time, and as usual, she got a trickle over the tops of the waders. She did not mind that, but in blaming me she got my shoes full of water. We caught a round dozen, and I showed Dinny how to use a worm and keep it off the bottom away from the eels that were newly in from the sea. We could have caught a bigger bag if we wanted to, but a dozen trout ranging from one-and-a-half to two-and-a-half pounds were ample for the two houses.

After that we went up to Castle Evan, and raided the pantry. We had early tomatoes out of the hot-house, and strawberries and cream; and Uncle Tom joined us in the kitchen and ate his share. And we forgot to bring away our half of the fish. We were going through the arch at Castle Gillian when we got Sylvia's clear hail from the foot-bridge across the river, and we went back and met her at the haw-haw.

"I was thinkin' o' Sandy," she said, panting nicely. "He might like a wee Sunday trootie on a Monday."

"Hesht! who are them over there?" whispered Dinny. "Oh! Miss Mary and Robin!" He called him "Robber" no longer.

It was a clear dusk that would not grow dark till midnight, and we could just make out the two walking slantwise across the lawn towards the house. They were near enough to each other, but not touching, and they were silent, for they were already companionable enough not to need to make talk. Mary was wearing one of her light dresses.

"Wait a bit!" whispered Sylvia, and put a staying hand on my arm.

The stillness closed down on us again, a stillness coming down from the very stars, faint and far in a hazy blue. A countryman would not notice that silence until it was accented by a dog's bark in the distance, or the rasp of a corncrake in the grass, or the clack of a cart axle on the hill road. And by listening we could hear the Gullane sighing remotely down the long slide. And now we could hear Mary's quiet voice from the steps of the porch.

"Good night, Robin!"

"Good night, Mary!"

That was all. Robin drifted back on the grass, and hesitated. Probably he was making up his mind to go to bed, or to come looking for us. He wouldn't yet notice us against the bulk of the holms.

"Not even a good-night kiss?" murmured Sylvia.

"Did I ever give you one, fat-head?" I murmured back.

"And lose your nose! And we are not in love, you know?"

"That's right too," I agreed.

"What whould anyone be kissing for, I'd like to know?" wondered Dinny. "My granny used to be kissing me till I ran for it."

"Stick to that, sonny," I told him, "and your fortune is made."

A window went up on the first floor right of the portico. That was Mary's room. She had not lit her lamp, but we could see the pale glimmer of her as she leant on the sill. Whether she saw Robin's dark bulk on the grass I do not know, but she gave no sign. Neither did Robin. And Sylvia would not stand for that.

"Hush!" she whispered urgently. "Go on, Romeo! do your stuff!"

But that Romeo over there on the lawn had a tight hold on himself, whatever urge was in him. I gave Sylvia a push, and stepped away.

"Go back to your bed, you sentimental coot!" I told her.

"You go to hell, Gill Morris!" she said deeply, and surprised me. For she threw back her head, so that I saw her firm chin against the sky, and her great contralto voice, though only just above her breath, filled the whole valley of the Gullane. And the song she sang was by a man called Robin who knew all about the lornness of love:

> "O Mary, at thy window be,
> It is the wished, the trysted hour!
> Those smiles and glances let me see
> That make the miser's treasure poor.
> How blithely would I bide the stoure,
> A weary slave frae sun to sun,
> Could I the rich reward secure,
> The lovely Mary Morison."

Sylvia's voice vibrated and died, and a queer, waiting hush came down over the glen. And then Mary's soft, throaty chuckle came across the grass, and her window closed down with a little snick. That was all.

"Mary Morris—Mary Morrison! How easy the change?" said Sylvia, softly sibilant.

I had nothing to say. Sylvia's singing voice always did strange things to me, and my throat felt a little thick. I just turned on my heel, and stalked away across the grass towards where Robin was drifting through the arch in the wall.

II

And so the days went by. I sowed swedes, earthed up potatoes, and cut some first-crop hay. Robin helped with the hay, and Dinny and Sylvia made meadow cocks, and tumbled one or two. The work of the stable went on as usual: morning exercises, lungeing, mucking, grooming, bedding, measuring feeds, and all the other activities that did not interest me: the quiet of the afternoon, the evening stables, the talk and play under the roof, the distant rattle of head-chains in the night when horses were stoking up; all the old round day after day.

And Mary Morris worked harder than any of her men, in one final effort to hold her world together. And I will say that it was a world worth holding together all that halcyon summer.

Mary and Robin carried on as usual. There was no direct declaration, and no least sign of love-making. The two just sort of circulated about each other: working in a loose-box and stoking mangers together, measuring bowls of corn together, lungeing or exercising together, grooming and doctoring Benbecula together, lighting a cigarette for each other; and their hands might touch sometimes. That was all.

And I was wrong about Mary. She did not, in desperation, encourage Garret Ward; not that Ward made any particular advances. He came over as usual, interested himself in the routine, and Mary frequently went out on horseback with him. He did not seem to suspect anything, and, yet, I was not sure. He was wholly confident that he had Morrison's measure, and, it could be, that he was letting the iron twist deeper and deeper into the Highlandman's heart. Ward might be just biding his time, and, when that time came, Morrison would go; and so would Dinny Lane; indeed, there might be an entire new staff at Castle Gillian. And I would go too. Of this I am certain: Ward never once contemplated anything happening to save Castle Gillian. He did not believe in miracles either.

Mary was clear-sighted enough. No doubt she realised that she would have to decide between Robin Morrison and Castle Gillian, but she postponed that decision right up to the end. It was as if she had said: *Very well! I have these four or five months, and I will not be deprived of them. Let us enjoy them and have no bitter taste in our mouths.* And that she and Robin did in their own continent way. They were fine and pleasant months, not only for the two, but for us all.

We put aside foreboding, and came out from under our

cloud; and we did not realise how gloomy we had been, until we were again in the sun. The old gaiety returned, and, as old Timmy had said, there was carefree laughter about the place day and dark. I knew it was only an Indian summer, but I accepted it gladly as such. And Robin Morrison was the life of the place. He treated Mary as The-One-to-be-obeyed, and after that poked gentle fun at her, and made her the victim of one or two gay pranks. I never saw her so blithe, and it sometimes made my heart sore to think of what a wife and matron she might be in happier circumstances.

And without realising it Mary gradually yielded control to Robin. Soon she was doing nothing without consulting him, and shortly after that he was making suggestions himself, and carrying them out too.

Also, Morrison took to writing again—when he had time—going back to free-lance work; and pulling down several useful guineas from sporting and country-life journals. This largesse, Mary, as a matter of course, allotted between the stables and ourselves, and was quite fair about it, so that, individually, we were in better funds than usual. Sylvia was a trifle jealous about this, for she liked to be one of our resources in an emergency. Robin and I took her in hand and soon we had a contra account going that was beyond untangling by plain arithmetic.

Even my father felt the new surge of life in the place. He seemed to take more interest in things, and no longer prowled about aimlessly before returning to his decanter. He would always drink, of course, and never again be the man he once had been; but, given a good man in control, old Gillian Morris's advice and experience would be invaluable. For the present the good man about the place was Robin Morrison. My father was interested in Robin, but no familiarity had yet grown between them, and, though they often talked, the talk was formally couched, even when frank. I have heard my father say:

"This work is too much for a girl, Mr Morrison?"

"The salt of her life, sir!" Robin would hold.

"Surely! But where does it lead—without additional capital?"

"Raise some?" suggested Robin shortly.

"Not with the weight already on it. The only thing is to sell a share—a controlling share, I fear."

"You've had an offer, Mr Morris?" Robin said bluntly.

"I like to choose my own partner," my father had said and strolled away. The meaning of that was plain: he had to have a partner, and he did not want Garret Ward: and he might also be hinting that he would favourably consider an offer from another source, say from Robin Morrison. Robin Morrison could make no offer.

My father gave us a real surprise by carrying out his promise to Tyzack Lanc about Dinny. Old Gillian actually stole young Dinny from Robin Morrison and Mary. I suppose Dinny sensed the selfishness of lovers in themselves, and turned to the old man readily; and my father soon found that he had a worshipper in Dinny, and that pleased him mightily. He was like a grandfather whose first grandson claims him for his own. The lad trotted about with him everywhere, before and behind and sometimes actually under his oxter; and the old man talked to him quietly of stable technique, and watched how he behaved with horses in stable and training track. In a very brief time Gillian Morris realised that a diamond in the rough had been delivered into his hands to be cut and polished into a valuable gem: a rider of real class, with the hands, the balance, the poundage, and the spirit.

So my father took an apprentice in hand for the first time in years, and that kept him out-of-doors most of the day. The two took complete charge of Benbecula, lungeing him, exercising him, gradually building up a sound tendon in the hurt shoulder; and then, Dinny in the saddle and my father cracking a long whip, they schooled a sound horse progressively from low hurdles to regulation bush fences. Benbecula was no longer a showground jumper, but a racer taking anything in his stride. And Dinny got a bit beside himself, until Lant took the conceit out of him over three rounds. And Robin was now helping Mary to build her castle in Spain. He realised that, between them, they had a sound horse, and dammit! a horse has saved a Kingdom more than once!

III

And then one evening early in August, Sloper Jones came sloping into the Man's Room, and he was grinning widely. Dinny and his Sut dog were all over him at once, and Robin pounding his shoulder. I was the first to make a claim, for I guessed that camp was back, and back a full month before the end of the show-season. I shouted to make myself heard:

"My meat! I saw him first." I had a job for Sloper on the farm side.

"Ay faith!" said Sloper, "we're back at the Bridge, and I was sent up lookin' for a light job. Light, I said!"

"You have it," I said. "You'll be slinging tram cocks the morrow's morn."

I heard Dinny's light feet on the boards. He was making for the door full pelt, his dog a bad second, and I knew he was off to tell all his doings to his grandparents and uncle; and I knew, too, that they would see that we had done well by Dinny.

In about an hour Robin and I followed him, and we found the camp in its usual staid serenity, just as if it had been there all the summer: Tyzack in his canvas chair, lifting his book in silent greeting: Oonagh knitting and pleasantly smiling, and presently making tea for us: Jacus complaining that we had worn his poor little nephew to the last thread, and borrowing the pouch that I had specially filled: and Dinny, the expert in his own mind, circling round two yearling colts that Tyzack had bought at the Metro sales. I sat at Oonagh's knee and felt a finger in my hair.

Cousin Sylvia was already in the camp when we arrived, and she had given all the news. It was only later that I discovered that she had kept in touch with Oonagh all during the summer. Jacus put some of my tobacco in a paper twist, and handed me back my depleted pouch.

"Tell me this," said he, "has Garret Ward—God-forgive-him-I-won't—put his money on the board?"

"Not yet!" I said. "There's some hitch in the sale of his place at Monaglass." Out of the side of an eye I saw Tyzack's hand go up to his chin.

"Maybe he won't sell at all," said Jacus doubtfully.

"Oh yes, he will!" cried Sylvia who knew more about it than I did. "It will take about another month. He has a row on with his crofting tenants."

"'Twouldn't be the first time a crofter shot a landlord, thanks be to God!" said Jacus.

A little later Mary came into camp. This was, indeed, like old times, and we made an occasion of it. . . .

And then followed our brief golden age, the real halcyon weeks—only six of them—but they flowed full and free. Everything in the garden was fragilely perfect, but the serpent was already on the crawl in the stocky form of Garret Ward. No one seemed to mind. Everyone took the good time debonairly. The stable was still understaffed, but, with the additional help, some of the horses were adequately trained, and Mary won two races for owners who had been doubting.

Robin and Mary went to the races together, and took Dinny along to get the feel of things. My father no longer went to race meetings. We had Tyzack's two colts in paddock, and two fresh horses came in from reassured clients. With additional capital and a free hand, Mary might well restore the great days. Well! she could have the capital at a word, but alas! not the free hand—unless Benbecula——! but she must not think too much of Benbecula!

Jacus McGrath came fussing about the stables most days, and we—Sylvia and I—feuded and sided with him as of old. But Tyzack and Oonagh remained aloof in their own camp, and I think that only once in that six weeks did my father and the showman meet.

CHAPTER X

DINNY AND BENBECULA TO THE PROOF

I

IT was a fine evening early in September, and the green of the woods was dulling before blazing again into fall colours. Dinny and I went down to the bottom paddock to bring Benbecula in; the horse was in half-training now, and stabled at night.

We found Mary and Robin already there, and sitting on a rail. That had become a habit of theirs. After the day's work Mary would take a bath, change into her woman's clothes, and go off for a stroll with Robin. And Sandy Ythan would shake his head, and "wonder to Goad!" The two would work round to the paddock, and sit on the rail, not too far from each other and, yet, not too near, smoking and talking—but not talking a great deal—easy and confident in each other's company. But that community of mind in two vital young people, without the little intimacies of love, was not natural. Perhaps, they could hold it for the few weeks that were left them.

She was wearing vivid green this evening, and to look at her no one would take her for a hard-bitten horse-trainer. I leant on the rail at Robin's side, and blew smoke. They took no notice of me. Dinny vaulted the rail handily, and raced out into the paddock with Sut. Benbecula circled round them, neck and tail acurve, and there was no least trace of shoulder-yield. The horse was really in splendid fettle, its dark hide shining, and its brown-muzzled head held pridefully.

"That crowbait looks fit to race," I said impishly.

"A fortnight's steady work and it would," said Robin the expert, "thanks to your father, and no one else." He overdid the nonchalance, but there was some excitement underneath.

Mary laughed, "This is a secret!" she said: "Father is holding out on us. To-day he has been writing letters and sending off forms behind my back. Listen! That horse is being entered for a race somewhere."

Robin sat up interestedly. "No, Mary? Where? What class?" he put quickly.

"We shall see," said Mary offhandedly.

But they could not fool me. I saw what was in their eyes as they looked at each other, and it hurt me. Here was fear, here was hope, here was the one chance in a hundred! Only give them a stake on the board, and they would win happiness in the teeth of disaster.

"Steady, you fools!" I said. "You are having more company this evening. Oh, blast!"

My father and Garret Ward had just come round one of the hazel clumps. At this hour of the evening my father was usually in his own room, and, certainly, not sober; but he had been out with Dinny most of the day, and had not yet time to get loaded. He had some drink taken; I got the whiff of alcohol where he came to a halt at my side; but he was in full control of voice and movement. He chuckled, and nodded out towards Dinny and the horse.

"A couple of useful young animals!" he said.

"Thanks to you, sir," said Robin.

Garret Ward was leaning as close to Mary as he dared without touching her. He laughed with what he thought was irony.

"I don't care for the breeding of one," he said, "but I'd like to try the other a gruelling two miles over hurdles, and see how that shoulder stands up."

No one, carefully, said anything to that for a minute, and then my father spoke equably.

"We aim to try, Garret, but not for some time. Say a hurdle race in May, and a maiden 'chase, November!"

"May should decide, don't you think?" queried Ward.

"And the decision yours, Garret?" I said.

"I would not decide against a good horse," he said firmly.

"And that is a good horse," said my father, "and may turn out a National candidate!" He hesitated and went on. "Possibly, Garret is right in a way—he sometimes is—and we should soon try Ben with his peers."

"But not over jumps, Father?" said Mary, leading him on. "Say, a flat mile or so in amateur company?"

"I am glad you think so, my dear," said my father, chuckling. "As a matter of fact, I have entered Benbecula for the Apprentice Cup at Logantown in mid-September. Poor judgment—eh?"

My father knew that Mary no longer trusted his judgment. That was professional jealousy on her part, for, deep down, she knew that she'd never have her father's judgment, drunk or sober.

"You old rogue!" she called him, and went on judiciously. "Let me see! The Apprentice Cup at Logantown! That's a mile without whip or spur! But isn't the company a bit high-class?" She frowned.

"You don't know, my girl," said her dad promptly. "A maiden race for horses that mostly hope to go on to hurdles and fences: that's Benbecula's class, isn't it?"

Mary put a confident but clasping hand on Robin's shoulder and leant across him to look at her father. There was suspicion in her eye.

"An apprentice race, my man! What apprentice do you put up?"

My father would not meet her eye. He nodded towards where Dinny was leading Benbecula towards the gate in the rails.

"That young man is qualified to ride," he said carelessly.

"No—no!" cried Mary, very seriously now. "Dinny is too young! It is not right—it is not safe! You might break his nerve amongst tough young devils! What do you say, Robin?" There she was, again doubting her father's judgment, and appealing to Robin as the natural thing to do. But she also showed a nice trait: she would not risk young Dinny, even with Castle Gillian at stake.

Robin, the Scot, was carefully non-committal. He said:

"No doubt, Mr Morris has consulted Dinny's grandfather?"

"Exactly, Mr Morrison!" said my father with satisfaction. "I put it up to Tyzack Lane, and he sees it as I do. That lad out there has the makings in him. He can take Ben over a bush fence, and why not over a flat mile with a wide curve and a long run-in? I want to see him try his hands, balance and judgment against opposition in his own class."

"Then you will be going to Logantown, Dad?" There was life in Mary's voice; for she had an idea that Father might pull himself together if he went racing again.

"This once, to see my lad blooded," her father said, and turned away from the rail.

Garret Ward had been silent for a while, and now he changed his tone. He said:

"I'll back your judgment any time, Uncle. Do you think that horse has a chance?"

"As good a chance as anything in the race," my father told him. "Depends how he is ridden out, but I'll be disappointed if he's not placed." He strolled off towards where Dinny was waiting at the gate. Garret Ward did not follow him, and I stayed on too; I would not trust Ward.

He turned his back to the rail, put his hands on it, and leant well back, so that he could look up into Mary's face. There was a queer secretive watchfulness in his eyes that I had never seen before.

"I never wanted to buy you, Mary, but you'll come to me anyhow." He laughed. "Silly and Gilly—maybe others—work overtime on my reputation, but, honestly, I want you to win this race."

Mary smiled, and her eyes met his steadily. "Nonsense, Garret! Silly and Gilly couldn't convince me that you would want the stables to lose. Why should you?"

"Why should I, indeed?" He grinned mockingly, but there was an odd quality in his grin that was more than mockery. "It hasn't crossed your mind that this race is the opportunity of a lifetime?" There was a sardonic note in his voice, though he tried to hide it.

"Tell me, Garret?" said Mary simply, not wincing, though he was playing on the raw nerve of her dream—and Robin's.

"Can't you see? This race was made for you. It is completely open. There will be twenty runners at least, all horses of about the same class who have never won a race, but whose form is known—all but Benbecula's. Benbecula, who is not known at all, and ridden by an unknown apprentice in his first race! You'll be able to get twenties with the books. Back Uncle Gillian's judgment; he expects to win—you could see that. Raise all the money you can. At twenties you could easily win five—ten thousand pounds. Ten thousand pounds! and Castle Gillian is yours—and our dear friend, Mr Robin Morrison, need not leave his cosy nest forever and a day."

Mary was in complete control of herself, and gave no sign of a hurt.

"That's very nice, and thank you, Garret," she said dryly. "But I don't see myself making a pile on a half-trained horse. That's not done outside a novel, you know." She was using reason now, in defence; but what has reason to do with wishful thinking?

"It has been done," Ward insisted. "Take my advice and try it. If you pull it off, Castle Gillian is yours, and I'll take my chance of winning you fairly."

That's a damn lie! I thought, and had a new conception of Garret Ward. No matter what Sylvia had said, I had thought of him as an arrogant, insensitive oaf: a crude bully who enjoyed beating up weaker men. I was wrong. He did not lack subtlety. He had just let Mary know that he knew that her secret hope was centred in Benbecula; he had let her know that he knew that Robin Morrison attracted her; and he was making fun of her dream by showing how easily it might be realised. He was piercing Mary to the quick, and liked it.

"You forget one thing, Garret boy!" I said, and I was coldly angry to hear him baiting Mary.

"Keep out o' this, Gilly!" he ordered.

"No I won't," I said quickly. "You forget the villain."

"What villain?"

"Yourself, afraid for the first time in your life."

That touched him, for it was true, and I had just found out.

"Afraid! Afraid of what?"

"Afraid that you are losing the game, you hound!" I wanted to get this over.

"Damn you! I'll clout your lug for that," he blared, and took a stride towards me. I straightened and turned, and set my buttocks against the rail. That would give

217

me a good drive to take him off his splay feet; and after that, if I had time, I would bite his ears off.

Robin Morrison had played a very careful hand with Garret Ward for four months, never addressing him, and replying briefly when addressed. He had made up his mind to play fair with Mary, and give her no cause for bias one way or the other. Now he, also, showed his hurt. He pivoted round over the top-rail, and leant forward, hands on knees. His shoulders were twitching, his face drained of colour, and his eyes grey stone.

"Just you try it, Ward!" he invited softly.

Ward's hands slowly clenched themselves, and he turned head in a curiously leisurely way. Robin had a toe on the second rail, ready for launching, and his brows were down over his deep-set stone eyes. There was a queer waiting pause, and, then, Ward's hands slowly unclenched. Somehow I was glad to see that, for I did not want to pile him in double-harness.

"Get going, Garret, or we'll take your hide off!" I said.

He stepped back and laughed quite cheerfully. "Oh, no! you don't! but I'd love you for to try. But not yet! I'll deal with you, Morrison, and you too, Gilly, when the time comes, and it won't be long now." He glanced at Mary's back. "So long, Mary! Sorry your thugs can't take a bit of fun!" And he went striding away in that thigh-swinging, stiff-kneed, splay-footed way he had.

"Nice sense of fun he has!" said Robin grimly. "But he's right in one thing: the time has not yet come, but it won't be long now."

Mary had not said a word, and she had not moved. She sat with her back to us, and looked down at her hands in her lap, and, for the first time, there was a little hopeless droop to her shoulders. Garret Ward had smirched her dream for her. Robin pivoted round on the rail, and sidled closer.

I left the two there comforting each other, and slouched off along the rail and up the slope towards the house. I did not like this new insight into Garret Ward's character. I knew he was lying when he said he would prefer to win Mary fairly. Garret Ward would prefer to have Mary forced into his arms. He had shown a strange obtuseness about the growing friendship between Mary and Robin, but he surely was not ignorant of it. Yes, he knew they were in love, and he had just suggested a plausible scheme whereby Mary might have her cake and eat it. I had read his intentions correctly. He would love to close the net about her, show her an opening, close it again, and finally hold her, a bruised victim to be discarded when the fancy took him. His vice was sadism, the most atrocious of all vices. And he would be my brother-in-law!

II

Logantown Racecourse is finely situated. Behind the paddock and the stands the green-and-brown hills rise up fold on fold; in front, the two-mile oval, within its white rails, spreads its emerald green; and at the far side, beyond the ruddy-toned brick of the Railway Station, the wooded, mansion-dotted countryside slopes up to the craggy grey granite of Culin Head. From the top of the Members' Stand one can see the green northern sea shattering itself to white against the flank of Culin.

A good few of us were up from Gullane to see Benbecula run. My father and Tyzack were somewhere about; and Tyzack, in his quiet way, would be orienting my father away from the Members' Bar; Mary, the business woman, was contacting owners as if her world was wholly secure on her atlas shoulders; Robin was with Dinny,

getting ready in the Jockey Room; Sandy Ythan and
Dan Shea were with Benbecula in the open-fronted line
of saddling boxes under the trees, back of the parade
enclosure; and, finally, Jacus and I were out in the
paddock in front of the tall, checkered number-board;
and Jacus's new check suit was nearly as formidable as
the board. There Sylvia rejoined us after a while. She
had been out front to see what the books were offering
on Benbecula. If Garret Ward was there, and he was,
I did not set eyes on him.

The crowd was a good one, but not a close pack.
Men, intent on horses or in picking winners, moved
constantly about us, paused to talk, and moved on again;
women moved likewise but not so intently. Women, as
a rule, though they gamble readily, don't go to the races
to see horses gallop; but, if you must see a woman at her
best, visit a racecourse, and, if you are interested in
horses, try and forget the women. Not being greatly
interested in racehorses, I observed the women. There
was nothing wrong with them, but not one of them had
anything on our Sylvia, tall and slender in her flowered
dress, parasol over shoulder, her eyes brilliant, and her
lovely hair not quite demure under a little caricature
of a hat with a small high crown. She had hold of
Jacus's arm, and the contrast between her and the
squat, checkered, blue-jawed man made men stare
and women smile. Sylvia didn't care; she was debonair
to-day.

Horse-racing did not interest me, but I admit that I
was interested in that race to the point where one's heart
sometimes comes up into one's throat, and sometimes
sinks into one's stomach. Even my voice was not too
steady as I enquired carelessly:

"How are things?"

"Benbecula opened at sixes," said Sylvia cheerfully.

"Sixes!" squeaked Jacus painfully. "Sixes! on a bastar' that hasn't a chance in hell!"

"Only a feeler!" said Sylvia confidently. "As soon as the favourite shows in the money Ben will go out to tens —or worse. Damn Mary! She's too conservative——"

"Stop it!" I snapped.

"But look, Gill! She insists she'll put our money on as soon as the price touches sevens." Sylvia was disgusted. "Blow! I'll have a bet of my own at tens."

"Safer at sixes!" I said. I knew the fear I had.

"I wouldn't move a hand towards me hip till I saw twenties chalked on the board," said Jacus valiantly.

Let me say here that I had fallen for Mary's castle in Spain. We all had. I had sold a field of standing wheat; Mary had sold her trick jumper; Robin, swallowing his Highland pride, wrote a brother in Moidart, who promptly replied with a cheque for a hundred, as a Highland brother would; we even allowed Sylvia in with fifty. After scraping the bottom of the pot we put five hundred pounds in Mary's hands to gamble with, her heart on the board. And if Mary had put it on at——! But what's the use in talking?

Jacus rammed his brown bowler firmly on the back of his poll, and looked up truculently at the number-board.

"Wan—two—three—are they all running, in God's name?" he wanted to know.

"Don't think that Providence has anything to do with an apprentice race!" I said.

"One to fifteen—six and ten non-starters—thirteen in the field," Sylvia informed him.

"Jacus! an' that's an unlucky number! No. 7, D. Lane! There he is stuck in the middle, and there he'll be first and last. What chance has he amongst a pack o' weasels. Ay! No. 7, D. Lane!" He was as proud as

Punch to see his nephew's name up there in the public eye.

"Devil a chance he has!" I agreed with him, to his chagrin.

"Jacus! he has a small chance anyway!" he protested, and looked at his card. "Benbecula, eight-seven—he'll be loaded with a ton o' lead!"

"Twelve pounds of it," I amended.

Sylvia tugged at his arm. "Let's have a look at Ben," she suggested, and we threaded our way up over the green September grass.

Sandy Ythan and Dan Shea were saddling Benbecula in one of the open-fronted boxes. Jacus moved hurriedly, hopped from one foot to the other, and was petulantly authoritative.

"Jacus alive! Are your fingers all thumbs, Dan Shea? Take it in wan more hole. Wan, I said! Are you for cuttin' the crathur in two halves? Let me feel that girth. It will do—barely—and, if the saddle slips, I'll have a thing or two to say before and after wakin' Dinny Lane. An' where the hell is Dinny Lane?"

"Bawlin' his head off on the road back to Gullane, I would say," Dan Shea said derisively.

Ythan took no least notice of Jacus. He patted the horse's shoulder.

"Lead him out, Dan! Easy, boy, easy! Our hopes are on you, and our shirts forbye."

Sylvia was again tugging Jacus. "Let's see how he compares in the enclosure," she said.

Eight or ten horses were already being led round the long oval of the clay track: some sedate, some nervous, some skittish. Benbecula was there, and he was one of the sedate ones; he was used to crowds from his show-ground experience, and was looking around him with quiet curiosity. He was as good-looking as anything there, taller than any, and with better shoulders and thrust than most. Perhaps he was a little too sleek, as if short of a week's preparation. On the yellow horse-cloth I saw the red monogram of our once-famous stable: CMG—Morris of Castle Gillian.

The rail of the enclosure was lined by observers, and we moved along looking over shoulders; and I kept an ear open for passing remarks. Many of them were about the tall young horse that took the eye. *No. 7—good-looking black! No, brown gelding! On the tall side, more of a hurdler I'd say. Benbecula? never heard of him! Ah—Black-thorn blood—a young lepper out for a gallop, I suppose! Five, rising six—and never raced—what's wrong with him? Trainer-owner Gillian Morris—the Gullane stables begad!—coming again they say! Who is the apprentice? D. Lane—never heard of him either—a stable-lad! Walton is the lad with the hands in this bevy—and the mount too! Come and see what the books are doing!*

There was a stir amongst the crowd. The jockeys, in ones and twos, were trickling across from the weigh-room: slim young runts, most of them, but one or two stockily undersized. Dinny was walking at Robin's side, and Robin was talking down at him easily. Dinny was pale under his tan, but his mouth was all right. His black curls were tucked away under his tight-fitting, peaked cap, and he looked a neat, light-legged, mature little man in our famous old colour: white, green square back and front, green collar and cuffs, green cap.

My father was in the enclosure now. Dinny ducked under the rail and went to him; and my father put a hand over Dinny's shoulder.

Sylvia was again hauling Jacus and me along. "Come down to the side-gate and give Dinny a cheer."

Jacus protested. "Jacus, girl! 'tis unlucky to encounter a woman on the way to the post."

"That's a red-haired woman. Come along!"

We went. After a time the horses came leisurely, led by grooms. Sometimes a trainer or owner walked beside to give the final word. Sandy Ythan was leading Benbecula, and Dinny was squatted neatly, well up on the withers. My father was walking by one of Dinny's knees, and Robin Morrison by the other. There was a fine deep note in Sylvia's voice:

"Fine man yourself, Dinny Lane! This is your very own day."

"Thank you, Miss Syl!" Dinny's voice was thin, and his smile wan. Luckily he did not know what was depending on him, or he might have fallen out of the saddle.

The horse paused in the gate, and my father touched Dinny's knee. His voice was easy-going: "Only a trial gallop, young fellow, but win if you can! Sit still, and edge out to the top curve I showed you this morning; come wide into the straight, and ride him right out with your hands, first or last—we want to know." That was keeping Dinny out of all danger, and giving him a chance to show his style in a long run-in.

Jacus and I were chattels in Sylvia's hands; she was sweeping us along again. "Hurry now! I should get tens."

If I were writing a romantic story I would, of course, make this the climax. I would have subtly and gradually drawn the interest about Benbecula and directed it surely to this race for three hundred pounds, and a cup, and a couple of hearts, and an eternal soul, and an old house, and a way of living, and quite a lot of things. I wonder does a thing like that ever happen in real life. Why not? I once knew a man who borrowed a ten-pound Bank of England to go to a race-meeting, put it on one horse at tens, and found that he had won ten thousand pounds. The note was a thousand-pound one.

Nothing like that happened at Logantown. Let me say that at once, and then say that quite a lot happened.

We went through the arch by the weigh-room, and round the corner to the Members' Enclosure in front of the long red-and-white stand. A band was playing on the lawn, and waves of sound filled the sky; and the ocean of sound was punctuated by the loud clear or husky voices of the ring book-makers lining the rails on our left.

"Three to one the field! Three to one bar one."

And the extraordinary thing was that the horse barred threes was our Benbecula.

No one knows all the reasons why a horse is made favourite in a race. In this case it might be subtle rumour gradually swollen to certainty: *Whisper! Benbecula is a dark horse brought from the south and specially prepared for this race, and isn't his apprentice specially trained to ride him? and is not his owner and trainer here on the course?— and that man has not been seen on a course for years; and is not the stable beginning to come out of the doldrums? Get your money on while the going is good!*

There was a press of punters on the rails; bets were being made on the nod; many hands reached soiled notes; and the odds against Benbecula kept dropping point by point. There had been sixes to begin with; now the figures were six to four; a little later one could not get better than evens. And Mary had not put her money on at sixes, and that was the end of that!

And yet odds of six to four against an untried horse in an open field were ridiculous. No mere rumours should have brought the odds down to that. There was a nigger in the wood-pile, and I knew who that nigger was. Enough said! But someone was piling the odds for a day of reckoning.

We found Mary and Robin standing on a seat at the front of the lawn, close to the rails. They were shoulder to shoulder, and Robin was carrying things off in one of his devil-may-care moods. He was making Mary laugh, but, when she stopped laughing, her mouth and her brows went in straight bars. She smiled down gallantly at us.

"Six to four was the best I could get, Syl," she said frankly.

"And good enough for a nest-egg!" cried Syl. "Who's downhearted?"

"That's the spirit!" said Robin. "Aren't we here to see Benbecula race, and Dinny Lane on top of him?"

"Win, lose or draw, and the divil take the hindmost!" cried Jacus. "Give me a hand-up, young woman!"

Mary hauled Jacus up beside her, and Sylvia hopped neatly up beside Jacus. There was no room for me on the seat, so I stood at the rails in front and a little to the side of Sylvia. I could see only the start and finish of that race, but I saw plenty of it through Jacus's eyes— and Mary's too. My father and Tyzack Lane were on top of the stand somewhere.

The dominant feeling I had then was relief. The tension slacked. I think that deep down we were all relieved, and a little ashamed too. We could win still, but we could no longer win enough to save Castle Gillian, and, *by the Lord! it was better so. Save Castle Gillian on a horse-race! Foil Garret Ward on a horse-race! That was a solution so cheap as not to be worth contemplation. Hell! but we had contemplated it? Very well! If there was no other solution let us go down the drain!* That is how I felt.

The thirteen starters had paraded before the Judges' box, and now cantered by in a loose string for the starting gate at the other side of the course. Benbecula strode along low and smoothly, head well in and legs well under him; and Dinny stood up in the stirrups and sat down again.

"Be aisy, ladeen! or you'll go over his ears," said Jacus in a small voice.

The band had stopped playing; the susurrus of sound was of a lower pitch; the book-makers were still offering and still taking bets:

"Four to one the field! Four to one bar one! Four to six Benbecula!" Some of the bookies pronounced it Benbeckyoola.

"Six to four on!" That was buying money in an apprentice race, where whips are not allowed, and anything may happen.

The mile at Logantown is a half-oval, with the home-side flattened to make a long straight. Just beyond the Station, against the trees lining the railway, I could see a medley of colours milling about, but could not pick out any individual horse or rider. Jacus's voice lifted appealingly.

"Holy Jacus! is that Benbecula makin' circles?"

I glanced back and up. Sylvia's mouth was clenched and pale, and I could see the flowered dress quivering over her knees; and her parasol was on the ground as usual; Robin's eyes were slitted, and his jaw ridged; Mary had her old scuffled racing glasses up and steady, and her voice was soothing Jacus.

"Give the lads time, Uncle! They are not yet under orders."

"Orders! and what the bloody wars is the starter doin'?"

"His job—walking up and down in front to give them confidence. Now they're straightened out! No! Darn you No. 5! Get round, Dinny!"

Jacus, used to wide horizons, had keener sight than I had. He screeched: "'Tisn't with your backside you're startin', Dinny Lane!"

"Not his fault," Mary said. "No. 5 is interfering."

"No. 5 is it? I'll get Dinny to belt that lad if he has a neck left."

"In line again, and walking to the wire," Mary murmured. "Under orders—there's the white flag! Steady! he has them! No! No. 5 is switching places. Steady! Now! Now! They're off! One left four lengths!"

I could see the burst from the wire, and I could see the horse left; and my heart leaped to drop plumb into the pit of my stomach, for the colours were something in green-and-white. Jacus's voice was acutely dolorous.

"My poor little Dinny! an' that's the end of him!"

"Shut up!" said Mary shortly. "That's five! Dinny is in the bunch with the leaders."

"Ten year o' me life down the drain!" said Jacus, "but sure I had me time."

I could see the bunch too, and green-and-white in the heart of it. Jacus bestirred himself.

"In the bunch, be Jacus! An' there he'll stick like a wren in a sally bush!"

I couldn't see the horses now for the crowd along the rails. I turned round and looked up at the others. Sylvia was breathing hard through her nose, and one hand was patting below her breasts keeping time to her heart; Mary's mouth was austere, and the eye-pieces of her glasses were reflecting yellow rings on her cheeks; Robin, however, was inclined to smile, and his jaw was no longer clamped; and Jacus's mouth was open and his eyes staring.

"It is rather a pack!" murmured Mary doubtfully through her teeth, and then her cheeks crinkled. "That's the lad, Dinny! Never mind a length or two, get out from under! Good boy! lying fifth, I think!"

"Hoo!" breathed Jacus. "Fifth an' losing ground. That brown bastar' is only fit for donkey races."

Mary was getting excited now. "It's a race! There's the top swing, and Benbecula coming wide but clear. Sit down on him, Dinny! You're a horseman! Sit down, lad!"

"I see him now," roared Jacus. "Wide is it? Wide! Round be the mountains he's comin'. Jacus! he's paralysed in the saddle."

And there the calm Scot, that was Robin Morrison, surprised us. He threw his clenched hands in the air, opened his mouth, and loosed a colossal volume of sound. The crowd were already shouting home a leader that was not Benbecula, but Robin's stentorian bellow drowned all other sounds. My spine tingled.

"Now then, Dinny! Now then, my bonny lad! Your hands! Your hands! Your hands!" And Robin kept swaying his hands in time to Dinny sweeping down the last furlong. I turned round.

I could see Dinny now, flitting like a bead on a string above the heads of the crowd. He was like a taut bent bow, perfectly balanced, and his hands were moving with extraordinary force and rhythm; and he was with the leaders. Jacus was shouting anguishedly:

"Is he up? He is—he isn't! Is that his nose? It isn't—it is! Daylight, and his tail to them, be Jacus! Up the middle an' down again! Up the men o' the Lanes! up the Gullane Glen! Two lengths—ten lengths —a hundred thousan' bloody million lengths! Hurroo!"

We were all shouting now—roaring—drowning all other sounds—bringing Benbecula home away out in front, and going like a steam-engine. The tears of excitement were running down Sylvia's cheeks. Jacus quieted suddenly and turned to Mary. His voice was piteous in its appeal.

"Was we in it, Miss Mary? Was it us at all?"

"By a street, Jacus! By a whole street!" She had dropped her glasses on her breast, and her arm was impulsively round Robin's shoulder.

Jacus straightened up, and hammered his chest resoundingly. His tenor carried far and wide.

"Be a street! Be two streets! Look at us now! Showmen o' the road? Never no more! Mr Robin Morrison, Esquire, and Co. gintleman owner, and Dionuusius Lane, leadin' jock! That's us! Huroosh!"

His hat went up in the air, he leaped six inches, and started to fall off the seat, his shoulder thrusting against Sylvia. And Sylvia came down in a flying disarray of arms, legs, and flowered dress. I caught her before she fell, and her arms tightened round me, her eyes blazing into mine, and her voice deep. "Gosh, Gill! We pulled it off!"

I loosed one arm, and wiped her cheek with the heel of my fist: "Unhand me, crybaby!" I said.

She shoved me off. "Three ribs gone, you gorilla!" She wrinkled her nose at me, "but 'twas worth it." What was?

Mary, Robin, and Jacus were in a heap. Jacus tottering had grasped at Mary, and Mary had tightened her arm on Robin, and Robin, having no anchor, used his strength and activity to get them all done in an easy tangle, Jacus underneath. Mary's fine hair was blowing over Robin's face. I untangled them on to their feet. Jacus groaned realistically and felt his middle.

"Me livers and lights in porridge! But sure what harm?" He looked at the other two suspiciously. "That was a quare sound I thought I heard. I mind hearing it once in me young days. I was kissin' a girl at the time."

The blood was in Mary's face, and she was busy with the ribbon in her hair. Robin was as calm as a post, but I noted the expression on his face. If I ever see a cat with that expression I'll investigate the cream jug.

The friendly racing people were laughing round us, with us and at us. We didn't mind. We had failed to save Castle Gillian, but we had won a race, and Benbecula and Dinny had proved themselves. Nothing else counted then. Still a horse unsaleable five months ago was now valuable. The stake was only three hundred and our winnings six or seven, figures immensely short of Mary's needs; but still the day was a notable one—and to hell with Kismet.

Mary led Benbecula in, and Robin walked at her side.

We made a night of it too. We had dinner together in the best restaurant in town, and had some good claret, that Jacus swore by his god was malt vinegar. Thereafter, my father, Tyzack, Dinny and the girls went to a show out of harm's way. We promised to follow them up in a minute, in a short while, in no time at all. As Ythan said, we'd ha'e the a'e sweetener in the Palace Bar. We had, but that first sweetener was not quite sweet enough.

We made a night of it. Robin, Sandy, Dan Shea, Jacus and I did what is known as a pub-crawl, and we got thoroughly lit up. We made speeches to each other, and mapped the career of horse and rider; we sang songs against all the rules of licensed vintners; and finally we got thrown out, but not in anger.

Mary and Sylvia ran us to ground in my room at two in the morning, and I lost a fistful of hair to Sylvia, for she blamed me for sending her to a tame show away from the fun. But we had some more fun. Jacus unexpectedly discovered, in his tail coat, a bottle of Paddy whiskey and one of sherry, and was, of course, accused of practising the chicken-stealer's art. The ladies, be Jacus! would drink the wan toast! To Benbecula! And wasn't there Dinny Lane too? There was. And wasn't the night young? It was.

Robin sang; Dan Shea gave us a "comeall-you"; the girls sang, and Sylvia brought down a flake from the ceiling; Jacus made a speech; and I had a few remarks to make. Robin stopped me with a pillow in ten minutes. And then Robin, dignified as a Highland chief, made a speech for and on behalf of the two ladies, and I stopped him with a pillow in fifteen minutes; and thereafter he recited "John o' Lorn" in manly sorrow for himself. And Mary hid her face.

> "But never more the heather nor the bracken at my knees,
> I am poor John o' Lorn, a broken man ;
> For an old Highland story I must sail the swinging seas,
> A chief without a castle or a clan!"

A long-suffering management requested us to leave at four in the morning. So, in a red September dawn, we set out for Gullane Glen in Sylvia's car and Robin's horse-box. And we were still singing.

It was our last fling, we thought, and we had no regrets.

Chapter XI

THE BEGINNING OF THE END

I

THINGS happened quickly at the end, and I was in the dark as to a good deal that happened right up to that very end. I knew then surely, for I was in it up to the neck.

The harvest was about over. The hay was in shed, the corn in stack, and, once we had the potatoes lifted, our winter stores were secure—for whom I was not yet sure!

Things began to happen on the last Tuesday of September. That was in the evening after dusk. I didn't know where Robin and Mary were, but Garret Ward had come earlier in his car, and was in the house with my father. He was in there for so long a time that I decided to do some prospecting.

I found my father and Ward in the gun-room, and both had been drinking; and that was unusual for Ward. He leant wide shoulders against the chipped marble mantelpiece, and near one shoulder was an empty glass and a water-jug. There was a fire of peat and green ash blazing brightly in the depth of the steel grate, and his stout, breeched legs were outlined against the glow.

My father was sitting aside in his carver's chair at the head of the table, an elbow on the board; he was facing the door, his profile turned to Ward. Near his hand, the empty Waterford decanter, slightly asymmetrical, squatted on a big, legal-looking document. I knew what that document was. Close by was the broken butt of a fishing-rod.

"Want a drink, Gillian?" my father said as I came in.

His husky voice was slurring a little, but he did not show any other signs of being drunk. He never did.

I shook my head, sat with a thigh over the side of the table, and looked at Garret Ward. He grinned at me. It was the light from the hanging brass lamp shining in his unfocussed black eyes that told me he had drink taken.

My father picked up the broken butt and hammered the hard-rubber end of it on the misused mahogany. Old Timmy at once shuffled in, as if he had been waiting close outside the door. He had a half-full decanter of pale whiskey hanging from one hand, and, as usual, he was grumbling away to himself.

"This is the last dropeen in the house, an' anyone that likes can squeeze the jar." That was an oft-told lie, as my father knew.

"I told you 'phone Maney's to-day?" my father said.

"An' didn't I? It'll be here to-morrow." He picked up the empty decanter, placed the half-full one carefully in its place, and stabbed it with a forefinger. "Make kitchen o' that! Divil the drop more anyone'll get this holy and blasted night."

My father gestured a loose hand. "One for the road, Garret?"

"No, please! I'm driving." He shook his massive head. "Not my vice, you know!"

Timmy turned from the door, his voice casual. "Sure every san of a bitch knows Garret Ward's vice!"

Timmy was wrong. Woman was not Ward's vice.

"Not any more, you old devil!" said Garret Ward amiably. "I'm all for being a happy Benedick now."

"Saint Benedict! no dam' fearo! 'Tisn't in your marra, or your father's before you. But how do I know? Some of them ould divils of saints was gay bucks while they had their strength. Be jabers! they had it comin'

234

and goin'. I would myself." Timmy shut the door behind him.

The decanter neck click-clicked the rim of the glass as my father poured a half-tumblerful. By that I knew he was near his plimsoll mark. He gestured away the water-jug that Garret reached him, put the decanter to one side, gulped deeply, and placed his long lean hand on the legal-looking document.

"This is it at last, Gillian!" he said evenly, "the thing that Mary has been holding off for so long."

"I gave her all the time there was," said Garret Ward. "That's right, Gilly! In three days Padderson must have his three thousand, and that document is the answer."

"When executed," added my father.

"If it isn't——" The sweep of Ward's hand told us what would happen. "I have sold Monaglass, and the cash is ready."

"I know, Garret." My father pulled the document towards him and opened a folio. "Look, Gillian?" I went round to his side, and looked where his finger traced a line: "A name inserted there"—he turned a folio—"and my signature there before a Commissioner for Oaths, and someone owns a controlling share of all Castle Gillian." He tapped the paper. "It has to be done. A name must be inserted, and one name I do not want."

"Yes, Uncle!" said Garret Ward. "I know you have been doing your damnedest to find another partner—and I wonder why?"

"No you don't, you rogue!" said my father genially. "Begad, Garret! I'd love to double-cross you the last minute."

"Keep on trying, Uncle!" and then some of his basic character came to the surface. "Who will partner Gillian Morris in a broken-down stables?"

I suppose I should have jumped him then, and taken my licking. But what was the good? I said:

"You say the thing has to be done, Father?"

"Or we lose Castle Gillian."

"You have consulted Mary finally?"

"I shall. The decision is hers."

"Where is Mary?" Ward put quickly.

"Around with Robin somewhere," I said, I fear, a little spitefully.

"Our broken-down gent—among the other broken-downs! The moth and the candle—eh? Ah well! in three days' time the whole showman brood gets kicked out of here."

"Don't tempt us too far, Garret!" I said softly, and took a step towards the door.

"Wait, Gillian!" my father called, and I turned. He looked at me; his eyes were focussing intently and one hand was rubbing his bush of hair desperately. For the first time I saw his fatalist calm broken. "You will have sense, my son," he said sternly. He struck the document with his fist and his whiskey splashed. "I will deal with this now—and later—and the decision is not your sister's. If I sign this, at least there is the chance that her son will own all of Castle Gillian."

"I hope so," said Garret Ward firmly.

My father's mood changed. He turned his head whimsically to look at Ward.

"There's a certain risk, Garret. I wonder what sort of hellion your son would be?"

Ward straightened from the mantelpiece, and his voice rasped.

"No worse than your father's son, Gillian Morris."

"I asked for that," said my father equably.

"And you'll get more. Would you like my son to be like your son, Gilly without guts?"

236

My father leant to him. "You are an obtuse fool, Garret. My son warned you just now, and you had better take heed. Listen, Garret! I hope Mary marries you soon, and has a son, so that I can break your neck to save Gillian doing it——!"

II

It was at that juncture that Mary came in. This evening she had not changed her jodhpurs for a skirt; and she looked tired and depressed. Her resilient spirit had failed her at the end, and my father saw that. He tossed off his drink, and rose to his feet; and there was in him a resolution that conquered alcohol.

Mary said spiritlessly: "Have you finished this business?"

"Yes, Mary." He pointed to the table, and his voice did not slur. "There is a blank deed of transfers. To-morrow I go up to town to execute it. That is my final decision. Good night!"

I opened the door for him, and he walked out as if on a chalked line. For the first time, that I could remember, he had left his decanter behind him.

I stood at the door and looked at Mary. I think she was relieved that the final decision had come so abruptly, and from her father. She was leaning over listlessly, and reading the deed, but without interest.

"It means such a lot, but it is very easily done, isn't it?" she said tonelessly.

Garret Ward was at her side, a hand lightly on her shoulder; and, with his free hand, he pushed the paper away from her.

"No need for that dam' thing at all!" he said strongly. "Mary, promise to marry me, and I'll ask for no more."

I knew exactly what was in his mind. He wanted Mary. He must have Mary. But he was no longer sure

237

that he could win her or conquer her in a year. Get her to promise now, pay off Padderson, and then she would never break her word. My mouth was open to warn her, but she forestalled me.

She leant forward before his hand could tighten, drew the document back and shook her head wearily but negatively. "No, Garret! I will have this deed."

I shut the door behind me, and left them to wrangle it out.

I went through the baize door into the big, echoing, unlighted hall. Timmy was aye forgetting to light the hall lanthorn, and had a hellish habit of moving the big bronze pots here and there. Usually I moved carefully in that dark cavern, but to-night I did not, and in half a dozen strides stubbed my toe against a pot. I did not hesitate for an instant, but at once kicked that vase in collision after collision clear across the hall; and the brazen clangour was nearly enough to bring the ceiling down. The glimmer from the windows at the front showed me where the door was, and I shuffle-footed that way.

Timmy's voice from the baize door made prayer to high heaven:

"Jesus, Mary, and Joseph! Is anyone kilt?"

"Come on over, and there will be," I invited. "You inveterate old son of a blunderbuss!"

"I'll complain you to Miss Mary for misapplied langwidge!" Timmy threatened.

"Complaint noted!" said the voice of Mary behind him. "Mind your temper, Gillian!"

"Go to—glory!" I shouted, and opened the front door. I left it open behind me. That kicked pot had served its purpose: it brought Mary out of the gun-room; and the open door would not have her fumbling in the dark in the vicinity of Garret Ward.

It was not quite dark outside, and I could see Ward's car like a squat beast on the gravel. The sky was overcast, but there was a moon somewhere, and there was enough light to show the black bulk of Castle Evan hill. I could not make out the house itself, for none of the dormer windows were lighted. I sat down against the wall by a pilaster well away from the door. That was not my usual seat, but I did not want Garret Ward walking over me, and I wanted to stay near at hand.

The night was fresh but not cold, and a fitful breeze, blowing up from the river, brought the remote, sighing sound from the long slide in slow pulses. That was the only sound until, suddenly, the night shivered to the hysterical cry of an alarmed cock pheasant. That cry came across the water from one of Uncle Tom's stocked coverts. *A fox—two-legged or four!* I said.

Mary did not stay long in the house with Garret Ward. She came out on the porch, and he was close behind her. They did not see me sitting low against the wall, but I could see them clearly against the sky where they faced each other at the head of the steps. They were at the end of their wrangle.

"You will not give me an answer, then?" he put, patiently impatient.

"Not for a year—and not then if——"

"Don't say it, Mary!" I heard him draw in a long breath, and he held it while he spoke tightly. "All right! I'll not press you any more—now. Good night—partner!"

He reached her his hand and she took it slowly. Probably in her spiritless mood she let herself be drawn, for, next instant, she was in his arms, and he was kissing her, holding her tight and trying to draw response. But he must have felt the slackness of her, the absence of any stir of emotion; for he held her away from him, and shook her angrily.

"Don't you see, girl?" he said throatily. "You will be compelled to marry me!"

"A fly in amber, Garret! but not yet. Please let me go?" Her voice was cool and toneless.

I drew my feet up, but he released her without another word, and she went into the house a little uncertain on her feet. He made no move to follow her. He struck his palms together, and his low rumble of a voice had chagrin and gloat in it:

"Blast! I nearly had her that time—but I'm not rushing my fences!" He went down the steps to his car; and for a moment I wondered if I could not kill him with my bare hands down there on the gravel.

The door of the car banged, the self-starter purred, the engine roared, and the lights went on. And there, coming up the drive, in the splaying path of the lights, was Robin Morrison. The engine slowed to a soft purr, the roof-light went on, and the near window came down. I could see Garret Ward leaning aside, and his black head in the opening. His deep voice commanded:

"A word with you, Mister Showman!"

Robin's pace never varied. I think he was going to pass by the car without stopping, but Ward spoke again:

"I am giving you notice now, Morrison!"

Robin pivoted on his heel, and his restraint went. No doubt he knew what was in the wind, and that his truce with himself was no longer needed.

"Go to hell, you and your notice!" he said, contempt in his voice.

Ward kept his control for the moment. "Listen, you scum! Day after to-morrow I am in control. If I find you here then I'll kick you straight into hell."

Morrison's voice grated. "Why don't you come out and try some kicking now?"

The head was withdrawn, and the door was opening.

Yes, this was as good a time as any. I was on my feet, a red spark flicked across my sight, and I took the steps in a bound. I wonder what would have happened if I had not shouted.

"Come on, Robin! Let's show the dog before it's too late!"

The door wavered and banged forcefully, and the engine roared again. I had my hand on the handle when Robin slung a strong arm round my chest and jerked me away. He had heard something in my voice that made him take a clove pitch on himself.

"No—no! Gillian!" he cried, and his arm tightened.

I strained only for a moment. The wheels spurted the gravel, and the car jerked off, gathering momentum down the drive. Robin released me, and spoke quietly.

"Come on up to the Rookery. I want to talk to you!"

I caught his sleeve as he moved. "Talk—talk—talk!" I mocked him. "All the talking has been done long ago. Now it's action."

"You mean——?"

"I mean that Garret Ward spoke a mouthful. I mean that my father is going up to town to-morrow to execute a deed of transfer. I mean that Garret Ward will be in control here, and you out on your ear—whoever does the kicking. That is what I mean!"

"And your language is plain." He drew his arm away. "And Mary——?"

"Ay, Mary! You are in love with her, aren't you?"

"From the first hour," he answered quietly.

"And she is in love with you, and what are ye going to do about it? Will you let her stay here under Ward's hands for a year? Will you?"

His voice did not change. "You were right, Gillian! We must do something. And it is not too late yet."

A voice harshly stern spoke across from the porch:
"Will you boys stop that nonsense?"

That was Mary. She had lit the hall lanthorn, and the dim glow of it through the open door outlined her long legs at the head of the steps. Robin walked straight across and up to her. I stood at the foot of the steps and looked up at them; and I was in the mood to force my will on theirs. She put a confident hand on his shoulder, but he made no move to draw her close. She said gently:

"The good days are over, Robin!"

"How do I know?" he said steadily.

"They were good days—you found them good days, didn't you, Robin?" She was softly persuasive.

"They were good days, Mary," Robin said.

"Blast you, Robin!" I cried. "Don't let her grow sentimental on us—she's in the mood for sacrifice."

"Don't mind Gill!" Mary pleaded. "Robin dear, don't let him or you spoil our memories by a mad act."

"Wait, Mary!" He would not promise her anything. "You are signing on for a year; have you any feeling at all for Garret Ward?"

"Fear only; he has a devil in him." She gave way then. "Oh, Robin! I've lost my nerve. I—I don't seem to care what happens to me."

Her head was against his shoulder, and his arm was around her, and she was whimpering heart-brokenly. I flared up at them:

"It's up to you now, Morrison! Leave it to her, and she goes drifting! Take her away! She won't go? Abduct her, blast you! Take her away in your horse-box!" I was shouting. "Take her right away! Seduce her, if you have to, and make her marry you!"

And there I left them, turning on my heel, and forging away into the dark of the drive.

It was dark enough under the trees, but I could see the sky, like an upside-down avenue, between the double line of foliage, and so was able to keep the middle of the road. The early fallen leaves whispered about my feet, and the rustle of air in the branches had the sere, dry rasp of the fall.

In half a mile I came out on the county road through our main gateway. The massive, crested, granite gate-posts were indestructible, but the old rusted gates were sagging open, and the gate lodge was empty and falling into ruin. *Garret Ward will see to that*, I thought, *and, lacking Mary—or holding Mary—keep a kept-woman in the lodge.*

I turned down the hill towards the Gullane, but I didn't cross the bridge. Instead, I stopped to lean over the wing parapet on our side. There in its sheltered nook within sound of running water was Tyzack Lane's camp, the fitful air blowing about it, and making a small resonant boom under the arch of the bridge. There was a red-curtained glow in the high-set, small window of the old van; Sloper Jones would be in there, and, possibly, Jacus. There was a brighter pink glow in the arched window of the modern palace van that was Oonagh Blake's domain. *I bet a hat they're drinking tea*, I said as I slid down the grassy slope.

They were drinking tea.

"God save all here!' I greeted, and shoved the door shut with my shoulder.

"And you too, Gillian," greeted back Oonagh. "You're in time for a cup." She was presiding at a round table.

It was cosy and homelike inside that van, and there was plenty of space economically used. It was a cultured woman's small room, pinkish in tone, and the hooded petrol lamp shone softly on white napery, flowered china and polished silver.

"Be Jacus! he can follow his nose this fellow!" said Jacus. His hat was off, as it must be in his queen's parlour, and his bald dome gave him a queer look of truculent benevolence.

Sylvia Gayne, in slacks, was sitting cross-legged on a cushion on the carpet, a saucer balanced on her knee. A fragment of lichen was adhering to the flat heel of one of her shoes, and I knew where she had picked that up. She looked at me intently and kept on looking, and when she spoke her voice was soft and deep:

"What is troubling you, Gillian?"

"It will keep—I want some tea," I said.

Tyzack was watching me too, but said nothing. He moved a book and tapped the cushioned flap-bench at his side. I sat down by him, and found that I was weary for no reason. I needed the tea, for my mouth was dry and my throat harsh. I suppose that was due to the adrenalin that had drained into my blood.

I drank my first cup too quickly, and nearly burned my tongue off. I sipped the second. No, I wouldn't have a biscuit, thanks! Had I any news? I would get round to it my own way. I said, leaning aside:

"Jacus McGrath! let me see your shoes?"

"Jacus no! I want 'em for myself," and he thrust his feet back under the bench opposite.

Sylvia said "Damn!" startledly, and, when I looked, the scrap of lichen had gone from her shoe-heel.

"There are two people here without any discretion, Oonagh Blake," I said.

"Tyzack and myself? yes, Gill!"

"No! you two would know that a cock-pheasant does not go to sleep on a bough till black dark."

"Wait there! Wait there!" yelped Jacus. "Who are you referring to, me dear man?"

"Put on your hat and see if it fits," I said.

"Holy Jacus! was I outside the door this blasted night —barrin' for a minute? Was I, Ty Lane?"

"Oonagh would know," said Tyzack cagily.

"A minute—not less," said Oonagh oracularly.

"And where would the poor old cripple be?" said Sylvia. "Wasn't he with me for that minute?"

"And there's two sound witnesses for you, me hayro!" cried Jacus, "but less of the cripple, all the same!"

I put a hand on Tyzack's arm, and leant across him to Oonagh. "No more pheasants out of Uncle Tom's coverts, Oonagh!" I said. "No more of Mary's chickens rambling off to lose themselves!"

"Has it come to that, Gillian?" Oonagh understood.

"It has, Oonagh. I promised to let you know when the crisis came. It came this evening. Garret Ward has sold Monaglass, and his money is on the board; and my father is signing a deed of transfer day after to-morrow. That's all."

"Oh, dear! Oh, dear!" cried Sylvia grievedly. "Tell us all that happened, Gillian."

I told them, as I had always told them, and Sylvia, from the beginning, emphasised the high lights.

"Monaglass is sold—that's sure?"

"And cash in hand—he said so."

"And Uncle Gillian going to town to-morrow?"

"He is," I said patiently.

"To make the transfer?"

"What else? The deed—I saw it—only needs name and signature."

"And the whole showman brood kicked out of here— Robin and all?"

"If they don't go to-morrow, they will be ordered off next day."

"And he mocked drunken Gillian Morris, who could not find a partner?"

"Not forgetting his son, Gilly without guts. Blast it, girl! Stop that!"

"Blast yourself!" she flared. "Why did you not drive the words down his gullet?"

"Very well, Syl!" I said. "I will do more than that to him."

It might be my voice, or jaw, or eyes that showed her the savagery in my mind. She was on her feet and over me almost in one movement. But she was not angry any more. She had me by the shoulder, her eyes close to mine as if to make sure, and her voice hurt me.

"No—no—no, Gillian!" She shook me, but not roughly. "You will not! You must not! Oh God! what am I going to do? What am I going to do at all?" She turned from me to Tyzack. "Can you stop him Tyzack? I can't move him any more."

Tyzack was on his feet, his hand out. "I can, my dear, and you are coming home with me," he said firmly.

She gave him her hand like a child. "I am going home to my father," she said in a small voice.

She did not look at me again, but went out ahead of Tyzack. From the door Tyzack turned and gave Jacus a double-sign, using both hands. I knew some of their sign language, but that double sign I did not know.

I sat on, leaning back against the side of the van, hands in pockets, and head on chest. I had no more to say, and it was easy to sit talkless with these two people who understood the black dog that was on me. Oonagh took up some knitting, and softly crooned a soothing old Galway song. Jacus got up and put on his hat, and looked at me, plain truculent; then took off his hat and sat down again, his blue jowl propped on his fist. After a while I realised that he was waiting on me, and I got on my feet.

"*Oidhce mhaith!* Good night, and sorry for troubling!" I said.

"Good night, Gillian dear!" said Oonagh, her voice lifting and falling softly. "Tyzack will see you later, and you will take it easy till you see the end of the road."

I thought I was seeing the end of the road then, and I was not going to take it easy.

IV

Jacus went out with me, and up to the road, and along it. He put his hand on my arm.

"The ould feet are not so good in the dark," he lied. He could drift through a wood in the dark safely as an owl. I had often noted that in the night, alone with me on some ploy, Jacus had another self, a quiet self, his real under-self. Even his voice lost its turbulent note. He talked quietly to me now, and I said nothing, but I thought: *That was what Tyzack's sign meant: see mad Gillian home, and talk his mood out!*

He told me things about himself, and he was not boastful: about the foolish bits of mistakes he had made in haste: and about the one terrible mistake (his secret and, now, mine) he had made, and need not have made if he had waited another—one other day. He was pointing a moral. "I was never the same man again after that; I was no man at all, till my brother took hold o' me— but 'tis only an imitation man I am after all!"

"Heart o' corn only!" I said.

"Och! wishan-wishan! But why didn't I make sure first? That's the way: make dead-sure beforehand, and, then, maybe nothin' is called for. Jacus! here I

247

am at your own door with all your talking! Good night, son!"

"I'll make dead-sure Jacus," I told him. "Will I convey you back the road a bit?"

He chuckled. "Back and fore all night like the two brothers in the drunk story. Go to your bed, boy!"

I went along by the wall to the arch leading to the Man's Room. At the mouth of it I looked back. The front door was still open, and the dim lanthorn light splayed out and cast faint shadows of the pillars. Jacus was standing at the foot of the steps, and as I looked, he mounted them and went in at the door.

But I did not go to bed that night. I did what I had done once or twice before. I sought the hollows of the hills, and let the waves of desolation roll over me. I lay on my back amongst the furze, and their dry flavour was all about me. And I did not sleep at all.

And there, some time before the dawn, the thing that I had to do came to me. It was so simple and easy that I wondered why I had not thought of it before. I would go down to Castle Gillian, get hold of that blank deed, tear it in pieces, lock my father's door, and hold the house against all comers for as long as was necessary.

My father's train did not leave the local station until 8 a.m. I calculated that I had three hours to wait, and I could patiently wait, now that my mind was made up. And, my mind easy, I fell asleep.

When I waked it was clear day, and I got to my feet and ran. But I was late. My father was gone; he was gone an hour. *That Kismet of his is working out faithfully*, I said.

Chapter XII

BOSS BEFORE HIS TIME

I

In the Man's Room the peats were blazing on the open hearth; the hanging lamps were lighted; and Sandy Ythan, the Shea brothers and myself were playing Spoil Five. Dinny Lane was there too, but Ythan's queer moral code forbade Dinny to play, though Dinny knew more of the finesse and finer points of the game than Ythan ever would. Ythan was dead against gambling: he would not countenance poker or solo or nap, looked askance at Bridge, but, for some obscure reason, thought cut-throat Spoil Five a simple and innocuous game, and loved to play it for pennies—and never understood it. If Ythan was flush of "siller," and we, including Sylvia, wanted some of it, we used to induce him into a little game, take a couple of half-dollars off him, and call it a day.

It was Lant's deal. He turned up the ace of hearts as trumps and claimed it. A club was led, and Sandy sitting at Lant's right hesitated. He had an idea that at all costs he must stop Lant from making his ace of hearts. Dinny, who had flitted round the table for a peep, slipped a forefinger to the king of clubs in the old fellow's hand. Lant yowled to heaven, and Sandy said: "Awa', laddie! I kent this game afore ye were born!" and put the knave of hearts in to Lant, who promptly struck it and the table with the leading trump—the five of hearts—led back the ace, cleaning out Sandy's remaining trump, took the third and winning trick with an outside queen, and, chortling, gathered in a little pile of pennies.

"You played that hand right weel, Mr Ythan!" said Dan, mildly satiric.

"I couldna ha' stopped him, could I?" enquired Sandy doubtfully.

"Jerusalem!" Dan's voice was warmer. "Hadn't you the knave guarded?"

"Let me see! Ay, had I."

"And wasn't clubs led?"

"Was they?"

"Mother o' Moses!" roared Dan, "and Dinny's finger on the king for you! That would force Lant's ace, and you still had your knave guarded agin' the five." He walloped the table angrily and exploded. "To hell wi' the game!" and quietened just as suddenly. "Very well so! deal us one other hand."

"Wait a wee, my bonnie lad!" Sandy started to argue against irrefutable fact. But at that juncture Garret Ward came in at the door from the stairs, and threaded his way across between chairs.

"The new boss — ugh!" said Sandy with a deep growl.

"Not yet," I said, and shuffled the cards for dealing.

Garret Ward stood well back, legs wide, feet splayed, hands on hips, and in one hand a riding crop. He looked insolently round the table, and thrust his head forward.

"You fellows might get on your legs!" It was not quite an order. Sandy hesitated, and put his hands on the board.

"Sit still, Ythan!" I said. "Jack is as good as his master in this room. You ought to know the rule!"

Ward nodded, and grinned at me. "All right, Gilly! Have your rule for to-night! To-morrow I'll make new rules—and one for you too."

The others sat still round the table. Dan Shea, his clenched fists on the board, looked underbrow at me.

Dan was prepared to back me in anything.   Garret Ward went on talking:

"I just dropped in to let you fellows know what the situation will be here as from to-morrow. Mr Morris is in town executing a deed in my favour, and, in fact, at this moment I own a controlling share of Castle Gillian—house, stables and land. Do you get that?"

"It is verra clear, Mr Ward," said Sandy.

"I'll make it so. It means that I run this place, engaging or dismissing any or all hands. You are a good-enough man for a Scottie, Ythan, and if you want to stay on as head-groom——"

Ythan sat up. "A meenit, sir? About Mr Morris——"

"Mr Morris is no concern of yours," Ward stopped him.

"And there's Miss Mary——?" Sandy wanted his point.

"No concern of yours either—she stays to train, of course."

"I'll stay wi' her," said Sandy, and sat back resignedly.

"You stay as long as I am satisfied," Ward told him. "As regards these two brothers——"

Dan Shea, his back to Ward, addressed himself to me:

"Is Robin Morrison gone, Master Gill?"

"You young hulk!" Ward took a stride forward. "I'll answer that."

Dan turned in his chair, his hands clenching and un-clenching, but he spoke mannerly enough: "Yes, sir?"

"Was Morrison here to-day?" Ward asked.

"No, sir!"

"Because I gave him his marching orders last night, and he took them—apparently. Tinker Morrison is out for good."

Dinny was pressing close to my side, and he whispered desperately:

251

"Oh—oh—oh! is Robin gone on me?"

Dan Shea got on his feet, walked across to the fireplace, and looked down before turning round. I knew he was placing where the long thighed peat-tongs stood in a corner. I had placed it already. When he turned round I was struck by the queer, proud, desolate look on his face. His voice was grim and steady.

"Robin Morrison is gone, and Gill Morris is goin'. Very well so! I am goin' too. Not even for Mary Morris will I work for you, Garret Ward."

So that was why he was desolate: he was leaving his Mary Morris.

Lant scrambled to his feet, and went to his brother's side: "I stand be that!" he cried, his voice breaking shrilly.

I thought, for a moment, that Ward was going to use his riding crop. But he recalled his dignity in time, and merely shrugged his shoulders.

"I'll take that for notice," he said, "and my stables will be well rid of you." He took a step nearer and contemplated Dinny shrinking against me. "As for you, young Lane! I have nothing against you! You're a dam' useful lad, but I don't like your breed——"

"All right—all right, sir!" cried Dinny eagerly. "I'll take Benbecula, and go back to my granda."

That eagerness did not help Dinny. Ward was about to order him off too, but he noted the lad's eagerness to go, and, visibly, I saw the change coming in his sadist mind. "Oh no, my lad!" he said half-coaxingly, half-tauntingly, "you and Benbecula stay. That horse is a valuable one and belongs to the stable——"

"No—no——!"

"Shut up!" Ward rapped out, and grinned at me. "You didn't know I made a killing at Logantown, Gilly? A hundred at fives; and so had all my friends——"

"That would be about two in all," I said.

"Enough to bring the price down to six to four on."

"Enough to allay your fear?" I said.

"Fear! I'll show you what fear is one of these days," he grated, and returned to Dinny. "Look here, young Lane! You're an indentured apprentice and you stay in stable——"

"No—no——!"

"Then I'll soak your grandfather in penalty damages."

"I will not stay," cried Dinny, fiercely desperate. "And I will not leave Benbecula either——"

"You impudent little thief!" Ward took a stride to come round the table. I rose to my feet and put Dinny behind me.

"Just a moment, Garret," I said as quietly as I could. He stopped and looked at me grimly, and the knuckles of his right hand whitened as he gripped his riding crop. He was remembering last night, and had come armed to-night.

I looked aside and savagely at Ythan at the top of the oblong table, but he shook his head at me, and then nodded.

"Right!" I said. "I'll take your place for once," and turned to Ward. "Listen for a minute, Garret, and then please yourself! I am head in the Man's Room to-night, and my orders will be obeyed. You are going now. Get out! That's an order. Dan and Lant, leave this to me!"

Dan had the long tongs, Lant a sod of solid, coal-hard peat, and they were crouching ready. I leant my fingers on the table. I would get on top of it and take him from above. It was up to Garret Ward! But Sandy Ythan was on his feet now, his arms wide-open between us.

"No—no! I'll no' have it!" he cried urgently. "There'll be no blood shed in this place. Miss Mary wouldna have it. Ye'll gang, Mr Ward?"

253

Perhaps it was Mary's name that decided Ward. He certainly was not afraid of me—or of all of us together. He stepped back, and gestured with his riding crop.

"Right you are, Ythan! We'll not begin with bloody noses. You know my orders? These two louts go, young Lane stays, and as for you, Gilly! before you are two days older I'll give you a lesson you'll remember the longest day you live." He swung round and went off stiff-kneed and splay-footed. Near the door he struck savagely with his riding crop at the top of an old sideboard.

Dan Shea crashed the tongs into its corner. "Blast it all, Ythan! why didn't you let Gill take him?"

"Thank you all the same, Mr Ythan," I said.

Ythan shook his old head at me. "Maybe I was wrong too, but ye ken I didna think the time was ripe. The time it is there'll be nane to help or hinner ye, my lad."

"That's the time I fear," I said.

Dinny lifted up his voice. "Is it true that Robin went away without me? He wouldn't—he never would!" The lad was suffering a grief beyond our kenning.

"He'll be at the camp, I've no doubt," I said to help him.

"That's a fact, and whaur else would he be?" Sandy agreed.

"He didn't sleep in his bed last night, same as yourself, Master Gill," said Lant, who was our makeshift for a chambermaid.

This was news to me. Had Robin taken to the hills too? But where was he now?

Dinny lifted head out of a thought of his own, and looked at me.

"It was your deal, Master Gill," he said brightly.

"So it was," I said, and picked up the cards, but in

254

my own mind I said: *Oh ho, my son! there's something in your mind, and I'm watching you.* I winked at Ythan, and dealt four hands, and we played a game or two spiritlessly. The blight of Garret Ward was already on us.

I kept an eye on Dinny, and so did Sandy. He slipped away from the table and fireside, and drifted into the passage to the Rookery, his dog behind him. *That's telling us he has gone to bed*, I said. But, presently, he came sidling out softly and along the wall, keeping pieces of furniture in our line of vision. His dog, more direct, went straight to the door, and waited for him; and the two disappeared into the head of the stairway.

I sacrificed that game to Ythan, rose to my feet, and said: "Leave me out of the next!"

"And me, as well!" said Sandy, and made to rise too.

"I think one will be enough," I said, moving off.

"Oh, verra well! You're no' for stoppin' the laddie?"

"No—whatever you mean! Keep the boys in."

II

I crouched in the dark of the narrow arch leading to the stable-yard, and was just in time to see. The night was faintly clouded, and the half-moon, thinly veiled, showed me the other side of the yard.

Benbecula's loose-box door was a black gape. I could hear a rustle in there, and the muted rattle of a head-chain. Then I caught a movement, and something big bulked in the doorway. A shod hoof clacked on wood, and muted on gravel, and Dinny Lane led his "little" Benbecula across the yard and through the southern arch. He was breaking his bond, and stealing a horse. But the horse was Robin Morrison's, though Garret Ward did not know that. And the strange thing was: Garret Ward was the only one who did not know.

255

I did not stop Dinny. But I followed horse and boy at a safe distance down the avenue. Once Sut heard me, and barked enquiringly, and I leant against a tree trunk and waited. I did not see the dog till it startled me with its cold nose against my hand.

"Wow! away, boy!" I whispered, and patted it softly. It disappeared like a black shadow.

I trailed Dinny to the camp, but did not follow him down. I sat under the wing parapet for a long time, and wondered if there was anything I could do. There were a few points that troubled, and I decided, at last, that I would try and get a little light on them. I rose to my feet, leant over the coping stones, and listened. There was only the sough of the slide and the forlorn murmur under the arches. Both vans were lighted, and I wondered if Robin Morrison was again in residence. If so he would be in with Oonagh and Tyzack at this early hour. I did not want to see him. He had done nothing elemental at the end. He had left Castle Gillian and Mary who loved him; and Mary was back there in her room, waiting for Father to return and tell her that her kingdom was broken. I was disappointed in Robin Morrison, but why should I be? He had but returned to his negative philosophy, and become a drifter again. Was I any better? But I liked Robin Morrison, and I was sorry.

After a while I circled round through the whins, to the rear door of Sloper Jones's old van. There was no sound from inside, and I scratched on the wood in a way Sylvia and I had when some game was on. I heard a fumble then, and the top half of the door opened without a sound. Sloper's cropped head was in the opening, and the soft glow behind him shone through one ruined ear.

"Gill Morris?" he whispered.

"Right, first time!" I whispered back. "Come on out—I want to talk to you."

He opened the bottom half of the door, and slid to the ground; and I led him round to the side where we could not be seen or heard from the other van.

"You're the very devil, Gill Morris!" he said. "You'd go poachin' and the sky fallin'."

"The sky is fallin', and I'm not going poachin'. Dinny about?"

He hesitated for so long that I knew he knew.

"Dinny Lane?"

"Come off it, Sloper!" I said, "I followed him down. Where is Benbecula?"

"Dinny is in with his grandma and Jacus."

"And his granda?"

"No!" Sloper again hesitated. "Ty Lane is away for the day."

"Seeing his winter camps, I suppose! Where have you hidden a horse?"

"I haven't. He's in his box."

"You'll have to hide him better than that!"

"Why so?"

"Garret Ward will come looking for him to-morrow."

"He's not Ward's horse!" Sloper said indignantly.

"Ward thinks he owns two-thirds of him, and he'll just take him away from you pronto."

"I'd like to see him try," said Sloper wickedly, "but maybe you are right."

"I am. Where is Robin Morrison?"

"Should I know?"

"You should, pig-head! I gather he is not in camp. Is he with Tyzack?"

"Ay! he's away with Tyzack." Sloper was still hesitant.

"Back on the old routine," I said, "and he'll leave with you when you leave to-morrow?"

"Who's leavin' to-morrow?"

"You are—all of you—and I'll bet a hat on that."

"That's one bet I'm not going to make," he said cryptically, "and I'm needin' a hat." Usually Sloper was prepared to bet his shirt on anything.

For a time we leant silently against a wheel, and listened to the sounds of the night. I had got some information I wanted. I suppose our thoughts ran in the same channel.

"You think we are for the road, then?" he said.

"Yes! And I'm sorry for you, Sloper boy, wantin' your quiet place in the hills. Man dear! I'm sorry for all of us. But we never had a chance."

He put a hand on my arm. "Don't be mournin' for us, Gill. There's no cause. You and Miss Syl did your damnedest to help—an' to-morrow is another day!"

"The day of evil! Poor old Syl!" I said sadly, and I was sorry for her. "She's not in with Oonagh, is she?"

He hesitated again. "No—she isn't."

"Do you have to spell your words before mouthing them? Is she up at Evan—or is she gone away, too?"

He didn't hesitate this time. "There's wan way o' findin' out: run up and ask, and, if you are afraid of the dark, I'll go up with you."

I shouldered him away. "Go back to your bed! If you are holding out on me—and I think you are—I'll tan the tough Welsh hide of you."

"An' 'twas myself taught you, like a dam' fool." He turned from the corner of the van. "An' 'tisn't old Sloper Jones you should be tannin', Gill Morris," he said, and ducked away.

They all knew the man I should be tanning. I knew him myself. I had tried to make a beginning more than once, but kept falling down on the job. Damn! I had a Hamlet complex.

I went up the river-path by the holms. It was dark
under the evergreens, but the river on my left was shining,
for the moon was out from under the clouds now. I
went out on the foot-bridge, and leant on the rail, as
usual. The breeze whispered in the stiff green leaves,
and the sigh from the slide came in irregular pulses.
The shadows of the trees were cast faintly on the silver-
and-black mirror of the pool, and the moon looked up
at me from the deeps of an abyss. I seemed to be hung
in a canyon of space between two immense skies.

I was thinking of Sylvia. I was sorry for Sylvia. She
had been sore hurt last night. All her schemes had
tumbled about her, and no time was given her to build
them up again. Mary had failed her, and Robin, and
Tyzack—and I hadn't helped much. Well! my father's
Kismet ruled the roost, and she should not have played
with fire. But still, let one be fair to her! She wasn't
thinking of herself. She had tried to help Mary and Robin
and Dinny, put up a mighty good show, and only failed
at the end where failure was inevitable. Should I say,
in passing, that the musing Gilly Morris, leaning over
the Gullane, was minus one eye and blind in the other?

Sylvia would be disconsolate now, mooning about the
huge old house, ashamed of herself, and mad at the rest
of us. And no one had gone to see her! I would. We
had fought our little wars in the past, but we had been
allies oftener than not. Right! I would say a few words
to her to-night, even make her enough mad to discharge
her choler on me. And to-morrow! To-morrow was
another day, as Sloper Jones had said. . . .

I went up through the oaks, and over the haw-haw,
and across the lawn clumped with shrubs and flower-beds,
where the light was not enough to show the gaud of the

chrysanthemums. There was a light in the hall, but the front of the house was in darkness, and Sylvia's dormer window was blank as a dead eye. From the back of the house I heard the soft thud of the oil engine of Uncle Tom's lighting plant.

I didn't pull the clangorous old bell by the hall door, for, as usual, the door was unlocked, and I opened it to the soft glow of hooded electric lamps. That hall was luxurious, but nicely luxurious, not like our bare echoing one. Mary was, surely, a chatelaine but never a house-keeper. Sylvia was no chatelaine, but, surely, she could keep a house. That was one of her many contradictions.

I made straight down the hall, and under the stairs, for Uncle Tom's den: what he called his Reading Room. If Sylvia was not sulking in the dark in her own quarters, she would be in here, with her father, reading. I tapped on the door, but it was not Sylvia's voice that called: "Come along!" That was Uncle Tom.

He was sitting in his big leather chair at the other side of the fire reading a newspaper. The room was full of books, books that Sylvia read, for that was another of her contradictions. Uncle Tom read three dailies, a Sunday journal, two financial weeklies, and nothing else. He was reading a daily now, and the two others were on the desk at his elbow under a big volume that looked like an account book. Also on the desk was a tray holding a decanter, some glasses, and a syphon. The standard lamp was behind his shoulder, and the pink hood of it left the room in a soft light.

Uncle Tom was in his evening uniform: an outrageous, felted, befrogged smoking jacket—and he did not smoke —and a round, flat, tasselled cap. He looked exactly like Squire Johnny Bull taking his ease out of his reds and leathers. But if there was any Anglo-Saxon blood in him I had never heard about it. Unlike the Anglo-

Saxon, he was too conceited in his own way, and, if he couldn't have it one way, he took steps to have it another.

His face lit up when he saw me. "Welcome, Gillian, lad!" he greeted me warmly. "You are a great stranger these days."

I came to the point at once: "Syl about, Uncle Tom?"

He looked at me questioningly and hesitated. *Blow! everyone was hesitating with me to-night.*

"No—o!" he said then. "Were you expecting her back so soon?"

"I didn't know she was away," I told him.

He opened his eyes. "You don't know where she is gone—you generally do?"

"I don't know a dam' thing, Uncle," I said disgustedly. "Everyone is holding out on me."

"Do you tell me so?" He was getting cagy. "Ah well! Sylvia will be back—probably to-morrow. She went off in her car early."

Sylvia frequently took jaunts like that. Sometimes I went along, but, if I didn't, I always knew where to contact her. But not this time. *I wouldn't be surprised if she's off with Tyzack and Robin to visit a winter camp*, I thought. *But Slope would have told me that—or would he?* Aloud I said:

"It does not matter, Uncle! I'll not keep you from your news-hounds. Good night, sir!"

He dropped his paper on the floor, and there was an urgency in his voice that was almost a command.

"Wait, Gillian! There's something I want to tell you." He moved a hand. "Have a drink?—help yourself."

I am not a whiskey drinker, but I needed one just then. I went to the desk, poured myself a stiff one, squirted a little soda, and tossed the mixture straight down on the pit of my stomach. The shock of the alcohol made me shiver, as it always did, and the little maggots of it started crawling almost at once.

I sat down in the chair that was Sylvia's, and caught a faint aroma of the verbena, or whatever it was, that she used on her hair. I snuggled well down, and had a strange nostalgic feeling.

"Yes, Uncle?" I said, and waited. He had something to tell me, had he? Something he wanted, maybe? I had nothing for him any more—or for anyone.

He leant back in his leather chair, and his smoking-cap tilted itself ridiculously over one eye. Those shrewd blue eyes of his contemplated me over his tapping finger-tips, and he was slow to begin.

"I don't like telling you this, Gillian," he said at last.

"It can't be worse than what I know already," I said, but I was disturbed all the same.

"I know, boy! It is nothing like that. Sylvia is going away."

"Going away!" I repeated. "You mean she is gone already?"

"No—no!" he said quickly. "I mean she is going."

So that was it. Sylvia, having made her hash, was going away. Well! Why not she go away? It was no business of mine, though my breast was hollow.

"She took it badly last night, Gillian," my uncle said. Sylvia hid nothing from her father.

"Yes, Uncle! Was she distressed—you know?"

"Terribly distressed."

"At the weeping stage?"

"She nearly broke my heart." There was, even now, a tremor in his bluff voice; he bent over to hide his face, and threw some brown sods of peat on the fire from an oaken tub.

From her earliest years, Sylvia nearly broke all our hearts when she wept. She very seldom let herself go, but when she did, it was an experience of utter poignancy, her grief was so complete, so whole-hearted, so pitiful. It surely was not soundless, but it did not contort her face, though the tears poured. It was wordless, yet it was a lament, a *caoine*, a threnody, a mourning for something that could never be restored. Sitting back in that chair, her aura all round me, a lump came into my throat thinking of Sylvia's grief.

"Oh, dear! Oh, dear!" I said. "Yes, Uncle, she must go away for a time. She had her mind set on something, and she failed to pull it off."

"That is what she kept on saying: She failed—she couldn't stay here—she wouldn't come back ever. I could not comfort her at all, and in the end I agreed to go away with her. It is not convenient for me to go away just now, but I could not let her go alone—I suppose?"

"Why not, if you don't want to go," I said, and the whiskey was moving in me. "Sylvia is safe anywhere. Sylvia is all right. Sylvia is fine. By hell! Sylvia is the finest girl in the world."

"Next to Mary—eh?"

"No, by God! I'll put no one equal to Sylvia." I should avoid alcohol, for no man should carry his heart on his sleeve.

Uncle Tom made no remark on that explosion. He said:

"We shall be away some time, Gillian: a year—two years—round the globe somewhere. You know, I was never very keen on this big barracks of a place. A town bird—business shark you used to call me—I always preferred my place in town. Sylvia and her mother loved Castle Evan; and now Sylvia is leaving, and not coming back—or so she says. I don't believe that. If I did, by dam! I'd close a three century chapter, and sell out." He looked at me and away. "Once I thought to see the start of a new chapter, and leave ye at it——"

He looked at me again, but I shook an obstinate head.

"I know—I know!" he said almost angrily. "You and Sylvia! I know how it is with ye——"

"You don't—not quite," I said.

"Bah to you, Gill Morris! All right! I am not interfering. Ye have yere own views, and bedamned to them! But carry on—carry on! There is a more important thing in my mind, young fellow, and I am going to say it to you as if I were your real uncle. Will you believe that?" He sat up and looked at me intently. Maybe he was sincere at that.

"Yes, Uncle Tom," I said.

"Fine! What I want to say is this! You are talking of going away yourself, but, in the present circumstances, you should stay near Mary for some time."

"That was in my mind too, but—I am afraid," I said.

"You can face your fear any time you want to."

"That is a different fear—what do you propose?"

"There is this house here—it's an old Morris home, not a Gayne's! Wait! Remember, Sylvia and I will be out of your way." He put his hand on the big account book. "You know what this is?"

"I have seen Sylvia at it—she wouldn't let me see."

"No, she's not very proud of it. She's a whale at figures, and this is her profit and loss account for Castle Evan—mostly loss!"

"And that's a dam' shame," I said, "but don't blame Sylvia."

"I'm not. This place is only a plaything of mine——"

"God forgive, Tom Gayne!" I said.

"I hope so. Let me ask you two questions: The place is stocked—a staff of men, cattle, implements, machinery and so on—could it be worked at a profit?"

"Yes and no!" I said.

"Blazes! What sort of answer is that?"

264

"Wait!" This was my subject and I livened up. "The place is stocked, you say: men used to bone laziness; machinery galore, some useful but mostly expensive gentlemen's gadgets; Connemara ponies, fallow deer, hand-reared pheasants, ornamental cattle and scrub cows. No profit in these, business man!"

He tapped the book. "It's all there in black and white. Well?"

I was warming up, and the whiskey had loosened my tongue:

"If you would stock the place properly, go in for mixed farming in a big way, with fruit and tomatoes on the side, you'd make a tidy income—and to hell with huckstering in limited liability companies!—Two blades o' grass where one grew before! that's my motto. You'd have to spread some capital at first, of course."

"Very good!" said my uncle with satisfaction. "Suppose I were to put up some capital—say three thousand pounds at five per cent——"

"Oh no! you don't, business magnate!" I stopped him. "Say, five thousand pounds at two and three-quarters per cent—not a farthing less and not a fraction more—it is the agricultural rate."

"Do you tell me that? Ridiculous! I could get— but let it ride. Five thousand pounds at two and three-quarters per cent—and half the net profits——?"

"Not by a jugful!" I told him firmly. "You change a dead loss on a plaything to a tidy income on a valuable property——"

"Problematical!" he interjected.

"A tidy income," I insisted, "and enhanced values, and you sit back and twiddle your thumbs. No, suh! A fourth of the net profits is a fair return, and no one is trying to cheat you."

"And you call me a business shark?" said Uncle Tom

warmly. "Begad, you are a tough one, but I won't haggle." He leant forward. "This is my second question: Will you, young Gillian Morris, work Castle Evan on these terms? Wait, now! You will have full responsibility, and Sylvia and I will not be under your feet. And you will be near Mary. I will give you a five years' contract, and if Sylvia don't want the place I'll give you a lease, That's a plain business proposal and no catch in it." His voice hardened. "If the proposal does not appeal to you I'll just let to graziers or sell out. That's all!" He sat back and waited, his eyes keenly on me.

It was a business proposal, and it had its appeal. At any other time, as often before, I would let my fancy flow to all the things I would do to Castle Evan. But, put up to me like that, concretely, in this dark hour, I found I could no longer think optimistically. I had got out of the way of thinking optimistically, and to-night I couldn't think at all. A mood of fatalism was on me, and I could not make a decision. Uncle Tom saw that, and patted a hand at me.

"Leave it at that, lad, for the present. There's no great hurry, and your mind is troubled. But, sure, to-morrow is another day!"

Sloper Jones had said that too, but I was not looking forward to to-morrow.

"Thanks, Uncle Tom!" I said. "All I will say is, that your offer appeals to me."

"Fine, lad! Fine!" A whimsical, sad little note came into his voice. "If Sylvia and you had settled down together that is the offer I would have made to you—but I'd have stood out for better terms, you rogue. You'll be nice to Sylvia before she goes away, Gill?"

If Sylvia and I had settled down together! But Sylvia was going away. Desolateness overwhelmed me. I would be working Castle Evan, and Sylvia not there! What would I be working Castle Evan for?

I got to my feet and walked towards the door so that my face was hidden.

"No, Uncle!" I said. "I will not be seeing Sylvia, and I cannot see myself accepting your offer either. I am sorry, and Good night, sir!"

"I am not accepting that for an answer to-night," he called after me firmly. "Second thoughts are best. Good night, boy!"

IV

I went out into the night, and the weight of lonesomeness was heavy on me. I was no longer part of my surroundings, and my own Gullane Glen held itself aloof. For the first time in my life I found that I did not belong. The glen ignored me, went on in its own primeval way, oblivious of me and of all the midget bipeds that marred and scarred it. The air that hushed in the leaves, the river that sighed down the long slide, the little lives that rustled in the coverts were concerned with things altogether outside humanity, carrying on in an existence of their own that would go on when man had gone the way of the mastodon.

I was cut off from elemental life, and I was frightened. I was for a moment outside that place where, alone, man can live sanely: the self-centred centre. I wanted to hide in a corner made by man away from the elementals. I was close to the thin edge of insanity. But, desperately, I refused to be ignored.

"No—no—no!" I said to the night, to the glen, "I will not be shaken off like a dead leaf. You can do your damnedest, but you will not frighten me into a hole!"

That night, again, I did not go into the house. I went

round it, back of the stables, and climbed up through the trees to the crown of our little hill that was clothed with larches.

There is salubrity, even in winter, in a larch wood. That was only the end of September; there had been no rain for days; and the harvest sun had warmed the ground. The trees were still in green—a dulled green—but many needle fronds had drifted down and settled. I lay on my back on a brown carpet, arms and legs extended, and let the earth currents flow through me.

And slowly, but surely, I was taken back into the fold. The larch trees, that are never silent, were hushing me into their own contentment; the moonlight was making a lace pattern to please my eye; the rustle of a field-mouse was the friendly stir of another life kin to mine. I was afraid no longer.

I knew then that, while everything mattered, nothing mattered much; that I had been making mountains out of molehills, and would go on making them in my many foolish hours; that a man should not be trammelled by possessions in time, place, or eternity; that a crisis could be faced debonairly, and, if not, could be evaded; that man, the sojourner, could always break camp and be free—as Robin Morrison was free, as I would be free. . . .

After a long time I fell asleep.

Chapter XIII

DRAMA AT CAERLINE

I

I SLEPT the round of a clock, and when I waked I knew that it was the first real sleep I had in weeks. The sun was my clock that morning, and I knew, by the slant of it on a tree bole, that it was about eleven o'clock, summertime.

I lay and considered myself, and felt hale and whole; my mind was clear as crystal; and that mood of serene indifference was still with me. But I was not indifferent to the hunger that ravened in me. I rolled to my feet, kicked a stiff leg here and there, and sidled down the hill, fending myself off the straight-growing trunks of the larches. I ran down old Timmy in his acre of kitchen, and found him humming and grumbling away to himself, as usual.

"Drinkin' himself drunk an' sober at the Cross all night, and here he is now, an' I know the first thing he'll say!"

"Is there a bite in the house, Timmy Tadg Shawn?"

"What did I tell you? But haven't you given up atin'?" He looked into my eyes. "If it's drinkin' you was, divil the ha'porth o' harm it has done you, be japers!"

"I drank of a deep well," I told him, "and now I want food. Where is Mary?"

"Out—out somewhere! Eat first, and I'll question you after."

While Timmy prepared a late breakfast, I had a shave, a cold plunge, and a change of clothes; and then Timmy fed me bacon and eggs, hot-butter'd toast, marmalade,

269

and strong tea. He fussed about me, pouring tea, and buttering toast, and said: "Japers, boy! don't choke yourself!" but he did not open with his guns till I was filling a first pipe.

"There was near to blue murdher in the stable-yard this mornin'," he said, "and there's a robber—not far from here, aither!"

"Nor from here," I said. "What did you rob?"

"Nothin' this long time—and she was a widow woman's daughter." He was watching me closely, though pretending to be busy gathering delf. "Some thief o' the world up an' lifted that nice black-hided colt, Benbecula."

"And I'm that thief, you think?" I put him calmly.

He pointed a fork at me. "You're takin' it dam' cool —an' your bed wasn't slept in?"

"Was Robin Morrison's?"

"No, then! but I knew where he was."

"You did? Have the police been looking for me?"

"Not yet. Listen! I rolled about in your bed early this mornin', and didn't I hear you snorin' the livelong night?"

"So you did. Listen you, Timmy! I did not steal Benbecula, but I know who led him off."

"So do I," said Timmy, "but I took me few precautions all the same. Man, Gill! There was red hell in the yard when Garret Ward found the horse was gone."

I sat up at that. "He has found out already?"

"He was here early to take charge, and showed his teeth plain. He gave Ythan notice first thing, an' set out to kick Dan Shea off the primises. Miss Mary had to come between them, an' didn't she blister the skin off Garret Ward?"

"She would. Where is she now?"

"Off to Caerline, riding horseback."

"Whatever for?"

"How would I know? To see her man-o'-law, what else? or meet her da off the train!" Yes, Father would be home in the afternoon, probably, with the deed executed.

"Where are all the others?" I asked then.

"Every dang one o' them looking for that horse—under Garret Ward's orders."

"Sandy Ythan could find that horse—if he wanted to," I said, rising to my feet, and moving towards the back door.

Timmy came, shuffling his carpet slippers, after me, and put a hand on my arm. "You're in one o' them cold moods, Master Gill! You'll do nothing foolish, with the help o' God?"

"With the help o' God, I will," I said, and shut the back door between us.

There was no one in the stable-yard. Benbecula's loose-box was open and empty, and there was a queer feeling of forlornness about the place in the noon sun—almost a feeling of decay. Some of the horses were whickering and uneasy, for horses do sense confusion and unease amongst their menservants. They had not been exercised that morning or attended to in any way, and I did not like to see horses—even blood horses—in discomfort. I spent a busy hour or so, got my head nearly kicked off, and was at a rough finish, when I heard a horse's hooves on the cobbles under the arch. I jumped out hurriedly.

II

Lant Shea led Benbecula across the yard to me. The horse was none the worse for his night out, but I could see by Lant's cheeks that he had just done bawling. Now he was getting ready to bawl some more.

"Oh, Master Gill!" he cried shrilly, "we're ruined for ever, and them all in jail for night robbery."

He opened his mouth wide to make lament, but I moved in quickly and dealt him a firm thump on the shoulder.

"Take it easy, Lant!" I said. "We'll box Benbecula, and then I'll talk to you."

I took the horse from him, and he followed, gulping air. We were busy for a minute or two. I tied the head-rope, slapped the horse's sound shoulder, and spoke casually:

"Good old Ben! I wonder who is in jail, anyway?"

"Dinny Lane and Jacus and Slope Jones—for stealing Benbecula," Lant said, steadily, now.

"But this is Benbecula back in stable, and he was not stolen."

"Garret Ward says different, and he's the new boss."

"All the worse for Garret Ward. I know what happened last night, Lant. You stop swallowing your palate, and tell me all that happened this morning."

We went out into the pleasant sunlight and Lant told me confusedly what Timmy had already told me. "I had a stirrup-iron nice and handy," he said, "when Miss Mary stopped us. Gor, Master Gill! why weren't you there, and we'd ha' crucified him?"

"I'm never there at the right time, Lant. Go on!"

Ward had looked for Dinny, and, then, had gone off by himself, apparently to the camp. He was soon back, and, under his orders, they all went down to search. Oonagh and Jacus and Sloper Jones were in camp, and so was Dinny. Tyzack and Robin were away some place with Miss Syl in her car—Lant had seen the three of them collogin' night before last.

"I see or hear nothing myself," I said sourly. "Go on! What did Jacus say?"

The strange part of it was that Jacus had said absolutely nothing. Oonagh wouldn't let him, and I gathered from Lant's garbled version that the only thing Oonagh had said was: "Whom the gods destroy they first make mad."

The stable party had done some desultory searching. "I could find the place in a minit," Lant boasted, "an' so could Ythan—his father was a sheep-stealer. But we kep' edgin' away from it, an' Garret Ward, cursin' all of us, got madder and madder, an' went straight up to the Cross an' brought down the Sarjint o' the Guards— that new buck from Mayo, used to chasing stills in the mountains—an' he found the horse in no time at all. It was in them big furze bushes at th' other side o' the road where meself an' Dinny had made a sort of cave—you know?"

"I know," I said, "a place for an apprentice's smoke! —Ythan told me about it."

"Th' ould divil! Man, it was a fair cop, an' what could the Sarjint do but haul the three boyos off to Caerline, Garret Ward accusin' thim of stealin' an' hidin' a valuable race-horse be night time." Lant's cheeks began to tremble. "In America, where they have no Christianity, I hear tell, you can be hanged for horse-stealin'. That's not the law here, is it?"

"No, you donkey! That horse was not stolen. You know the owner, don't you?"

"O' course, I do: Robin Morrison."

"You all knew: Ythan, Dan—Dammit! even Timmy knew—Mary, my father, Oonagh, Dinny, Jacus, Sloper— every one of you. But not Garret Ward! And will you tell me now, my lad, why none of you said a word to Garret Ward?"

"Manalive! what do you take us for?" he said indignantly. "If Miss Mary wouldn't say the word, how could we?"

273

"I take you for a pack o' rogues," I said. "Some of you would kill a man if Mary pointed a finger."

"Dan would," said Lant, "and I would if your Miss Syl put me up to it."

I slapped his shoulders. "Garret Ward has put a rod in pickle for himself, and he'll taste it, Lant."

"Gor! will he, Gill?"

"Ay! he'll learn that Castle Gillian can bite deep even in its death throes, and Mary Morris will be his teacher. Come on!——" A thought struck me. "Say, where are Ythan and Dan?"

"Garret Ward took them off in his car to be witnesses."

"He is in for some hard swearin', then. Come on! Your horses are attended to. Get out the old bikes, and we'll go jaunting!"

Cycling down the drive at my side, Lant grew quite cheerful, and whistled one of Ythan's two tunes: *At the Back of Benachie*. At the Bridge we dismounted, leant our cycles against a parapet and went down to see Oonagh Blake.

I was worried about Oonagh. I need not be. She was sitting, her neatly shod feet in the mild sun of the fall, in the doorway of her resplendent van, and her softly moulded hands were busy at her knitting. She smiled pleasantly at us, and her voice was placid.

"If you boys don't hurry you'll be late for the show."

I looked closely at her. "You are not troubled about this, Oonagh?"

"Not any more, Gillian." Her mass of hair lit up as she moved her head. "Once, not so long ago, I was troubled about you."

"A sour dog, wasn't I? You are not leaving here to-day?"

"Nor to-morrow."

"Does Sloper need a new hat?" I asked then.

"He said you promised him one."

"The devil I did!" I leant a shoulder against the door-post and looked down at her contemplatively. She was always placidly equable, but now there was something additional that in anyone else I would call smugness.

"Look you, Granny Lane!" She had the hale woman's objection to grannyhood. "Don't be lickin' cream in my face! There has been something going on here, and you're hiding it from me."

"No, Gillian my dear!" she protested sincerely. "You've been keeping yourself aloof of late, and when things really began to happen you had taken to your refuge in the hills. I haven't had a chance to tell you. Well! I can now." She glanced at Lant, who started to move away. "No, Lant!" She thought for a moment, and smiled playfully. "Do you know? I think I'll let you see the finish as an onlooker, and that will be nice for you. Off ye go!"

"Where to?"

"Caerline. Where Jacobus is there the show will be. Listen! You know my Tyzack? A good man? Surely. I know him better, and he is a good man. But he has the cold gipsy kink in him: he never forgets and he never forgives. But he is not vindictive, and he never takes action until he is forced to. Then he chooses his time and bides it, and waits patiently for the full effect. Waiting is good hunting! And the time is now! Go down to Caerline and see. I'll have a meal ready for you when you come back, and prove once and for all that I am a better cook than Jacus."

"You're not," I said, "and never will be, and Sylvia will tell you the same."

"All right! We'll put it to Sylvia. She'll be here."

Then I will not be here, I said in my own mind.

The Courthouse at Caerline is at the corner of Morris Square, but the main entrance is in the narrow side-street, Morris Street, and across from it is the Morris Arms Hotel fronted by a white, balustraded porch. The Morrises, in the days of their power, had left their mark on Caerline.

Lant Shea and I mounted the wide limestone steps— a baker's dozen of them as I had often counted—and the uniformed guard before the door of carved oak nodded familiarly.

"Just in time, Gill!" he said. "It's my bloody luck to be posted out here! There'll be a circus going on inside, and the devil to pay!"

"He'll be paid," I said. "Slip us through, Bill?"

"Is Lant old enough? He is! In ye go!" He opened a slit of door, and the drone of a casual voice came out to meet us.

We slipped through and into the first empty bench, to the right, just inside the door. There was a good sprinkling of citizens on the benches that sloped slowly down on either side of the drugget ed passage. This case, only a few hours old, had already made a stir; but, of course, the alleged stealing of a race-horse would be of import in the capital of a horse-breeding county.

I had a look round to place the people I was interested in. I saw Mary at once. She was just across the passage from us, all by herself. Our eyes met, but she did not nod, or even smile; she just gave me one searching look and turned her face from me; but I saw at once that she was bearing up all she knew against some hard inner strain. Her eyes looked black in a face that had lost most of its lovely colour; and her arms hung stiffly to her clenched brown hands.

You can quash this case any time you want to, my girl, I said. *What are you waiting for? Damn! there was something going on behind my back.*

I looked over the heads of the public, and, directly facing me, was the Justice's dais behind its panelled oak screen. The Justice sat alean in his high-backed, carved chair, his eyes on the groined ceiling, and his face ruddy above his black robes and below his dogean cap: a man not many years older than myself, and an old friend: Ned Dowling, a gay devil off the Bench—and sometimes on it. He knew Jacus McGrath nearly as well as I did, and, in his time, had had the gloves on with Sloper Jones. And he knew Garret Ward too. His justice might sometimes be questioned, but never his equity.

Below him, outside the screen, sat his clerk, busily working at his notes, and by the clerk's side sat the court usher, who did not guess the busy time he was in for. Fronting the two was a low wide platform, whereon stood a single Windsor chair: that was the witness-stand. At each side of it were the leather-upholstered benches for lawyers and counsel. At the right side, a tall man in a smoky-blue uniform was on his feet addressing the Bench: he was the Superintendent for Caerline, a recent appointment, and not yet of my acquaintance. He would, probably, know nothing of Jacus McGrath other than that he was a showman and the proprietor of a boxing-booth, and so needing the whip of the law.

On the near side of the witness-stand were two long wooden benches railed off from the body of the court: these were for the witnesses. In the front bench I saw the massive, black-lacquered head of Garret Ward; and behind it was Ythan's bald dome and Dan Shea's red bush.

Mary Morris should be down there too—if she's not double-dealing! I said to myself.

And, finally, facing the Superintendent, at the other side of the witness-stand, was the high-railed prisoners' dock. There my eyes stayed. There was Jacus, his jaw truculent and his brow benevolent, sitting erect, his two fists firmly grasping the rail in front of him. His profile was to me now, but ever and again he turned his head for a quick look at the door near my shoulder. He had seen me come in, held my eye for a moment, and, as he turned his head away, gave that downward twist of thumb that meant "Pipe down!" I was under orders too—and perhaps Mary was!

Sloper Jones sat at Jacus's side solemn and composed as Buddha, and one bulbous ear looked like a roughly-carved piece of red granite; and pressing close against him was Dinny Lane, and Sloper's arm was around him. Dinny, I could see, was frightened and dismayed. He was the real guilty party, he felt, and had brought two men he loved into the jaws of jail. Two tall guards stood up behind the prisoners, and looked bored. Not for long.

I could not see Tyzack or Robin or Sylvia anywhere, and as Jacus still kept turning head doorwards I calculated that he was on the look out for them—or for someone.

A shaft of sunlight slanted in through a tall window above my head and touched the edge of the witness-stand. Motes danced in it, and I said: *It is three o'clock in the afternoon, daylight-saving time.*

We were just in time. The formal preliminaries were over. The Superintendent put a foot on the platform, a hand on his lifted knee, and addressed the Justice. His voice was casual, the voice of a man making a request that had merely to be made and granted.

"It is alleged, Your Honour, that the prisoners—the accused—Jacobus McGrath, Lloyd Jones, and Dionysius Lane, a minor, stole and concealed a valuable race-horse, the property of Mr Gillian Morris of Castle Gillian. Mr

Morris, an essential witness on the point of ownership, is unavoidably absent; and I request that the accused be remanded in custody to the next sitting of the court." He lazed down into his seat.

Good Lord! not in custody, I said. *Mary can't allow that, and she's the essential witness, not my father!* It was natural enough that a new Superintendent should ask for a remand in custody in the case of a showman and his broken-down pug.

The Justice sat forward, his forearms across his Case-Book, and looked down, head aslant, at the Superintendent, and on his face was a look of curious interest.

"Just like that, my dear Superintendent?" he said coaxingly.

The Superintendent moved hand and head affirmatively, and frowned. He was not used to Ned Dowling's brand of justice.

The Justice held him with his eye. "You are not joking, are you? Remand in custody! Remand, possibly, but before you get me to remand in custody"—he pointed to each prisoner—"Jacus McGrath, old Sloper Jones, and Ty Lane's son, a minor, you'll have to show cause and plenty of it."

"Hu—hu—hoo!" That was Jacus's high tenor. "That's the way to treat a new broom, Your Honour!" Jacus was trying a pipe-opener.

"Silence in court!" shouted the usher, on his feet.

The Superintendent was on his feet too. "Your Honour misunderstands me." His voice was no longer casual. "I shall, of course, show cause, and to do that I hope it will be only necessary to call the witness who laid information. Mr Garret Ward!"

The usher half rose and shouted: "Garret Ward!"

"Just a moment!" said the Justice, glancing at the Lawyers' Bench. "Are the accused represented?"

"I'm conducting me own offence, Your Honour, and well I'm able," cried Jacus promptly.

Jacus would, and Jacus could. There was no one to tell him to "pipe down" to-day. Garret Ward had taken what looked like a good opportunity to show his enemy up and, possibly, get him a few days' incarceration. And now Jacus was going to show his mettle. At this juncture, he, and he alone, was the man-in-the-gap for us all. Not Tyzack, not Robin Morrison! Just Jacus McGrath, himself alone.

Garret Ward rose and hopped on to the witness-stand. He was not neat on his feet, and he did it awkwardly. Followed the unimpressive oath-taking, and Ward sat down easily in the Windsor chair. I could not see his face, but the set of head and shoulders showed a nonchalant confidence. The Superintendent set out to do things thoroughly this time.

"You are Mr Garret Ward of Monaglass?"

"Mr Garret Ward of Castle Gillian," amended his witness. "I have sold Monaglass."

There was a stir in court. The prospective change in Glen Gullane had been widely bruited, and here it was at last—the end of Morris of Castle Gillian!

"Of Castle Gillian, then." The Superintendent nodded. "You know the accused?"

"All three—yes."

"To your knowledge was the youngest prisoner, Dionysius—commonly known as Dinny Lane—employed in the stables at Castle Gillian?"

"He was an indentured apprentice."

Jacus leant forward to give a bit of confidential information to his friend, the Justice.

"Apprentice jock to Gillian Morris—with a good winner already, Benbecula, his first mount—an' keep your eye on that horse, Your Honour!"

"The horse that was stolen!" rapped the Superintendent, and scored a point.

"Stolen your gran'mother!" said Jacus succinctly.

"Order in court!" shouted the usher, his nose crinkling.

The Justice lifted a pencil. "You keep order too, Jacus."

"Not another word out o' me, Your Honour," Jacus promised.

"The accused, Dinny Lane, lived-in at Castle Gillian?" went on the Superintendent, controlling his temper.

"Yes, in the men's quarters."

"Where did his people live?"

"His grandfather, Tyzack Lane, travelling showman, was in camp on Castle Gillian ground at Gullane Bridge, half a mile from the house, and so were Jacus McGrath and Sloper Jones."

"Yes, the other two accused! Will you please tell his Honour what took place at Castle Gillian the night— that is, the night before last at Castle Gillian."

"I visited the men's quarters at the top of the house. There were present Sandy Ythan the head-groom, two stable hands, Dan and Lant Shea, the apprentice Dinny Lane, and young Gilly Morris. I informed them of the changes that were taking place in the control of the stables, re-engaged the head-groom, gave notice to the Shea brothers"— another item came to him —"and also informed them that on the previous night I had ordered off one Robin Morrison, a hanger-on at the Lane camp, temporarily employed in the stables——"

Jacus could not stand this. His voice lifted. "Wait there! Tell me, me darlin' Garret Ward, what right had you to order anyone off in Gillian Morris's stables?"

Before Ward might answer, the Justice rapped sharply on his desk. "Order—order! This will not do, McGrath. I see your point, and when the witness has completed his evidence I will give you an opportunity to cross-examine him."

"The very thing, Your Honour!" said Jacus agreeably, and made a vulgar gesture. "An' I'll crack him like that between me two thumb nails."

The usher's "Silence in court!" was not quite in time. The Superintendent was not having the smooth course he expected, but he stuck to it.

"Now as regards Dinny Lane——?"

"I told him that I was pleased with him, and that, of course, he would stay on as an indentured apprentice. For some reason he refused. The words he used were: 'No! I will go back to my grandfather and take Benbecula.'"

"That is the horse in question?"

"Yes. I forbade him to leave the stables or take the horse. Then I left."

Lant nudged me and whispered in my ear: "A split second afore you thrun him downstairs." And there he added an unusual thought in a shocked way. "Gor! what a gran' lie you can tell be stickin' to the bare truth."

The Superintendent went on building up a case for Garret Ward.

"This horse Benbecula was in stable at Castle Gillian that night?"

"It was. I saw it there."

"Can you state definitely who is the owner of the horse?"

"Not definitely, but it is trained by Gillian Morris, and raced under his name and colours——"

"And ridden by Dionusius Lane," added Jacus.

I looked at Jacus and waited. Now was the time to clout Garret Ward, and call Mary Morris to witness. Jacus looked at Ward, nodded solemnly, and never said a word. But he lifted a hand carelessly and again twisted down that thumb. Was that signal for me? I looked aside at Mary. She was smiling faintly but grimly. Yes, the signal was for her too, and she knew more of the sign language than I did.

"Now, Mr Ward, when did you discover that the horse was missing?" queried the Superintendent.

"This morning."

"What steps did you take to recover it?"

"Naturally I suspected young Lane, and at once went down to the camp at the Bridge——"

"Ay faith!" cried Jacus, "and left it at the double, meself and Sloper after you with a hatchet!"

Sloper's face crinkled its mask for the first time, and the usher failed to stop the laughter in court.

Lant whispered in my ear: "Jacus is as good as a circus any day."

I was watching Ned Dowling's eye and I whispered back, "Jacus is going to take the rap for contempt any minute."

Ward saved him. "Yes, Your Honour," he said, "the accused were threatening and abusive, so I left and returned with my grooms. Young Lane was in camp, but Tyzack Lane was not nor was his hanger-on Morrison——"

Jacus winked placatingly at Justice, and put a hand to the side of his mouth. His whisper carried. "They'll be here any minute now, Your Honour, I'm on the look out for 'em, melt 'em!" And to Ward, "Go on with your complaint, me man!"

Garret Ward's shoulders stiffened. Jacus was getting under his skin. He went on.

"The accused were still threatening" (that was a straight lie) "and I went for Sergeant Mongan at Gullane Cross. With his aid we found the horse hidden in some whins near the camp, and I took charge of it——"

"Be Jacus alive!" Jacus hit the rail. "There he was after abductin' the horse himself. There's the first robber in the case, and I'll have the law on him."

I think it was then that the Justice decided that nothing could be done about Jacus; and I think the Superintendent was afraid to tackle him any longer, for he made his finishing statement there and then:

"Sergeant Mongan can vouch that the horse was hidden," he said, "but I propose to offer no further evidence at this juncture. The horse is a valuable one; it was taken out of its stable in the night and against direct prohibition; and was found hidden in Lane's camp. If there is any question as to ownership, why hide the horse away? That at once implies a guilty conscience. I emphasise that. The horse was removed against orders and hidden in the accused's camp, and they hindered in the search for it. In the circumstances I consider myself justified in asking for a remand in custody. You may stand down, Mr Ward."

To be fair, he was justified, but he reckoned without Jacus.

Garret Ward rose to his feet, but Jacus yelped appealingly.

"Stop him—stop him, Your Honour! I want to use the curry-comb on him!"

The Justice shook his head resignedly, and gestured Ward back into the witness-chair. Ward hesitated and obeyed; he was not nonchalant any longer.

"Jacus, you old terror," said the Justice, "I should fine you for contempt of court, but what's the use. There's your witness, and serve the ends of Justice if you can."

"Just a few triflin' bits o' questions, Your Honour," said Jacus agreeably, "and all I ask of you is not to let 'em in one ear and out the other."

He got to his feet and leant confidentially over the rail,

and the moment he opened his mouth I knew that he was playing all he knew for time. Probably the Justice knew that too, and gave him free rein.

"You know me, Your Honour, and I know you and-your-father-before-you-a-dacent-man-God-rest-his-soul! And that bein' so, you will be knowin' the friendship between ourselves and the young people of Castle Gillian. Twenty-five year, man and boy, we been campin' off and on in the Bridge field of Gullane." He held up two fingers and his voice resounded. "Twenty-five years! and we been as close in friendship as them two fingers with the gentry of Castle Gillian—an' Castle Evan too. Gintlemen and ladies they were, and above pride! The children were the same as our own, and are yet, an' like our own they made me hair bald—an' I'm losin' some of it this day. We ate with them and off them, an' they ate with us. We had the same fun together, and their sorra was ours. We saw Castle Gillian in its good days, and in its bad days; and the bad days have come to this. To what have the bad days come? To a man, to that man there, claimin' that he has the power and the right to break the old tie and the old custom." He struck the rail. "He hasn't the power if he lived a million year, and I challenge his right to try here in this court."

He leant down towards Garret Ward. This was a new Jacus McGrath, a dominant, formidable man dealing with his enemy. He put a quiet question.

"Garret Ward, have you sold Monaglass?"

"I have sold it," Ward told the Justice, not turning his head to Jacus.

"Then you are a landless man, without an acre to your name." There was iron in Jacus's voice. A confused thought came into my mind, but I put it aside, though my blood stirred.

"That is a lie," said Garret Ward. The Justice let it go.

Jacus pointed one finger. "Listen! You got rid o' the sour bogs o' Monaglass, and you had a hunger for the fat land of Glen Gullane that bred your race. But what right have you to lord it in Castle Gillian? Answer me that! What right have you to accuse us of stealing a horse from Gillian Morris? Answer me that! Answer!"

Garret Ward turned his head like a baited bull. "I have controlling rights by purchase," he said, fiercely contemptuous.

"And I have you where I want you," said Jacus grimly, and straightened up. He spoke quietly to the Justice. "Your Honour, I ask Garret Ward to prove his right here in your court?"

Jacus sat down. He had not done badly. I glanced sideways at the door. It was still obdurately shut.

The Justice, who had been sitting back in a rather negative attitude, now sat up, and put Ward a question.

"Mr Ward, do you claim controlling rights at Castle Gillian?"

"I do, sir—house, stables, and lands," Ward answered firmly.

"Jacus McGrath asks you to prove that claim? Wait! I want to consider this." He lifted his head and looked up the slope of the courtroom. His eyes met mine and half-hooded themselves, and I was inclined to wink, but did not. Again his eyes shifted and I knew they were on Mary; and Mary remained as still as a mouse.

The Justice spoke thoughtfully. "It is a serious thing to accuse a man of stealing a horse. There are two people in court who might have made that accusation, but have not. Since your standing in the case, Mr Ward, depends on your right to take precedence, the accused is entitled to ask for proof. Well?"

"My very words, Your Honour!" cried Jacus, waving an eloquent hand.

Garret Ward lifted a hand too. "Let me explain, Mr Dowling. The negotiations for sale have been going on for some time. Two days ago Mr Gillian Morris went up to town to execute a deed in my favour. He should be back this evening; but the deed would have been executed yesterday."

"But at the moment you have nothing to show for proof?"

"Damn the ha'porth!" put in Jacus.

"Proof will be forthcoming," said Ward confidently.

"And so I ask for an adjournment," interpolated the Superintendent.

The Justice looked at Jacus. "You are not satisfied, Jacus?"

Jacus was not looking at him. He was looking at the door near my shoulder, and his eyes were batting. And there and then he stole the Justice's own court. His voice rang.

"The case before the coort is: did we steal this horse, Benbecula?"

He leant over the rail, and his voice was dominant.

"Look at me, Ward! Young Gill Morris is in court. If he says that we did not steal the horse——"

Ward stopped him. "I'll accept nothing from Gilly Morris—you and he make a pair."

"Liars the both of us!" said Jacus. "Listen! if Miss Mary Morris—she's here too—says the horse is not her father's——"

Ward stopped him definitely. "Why ask her? Mr Gillian Morris is the man to ask."

"Then your minute has come," cried Jacus ringingly.

"Here is Mr Gillian Morris, and anyone that likes can ask him. Thank you, Your Honour!"

The time that Jacus had been stalling for had arrived. A murmur lifted and died in a waiting hush. Here was drama, and everyone in court sensed it.

IV

The door had opened quietly. My father came in, bareheaded, eagle-faced, full of old-world dignity. No whited sepulchre he. Every eye was on him as he walked slowly down the drugged passage, and he was not walking his chalked line any longer.

He was not alone. Behind him came the broad grey figure of Tyzack Lane, and Tyzack's face was as composed and saturnine as ever. He took the seat just in front of us, and moved his head gravely in my direction.

And behind him came Robin Morrison, also grave, but holding in excitement. He gave one glance about him, saw where Mary was, and did not hesitate a moment. He was at her side, and her eyes and her mouth gave her away; the hands that met and held had nothing to add. Mary had surrendered; she had to have her Highlandman, and what Garret Ward had no longer mattered. Mary Morris no more! She was for ever "lovely Mary Morrison."

And, strangely enough, behind Robin came bluff Tom Gayne. He gave me a shrewd side-glance, hooded one eye knowingly, and sat down by Tyzack Lane.

There was a pause then, and my mind said blankly: *And that is all!* No! the damsel debonair made a good entrance. The door opened wide, and there was Sylvia Gayne. She was wearing a long, tan driving coat, and her hair was hidden under a bright blue kerchief. Her eyes were brilliant, and her face colourless. She saw me, threw back her head, looked down her nose at me, and moved to sit in front at her father's side; but she changed her mind at the last, and went two seats forward. I knew why: she was afraid of losing a fistful of her back hair.

This could never have been stage-managed, I said, *yet here it is!* But it had been stage-managed. Jacus had done it, by delaying proceedings and withholding the evidence that would have quashed the case right at the start.

Lant's eyes were bulging. He nudged me and whispered: "Gosh, Gill! this is the best yet, an' I'd ha' missed it but for you."

Garret Ward had turned in his chair, and was now on his feet, a confident smile on his face. Jacus McGrath had been turning the tables on him, but now Jacus was delivered into his hands, and Jacus was going to get it in the neck.

But Jacus was leaning back comfortably, eyes aloft, and his head actually resting on a guard's broad chest: the great god Jove taking his ease, no longer interested in the little mundane affairs that he had finished ordering.

My father was now at the witness-stand. Garret Ward bowed to him and his hand was inviting: "Take the chair, Uncle Gillian!"

I looked at Ned Dowling, the king-bee in his own court. He was sitting forward interestedly. He sensed the drama too, and was not going to spoil it by insisting on judicial ritual. He removed his dogean cap of office.

Garret Ward sat on the front bench; my father stood easily behind the witness chair, his hand resting on the circular top. His cool, husky voice filled the room.

"I am at your service, Mr Dowling. A guard outside informed me that my testimony was required. Some ridiculous nonsense about stealing a horse?"

Ned Dowling took his cue. He put his elbow on the bench, his chin aside in his hand, and spoke as friend to friend.

"I am ashamed to confess, Mr Morris, that all the rules of my court have been broken to-day, and it is now too late to restore them. We will keep this informal for a few minutes. I am not going into the case with you." He gestured towards the prisoners' dock. "These three—you know them?"

"Very well indeed, sir."

Jacus sat up, and he and my father saluted each other with old-world dignity. Sloper Jones showed his gapped mouth, and Dinny smiled shyly at the man he worshipped.

The Justice went on, "Mr Garret Ward accuses them of stealing one of your horses, and hiding it away in Tyzack Lane's camp."

"And the horse, sir?"

"A valuable young horse, Benbecula."

My father spoke clearly and slowly. "Mr Garret Ward is wrong. I am not the owner of Benbecula."

Garret Ward, who had been sitting head-forward, straightened up neck-stiff. Before the Justice could ask another question my father went on, carefully explaining:

"I train Benbecula at Castle Gillian stables, and, by arrangement, I raced him under my name and colours, but the absolute owner is Mr Robin Morrison."

"Mr Robin Morrison?" The Justice had heard that name twice already, but it had scarcely registered, and my father saw that.

"Yes, sir!" he said, "Mr Robin Morrison, a writer, whose present headquarters are with Tyzack Lane at Gullane Bridge."

That registered. Ned Dowling knew Tyzack Lane and respected him, but Justice Dowling was going to be fair and thorough. He said slowly:

"The horse was not stolen from *you*, Mr Morris, but the horse was taken from your stables at night, and——"

My father stopped him definitely. "I can assure you, Mr Dowling, that the horse was not stolen from anyone."

At that point my father could have called on Robin Morrison, but elected not to. Instead he said:

"The horse could have been taken away at any time. If it was taken back to Tyzack Lane's camp, that is where it came out of, and that is where it belonged. I have no complaint to make."

That was definite enough. It finished the case, and if my father had left it at that the whole thing might have gone off sedately and respectably, without implicating me. But my father was frankly puzzled, as his voice and gesture showed.

"But, Mr Dowling, my daughter Mary could have told you all that. It was she who made all the arrangements with the owner, Mr Morrison!"

I did not look at Mary, but I hope she blushed. I was watching Garret Ward, the one man who had been kept in the dark. He half rose from his seat, and sat down again, and his massive head sank between his hunched shoulders dangerously.

I did not catch Ned Dowling's next remark, but, judging by his lips, it was: "*Well, I'm damned.*"

Everyone in that court knew that only the fringes of the drama had been touched. There was more than the stealing of a horse involved in this. The very fate of Castle Gillian was behind it. How, now, did Garret Ward stand in relation to Castle Gillian—lord of the Glen or a landless man? There was a waiting silence.

But in real life, drama has a trick of stopping short of the final curtain. It did that now. My father was never a vindictive man, and, possibly, he was a bit ashamed of himself too. The affairs of Castle Gillian were our own private concern, and here in public he would not humiliate even Garret Ward more than was necessary. I think that at that point something passed between him and Ned Dowling.

For, suddenly, the Justice rammed his dogean cap flat with his fist, and his face flamed. He was on his feet and blaring:

"A sheer waste of time! I'll not have my court turned into a playhouse. The case is dismissed, and get out of here every damn'd one of you!"

I was one of the first to obey. The implications of the new situation, as I guessed at it, were beginning to intrude themselves confusedly, and I wanted to get away by myself to consider them. I did not get away as easily as I hoped.

Chapter XIV

A SADIST COME TO JUDGMENT

I

It was here I came into the limelight to make the finish historical—or should I say, notorious. The citizenry of Caerline talk about that finish yet, some of them reprehensibly. And I am not proud of it.

When I got outside I hesitated, and decided that I would stay at hand until Garret Ward took himself off. I honestly wanted to have nothing more to do with him, but I was not sure how he might act when he realised the finality of his disaster. I stood aloof below the balustrade of the hotel porch, and my eyes were watchful on the courthouse steps.

The court emptied quickly, and there was quite a crowd in the narrow street. Mary and Robin were there very close together; Tyzack and Jacus were there, but Jacus's tenor voice was absent; my father was there; Tom Gayne was there; and there was Sylvia at the foot of the steps. She had a quick look round, saw me, and carefully turned her back. That hurt. A week ago we would have sidled about and found ourselves side by side.

All right, Syl, old girl! I said. *I will take myself off, and not trouble you.*

Garret Ward had not appeared, and I decided that he had slipped away from the public gaze by a side door into the Square. I turned to go round the corner where my old cycle leant against a wall. A queer sudden hush made me turn again.

Garret Ward was standing at the head of the court-house steps. He stood in a characteristic attitude, feet

293

apart, hands on hips, and head forward. His black eyes were slitted, his face livid, and his jaws grinding. He spoke gratingly, clamping his teeth on the words.

"The double-cross! I'll let no woman and her tame dog get away with that!"

He came down the steps, not bounding or hurriedly, but almost leisurely, solidly, step by step. People got out of his way. They had to. He did not see them. And there he was, facing Mary. He showed her his teeth in a mirthless grin.

"A neatly-played trick, Mary!" he said softly. "And it was you put it across."

Mary pulled herself up and spoke coldly. "You poor foolish bully!"

"Foolish?" His voice grated. "I'll show Castle Gillian who is the dam' fool before another day is over you!"

It was then that I realised that Garret Ward's obsession had made him as blind as a bat. Jacus McGrath had called him a landless man, but the implication had never come home. My father had been to town to execute a deed in his favour, and my father was now back; therefore he, Garret Ward, now controlled Castle Gillian. But there was one thing that he did realise there and then: no matter what he had gained he had lost Mary Morris. He knew it and it maddened him. His taurine voice broke and went queerly high:

"You treacherous little bitch! Oh! you treacherous little bitch!" And forthwith he slapped her wickedly across the face.

Mary surprised me then. Her voice pealed anguishedly, and my hair stirred, for it was not to her lover she called.

"Gillian! Oh, Gillian! Where are you?" She knew deep down and for a long time that it was her brother who had to settle with Garret Ward.

That red spark flicked across my sight. The time had come, and I was ready and not afraid. I had no voice to speak, but I moved quickly. Even so Robin Morrison very nearly beat me to it. He would have if Tyzack Lane had not actually scooped him off his feet, and slung him into Jacus's arms. Tyzack knew, Jacus knew, my father knew, Sandy Ythan knew, Sloper Jones knew, and, finally, Sylvia knew that some day Garret Ward and Gillian Morris had to come to this. This was the day they had waited for, and that some of them had planned for.

He was half-turned from me, ready for Robin. I caught him by the shoulder, and jerked him round forcibly.

"You'll remember this the longest day you live, Garret!" I said.

"Get away, you pup!" he blared. "You are not the man I want!"

He flung a contemptuous unclenched hand at me. I went under it and smashed him, left-handed, flush on the mouth.

"Right! I'll take you all on!" he growled in his throat.

He tried to whip off his jacket, but I hit him right-handed in the split of the breast-bone. "I'll strip you, Garret," I said.

He leaped at me in that awkward way, his hands clawed to tear little Gilly Morris apart, before facing a foeman more worthy of his steel. I was quicker on my feet; I was under his arms and out again, and again gave him all I had with the left on his bleeding mouth. I stopped him, right back on his heels, got in again and away and gave him the first taste of his own medicine, a right jolt to the ribs. I knew then that I need never have feared him. I knew I had him if it took me a year. It did not take me a year, but it took me some time, and I knew I had been in a fight at the end of it.

The fight was on. This was no boxing-match in a booth. This was a brutal and elemental fight, and people will go on talking about the savagery of it. Some even say that teeth were used. I did not have any teeth marks on me at the end, and I did not need to use mine, but I would have hung on by them if I had to.

I do not want to boast that I did a mighty deed in licking Garret Ward. He was taller than I was and heavier, but my reach was just as long, if not longer. He had heavy arms, slow in the swing, and his only method was to get close in, and break a man in two with body jolts. I was quicker, and tougher, and fitter after a hard harvest's work; my toil-hardened hands were in good shape and his gentleman's hands, unprotected by gloves, soon puffed. In a clinch he could throw me by sheer strength, but in time I found that a smart cross-buttock twisted him off his splay feet. And in time I solved the problem of his body rips by countering to the head as soon as his hands dropped: countering, side-stepping, and lacing the right to the ribs.

And he went berserk, as usual. No, not as usual, not as in a two-minute round with a minute to rest. He was insanely berserk all the time, and that was not good for his wind. And I think he panicked after a time. Gilly Morris couldn't do this to him! But Gilly Morris was doing it.

I was so sure of myself that I had a double vision. I could see our shadows leap and flow in the evening sun; I could see every move that Ward made, and counter it. But also I noticed every move of the people about us. The courthouse steps were crowded. My father and Mary and Uncle Tom were up in the hotel porch, and the red weal on Mary's face put pith in my blows. Dinny and Lant were up there too, out of harm's way, and they were screeching at me most of the time, and bawling dolorously once or twice. Tyzack's mighty shoulders, Jacus's squat solidity, Robin Morrison's suppleness, Ythan's wiry toughness, Sloper's driving elbows, Dan Shea's poundage, these kept the ring open for me. The fight swayed across the street and back again; sometimes we were on our feet, and sometimes we rolled, but always my friends kept a clear ring around us. I could hear Jacus's high bellow. "Room! Room! Give a man room to use his feet." And I did use them. It was those slightly-intoed feet, those tireless slightly-bowed legs that won the fight for me.

And Sylvia—my Sylvia Gayne—where was she? She was right there in the heart of it, her dust-coat off, and her blue kerchief in one hand. She was actually in the ring, slipping here and there like a pantheress, her hair flying, her eyes blazing, and her face dead white. Everyone there knew on which side Sylvia was, for Sylvia could not keep her mouth shut. Sylvia was rooting, as she had once promised to root. Sylvia gave herself away.

Early on, before I solved my problem of attack and defence, and looked to be doomed to demolition, Sylvia lifted her great contralto voice:

"Go on, Gillian! Gillian, you will! Gillian, don't break my heart! Gillian, I'll die! You are not beaten, Gillian! Up, Gillian!"

But when I got going good, her voice was a slogan cry: "Gillian! Gillian! Gillian!"

No! It was not my tireless legs won the fight for me. It was Sylvia's slogan. I knew what Sylvia meant.

But along towards the end my vision was not so good. It was blurred a bit, and Sylvia's voice was coming from far away—but still coming.

I have a hazy recollection of a dog's fall at the foot of

the courthouse steps, and feet leaping over us, and finding myself, somehow, flat at the top of the steps with Ward underneath, and rolling under and over him to the bottom. I remember the face of Justice Ned Dowling, nostrils flaring, over the shoulders of two uniformed men in the doorway. Some folks said afterwards that he was restraining the guardians of the peace from interfering in a brutal street brawl.

It seemed to be the next instant that our hurtling bodies crashed through the porch railing close to Mary, and I heard the thrum of the boards as we rolled and pitched down on to the street again.

Strangely enough I remember the end clearly. I saw Ward trying to lift his heavy arms, and I hit him left-handed below the breast-bone. His head came down, and I brought the right up. He fell flat on his face, one arm under him and one thrown helplessly wide. He did not move; I put my foot firmly between his shoulder-blades, and turned my thumb down. And his shoulder-blades were naked. I was the more brutal of the two, and had about stripped the clothes off him—and some of the hide too.

Someone yelled high and clear, a savage cry of exultation.

Do you know! when I come to think of it, and all is said and done, I do not deserve much credit for licking Garret Ward.

Chapter XV

MASTERED AT LAST

A DEEP, fierce young voice said: "Give him to me!" And a strong young arm was around me.

I started to let myself go then, but the voice, stern now, pulled me up. "Walk out on your feet, Gill Morris! and let them see."

I found myself walking, without touching the ground, it seemed to me, and Sylvia's arm was in mine, and her shoulder was like an ash sapling, so lithe and so strong.

There was some shouting that died away behind us. Tyzack was at my other shoulder, saying nothing. Robin was steadying Sylvia at the other side, and his "Mary Morrison" was holding on to him. I had all my senses, but I was in a vacuum of my own, and voices came from far away.

I heard Dinny and Lant, a mile or two in the rear, accenting high lights in high voices. Jacus went along soberly in front. His head was down, and he was blowing his nose into a red handkerchief. *What is Jacus crying for?* I wondered. Ythan was ahead too; he had his peaked cap in his hand, and was tapping it rhythmically on Sloper Jones's shoulder, and saying over and over again, "I aye said it! I aye said it, didn't I? No one to help or hinner him when the time came!" And Sloper said: "No help was needed, and the whole town couldn't hinder him." And Dan Shea said: "I didn't think there was a man could handle Garret Ward that way!"

There was a small blank then. And Tom Gayne's voice was close behind me.

"Let her take him—she knows!"

And my father's husky voice, trembling a little, said:

"Yes! Give him to Sylvia."

I found myself in a car, and my face was being wiped. . . . And after that I was going out of town on the Gullane road, and Sylvia was driving fast, and I was alone in the car with her. There was a great ringing in my ears; the wide plain of Moymore was tilting up and down, and our little hills were buck-jumping; and the insides of me wanted to turn a somersault.

"Hold it! Put your head down, and you'll be all right!" said Sylvia easily.

I dropped my head down as far as the dash-board would let me, and the ringing stopped after a while. I lifted my head a little and drew in long breaths. One of my ribs hurt, but it was not broken. I lifted my head some more, and things steadied themselves. I was all right now, and I knew it, because I began to feel the weariness in my arms and the ache in my right thumb. The knuckles of my left hand were grazed, and my left sleeve was missing from the elbow down.

I knew all about Sylvia and myself now. But I would have to move very carefully with Sylvia, who had given herself away. I kept my head half-down and said carefully:

"That was a nice exhibition, yon?"

"Whose—yours?"

"No! Miss Gayne's."

"I don't care," she said belligerently. "I'd have died if Garret Ward had licked you, and I was afraid he would."

"We all heard you," I said.

And there without any warning she started to weep. The tension had slacked down, and she could not hold herself any more. As I said, Sylvia's weeping hurt one inside, it was so whole-hearted, so—well! somehow so lovely and so sad. It was like an old Gaelic *caoine*. And in her keening there were no words at first, but after a while I got a broken sentence or two.

"I shamed myself—oh—oh—oh! I don't care—I don't care any more—oh—oh—oh! I am going away—I'm going away to-morrow—oh—oh—oh! I can't stay to be shamed—oh—oh—oh!"

I sat up and looked at her, and she had the face of a child. Her glistening eyes were wide-open and unwinking, and the glistening tears were running down her cheeks. And she was driving like the wind.

"Turn it off! or you'll ditch us," I said heartlessly.

"No—no—no!"

There was a clean dust-cloth in the dash-board pocket. I picked it out, turned to her, and put a hand on her shoulder. She stopped as if a tap had been turned off, and her shoulder tremored under my hand. That moved me strangely.

"Look where you're going!" I warned, and carefully dabbed her cheeks and chin.

"So you are going away?" I said.

She moved her head away from the cloth and steadied her voice.

"What have I to stay for? Please don't make me cry any more, Gillian! It was you that made me cry always."

That was true, and I nearly cried myself then. But I said:

"I can't promise you that though you live to be a hundred."

I put away the dust-cloth, sat with my head over the back of the seat, drew in slow breaths, and looked sideways at Sylvia. Her fine hair, sun-bright, was blowing about her ears, and the light freedom of it was in contrast with the firm, grave line of her profile. After a while I said:

"You been jaunting about the last couple of days?"

"No, I wasn't," she denied at once.

"No, not jaunting! On business bent, I should say! At a guess, Tyzack Lane and Robin Morrison were with you?"

"That's not a guess."

"Ye were up in town—and that's not a guess either—and ye had a business appointment with my father? Look, Syl! I'm all in the dark. Who are the new owners of Castle Gillian. Garret Ward is not one of them?"

"No," she said firmly, and added quietly, "You are not one either, Gill."

"No. Garret and I are landless men! I can make a good guess at the new owners, though—three of them?"

"Go on!"

"My sister, Mary——"

"Wrong, wrong!" snapped Sylvia. "Mary knew nothing about it."

"I am glad to hear that," I said. "I was afraid Mary was double-crossing."

"Mary never would."

"Not quite! But my father holds her share for her. Yes, that's right! And Tyzack Lane holds a share for Dinny? That's right too? Yes, Tyzack bided his time. His grandson has a share in Castle Gillian, and Garret Ward has not an acre to his name. The third is Robin Morrison, but what did he use for money?"

"His horse is worth a thousand or two?"

"That's right! And Tyzack advanced him the cash. You did one fine job, Syl! No, don't pipe your eye! I suppose Mary and Robin will be for marrying, the young fools? I don't care a cuss! I'll be out of Castle Gillian."

"Five thousand miles!" whispered Sylvia, her mouth quivering.

"Not so far," I said. "I got a job of my own."

"A job?" I saw a shoulder twitch.

"Yep—a crackerjack! I got a five-year contract from one Tom Gayne to run Castle Evan my own way. He is going away with you?"

"Yes," she said, almost whispering.

"I'll be in complete control. By gum! I'll be like Garret Ward hoped to be in Castle Gillian, only more so, for—you're sure you are going away?"

"You're not punch deaf are you?" she said warmly.

"Fine! I'll have no woman under my feet. I'll surely make Castle Evan hum, and take most of the profits. And if I wanted I could keep a wife—in a frugal way—but I'll have years to look for a useful one."

"God help her!" said Sylvia, and looked at me sideways.

I left it at that for the time. Sylvia drove as fast as she knew how, as if in a hurry to get rid of me. No easy tooling along this evening with a song in her mouth. The keen air blowing about my ears revived me, and the ache was going out of my arms. The plain of Moymore below us was resplendent in fall colours, the Midland Mountains were a purple haze, and our own little hills were green and grey, with still a few blossoms on the furze.

The car slowed down for the gate of Castle Evan, and Sylvia spoke at last, coldly.

"You say you are in control here. Going up?"

"To-morrow will do. You can drop me here if you like."

"I will not," she said firmly. "I am taking you home to bed."

"You're not," I said, "but drive on for a bit!"

We slid down the slope, and slowed again over the switchback of the bridge.

"Stop here!" I said.

She stopped the car and looked at me. "Want to do a gloat?"

"Not yet," I said, "but Oonagh Blake said she'd have a meal for me."

"Gosh!" she snapped. "You'd eat and your belly hanging by a string."

"Let me out," I said indignantly. "You're a rude—damsel!"

I got out fumblingly, for I knew she was watching me. I had to be careful too. On my feet, I took one step and staggered another, wavered, steadied again, and put a hand over my heart.

"Oh, Gill! Gillian!" That was Sylvia's frightened voice. How she got out of the car I don't know, but her hands were on me, and I turned to face her. Her arms were around me, her whole, lithe young body yielding to and supporting me. I had the firm grip of her that I wanted.

"Your heart is it?" She whispered, terror in her eyes.

"My heart it is," I whispered back.

"Oh, my God! Did the brute drive in a rib?"

"No! This hurt is five months old," I told her, "and I can't stand it any longer."

We were looking close into each other's eyes, clinging to each other, two foolish youngsters mastered at last.

"I can't do without you, girl," I whispered. "Don't go from me."

"Oh, my Gillian," said Sylvia deeply, and said no more. We had hungered for each other long enough. . . .

After a while I lifted my head, released an arm, and shook a finger under her nose.

"Look you, my girl!" I said sternly. "There's one thing I will not have."

"Yes, Gillian dear?" She looked at me puzzledly.

"A double wedding! I'll not have it. It's too——"

She pulled my head down.

"Leave it to me, you little thug!" she said.

So I left it to her. And it was a double wedding.